PUSHKIN PRESS

THE SALT
OF THE
EARTH

'One of the great Central European war stories, on a par with the works of Jaroslav Hašek'

Los Angeles Review of Books

'A volume to be read again and again. It has the satisfying quality of good music'

Virginia Quarterly Review

'One of the small number of contemporary works which extend into the sphere of the mythical and epical'

Thomas Mann

'Cocteau's *Thomas the Imposter* meets Brecht's *Mother Courage* and Erich Maria Remarque's *All Quiet on the Western Front*… The dark tragedy of a world war, the collapse and eradication of an entire topos of history, humanity and culture becomes a tensely rhythmed black comedy'

Bookanista

D1426829

Windsor and Maidenhead

95800000129893

JÓZEF WITTLIN was born in 1896 and served in the Austro-Hungarian army during the First World War. His experiences inspired him to write *The Salt of the Earth*. Published in 1935 to great success, it received the Polish National Academy Prize, won Wittlin a nomination for the Nobel Prize, and has since been translated into 14 languages. Wittlin was also a translator and poet, penning numerous essays such as 'My Lwów', included in *City of Lions*, also published by Pushkin Press. With the outbreak of the Second World War he fled to France and then to New York, where he died in 1976.

PATRICK JOHN CORNESS is a literary translator from Czech, German, Polish, Russian and Ukrainian, and is currently Visiting Professor of Translation at Coventry University. Polish authors he has previously translated include Olga Tokarczuk, Krzysztof Jeżewski, Cyprian Norwid, Jan Twardowski, Stanisław Wygodzki and Franciszka Urszula Radziwiłłowa.

PHILIPPE SANDS QC is Professor of Law at University College London and a practising barrister at Matrix Chambers. He is the author of *East West Street*, which was the winner of the 2016 Baillie Gifford Prize and the 2018 Prix Montaigne, and also contributed to *City of Lions*.

THE SALT
OF THE
EARTH

Józef Wittlin

Translated from the Polish by Patrick John Corness

With a Foreword by Philippe Sands

PUSHKIN PRESS

Pushkin Press
71–75 Shelton Street
London, WC2H 9JQ

First published as *Sól ziemi* in Warsaw, 1935 © 1937 Verlag Allert de Lange, Amsterdam.
Translated from the Polish by I. Bermann, revised by Marianne Seeger

© 1969 S Fischer Verlag GmbH, Frankfurt am Main
English translation © Patrick John Corness 2018

First translated into English by Pauline de Chary and published in New York by Sheridan
House, 1941

This translation first published by Pushkin Press in 2018
This edition first published in 2019

This book has been published with the support of the © POLAND Translation Program

9 8 7 6 5 4 3 2 1

ISBN 13: 978-1-78227-472-8

Designed and typeset by Tetragon, London
Printed and bound by CPI Group (UK) Ltd, Croydon CRO 4YY

www.pushkinpress.com

Contents

Foreword

Józef Wittlin came into my life by chance. When I was invited to travel to the Ukrainian city of Lviv to deliver a lecture, a colleague in Warsaw sent me a photocopy of *Mój Lwów*,[*] a slim volume published in Polish in 1946. The author, an émigré poet, born in 1896 in the small Polish village of Dmytrów, reached the United States in his forty-sixth year. I did not speak Polish, but appreciated the grainy black-and-white photographs of buildings. They seemed significant to Wittlin. I wandered around the city in search of the monuments that touched him, a fine introduction to a city that melded pre-war Austro-Hungarian and interwar Polish style.

By the time of my second visit to Lviv a year later, I obtained a Spanish translation of Wittlin's book, published with the assistance of his daughter Elizabeth, who lives in Madrid. My understanding of Spanish is bare, but with the help of a friend from Barcelona I was able to appreciate the magical quality of Wittlin's lyrical prose. His words brought to life a world that was lost yet deeply present. Reassuring,

---

[*] Included in *City of Lions* by Józef Wittlin and Philippe Sands (also published by Pushkin Press).

full of life and energy and hope even during the dark periods from which he emerged, Wittlin opened up the imagination, helped me to feel what it might have been like to occupy those spaces at the time he walked them. He brought the past alive, and made it even more relevant.

I wanted more Józef Wittlin. Eventually, I found a copy of his only published novel, to which he gave the title *Sól ziemi*, or "The Salt of the Earth". Inspired in part by Homer's *Odyssey*, which Wittlin had translated into Polish in 1924 and for which he was honoured by the Polish PEN Club, the novel was first published in Polish in 1935, to considerable acclaim. A German edition appeared a year later, with a preface by Josef Roth. "He finds out through the loss of his soul", wrote Roth, "that there is something mightier than the emperor and even death." More translations followed—French in 1939, English in 1941. The book won awards, and led to Wittlin's being nominated for the Nobel Prize in 1939, the year in which the war that defined the essence of the poet's being was resumed.

The novel was intended as the first volume of a trilogy entitled "The Saga of the Patient Foot Soldier", but the drafts of the two other volumes were lost in the small French seaside town of St Jean de Luz on 22nd June 1940, when a soldier threw one of his suitcases into the sea. Only the first section of the second book, *Healthy Death*, survives, and is included at the end of this edition. The main protagonist is a railwayman, Piotr Niewiadomski, "Peter Incognito", a lowly worker on the Lwów—Czerniowce—Ickany line. The inhabitant of a small village in the Carpathian mountains in Eastern Galicia, a Catholic, son of a Hutsul mother and a Polish father, like millions of others he is summoned to war by Emperor

Franz Joseph, into the Austro-Hungarian Army, to defend the Empire. "He did not always comprehend this tragedy," Wittlin wrote of him in an essay. "He did not always know what he was fighting for or for what he was dying." Through the eyes of this exceptional being, a filter perhaps for Wittlin's own experiences and assessment, we come to a sense of war.

Plucked out of a simple life, Piotr Niewiadomski is thrust into a heaving, anonymous mass, fellow conscripts—Poles, Hungarians, Jews, Rumanians, Bosnians and others—who made up the Empire:

> Sweaty, breathless, drunken numbers of heads, arms, legs and torsos flow like lava towards the east and the south, from east to west, from south to north, to satisfy someone's ambitions, to someone's greater glory. Healthy, strong lungs, hearts and stomachs set off in their thousands, tens of thousands, hundreds of thousands, to all corners of the earth to a tournament of their own suffering, hunger and fever.

The organizing, unifying force the Emperor—and his world of absurdity and lies—is the anvil on which the fear that grips these young men is hammered out, as they prepare for war and death:

> Until then, fear had been something external; now it settled within them. It penetrated into their bodies from the coarse fibres of the uniforms. They all felt that this fragrant apparel smelling of malt consigned them to death. A miracle had occurred; this undrilled crowd had been overtaken by Discipline. It crept into their bones, mingling with the

marrow and stiffening their movements. It even altered their voices.

Wittlin knew of what he wrote. Having attended a gymnasium school in Lwów, some seventy kilometres north-east of the small town where he was born, he enrolled at the University of Vienna. The studies were interrupted by two years of service in the Austro-Hungarian Army, in its Eastern Polish Legion. "Mythical and epical," Thomas Mann wrote from California in the autumn of 1941, in a letter to the author. The words were directed at the novel's subject matter, but they might equally have been written for the man:

> There is humour and the lyrical, extraordinary detail that allows us to begin to understand some greater truths. There is irony and pity. There is a cry against horror and absurdity. There is the focus on the individual in the group. There is a tale, simple and extraordinary, that is perhaps for our times, once again, as greater forces propel us in an increasingly unsettled direction.

"Throughout his life," Wittlin's daughter Elizabeth tells me, "my father would always run off to the railroad station to search for a porter to speak with, so as to resuscitate Piotr Niewiadomski." Sickly and underweight, she adds, as he could not carry his own suitcases "the porters—the red-caps—were crucial to him".

As they should be to us. As the drums of nationalism and conflict start to beat again, amidst forces unknown that threaten to overwhelm, this "poetic representation of the First

World War"—this was how Wittlin characterized his novel about a "little Galician porter"—offers a salutary reminder. Of where we once were, to where we may return, of the power of the novel, of who we are and who is truly around us. Nothing is ever quite what it seems.

Philippe Sands
Bonnieux, July 2018

THE SALT
OF THE
EARTH

Ye are the salt of the earth: but if the salt have lost his savour, wherewith shall it be salted? It is thenceforth good for nothing, but to be cast out, and to be trodden under foot of men.   MATTHEW 5:13

Prologue

I

The black two-headed bird, the triple-crowned eagle, convulsively grips in its talons a golden apple and an unsheathed sword. What is the reason for its sudden appearance above our heads, darkening the sky with its massive black plumage? With a rustle of its wings and a clanking of its golden chains festooned with coats of arms, it escaped from the black-and-yellow sign above the tobacconist's where my brother used to buy cigarettes. Like a startled cockerel, it suddenly tore itself away from the metallic shield above the entrance to the post office, just as I was sending a telegram to our village to tell my mother about the birth of my son. It abandoned the cosy, warm nests it built years ago above the doorways to the school, the courthouse and the prison. It took flight, abandoning the round red seals on baptism, marriage and death certificates. It suddenly vanished from my tattered national identity certificate, and it scarpered from the official notice imposing on me a fine of 10 crowns for jay-walking across the railway tracks. It deserted from the postman's brass buttons, the cap of the guard at the savings bank and the gendarme's helmet. Like a gigantic black-and-yellow aircraft, it is swaying overhead with the sword in its grasp.

My brother is a reader of the boulevard press. My brother is a messenger in the offices of a certain commercial company. My brother sees—my brothers see—the eagle circling in the air, menacingly wielding the heraldic sword in its claws. The keen sword glints in its sharp talons like a thunderbolt from heaven, then abruptly plunges from on high to pierce the distant heart of my mother, our old mother who works on the land, her back bent as she struggles to wrest potatoes from the earth with her hoe—the last of this year's crops.

My brother is a simple man. My brothers are simple folk—barbers, cobblers, railway workers, tram conductors, foundrymen in vast iron foundries, clerks, waiters, peasants. Peasants.

My sister is a simple woman. They are all like her—simple and loquacious. Market-stall sellers, washerwomen, milliners, seamstresses, "maids of all work", nannies of children better situated than mine.

They have seen, they have heard, they have read their local papers, they have seen coloured picture postcards. I may have seen, heard and read myself.

II

Everyone stood up. The old rococo armchairs heaved a sigh of relief, suddenly free of the burden of venerable bodies. Below, outside the gateway, the crash of the palace guard's hobnailed boots rang out. Traditionally, soldiers of the 99th

Moravian Infantry Regiment had the privilege of guarding these sacred places.

"*Gewehr heraaaaaus!*" yelled the sentry, like a locomotive whistle administering the last rites to victims of a disaster. The guard presented arms.

A tall, bald-headed, distinguished-looking man, smiling frostily beneath a thin black moustache, cleared his throat. Today it was he who was to fulfil the most important role. Already as a child he had been fond of history. Very. Once more he glanced provocatively in the direction of the ministers poised stiffly in anticipation. Their faces, which now took on a ceremonial expression, though they were customarily sour and morose, bore witness to a severe hardening of the arteries. The worn-out vessels were now having difficulty pumping these gentlemen's true-blue blood to their hearts. It was common knowledge whom these hearts were beating for. History itself would testify to whom they had promised to give the "last drop" of their blood. Especially as nobody had asked it of them. Meanwhile, the blood was battling against its own degeneration.

The agreeable gentleman's gaze next came to rest on Maria Theresa's silver wig; from the enormous portrait, she was sizing up the bald heads and beards gathered around the table with her large, unashamedly masculine eyes. Above the wig, over the gilt frame, the large stones set in the crown of St Stephen surmounted by its leaning cross glowed with fiery reds, greens and purples. The crown blazed in the glow of the setting sun; it shed multi-coloured tears, but the Empress's eyes glowed even more intensely. Her arteries had never hardened.

A carriage rumbled up to the gateway. A crash of rifle butts on the command to order arms. Down below a dry cough.

The magnificent double doors were flung open. Two svelte guards officers had assumed their positions either side of the entrance, as motionless as two statues in the foyer of the court theatre. A secret ritual suddenly enclosed the two living bodies in deep silence, as though in chilly niches of marble. The ringing of the spurs, sounding like broken glass, was muffled in that silence.

Ceremonial expressions rapidly came over the gentlemen's faces. The short, stocky Chief of the General Staff knitted his bushy eyebrows. He inclined his greying, close-cropped head slightly to one side towards his left breast, where the most illustrious crosses and stars were soon to blossom. The bald, elegant gentleman, the Foreign Minister, shifted impatiently from foot to foot. The patent-leather shoes that he had to wear on official occasions had given him bunions. One had to create a good impression at the embassy! He was the only one in this company to wear a fragrance. Very discreetly, mind you. He was accustomed to importing his fragrances directly from Paris. He didn't trust the local products.

All of a sudden, two old men in general's uniform, with sashes the colour of scrambled eggs draped across their chests, escorted in a third old man in a bright blue tunic. He was stooping, leaning on a silver-handled cane. All three of them had grey sideburns and they were as alike as peas in a pod. The life they had shared over many years—the shared boredom and the shared pleasures—had conferred on them the same appearance. If it were not for the Golden Fleece beneath the third button on the breast of the stooping figure, a stranger in this house would be unable to tell which of the three old men was by the grace of God Emperor of Austria, Apostolic King of Hungary, King of Bohemia, King of Dalmatia, Croatia and Slavonia, King of Galicia and Lodomeria, King of Illyria, Archduke of Upper and Lower Austria, Grand Duke of Transylvania, Duke of Lorraine, Carinthia, Carniola, Bukovina and Upper and Lower Silesia, Prince-Count of Habsburg and Tyrol, Margrave of Moravia, King of Jerusalem, etc., etc., and which were the two aides-de-camp, Count Paar and Baron Bolfras.

The ministers and the generals bowed their heads. Just one of them, a third replica of His Majesty with sideburns, stood erect. He had the right to do so. On his breast—considerably younger than the Emperor's, it's true—he also wore a Golden Fleece. He was, after all, the grandson of the victor of Aspern, Archduke Karl.

The armchair the Emperor sat down on was covered in red plush and it stood close to Maria Theresa's portrait. For a moment, the Empress's eyes seemed to be searching, over the top of Franz Joseph's head, for the bushy eyebrows of little Baron Conrad, Chief of the General Staff, in order to remind him that the highest decoration an officer of the Imperial and Royal Army could be awarded is, was, and always would be her own Order, the Order of Maria Theresa. Conrad knew how one gained it. He knew Heinrich von Kleist's *Prince of Homburg* virtually off by heart.

Just then, dusk began to sprinkle fluff on the old portraits, exaggerating their outlines. The portraits grew and grew and grew, eventually merging into a continuous grey mass along with the wallpaper and the wood panelling of the elegant room. Prince Eugene of Savoy, with a final glint of his sleek, mirror-like black armour, disappeared into the gloom, where only a moment earlier his golden sceptre and the signet ring on his finger had clearly stood out. Maria Theresa's crinoline billowed like a gigantic, bulbous cushion filling with water. One might have expected that at any moment the old matriarch of the Habsburgs would emerge from her gilt frame, powerfully elbowing aside these old sclerotics, and casually sit down next to the wilting offspring of her exuberant lifeblood. She would embrace the old man in her plump arms, injecting vigour into his pale, withered being, and burst into lusty peals of laughter.

But the lights in the crown of St Stephen are going out one by one; the fiery glints in her eyes grow dim.

A valet enters. He turns on the electric lights in the crystal chandeliers. Not all of them, however, because His Imperial Majesty cannot bear bright lights. With a trembling hand, he dons his spectacles. After a short while, he removes them again and spends a long time cleaning them with a handkerchief. At this point the bald Count Berchtold, the Foreign Minister, loses his patience. He takes some documents from his briefcase, casting his gaze sternly, yet respectfully, in the Emperor's direction. His Parisian fragrances not unpleasantly tickle the nostrils of his immediate neighbour, His Excellency von Krobatin, the Minister for War. This aroma at dusk arouses in him memories of his youth. Those wonderful Hungarian girls really know how to kiss!

The Emperor has finished polishing his spectacles. The starchy faces of the highest state dignitaries come back to life. Not a trace of sclerosis now.

The Emperor is speaking. In a dull tone of voice, he is thanking them for something or other. What his dear Count Berchtold spoke about yesterday had greatly saddened him. If he was not mistaken, that meant—if his memory served him correctly—Belgrade? He was happy to acknowledge that feelings were growing strong among his beloved peoples, who were demanding, demanding…

The Emperor could not recall what it was that the beloved peoples were demanding.

So they began explaining to him. There was something the Emperor, despite everything, was still unwilling to understand at any price, apparently. At first, they explained matters to him patiently, like a mother to her child, but eventually they lost their composure and started gesticulating. When the light finally dawned, they began bargaining with him. The Emperor went on the defensive for some time, resisting, hesitating, coughing, and recalling the murdered Empress Elisabeth. At one point he even stood up unassisted, striking the table so forcibly with his silver-handled cane that the two statuesque guardsmen flinched and Maria Theresa's eyes sparkled.

Archduke Friedrich, the grandson of the one of Aspern fame, leapt to his feet. He approached His Majesty and bent over the pink ear from which wads of grey cotton wool protruded. At some length, he poured certain weighty words into that ear. As he bent over, the two Golden Fleeces on the Habsburgs' chests found one another and for a few moments they swung in unison. Then the Emperor conceded. He yielded to the will of his beloved peoples.

He had just one wish; let them display the traditional oak leaves on their helmets. And they must sing. Here the monarch was interrupted again by Archduke Friedrich, who spoke up to remind him that in the twentieth century his soldiers no longer wore helmets, only soft caps. The Emperor apologized; he hadn't been on manoeuvres for such a long time. He was visualizing the old heads of veterans of Novara, Mortara and Solferino, the Pandours, Radetzky… Shamefacedly, he turned to the Minister for War as a pupil to his teacher.

"Perhaps Your Excellency will be so good as to remind me how many troops I have?"

"Thirty-eight divisions in peacetime, not counting the Landwehr or the Honvéds."

"Thank you. I have thirty-eight divisions!"

Thirty-eight divisions! Franz Joseph relished in his imagination every division individually, delighting in the multitude and the diversity of colours represented by these numbers, sworn to serve him in life and death. He conjured up in his mind the last parades at which he had been present, the last simulated battles, in which the enemy's soldiers were identified by red ribbons in their caps. On that occasion he had personally, on horseback, led one of the warring armies, and his adversary had been none other than Franz Ferdinand, the heir to the throne, murdered four weeks earlier. His memory did not fail him here. That was unforgettable! Old passions were revived in the old man as he recalled it. For a while, he felt the old aversion for his mock enemy in the manoeuvres, whose actual death he and the entire Imperial and Royal Army were now bound to avenge. The old man felt a rush of blood to his head at the thought that this obstinate opponent, who had waited in vain for so many years for him to die a natural death, still gave him no peace even after his own death. Something in the old man's mind declared, triumphantly, "Look, I have outlived him after all!" But even this single unspoken victory was moments later overshadowed by sorrow for his unforgettable only son Rudolf, who had also been unfortunate: *"Mir bleibt nichts erspart!"**

An uncomfortable silence descended on the room. Berchtold's cloying perfume was in the air, drifting like incense over the bodies of the murdered. "Adieu, Parisian perfumes!" The road is cut off. The Triple Alliance, the Triple Entente! Count Berchtold knew very well what this meant. He recognized the odour of the impending course of history. It smelt of restriction to local products. But in the eerie silence not even the jovial Krobatin noticed that scent. He had never smelt powder either, but he was Minister for War, nonetheless.

The Emperor was deep in thought. His light blue, watery eyes grew dim behind his spectacles. His clean-shaven chin sank into his golden collar; only the whiskers of his sideburns protruded. The glittering cross on the crown of St Stephen leant even farther, threatening to fall on the old man's head. He remained silent, engrossed in the sombre catacombs of cadaverous recollections.

The tension continued to mount at the round table. The old armchairs were creaking. The sclerosis in the veins of the paladins advanced another step. Eventually, the Crown Council's impatience broke the bounds of etiquette. The generals began to whisper.

---

* "I am spared nothing!"

"Time is running out! He must sign."

Krobatin could not last any longer without a cigarette. At this point, Berchtold touched Count Paar's elbow. The latter placed a large sheet of paper before the Emperor. The second replica of the Emperor held a pen with (as court ceremonial procedures dictated) a new, unused steel nib. All eyes were turned towards the Emperor's dried-up, frail hand. At last, he came to and adjusted his spectacles. Everyone heaved a sigh of relief.

The monarch spent several minutes coldly perusing the rigid black rows of letters. He paid strict attention to every word, every punctuation mark. But after he had read the first sentences, his eyelids reddened and he had a burning sensation in his eyes. His spectacles misted up. Lately, the old man had found reading very tiring, especially in artificial light. He now looked away from the sheet of paper and, noting the Crown Council's impatience, dipped the pen with a trembling hand into the open black maw of the inkwell. The hand returned with the nib now steeped in the poisonous fluid and settled shakily on the paper like a pilot feeling for the ground below as he lands. Soon the left hand came to its assistance, holding the paper steady.

The Emperor was placing his signature, so long awaited by the ministers. As soon as the name "Franz" was written, the pen ran out of liquid breath; the ink ran dry. As the Emperor reached for the inkwell once more, the quivering pen slightly scratched the thumb of his left hand. A tiny drop of blood squirted from his thumb. It was red. No one noticed that he had scratched his thumb; he quickly wiped it and, with a single flourish, added "Joseph". The ink was blue.

Count Berchtold picked up the document. The following day it was translated into all the languages of the Austro-Hungarian Empire. It was printed and displayed at all street-corners in cities, towns and villages. It began "To my peoples…". For the illiterate, it was read aloud by town criers.

The Emperor rose with the assistance of his aides-de-camp. He was not accustomed to shaking hands with his officials. On this occasion, however, he shook the hand of the prime minister. In the doorway, he turned once more and said—it was unclear to whom—

"If I am not mistaken, blood will be spilt."

Then he left. Archduke Friedrich offered Finance Minister Biliński a Havana cigar. From down below, the crash of the hobnailed boots of the 99th Regiment infantrymen was heard. A crash of rifle butts on the command to order arms. At the nearby barracks the lights-out bugle call was sounded. It was nine o'clock.

At nine o'clock, the soldiers throughout the Austro-Hungarian Empire go to bed.

III

The guards locked the gates at ten o'clock, as was the custom, opening them to latecomers in return for the customary twenty-heller tip. The eagles stamped on the faces of the nickel coins they unceremoniously pocketed were old and worn out. No one hurried home, though. In Vienna, the beds of even the most respectable citizens remained unoccupied until long after midnight. Only the children were asleep.

Only the factory workers were snoring away, exhausted, concerned about nothing and prepared for anything, as the night shift had relieved them at eight o'clock. The sellers who set off to market every day at dawn were asleep; the postmen who had been going up and down flights of steps all day were asleep. Prisoners in their cells were sleeping, or pretending they were asleep. In hospitals, in clinics and smart sanatoria, bodies wracked by civilian diseases lay in a drugged stupor brought on by sleeping-draughts. In the cemeteries, the dead were sleeping. Somewhere far away the Emperor was sleeping.

The city was brimming with life. It was idly giving over its vast body to the pleasures of the night. It contentedly drank lemonade and ate sausages in cheap cafés, or squandered its superfluous means in costly establishments of unbridled excess.

Work proceeded as usual in the bakeries and printing houses. Bread and newspapers were produced during the night. Bakers, stripped to the waist, pushed lumps of dough into the ovens with long-handled shovels. Soon afterwards, they pulled out steaming loaves of bread, covered with a brownish glaze.

Compositors stood, bent over their type-cases, unconcern-edly baking early-morning bread for the souls of the populace. Steaming, odorous words. It was the compositors who were the first to start trembling that night. From the countless stores of microbial leaden characters, among which the history of the world lies atomized, the shirtless compositors had picked out three letters. Each of these letters is meaningless on its own, but when joined together they spell a chemical formula for disaster. While typesetting, the hand of one of the compositors began to shake. Then, for a moment, his mind went blank. When his confused consciousness returned to normal after a short while, he rubbed his eyes and realized that he had set a meaningless word: *waf.* Sadly, he removed the letter *f* and threw it back into the type-case, where hundreds of its brothers were resting. With a sense of guilt, he picked out the correct letter with hesitant fingers and confirmed the truth he could not believe. Then he washed his hands.

The row ended up crooked and entered the printing press like that. The dreadful word came off the press into the world, trailing in its wake a black, mournful train of printing ink smeared over the letters.

The apprentices kneading dough on long breadboards in the bakeries suddenly stopped working. Scraping off with knives the remains of the dough clinging to their fingers, they ran out into the street.

The trams suddenly came to a halt in the busiest parts of the city. With a hiss, green sparks flashed from the overhead cables, as if they were short-circuiting. The electric current ran along the nerves of passengers, conductors and drivers. They could not even wait for the next stop. They all got off in the middle of the road and made a dash for the newspapers. Then, for the first time, they noticed that the letters were black.

Mr M. Rosenzweig from Drohobycz, biggest shareholder of the Anglo-Rosenzweig Oil Company, who had interrupted his journey to Venice and was about to spend the first night of his honeymoon in one of the luxury hotels, got out of bed, dressed in a hurry and dashed collarless to the hotel lobby to obtain a copy of the special edition of the *Neues Wiener Journal*.

Even lovers embracing on benches in the municipal gardens or intoxicated with each other in the undergrowth at the Prater suddenly broke off. Love, startled by death's icy breath, deserted its perfumed or smelly refuges and made for the bustling boulevards. The rushing sound of Old Father Danube could be heard as usual beyond the Prater, carrying its eternal peace out to sea, into the Black Sea, for safekeeping. The Danube's last wave carried away with it for an age the enchanting melody of this city, a melody that would never return, just as good blood sapped from the people would never return to their hearts.

The news spread by word of mouth. The mouths bit it, chewed it, ground it and crunched it until suddenly a million mouths spat one word out onto the pavement like a bitter almond. War had already pervaded all the cafés, bars and restaurants. Orchestras everywhere were already playing Old Master Haydn's Imperial anthem. The one, two and five-crown coins, with the eagle on one side and the Emperor's head impressed on their obverse, made a sound different from the usual one; somehow, they gave a more metallic ring on the veined marble tabletops when alarmed officers called for their bills.

War took over all public establishments. It leapt over the fences of the moonlit, sleepy villas on the slopes of the Gersthof vineyards, squeezed its way through the gaps in the old inner-city walls, predatory as a she-cat in March frolicking on the Opera House's green copper roof. It lay in wait in the cloakrooms of the cabarets, and sprang at the throats of the

high-spirited, unsuspecting customers bringing their numbered tabs to collect their hats and coats. Like a sudden attack
of the plague, it began playing havoc with the citizens' relaxed
minds. Like a mysterious nightmare, it befuddled the brains
of happy Pilsner drinkers. A blissful yet deadly shudder shook
hearts prone to suffer from apoplexy. Vague, garish images
arose from old, long-forgotten school textbooks. Random
historical battle scenes, known only from cheap fly-blown
prints that used to hang in hairdressers' salons, began to
penetrate the sanctuaries of bourgeois souls, taking by storm
the long-lived peacefulness of previous years. There suddenly
appeared before one's eyes every wet-nurse's dream, familiar
from shoe-polish tins, a martial Hussar-shoeblack standing
to attention, with his upturned black moustache. Something
crumbled away in everyone's brain.

Lights are flickering at the windows of the barracks.
Something that hasn't been seen for many years—it's past
midnight, and lights on in the barracks! The soldiers are
rolling up their coats, fastening their backpacks, filling their
ammunition belts, cleaning their mess kits, oiling the knives
they call bayonets. In the stables, the cavalry officers stroke
their mounts' sleek haunches with a rag and comb their
manes. The poor horses whinny, noisily chomping on their
oats. The corporals are inspecting the harnesses and saddles,
cursing the Dragoons over missing buttons. The sergeants are
hurrying as though possessed from one office to another. In
the officers' quarters, the lieutenants' wives have been dragged
out of bed to wax waterproof socks and have thermos flasks
ready with hot tea.

It's the same in all the towns.

Only the villages are asleep, the eternal reservoir of all kinds of soldiery, the inexhaustible source of physical strength. The villages are asleep among Danubian meadows; the villages are asleep along the banks of the Vistula, the Dniester and the Inn. The villages are asleep behind enclosures in the Alps, in Transylvania and the Sudetenland. Everywhere, red-faced farmworkers lie in the straw beside their horses, their bellies full of potatoes and rye bread. They sleep sweatily. The cattle in the cowsheds are breathing heavily, calmly, in biblical peace.

A startled signalman in distant Hutsul country wakes up every now and then, rubs his eyes, pulls up his trousers, pulls his cap down over his sticking-out ears, and picks up his red flag. He keeps lowering the level-crossing barrier. So many trains that night, and all bound for Hungary.

"What's up?" he asks the engine driver of a stationary goods train.

"War!"

"War?" repeats the signalman, his jaw dropping. Either he hasn't heard properly, or he can't believe it. He stands stiffly to attention, saluting the windowless wagons carrying ammunition and pigs.

At dawn, a swarm of locusts descended on every town. The darkness of that night had spawned a swarm of blue insects—centipedes stabbing with bayonets, wasps armed with deadly stings. Are these the same soldiers who entertained us last Sunday with a fine parade?

Cars full of generals noisily speed along the streets. The tunics' red facings flash before the crowds of onlookers like matadors' red capes.

IV

Hurry, don't overdo the sentimentality. Seamstresses, no more kissing your boyfriends; stuff your crumpled photographs into their pockets and say your goodbyes. Cooks, dry your eyes with your greasy aprons, and with your fingers that smell of browning stroke the clumsily shaved heads of your lance corporals. Everyone must own something from which they could be parted. The wives have husbands, the mothers have sons. The children say goodbye to their fathers, highly amused by their new appearance, especially the whistle and the compass on its blue cord. They have realized at last that their parents are children too, especially when they cry. Somebody must have beaten them, or they are about to. Some children are pleased that their fathers are going into the field. There will be nobody to beat them now. Where is this field, though?

The magistrate's widow hurries to court to gift to the state her only keepsake, her gold wedding ring, receiving an iron one in exchange. After all, everyone must own something they could part with.

The fragrant Countess Lili has her hair cut short. Wearing a white cap and cloak, she goes to the Academy of Fine Arts, where the Red Cross flag is fluttering. She is keen to carry out the bedpans of the wounded in her dainty, feminine hands. The war has not yet lost its virginity; the hospitals are still empty.

The bridges across the river have begun vibrating. The reservists are already on the march from the railway stations to the barracks. Black wooden trunks on their backs, flowers in their caps. In the school playgrounds, the steam of boiling water is rising from the field kitchens. A young soldier, a one-year recruit who is a philosophy student, is eating meat with a spoon, for the first time in his life. An old reservist, an agent of the Provident Insurance Company, is lying on the bare ground, for the first time in his life. Uniforms have not been issued yet. The men are still in their own skins. A fitter from the Siemens works is dissatisfied. He does know that he will be assigned to a technical unit, actually, but that's still army. For now, he is enjoying the cigarettes he got from a pretty girl at the station.

Things have begun to stir. The new recruits are parting with their own personalities. This is the hardest parting of all. Full of contempt and sadness, they cast aside the former individual along with their civilian clothes, parting, as they don the worthy Imperial tunic, with their health and their life.

Cattle-drovers from Tisá, swineherds from the Puszta and mountain shepherds from the Carpathians are now wearing the blue uniform. First of all—to the canteen! Farmworkers from Galicia, Moravia and Styria have all taken on the same colour. The Bosnians wear a fez on their shaved heads. A gesture to Islam on the part of the Catholic authorities. The one-year recruit, the philosophy student, has never seen puttees before in his life. He consoles himself with the thought that Napoleon apparently wore them as well. The Dragoons wear helmets with shiny eagles, but they have to cover them with a greyish-blue slipcase, or wax them, so they don't glint in the sun at a distance, drawing enemy fire. For the same reason, the higher ranks cover up the insignia on their collars with a handkerchief. Only the Hussars keep their plumes, though they too must cover their helmets with oilcloths. You would look in vain for the proud cockerel plumes on the Chasseurs' caps. The Chasseurs will march in caps with matt buttons like the ordinary infantry. The priest has changed his clothes as well. He wears a habit, but he is still a captain and he will sprinkle holy water on the regiment as it sets off into the field. He will render unto God what is God's and unto Caesar what is Caesar's. He will bury the slain and absolve the seriously wounded of the mortal sin of killing. He will distribute books with comforting content in the field hospitals.

The corps, divisions, regiments and brigades have already been formed. In the first company of every brigade, stand-ard-bearers carry the flag. Endless retinues of mummers in weird attire obediently await orders from their directors. Only their faces lack masks. But faces are no longer of any significance. Today, all that counts is someone's torso, their limbs and what kind of stars and buttons are sewn onto them. Buttons! Above all, the buttons must be in order. Actually, masks will have their day too. Gas masks.

Following ancient tradition, the soldiers of the Imperial and Royal Army set sprays of oak leaves in their caps. In every soldier's trouser pocket there nestles, like a code and price label from a shop, a discreet metal identification tag, the death capsule, which will be removed from the dead by the orderlies. This concludes definitively the transaction with the conquered territory.

Attention! The lieutenants, field glasses and maps slung round their necks, are now leading their companies out. The captains are on horseback at the head of the battalions. They are followed by the adjutants and the buglers. With their sabres, the mounted regimental commanders salute the onlookers, who shout patriotic slogans, throwing flowers that are trampled under the horses' hooves. The regimental band strikes up the *Radetzky March*. Sweat runs down the faces of the Czechs blaring away on their brass helicons and bass tubas. A small drummer boy, a child soldier, beats away with all his might on the calf-skin of his drum. A little donkey carries the big drum on its back.

Mobilization. The officers' and ensigns' sabres glint. Oh dear, you sabres will not glint in the sun's rays much longer, will you? You will soon be done away with on the orders of His Excellency the Minister for War, so the enemy will be unable to distinguish officers from privates. Your place will be taken by the bayonet, the ordinary, crude bayonet.

Mobilization. The company bugles sound and the drummers' sticks start to beat. Oh dear, you drums will not beat time for the infantry much longer, will you? You will soon be done away with on the orders of His Excellency the Minister for War.

Mobilization. Men, horses, donkeys, mules and cattle are on the move. Iron, brass, wood and steel are on the move. Baggage trains rattle on, lorries start up grindingly, and ammunition wagons begin rumbling off, full of grenades, shells and bombs stacked in boxes like bottles of mineral water. Mortar, cannon and howitzer carriages lurch forwards. Animate and inanimate numbers are walking, driving, gasping, numbers worked out in the heads of the staff officers. In rows straight as a die, a host of heads in caps and helmets is marching, bodies in blue, grey and green tunics swaying like a field of wheat. Armies of buttons, whistles and belt straps flow upon armies of people in new, yellow, unpolished boots. The backpacks and grey mess tins sway on Polish, German, Czech, Italian and Hungarian shoulders. Haversacks, cartridge belts and bayonets are on the move, carried on foot, on horseback, by people, by horses, in wagons and in motor vehicles. Goods trains are loading up (40 men—8 horses) with masses of humans, animals, iron, wood, fabric, straps, and patience. Terror accumulated in such quantities does not know what to do with itself. For now, it is releasing itself in the form of trampling, clattering and rumbling noises.

In these processions man was fraternizing with beast, iron and wood. Rifles have now taken the place of wives, in place of brothers haversacks are befriended, and water flasks replace favourite children. Dear child, kiss the thirsty infantryman's parched lips.

The benevolent grey, chestnut and dun horses toss their heads. The donkeys loaded with machine-gun parts calmly and silently look round for the last time from the wagon ramp.

Mobilization. The railway stations at Vienna, Pest and Prague are weeping now, as are those at Lwów and Kraków. Answering sobs sound at stations in Belgrade and Moscow. Warsaw too.

The sweaty, breathless, drunken numbers of heads, arms, legs and torsos flow like lava towards the east and the south, from east to west, from south to north, to satisfy someone's ambitions, to someone's greater glory. Healthy, strong lungs, hearts and stomachs set off in their thousands, tens of thousands, hundreds of thousands, to all corners of the earth to a tournament of their own suffering, hunger and fever.

From all airfields, from all hangars, propellers buzzing, two-winged and four-winged moths and dragonflies soar up and away as though leaving their chrysalis.

They are advancing on land, at sea and in the air. Gunners on torpedo ships and battle-cruisers are keeping their powder dry. Submarines are preparing to dive; their periscopes scour the deep, seeking their prey. The equipment sings the praises of its inventors. Glory to the men on high, on land and under water!

A swarm of swarthy, moustachioed Serbs from the Drina, Sava and Timok is on its way to face the blue host under their black-and-yellow flag. They smoke pipes and march to the rhythm of their singing. They steal through the rushes and wade across the swamps in their own country—and wait.

Waves of Russians, urged on by blessings from their icons, roll on to face the Imperial host. Cossacks from the Amur, from Kazan and the Don ride their swift little horses. Slant-eyed Mongols bob along on their diminutive mounts. Graceful Circassians, slender-waisted like young girls, gallop with daggers in their belts on the banks of the Vistula, the Bug and the Niemen. Long, endless columns of Siberian infantry in fur hats and Caucasian front-line regiments in sand-coloured tunics head towards Poland at a rapid pace. Get the Kraut! Get the Kraut!

Balalaikas, shepherds' pipes and Jews' harps are heard. During extended rest stops, harmonicas play a Styrian waltz.

The 30th Lwów Regiment, the Iron Brigade, sings: "From Warsaw to Petersburg! Get the Muscovites, march on, march on!" *"Na zdar!"* call out the Czechs, their throats lubricated

---

* "Hurrah!"

with vodka and rum, as they pass by wagons full of Hungarians. "*Eljen!*" echo the Hungarian shepherds-turned-Honvéds. With responding cries of *Živio! Hoch! Ewiva!* and *Harazd!* the battalions of the polyglot monarchy greet one another as they pass. The trains race on like gigantic tin cans packed with human flesh, not yet drained of its blood.

In distant Hutsul country, young yokels stand waving their hats, their shirts hanging loose, gaping at the troop trains rushing past.

The man who is temporarily acting as signalman at signal box no. 86, on the Lwów–Czerniowce–Ickany line, cannot sleep. This signalman was called up the day before and he has joined his unit. Now he, a mere porter, has to look after the level-crossing barrier by day and by night, seeing to it that the movement of troops can proceed in orderly fashion, taking particular care to prevent "Muscovite sympathizer elements" placing blocks of wood on the track. He is amused by the graffiti chalked on the sides of the wagons, patriotic drawings of Tsar Nicholas and King Peter on the gallows. On one occasion, he was so distracted that he failed to hear an approaching locomotive and did not close the barrier. He nearly caused the death of a milkman who was driving across the track just as the train sped over the points. The nag took fright and could not be reined in; the shaft snapped. Virtually at the last moment, the "signalman" ran onto the track and just in time stopped the train, full of boisterous, singing Romanians. The racket the soldiers were making filled the entire Pokuttya plain. The stench of straw, human sweat and horses' urine mingled with the sharp aroma of the new-mown hay beyond the embankment. A major in command of the transport operation leapt down from a passenger carriage and asked, in an unknown language, about the cause of the delay. The man with the flag gabbled something in Ukrainian, then in Polish, even a few words in broken Yiddish, then he pointed out the pool of milk on the track and the Jewish milkman, who had by now managed to get across to the other side with his horse and cart.

"*Schweinerei!*" yelled the major. "—*Ja czi bende anzeigen, ti oferma!*—I'll show you, you idiot!"

Then he shook his riding crop at the Jew, gave a sign to the engine driver and returned to the carriage. The train got moving again, leaving the man with the flag alone in his shame.

"Idiot," he repeated.

Now he knew he would be joining the reservists. As a matter of fact, he didn't care. If it was war, then it was war, wasn't it? War had already broken out.

On 1st August 1914 a gunner on the *Temes*, an armoured cruiser on the Danube, aimed his cannon and fired on Belgrade. The Danube fleet began bombarding the city. On 2nd August, the German naval guns began to roar off the coast of Kurland, near Libau. On 3rd August, the French Alpine Chasseurs were deployed among the summits of the Vosges. That same day French pilots attempted to blow up bridges on the Rhine. German cavalry crossed the Golden Gate of Burgundy and advanced into the woods around Delle to reconnoitre. The first encounter between Austria and Russia took place on the frontier between Bessarabia and Bukovina, near Novoselytsia.

Unknown is the man who was the first to give his life in this war.

Unknown is the man who killed him. Unknown is the last man to fall in this war.

My word will raise him from the earth in which he lies; he will forgive me this exhumation.

Unknown is the Unknown Soldier.

Chapter One

I nto distant, forgotten corners of the Hutsul country—filled with the aroma of mint on summer evenings, sleepy villages nestling in quiet pastures where shepherds play their long wooden horns—comes the intruding railway. It is the only connection these godforsaken parts have with the outside world. It pierces the night's darkness with the coloured lights of its signals, violating the silence, violating the immaculacy of the profound night-time peacefulness. The din of its illuminated carriages rends the membrane of darkness. A long-drawn-out whistle blast awakens hares from their slumber and arouses people's drowsy curiosity. Like a great iron ladder nailed down onto the stony ground, shiny black rails on wooden sleepers stretch from one infinity towards another. Little white station buildings surrounded by hedges, vegetable plots, gazebos and flower-beds with coloured glass orbs on white-painted sticks, numerous little iron bridges crossing streams and countless small signal boxes give the lie to any impression that this part of the country was totally God-forsaken.

At the small Topory-Czernielica railway station, a man who had emerged from the darkness had been dealing for some twenty years in grain, timber, potatoes and casks of locally brewed moonshine. Darkness was his home and his element, no less than water is that of the fish and earth is that of the mole. Like a mole, Piotr burrowed his way through the darkness, digging out underground passages essential to his existence. In the fresh air he desperately gasped for breath, like a fish out of water.

He polished the station lamps, filled them with paraffin and swept the so-called waiting-room. When the need arose, he helped with repairs to the track, removing rotten sleepers, spreading gravel and occasionally riding the hand trolley with the inspection engineer. The fast trains did not even deign to do Topory-Czernielica station the honour of slowing down. They sped irreverently by, contemptuously puffing a cloud of smoke in its face. In summer, however, some townspeople would alight here. Schoolboys arrived with trunks they couldn't lift on their own. The train stopped at Topory for only three minutes, and the young gentlemen, in order to conceal their helplessness, would call out "Porter!" in a commanding tone, like seasoned travellers. Thereupon Piotr, although he was no porter, had no railwayman's cap, and did not even wear a brass porter's badge on his chest, would dash into the carriage, seize the luggage and carry it to the horses waiting behind the station building. Sometimes the Greek Catholic priest travelled to town and he had to be helped onto the train. Sometimes there was hunting in the extensive forests, and certain gentry preferred to travel by train so as not to tire their horses. This used to earn him a little something, and a few cigarettes some count gave him could be hidden under his cap. Those were the days!

And after the harvest came sacks of oats, and then of maize, so there were opportunities to make the occasional hole in a sack, saying, if necessary, that the sacks had been torn. They weren't sealed, anyway.

The stationmaster was human. Of course, he would box your ears, but he didn't dismiss you. When the stationmaster struck you, you had to kiss his hand at once, beating your breast and saying: "I honestly swear to God I'll never do it again," but you didn't have to return what you had stolen. That was the life!

Piotr's entire life involved carrying things. As a child, he had suffered from that infamous Hutsul affliction for which the human race had the French to thank, apparently. Its symptoms were the typical nose and certain defects of vision, which, however, did not develop further with age. Independently of the French influences, Piotr's body was also subject to English ones, the rickets. And so France and England, those two warring elements that had done battle in the historical arena over so many centuries, settled their differences in the body of a Hutsul child. To the end of his life, Piotr remained bandy-legged.

Not only that, but he wore his father's sheepskin coat, and bore his surname too. He had never known his father. His mother was a Hutsul and she smoked a pipe, even in her old age. She had a fine bearing, dainty feet, several beautifully embroidered shirts and jerkins, and numerous children too, who died virtually as soon as they were born. Only Piotr and Paraszka survived. The latter, in the opinion of many earnest folk, would have been well advised not to have survived.

The legendary father was Polish, apparently, name of Niewiadomski,* as—to avoid offending aristocratic gentlemen—children of uncertain paternity were known. But Piotr was a child from a legal marriage bed. The bed in question was situated in a cottage, now semi-dilapidated, at the far end of the parish of Topory. Thanks to this cottage with its thatched roof, Piotr had spent his entire life in Topory, not once submitting to the lure of Saxony, as he was frequently tempted to do. An orchard of just over an acre belonged to the cottage. One of the two apple trees had long since grown barren.

Of course, it belonged to Paraszka, who had gone to town and "decayed"—as the parish priest used to say—in a certain public establishment.

The neighbours' children gorged on plums from the six plum trees every autumn. Piotr did not have any land of his own. However, the railway granted him the lease of a small plot adjacent to the track. There he planted potatoes, beans, maize, cabbages and a few sunflowers. Actually, it wasn't he who did the planting, but a certain orphan girl called Magda. She was partial to sunflowers. After the death of Piotr's old mother in the Year of Our Lord 1910, she began to hang about near Piotr's cottage. Malicious female tongues wagged in the village, saying that on more than one occasion she brought him his milk in the evening and didn't leave until nearly daybreak, just before morning milking time. Piotr had no cow of his own either. When he was young, he had indeed driven his mother's cow and his mother's geese to pasture, but no

---

* "Incognito".

sooner was his mother buried than he sold the cow at market, sending half the proceeds to Paraszka, because that's how it should be, and drinking the rest. He took the geese to the station as a gift for the stationmaster's wife, just plucking a few feathers for himself first.

A dog represented his entire modest possessions. But what a dog! A dog such as this is more than a mere dog; it's an angel. True, it yielded no milk, but it was a good dog, meaning that it was fierce. Its mother was a mongrel and its father a wolf (Piotr did not care about the breed; he was cross-bred himself). The dog was called Bass, suggesting that he had a powerful voice. When he got a bit older, he did not exactly mellow, but he became indifferent and nobody in the village feared Bass any longer. He was porter Piotr Niewiadomski's one and only love.

Why didn't Piotr marry Magda? This was a question often asked by people who favoured the sanctity of marriage, and the Greek Catholic priest once even put the question to Piotr directly, at his Easter confession.

"I haven't had any children with her," Piotr told himself, "so I won't be having any now."

Disregarding the dreadful consequences to be suffered in life beyond the grave threatened by the priest—who was prepared to make an exception and even accept a reduced fee, since it was a matter of saving the soul of an inveterate sinner—Piotr declared categorically:

"I won't marry her, because she isn't a virgin."

But there were other reasons why Piotr, for the time being at least, had no wish to don the gold-plated crown customarily placed on the heads of the bride and groom as prescribed by

JÓZEF WITTLIN

the Greek Catholic marriage ceremony. Piotr Niewiadomski was a dreamer. He had in mind a quite different head covering. It might not be such a glittering one as the wedding crown, but on the other hand he could wear it to the end of his days and not just during the wedding ceremony. And if it really was a matter of outwardly resembling the great and the good of this world, Piotr was much closer to the mark in preferring a particular cloth cap instead of a metal symbol of doubtful value that was supposed to render him the equal of crowned kings. Anyway, it was only on playing cards that kings wore gold crowns, he believed, and he knew all about playing cards.

Long ago, perhaps as far back as Metternich's time, some state official in his wisdom designed the Austro-Hungarian uniform cap. He determined its shape, dimensions, cut and trim, and having gained approval at the highest level imposed it on the heads of all those who wished to serve the Emperor. The Emperor set an example by wearing one himself, as his own servant, and the Emperor's relatives wore it, as did his ministers, marshals and generals, his senior councillors and commissioners, officers and clerks, gendarmes (retired), members of military bands, cab-drivers, postmen, school caretakers, prison warders, and railway officials down to the last signalman. It was the Imperial headgear. His Imperial Majesty appeared in it on the balcony and in his carriage, raising his trembling white-gloved hand to its shiny black peak whenever he was greeted by his subjects, of whom he possessed so many during the sixty-six years of his most gracious reign. Of course, the cut and the trim of the cap had undergone all kinds of changes during the course of so many years. Many a defeat and many a victory had left its mark on the Imperial cap. Also, taking into consideration forms of service and hierarchical status, the wise inventors and renovators of the cap thought up various subtle variations, not always perceptible to the layman's eye. For example, officers' caps were made of black cloth with a gold cord running round the lower edge, incorporating a fine black zigzag pattern. Lower-ranking functionaries had a yellow thread rather than a gold one. Just one thing was common to all—the Imperial monogram, which had to be embroidered or imprinted, always taking pride of place, identifying the Emperor's servants like the Imperial handkerchiefs and the Imperial forks and spoons. So nobody could steal them, sell them or pawn them.

Piotr too belonged to the Emperor. He never ceased to be aware of who he served. On the face of it, he merely shifted loads for the young squires, on the face of it he served the Jews who dealt in grain and potatoes in these parts. In reality, he shifted all this for the Emperor. In return, the Emperor paid him and protected him with exceptional rights. Just let any merchant make so bold as to lay a finger on Piotr when he was on duty! This would constitute an insult to an Imperial and Royal personality, and it would therefore be no laughing matter. Such an offence was punishable by imprisonment.

However, Piotr was often wracked by doubt; indeed, a dark bitterness would creep into his heart. For, actually, why was he not supposed to wear an Imperial cap, like other railway employees? Why was he not supposed to command respect? Why, despite so many years of faithful service, did he still have the appearance of just any civilian? Why was he never promoted? Was he merely some supernumerary who could be replaced at any time? Was he merely some base kitchen spoon, considered unsuitable for inclusion among the treasury's grand dinner-service?

At such times, Piotr Niewiadomski indulged in self-pity, convincing himself that it would be better to give it all up, all these railway duties which just made him stoop-shouldered and gave him little pleasure. Perhaps it would be better, after all, to sell the house (with Paraszka's consent, of course, though she wouldn't be returning to it now), sell the orchard and go to Saxony.

However, these bitter thoughts never troubled him for very long. Such doubts were soon dispelled and his faith was restored that all was not lost, that the Emperor was good, God was just and that they would not harm their people. It was merely necessary to wait patiently, toil patiently, bear burdens patiently and patiently suffer abuse from conductors and senior porters. It was even necessary to put up with the stationmaster's wrath. An Imperial servant had the right to strike another Imperial servant in the face, because he was doing so in the name of His Imperial Majesty. But civilians—hands off!

So for many years Piotr anticipated that the day would eventually come when he would be promoted, having done enough carrying to deserve a pay rise and a cap. Perhaps this dream of an Imperial cap was a reflection of his unhappy childhood, when he'd pretended that an old pot he'd found disposed of on a rubbish heap was his military cap. No doubt that childhood memory still retained in Piotr's mind at the age of forty explains the undeniable fact that Piotr Niewiadomski would be delighted to be able to salute people instead of greeting them as a civilian would.

He would have liked most of all to be a railway crossing guard or an assistant guard on a goods train. Service on the railway was attractive to Piotr simply because he came into contact with trains leaving for far-off destinations. The whole wide world familiar to him from travellers' accounts passed through Topory-Czernielica station along with those trains. Piotr had seen carriages in which you could sleep under a blanket as comfortably as in a soft bed, and he had seen carriages in which gentlemen sat at tables covered by white tablecloths, eating, drinking and enjoying themselves. Often, curtained saloon cars with flowers in little vases in the windows flashed past Piotr as he stood rooted to the spot. By one window he would see a thick-set man in a tall white chef's cap leaning against the shiny bulkhead, pouring something from a copper saucepan.

Piotr also saw trains that had come all the way from Turkey, which is by the sea, where there are heathens who are permitted to have several wives at once, and he saw trains returning from Vienna, where the Emperor himself lives. True, he had little to do with those trains personally, as they naturally didn't stop at Topory-Czernielica station, but on a number of occasions he had the job of striking the wheels that had run on foreign tracks with a hammer. When he touched the wheels of goods trains that were destined for distant, unknown parts, it was as if he was touching the very secret of a world he had never known.

Why should he not become a signalman or travel on a goods train to the Romanian border? After all, he could recognize colours and distinguish red and green, even though he could not read or write. He also knew how to look after the points. Did people say he was stupid? Well, what if he was? The saints couldn't glue broken crockery together and King Solomon wasn't a guard on the railway.

If Piotr became a signalman—now, that would change everything! He would no longer avoid the wedding ceremony, though Magda would be even less in the running than before. Piotr the signalman would be highly eligible for many a respectable widow or even an older spinster, but she would have to be some well-to-do farmer's daughter, of course. Only then would he set up a home, a proper home with a proper woman. They would renovate the cottage, repair the leaky roof and thatch it with fresh straw, replace the rotten ceiling rafters and scrub the bedstead with a firm brush. Above the bed would hang a row of images of the Immaculate Mother of God, the Holy Virgin of Pochaiv, the Lord Jesus of Milatyn and various others. Above the icons there would be red paper roses on wires. They would buy a cuckoo clock, a mouse-trap and some saucepans at the fair; on the windowsill there would stand flower pots with fuchsias, red as radishes. They would paint the whole living room sky blue. The wife would undoubtedly bring decorated cupboards from home, in which they would keep shirts, a sheepskin coat, their money and prayer books. Magda would be able to carry on working if she wished, but now it would be his own cow she would milk, the one his wife would have to include in her dowry. No, he would not turf Magda out on her ear—Heaven forbid! On the other hand, she could no longer sleep with him. She would find herself another fellow.

These thoughts, which he did not mention to the priest at confession, kept Piotr at Topory and prevented him from taking a decisive step with regard to Magda. They combined his two life's ambitions in one joyful vision. Piotr always imagined his dilapidated house in a flourishing state, rebuilt and, in the absence of children, populated with chickens, ducks and even pigs, with which Bass got on famously. He always imagined his house as a place where happiness dwelt. At Easter, he would have sausages from his own pig, he would have a whole year's supply of pork fat, and feathers for his matrimonial eiderdowns from his own geese instead of stolen ones.

One day, at 5.20 in the morning, the Topory-Czernielica stationmaster summoned Piotr to his office. As a rule the stationmaster was still asleep at this hour, but today, though he was still unshaven, he was already fully dressed and had had his breakfast, as could be seen from the empty cup and half-eaten bread roll on a metal tray. Why hadn't the station-master finished his breakfast? This was Piotr's first thought on arrival at the office. There was a considerable delay before it occurred to Piotr to wonder why the old man had summoned him at such an early hour. The stationmaster was sitting at his telegraph machine as it clicked away. The red colour on his official cap contrasted sharply with his pale cheeks covered in dark stubble. He paid no attention to Piotr's arrival. He was engrossed in the long ribbon of paper he was feeding through his fingers, deciphering some secret messages. The machine clicked away incessantly. In the motionless silence that engulfed the office and the whole area surrounding the station, isolated among the fields, Piotr was alarmed by the dull, insistent clicking of the metal machine. He stopped observing the stationmaster, involuntarily turning his gaze towards the window, through which he had a view of the clear sky and several silent trees. The sky and the trees had a calming effect on him. All of a sudden, the machine stopped clicking. That was more ominous still. The stationmaster looked up. A great change seemed to have come over him. That severe, derisory expression that Piotr had found so daunting all those years seemed to have vanished overnight from his cold, gaunt, yet always contented features. Those eyes had so often caused him to endure hard times in his life. Piotr found them piercing even when, thankfully, they were closed. Those eyes were capable of stopping Piotr's heartbeat, penetrating the innermost recesses of his conscience. Beneath their gaze, Piotr would cringe and squirm so much that he had developed that false smile simple people assume in order to shake off the burden of contempt. Of all the burdens he carried in his life, the most onerous was the eyes of the stationmaster he felt on his back. Today, these eyes were extinguished; they were like the empty barrels of a double-barrelled shotgun. What has happened to the stationmaster?—Piotr wondered. He isn't looking at me as he usually does; he looks as though he has stopped being the stationmaster. Perhaps he is leaving for another position and his rule has come to an end here?

Piotr began thinking of his superior as his equal. Judging by his facial expression, the stationmaster was indeed on much the same level as Piotr Niewiadomski today. His eyes showed that look of consternation and sheer helplessness marking out those who vainly struggle to cope with life's cruel realities. Today, the stationmaster revealed his most human trait—his weakness. His rustic origins, which had been carefully concealed beneath his official tunic, were exposed too. In life, there occur moments that thwart people's efforts over the years to pull the wool over their own eyes and those of others, their perpetual efforts to emulate gestures they have observed. At such times, you might think, breeding somehow raises its head, drawn out by some chemical process. We are given away by a single involuntary movement of the hand, a single wry facial expression or a particular intonation. Something unusual must have happened that night for the stationmaster to be so changed. Perhaps he had suffered some loss in the family; perhaps he had been disciplined for something or other. Or had he been given to understand, by the officialdom whose ladder of hierarchy he aspired to ascend, that he was considered a simpleton?

No, no misfortune had befallen his family, no one had reported him for exceeding his authority and no one had reproached him for being the son of a cartwright in Rohatyn province. Quite different events had occurred that night... That night the timetable, which from time immemorial had been the ten commandments of the Lwów–Czerniowce–Ickany railway line, had collapsed. It had crashed in a single moment, never to recover from this ignominy. At that moment those secret instructions applying "in case of war" which the stationmaster, who had taken an oath on assuming his appointment, kept sealed in an iron box in the most secure place in the ticket office, had come into force. They were not issued by his civilian employers, who took their orders from the Mount Sinai of the railways at the Ministry of Transport, but by the Chief of Staff. That is how the strict Law that had been faithfully observed in blind obedience on the railways for so many years collapsed. Public transport was suspended.

The stationmaster cast a helpless, almost imploring gaze in Piotr's direction. He handed him two tightly rolled large sheets of white paper containing closely printed text.

"Niewiadomski," he said in a strangely soft voice, "war has broken out!"

It was a long time before Piotr took in the significance of these words. The word "war" crashed down on his head like a heavy clod. It penetrated his skull, penetrated the membrane and entered his brain. Piotr's brain was immediately inundated with images. In an instant, Piotr could see manoeuvres he had witnessed in these parts two years before. Vast numbers of soldiers were simulating a firefight. They fired from both sides, lying on either side of the embankment along the track, fighting for possession of this railway line, but none of them was killed because on hearing the sound of the bugle they all stood up and lit cigarettes, laughing and marching off towards the great forest to the sound of music. Piotr knew that in real wars people were killed. He had seen bodies of Serbs and Bulgarians in a colour illustration from the battle of Çatalca in some magazine a newsagent had shown him in Śniatyn. He also remembered illustrations from the Russo-Japanese war. And suddenly the word "war" performed a somersault in his brain; it fell into his aorta, which it would have burst had it not been carried by the bloodstream into his heart. From there it forced its way into his abdomen, finishing up there as a sharp pain, like a stab from an iron instrument. For a moment, Piotr was overcome by a fear of death. But the heavy blood, exhausted by this sudden unexpected rush, gradually flowed back to his brain, bearing the drowned remains of the dead word "war". Piotr regained his equilibrium. He realized that it was only soldiers who died in a war, and he was not in the army. He could now attend calmly to the stationmaster's next words.

"Take these posters and display them in the waiting-room, under the clock. Not too high up, and not too low down! Got it, Niewiadomski?"

As he was issuing the order, the stationmaster realized who he was talking to and attempted to inject a semblance of the former severity into his now timid voice.

"Take care not to tear them, and put them up straight!"

Piotr left, carefully shutting behind him the door bearing the prominent notice: "Unauthorized entry strictly forbidden". He stood in the dingy corridor, holding the war in his hands. It was not yet unfurled, coiled up like the leaves of buds in spring.

He did not unfurl it until he reached the waiting-room.

After Piotr had left, the stationmaster glanced at the great clock on the wall. He looked anxiously up at the clock every five minutes. Beneath the clock there ceremoniously hung a large tear-off calendar. The stationmaster's first duty each morning was to tear off a leaf from the calendar. Today the stationmaster had already been sitting for an hour in the office, but the calendar still displayed the date of the 27th of July. In this office, yesterday still persisted instead of today; it was intact. Why had the Topory-Czernielica stationmaster not cancelled the previous day? Could he be trying to hang on to the time when his timetable was in force, that of the railways, and not theirs? Could he be trying to hold on to the time when yesterday's world order was in force? Could it also simply be the case that, in the spate of work that had engulfed him that night, his usual daily routine had been forgotten? It was already 5.30. Six o'clock passed, but the stationmaster did not remove yesterday's leaf from the calendar.

At 6.25 there came a knock at the door. The stationmaster gave a start. His feet were entangled in snake-like coils of white paper covered in Morse code. Like a comic dancer at a ball, the ladies' favourite caught up among paper streamers, the stationmaster disengaged himself from the war around his feet, and he was free.

"Come in!" he called.

It was the trainee who was supposed to relieve him at seven o'clock. On seeing his deputy, the stationmaster came to terms with reality. He quickly approached the calendar and tore off the 27th of July. He crushed it in his hand and threw it into the overflowing waste-paper basket as though the latter was a communal grave for fallen soldiers. It meant that Topory-Czernielica station had bidden farewell to the last day of peacetime.

The waiting-room was still deserted. The window where the stationmaster issued tickets to the public was still closed. Twice a day people had the right to hurry to this window so as to catch the train in time. Today they no longer need to hurry. Nobody knows when it will open, or if indeed it will open at all. It is closed like the lips of a corpse. It will no longer accept any money and it will not issue any tickets. Perhaps it will be opened by the same power that abolished the Law last night.

To the left of the window, above the wooden benches, hung an enormous, majestic, yellow sheet of squared paper, with black lines separating main routes from branch lines. This was the wall timetable of the Imperial and Royal State Railways of the East Galician territory. Those able to read had always confidently used it to check the sacred hours and minutes of departures and arrivals, but today they were checking only dead memories. The official timetable hung there superfluous, unimportant, like an old funeral announcement at a house from which the deceased had long since been carried away.

Other posters and announcements were attached there too. A now very faded coloured poster, an invitation to attend the Vienna Eucharist Congress—ceremonies that had long since taken place and been forgotten. Pedigree turkeys and chickens invited you to the Third Regional Poultry Exhibition. A smiling, corpulent waiter in tails carrying frothing jugs of beer in both hands offered this beverage on behalf of the Lwów Brewery Company. An attractive sphinx-woman with massive earrings was smoking a cigarette wrapped in fine Abadia paper. All these adornments on the drab walls of the waiting-room at Topory-Czernielica station owed their presence over the years to Piotr Niewiadomski, who had pasted them up personally.

Two new notices had been drying out on the door for the last hour. Large, white, severe, bereft of illustrations, smiling waiters and sphinx-women. They were identical and inseparable, like Siamese twins, and their presence was also due to Piotr. There was a provocative freshness about them.

At around seven o'clock passengers began to gather. A gamekeeper in a green cap turned up, a couple of old women with baskets, a few Hutsul men in red trousers and some black-coated Jews. They all crowded round the new notices, talking loudly in their impatience and perplexity. Shortly, the stationmaster appeared. He wanted to announce in person that the passenger train was cancelled. That the line had been placed at the disposal of the military. Suddenly, glancing at the posters he had ordered Piotr to display that morning, he flew into a rage.

"Where's Niewiadomski?" he shouted. "I'll knock his block off!"

Niewiadomski didn't know why.

"The dozy nincompoop! The Emperor's proclamation—he's got the Emperor's proclamation upside down!"

It took him a long time to calm down. Finally, he dashed to the office for more posters and pasted them up himself. The people who had gathered in the waiting-room began reading aloud the words of the proclamation to the beloved nations. To begin with, one word at a time, if their reading ability allowed, then in chorus with the illiterates. They repeated each word like a litany in church. In these distant lands, their faith in Emperor Franz Joseph united Roman Catholics, Greek Catholics, Armenians and Jews in one shared universal church. Piotr involuntarily removed his cap as he listened open-mouthed to the Emperor's solemn imputation. The Emperor had despatched it here, to the very limits of his domains, so that good people might take pity on him and take up the cause of the injustice to his gracious person. The Emperor's faithful subjects did not disappoint him. In the universal agitation that overcame the Topory-Czernielica station waiting-room, Piotr Niewiadomski forgot his personal shame, because he was thick-skinned but soft-hearted. In a biblical, hieratic, moving style, the Emperor's proclamation railed against the wicked, subversive Serbs for obliging him to take up the sword instead of permitting him to eventually die in peace.

"What sort of sword?" Piotr wondered. "It must be the large silver pen-knife that His Majesty carries around in his pocket, and only takes out in the event of war."

Two days later, the stationmaster called Piotr into his office once again. Piotr thought he was going to be punished for the *lèse-majesté* he had committed by attaching the proclamation upside-down. By way of justification he could only say that he was illiterate, and that there were no illustrations on the Emperor's posters allowing him to tell top from bottom. However, the stationmaster received him calmly and amicably. Evidently, it was forgotten. Mobilization had smothered all else. For many a criminal, it brought a pleasant, unexpected amnesty.

"Niewiadomski," said the stationmaster, "you are an ass, but I have nobody else I can turn to. One after another they are being conscripted into the army. You have to go to 86; Banasik has received his call-up papers and he is joining the reservists. Today you have to go down to the track, take his cap and flag and look after the level-crossing barrier. Banasik will show you everything. The war won't last long, three weeks, four at the most. In a week's time we'll enter Belgrade, in two weeks we'll take Warsaw, and in three weeks we'll be in Moscow, God willing. Then we'll all return home; Banasik will return, unless he gets killed. Until then you have to stay at 86 and carry out his duties. Just don't let me hear any complaints, because war is no joking matter. You'll be out on your ear and not even the dog will bark for you."

When he said "we'll enter Belgrade" and "we'll take Warsaw", the stationmaster did not have in mind participating in the expedition personally, as he was, at least for the time being, exempted from that on account of his occupation and his age. He was merely using the pronoun "we" popular in wartime, as a manifestation of solidarity with those who go to war.

Piotr was not familiar with the subtle metaphors employed by civilized people since time immemorial. He took every word literally. So he imagined that the stationmaster would go to war together with the signalman. Piotr thought this was detrimental to his own interests. If Piotr had been able to think as civilized people do, he would have wished that the war might continue as long as possible, or that signalman Banasik would never return. For in either case he would have a chance of staying in signal box 86 for ever. But Piotr was not capable of such far-reaching speculation. He accepted the news of this so long-desired turn of fate with great calm, bordering on resignation. After what the stationmaster had said, he took his unexpected conditional promotion as more of a demotion. After all, he had become a signalman only by default and not in recognition of his personal deserts and abilities.

So Piotr Niewiadomski donned his dreamt-of railwayman's cap, his Imperial cap. It was in fact made of navy blue cloth, not black, and it did not have a little eagle with the Emperor's monogram, but it sported a fine metal railway-carriage wheel running towards infinity, with outstretched wings spreading on each side as though from the shoulders of an angel. Unfortunately this cap, received in such circumstances, was no promotion, and Piotr took no pleasure in it. Its charm had passed; its magic had vanished as soon as it became reality. Piotr was the victim of his own imagination.

The news that Piotr Niewiadomski was wearing a railwayman's cap was received by the world with indifference.

Piotr was not so naive as to look on the changes taking place on the 28th of July as being the result of his own promotion. Nevertheless, he was surprised that the people closest to him, who were not familiar with the details of his appointment, paid it no attention. Even Magda remained quite aloof. A young author, seeing his name in print for the first time, experiences similar feelings, surprised to find that people in the street don't point him out. Actually, Piotr had no worldly ambitions. The only thing that upset him was the fact that the high point of his life passed unnoticed, being associated rather with an unpleasant, downright humiliating memory, dissolving without trace in the general chaos and pathos of those momentous days. His head soon became so full of thoughts about the changes in the world that little room was left in it for thoughts about his actual role in that world. He did not even enjoy the saluting that was now his right, observing so many people in uniform who were obliged to salute.

He locked up his cottage and set off down the track, taking Bass with him. The signalman's wife continued to live in the signal box for a few days, but she soon left with her children and went to town to join her family. Niewiadomski was then alone; just once a day, at noon, Magda brought him food. The signal box stood on open land, high up on the embankment. Entry was gained via ladder-like steps. Before Piotr's eyes trains, trains and more trains began to flash by incessantly, loaded with military freight. He had ten sleepless nights; there was so much work with the level-crossing barrier. On one occasion, there was even an unpleasant event: a Jew and his horse were nearly run over, and it was Piotr's fault. Piotr lost his head completely after he started wearing the Imperial cap. It was rather too big for him, and it fell over his ears. The war intimidated him with the roar of the wagons, the rattle of the guns on their carriages, and the multilingual babble of the soldiers.

After ten days and ten nights, fewer and fewer military trains were sent along that line, and the soldiers' singing became less and less frequent. Finally, the transports ceased altogether in those parts. Everything went quiet. Passenger trains were gradually reinstated; however, the window in the so-called waiting-room at Topory-Czernielica station opened only once a day, and the timetable gave no guarantee of punctuality. Piotr was awakened in the night most often by goods trains. From time to time, such a silence descended on the track and the air was so fresh that he could hear the humming of the telegraph poles and the sound of the machinery at the distant sawmill.

Chapter Two

There was silence in the sky, there was silence on the ground, the dogs were not barking and the cocks were not crowing, when Emperor Franz Joseph announced general mobilization. The Emperor's voice did not reach as far as Hutsul territory, but the Emperor's post did. The parish clerks and the gendarmerie reached those places the post could not.

Sergeants and long-serving corporals sat in offices retrieving dusty, yellowing lists of conscripts, dating back to the earliest years. They extracted all the men's names, knowing nothing about these people beyond the mere fact that they had names. For each name, they prepared an individual call-up card and sent it to the municipality. Many of those being called up had long since been buried in the parish cemetery or lay rotting in foreign soil. Names do not die as quickly as people, however, and death keeps its records more diligently than the sergeants. So the Emperor was calling up the living and the dead.

Piotr Niewiadomski was on the call-up roster for the year 1873. He was unaware of this himself, not knowing much about figures, but the municipality knew. The municipality knows everything. The municipality also keeps records and fills in the forms on which is recorded in ink for all posterity who has come into this world and when, and who has departed for the next. In peacetime, the municipality identifies every man who has reached the age of twenty-one, and they all have to report for military service. Blind, lame, deaf, hunchbacked—it makes no difference. Once in their lifetime they have to report for military service, though, as in the Holy Scriptures, many are called, but few are chosen.

In peacetime, Piotr had been exempted. He was the sole breadwinner in his family, which consisted at the time of his elderly mother and Paraszka's illegitimate child. Soon afterwards they both died, first of all the bastard, then the old woman, but Piotr benefited anyway—he was not enlisted in the army. He thought they had forgotten about him by now, but he was mistaken, because the Emperor has a good memory. If necessary, he'll remember you even twenty years later. The Emperor had not forgotten Piotr, he was just putting him by for a darker hour.

That hour had now come, not the darkest hour, but an early evening time when it is still light, when a stillness comes over the earth as though it is being caressed by the hand of the angel for whom bells are ringing in all the churches. A clear sky like the Virgin Mary's azure robe softly cloaks the earth, dampening all conflict and din. Swarms of midges, exhausted by their endless circling in the hot atmosphere, muffle the buzzing of their wings. The oppressive heat begins to recede and abate, opening unseen valves. At this time even people's quarrelsome hearts beat more calmly and the most impetuous creatures of this world recognize the blessing of peace and quiet.

Piotr became very calm and settled. He had forgotten about the war raging somewhere beyond the disappearing horizon and beyond the boundaries of his weary senses. In the cooling atmosphere, the whine of the distant sawmill had finally ceased, and above the greenery of the bushes that hid the village from view bluish smoke began to rise from all the cottages. Everywhere supper was now being prepared. The cottages that had chimneys sent their smoke upwards in a vertical column that dispersed in the blue sky, whereas from the poor huts it spread out in a lazy, low-lying cloud. Piotr set about peeling potatoes. The last train of the day had passed signal box no. 86. It would be another two hours before a goods train was due. Piotr sat down on the doorstep of his little cabin and took off his cap. Bass was lying beside him with his nose to the ground, watching the ants milling around. In the quiet of the evening he did them no harm. His breathing sounded calm and regular.

All of a sudden, the dog raised his head and pricked up his ears. He had heard some suspicious rustling below the bank. A moment later he leapt up and adopted a watchful stance. Somebody must have bumped into the wires joining Piotr's lever to the level-crossing barrier, making them twang gently. They were slung low, just above ground level, and they continued to vibrate for some time in the prevailing silence. Something was moving in that silence, something was approaching the signal box. Piotr took no notice of the dog's concern. He continued to peel the potatoes, throwing them into an earthenware bowl filled with water. But Bass had sensed danger and he began to growl. As the rustling sound continued to draw closer, he could stand it no longer and started barking. He was barking so hard in his fear, anger and protest that he started to choke. The danger slithered silently, snake-like, through the undergrowth, gleaming golden flashes among the green vegetation; it was lost, and then flashed again.

"Quiet, Bass!" shouted Niewiadomski, pushing aside his potatoes. Bass lowered his head and stopped his angry barking, just growling softly. Among the bushes there was the flash of a bayonet, reflecting the rays of the setting sun like a mirror. Then the golden spike of a yellow helmet showed itself and suddenly war appeared over the embankment. It marched in black hobnail boots up the steps, bearing a rifle and sabre, to face Piotr Niewiadomski in the shape of the gendarme Corporal Jan Durek.

Piotr was always disturbed at the sight of a gendarme. Not that he had anything on his conscience, but a gendarme gives off the smell of jail and of the handcuffs he carries hidden in his leather bag, just in case. Corporal Durek was well known to Piotr. Piotr often talked to him at the railway station and he was proud to be acquainted with such a man. In Piotr's eyes, this gendarme represented the pinnacle of intelligence and good taste. The smell of a certain type of shaving cream used by the corporal never failed to make an impression on Niewiadomski. Above all, however, he was impressed by the gold tooth that shone in the gendarme's mouth whenever he opened it, whether this was on official business or privately. That tooth set Jan Durek apart from Piotr as a personality more decidedly than all the gold on his helmet and uniform, his ominous black chin-strap, or his rifle and sabre. It inspired respect for the man himself, so that even if Corporal Durek stripped naked that gold tooth would protect him from any familiarity.

On this occasion Durek opened his mouth on official business, but he embellished it condescendingly with a private smile.

"I have an invitation for you, Niewiadomski."

"Call-up papers?"

"No, tickets for a dance!"

Irony was something unusual in this part of the world, so at first Piotr did not take in the sarcasm of the gendarme's words. For a moment, Piotr imagined snatches of a *kołomyjka*, a Ukrainian folk-dance tune played on a piano accordion and a fiddle, with heavy, gaudily coloured skirts swaying before his eyes. He could almost feel the gorgeous warmth of those skirts on his cheeks. The gendarme quickly brought him down to earth, drawing from the bag in which he kept those handcuffs a small folded sheet of paper sealed with the Imperial eagle.

Gutenberg, Johannes Gutenberg, was the name of that man the devil had intoxicated with Rhine wine in Mainz in 1450, ordering him to invent a new torture for the illiterate and the slow-witted. Possessed by the devil, Gutenberg founded the first printing press, together with a certain Faust. Since that time the devilish seed had spread like a plague of cholera across the entire globe, disturbing, bewitching and poisoning by night and day greedy souls in thrall to their pride in knowledge. But although so many reams of white paper had been smudged by the devil's black characters that the entire globe could be wrapped up in it, in the year 1914 there were nevertheless many honest people in this world, especially in the Śniatyn province, who had not succumbed to the temptation. They were not even intimidated by the law introducing compulsory school attendance or by fines and imprisonment, preferring to pay the fines and suffer imprisonment rather than defile their descendants' souls with the Latin alphabet or the Cyrillic script. It is true, of course, that in this victorious struggle they had a silent but powerful ally, the budget of the Imperial and Royal Ministry of Religious Affairs and Education. In this way the government itself indirectly fought the devil, who inhabits all written words, even the Holy Scriptures. For this reason no God-fearing person would sign documents, recording only three crosses. These three holy signs drive out the devil from all contracts, receipts and promissory notes.

But the devil is vengeful. On all pathways of human life, including main roads as well as crossroads, he has placed signs and warnings, like scarecrows:

"No spitting here, no smoking there. Ignorance of the law is no grounds for exemption from punishment."

"It is forbidden to drink this water!" declares the devil on the large water-butt at Topory-Czernielica station. "Beware of the trains!"

Strzeż się pociągu!
Sterehty sia pojizdu!
Achtung auf den Zug!
Sama la trenu!

shrieks the devil in Polish, Ukrainian, German and Romanian on a pillar close to signal box no. 86, making out that he is a concerned friend looking after people's safety, as though human life, rather than death, were dear to him. But death is present everywhere, absolutely everywhere, and it must to be guarded against. Not only in wartime. Railway tracks spell death wherever they are found, and death can catch you unawares at any time. It lurks in the fresh air and the sunshine and suddenly falls on the heads of haymakers like a bolt from the blue. Death is in the water. Numerous bodies of the drowned are retrieved from the Prut and the Czeremosz in summer. Death lurks even in mushrooms and it finds its way into stomachs together with plums, bearing bloody dysentery along with their sweetness. The devil, that false friend, mocks human death. He speaks to the deaf and gestures to the blind.

Of course, sometimes there are ways to outwit the devil. For example, there is the level-crossing barrier. Horses, cows and Hutsuls are illiterate, but the good Lord has sent them a guardian angel, also illiterate, to save them from death on the railway track. Many a cow and many a Hutsul would have been taken by the devil, especially in these times of war, were it not for Piotr Niewiadomski.

Corporal Durek knew that Niewiadomski was illiterate. Despite that, he delivered the call-up paper to him with an expression on his face that made out that he was unaware of it. The fact that Niewiadomski would have to ask him to read it aloud flattered the corporal. To people who could read Durek merely communicated the orders of a higher authority, but in respect of the illiterate he felt not only that he was this authority's partner, a confidant of its intentions, but also that he personified education itself. For them, it was he who determined guilt and punishment. He was the holder of the keys to the prison cells, as well as of the keys to all secrets of the written word. This was why Durek could not resist the pleasure of confirming his superiority over Niewiadomski, although he had no desire to gloat over the latter's insignificance. Quite the opposite. Only an hour previously, he had been sympathizing in the hall of one of the nearby mansions, where he had gone to announce the requisition of hay and where he had been offered a drink of vodka, a piece of cake and cigarettes.

"Our people are still very uneducated, your Grace—at least eighty per cent of them are illiterate."

By referring to "them", he had wanted to give her to understand that he counted himself among the educated.

His hope was not in vain. Niewiadomski glanced helplessly at the sheet of paper and said:

"If you would, corporal…"

That was all the corporal needed. He had the satisfaction he had sought. He quickly broke the seal, looked at the date and announced sternly:

"In five days' time, at 9 a.m. sharp outside the recruiting office in Śniatyn."

He stressed the word "sharp" in a tone of voice that was meant to indicate that he, Durek, was fully in agreement with the senders of the call-up paper. However, Piotr wanted to know in detail what was written on the light blue paper, and he asked the gendarme to read it all aloud, from start to finish. Durek beamed. Not only that, but he also adopted an even sterner expression than usual, and his voice sounded like that of an actor announcing a death sentence. Durek placed particular emphasis on the words derived from Latin.

"Mr Piotr Niewiadomski," he declaimed, "is to report for inspection—"

"It can't be so bad if they address me as 'Mr'," Piotr thought, giving a sigh of relief. His ears gulped in every word as he struggled to digest it all. Some words were indigestible, however. They were as sharp and cruel as bayonets. "'The individual summoned for inspection is to report in a sober condition and washed'—I'll have to bathe in the Prut and tell Magda to wash my shirt—'Failure to report at the time indicated will result in forcible removal to the recruiting office and punishment by arrest and fine as under paragraph 324, article 12, and paragraph 162, article 3, of the regulations pertaining to civil mobilization, 1861.' What does all that mean? First of all they write 'Mr', addressing me politely, expressing confidence, but if anyone disobeys, then it's fixed bayonets and jail."

Piotr could already picture Corporal Durek getting the handcuffs out of his bag and holding a bayonet to Piotr's throat. He had once witnessed Corporal Durek escorting the bandit Matviy, known as The Bull, away in chains, by train.

The gendarme finished reading, carefully folded the call-up paper and returned it to the recruit, observing the effect of his declamation. Piotr was silent and he seemed unperturbed. The gendarme was dissatisfied by this. It had completely failed to have an impact. So, to inflate the gravity of the situation and at the same time to allude to his own authority, he said:

"But do you know how we deal with deserters now? Court martial and a bullet through the head!"

"That's how it should be!" retorted Niewiadomski.

Durek was taken aback. To conceal his consternation, he smiled, baring his gold tooth, and ostentatiously unslung his rifle. He examined the safety catch to make sure it was secured, and leant the rifle against the wall. He removed his helmet, mopped his brow with a handkerchief and sat down on the threshold. Then he took a shiny imitation-silver cigarette case out of his pocket, full of the cigarettes he had been given at the mansion. The hands which could at any moment change into the hands of justice presented it to Piotr. As Piotr took out a "lady's" cigarette, he noticed a beguilingly revealing pink female figure in lace underwear on the enamelled lid of the cigarette case. He felt a warm sensation in his spine as he recalled that Magda was supposed to bring the milk after sunset. They smoked in silence.

Suddenly, Emperor Franz Joseph's eyes were on Piotr Niewiadomski. He was observing him from a cross attached to the red-and-white ribbon on the gendarme's tunic, commemorating the sixtieth anniversary of his coronation. A golden bust of the Emperor, encircled by a wreath, was mounted at the point where the arms of the cross met, for God and the Emperor always accompany one another. Franz Joseph's cold, metallic eyes pierced Piotr's tunic and his sweaty shirt, penetrating into his very conscience. Anyone failing to voluntarily obey the Emperor's call from the cross at such a time would forgo the pardon of Jesus Christ himself on the day of judgement.

Piotr had appeared in court twice in his life. On both occasions as a witness, in cases of theft on the railway. He swore on the crucifix which stood between two gleaming candles on a green table. The judge, wearing a long black cassock and a cap resembling a priest's beret, pronounced the sentence: "In the name of His Imperial Majesty..." Then everyone had to rise, as in church during Holy Mass. The judge and the whole bench stood up, the gendarmes stood up, the accused and the witnesses stood up, the guilty and the innocent stood up. But they did not have to kneel. Above the green table, directly above the crucifix, there hung an enormous portrait of the Emperor.

Piotr finished his cigarette, and noticed that he had thrown the Imperial eagle to the ground together with the butt. The eagle was printed on the cigarette paper, for they were Imperial cigarettes.

"Everything in this world belongs to the Emperor. Or to God," thought Piotr. The Prut and the Czeremosz, the Carpathians and the cows, dogs and people belong to God. But the railway, all the rolling stock and the locomotives, the signal boxes and the level-crossing barriers, even every scrap of rusty wire, even a rotten sleeper, all is the Emperor's property. Anyone stealing a railway sleeper harms the Emperor and an Imperial gendarme places him under Imperial arrest. He has the right! The most important thing in the world is, of course, money. And whose money is it? It belongs to him whose head is engraved on it. The Emperor gives people money, just as God gives them life. Both of these are merely on loan. The Emperor has different interests from those of God, which means he has the right to take someone's life, borrowed as it is from God.

"Well," said Niewiadomski out loud, "then I'll join up."

But the gendarme had shouldered his rifle again, donned his helmet and fixed the black regulation chin-strap.

"You've nothing to fear. They'll take you in any case— they're taking everybody, but I reckon the whole thing will be over by Christmas."

He said "by Christmas", but he was convinced that the war would be over in four weeks.

Then he saluted and left. Piotr forgot that he was wearing an Imperial cap and he doffed it in civilian fashion. Bass jumped up again and started barking. Piotr silenced him with a kick. The wires twanged and the gendarme was now back on the other side of the track. His footsteps were soon lost in the silence.

The light blue sheet of paper rested in Piotr's motionless hands like a holy image between the stiff fingers of a corpse. He was afraid of the writing, which he could not understand. As long as the gendarme had stood here the letters had been human, but now the devil was in them, scaring him. This sheet of paper, this dead writing, had power over a living person. His fate now depended on these plump black circles, these straight, slender strokes. To be rendered so helpless by letters of the alphabet, not even knowing what words they made! Looking at the word "punctually", he imagined the word "arrest". A dark cell, iron bars in the tiny window. He sensed the chain of letters binding his arms like the links of iron fetters. He could already see the red welts they made. Then something was aroused in him resembling a sense of freedom, which he ought to defend. He did not understand how a sheet of light blue paper could take it away from him. He despaired at his powerlessness in the face of an enemy that he could crumple in his hands and tear to pieces, that would not even offer any resistance.

Perhaps none of this was true? What if the gendarme had deceived him? How could a lifeless piece of paper have any power over a living person? Why were people so stupid as to give credence to pieces of paper? Suddenly, to his consternation, he realized that train tickets are mere pieces of paper too, yet of course people pay money for them. And money is only paper as well, especially the most valuable—ten- and twenty-crown notes, and woe betide someone who loses them! He himself had suffered torment all his life in order to get 10 paper crowns and 5 silver ones on the first of every month. So this was all the devil's doing! What if somebody destroyed the call-up papers? At best, he would be cheating himself, not the devil. Until then, Piotr had thought that you were captured only when a living person stronger than you tied your hands, seized you by the neck and threw you to the ground. But a piece of paper? Today he knew that there were also invisible forces which can overpower you and take away your freedom. They exist somewhere else, but they know all about us and can determine everything to do with us, even sending us to death. Human intelligence and human will are of no avail, because those tiny black, lifeless letters are the ends of invisible threads running like telegraph wires all the way from Vienna and the Emperor himself. These words were written by the Emperor himself. That is obvious; otherwise they would not wield such power. So that's how it is? So the Emperor knows about me? He knows that porter Piotr Niewiadomski, son of Wasylina, has lived in the municipality of Topory-Czernielica, in Śniatyn Province, on the Lwów–Czerniowce–Ickany line, and served Him for many years? So the Emperor knows me? He needs me, and so he is addressing me as "Mr"? "Mr Piotr Niewiadomski!" That sounds good!

Piotr imagined the Emperor sitting in his Chancellery in Vienna behind a big desk with gilt corners, writing letters to all the Hutsuls. The Messrs Hutsuls.

Night was now beginning to draw its shrouds over the Hutsul land and move its shining lights across the sky. Mist and haze were rising from both its rivers. Piotr stood up, gave a deep sigh, took the pot of raw potatoes and turned his back on the sky, the earth and the night that was closing in. He left Bass in the yard. He went inside and placed the potatoes on the hearth, where the fire had gone out. He didn't feel like eating. He lay down on the bed with his boots on. Suddenly he gave a start. He went over to the door and turned the key in the lock. He had never done that. He lay down on the bed again, on his back. He was trying to see nothing and to think about nothing. There was much that he could see, however. So he shut his eyes. But that didn't help either. Reality crept into his brain even through his closed eyelids, tormenting him with images. Piotr could see and feel the hands of gendarme Corporal Jan Durek touching him, the menacing hands of justice.

At that time of day the cows, having had their fill of green grass and flowers, were returning from the pastures. The solemn procession occasionally came to a standstill on the way, scratching their backs with their horns and wishing to dispose of the excessive burden that oppressed their udders. They lowed skywards, like steamers' sirens. In this bovine chorus could be heard the primeval forces of life and vegetation, milk and maternity. The voices of the cattle were breaking, as though anticipating slaughter. In this plaintive call for relief, for relaxation, for sleep, Piotr Niewiadomski recognized the voice of his own soul. It was heavy and overburdened and it too was nourished by grass. It was now with difficulty digesting its fate, indigestible as raw meat.

The frogs had begun their nightly disputes, the crickets pierced the stillness with their chirping. Bass was also recalling former upsets, perhaps from a former existence, but he was not barking at the war any more. He just howled at the rising moon. He might have had toothache.

Piotr lay with his eyes open, staring dolefully into the darkness.

All over the world, gendarmes were spoiling people's appetites.

Chapter Three

During those days, men's bodies were weighed and measured. They were sorted by categories, picked over like potatoes, like fruit shaken off the tree of life. They were handled en masse, by the score, by the hundredweight, by the wagon-load, everything puny, tainted or sick being rejected. For there had been a great harvest of human bodies since the last war. Neither struck by natural disasters nor decimated by epidemics, two generations of bodies were now going to waste and decaying, not having experienced war. But the trust invested in the instinctive cultivation of the species had not been nurtured in vain. The service unwittingly rendered by the parents was being paid its due homage today.

For the first time in many years we were not being judged according to the way we dressed. On the contrary, today we were only worth anything without our clothes. Only as naked bodies could we display our greatest merits. All they were interested in was whether we were fit. They looked at our teeth as you look horses in the mouth at the sales; they looked us over from the front, they checked us over from behind, tapping our bellies to make sure our innards were not infested with worms.

Up till then, we had been mere names. All the calculations of the War Ministry and the General Staff were based on the numbers of names. The names moved around the world, grew fat and multiplied, to be converted on the day of mobilization into bodies.

The judging of bodies took place in vast drinking saloons, dance halls and popular inns. At the larger venues, the influx of bodies was so great that the premises of the district headquarters were unable to cope with it. So they crowded onto verandas, and nobody bothered if they broke the panes of glass. They waited for hours out in the gardens where intermingled melodies from the *Merry Widow*, *The Magic of the Waltz* and *The Gay Hussars* still wafted. Here and there, colourful Chinese lanterns still hung from wires stretched between the chestnut trees, like the heads of decapitated revellers from last Sunday's party. Lording it over the untidy garden in the distance, amid greasy wrappers and sausage skins, stood a bandstand which had been commandeered as a furniture store. Green armchairs and small green tables were piled up any old how on top of one another, crammed into the pavilion surmounted by a golden four-stringed lyre.

That's what it was like in the large towns, but Śniatyn is not a large town. The famous town of Śniatyn is a small town and the recruiting authorities operated in their own building there. They merely requisitioned chairs from the nearby pubs.

From early morning on, Piotr Niewiadomski waited his turn. It was a blisteringly hot day. Piotr felt like a drink of the beer which was flowing at Schames's pub a couple of feet away, but he resisted the temptation, mindful of the ban mentioned in his call-up papers. He would have a drink after the inspection was over. He waited among the crowd of farm labourers, Jews and various young gentlemen. He was surprised to see such a motley group of different social classes and types of dress. Every now and then, a fat little sergeant appeared in the doorway to the recruiting offices, minus his cap and sabre. The crowd fell silent. The sergeant read out surnames from large sheets of paper. Every name required the response in German:

"*Hier!*"

This word "here" sounded like a hiccup in the mouths of the peasants. They all had their eyes on the sergeant's lips, as the names hissed forth from them like so many buzzing insects. Piotr waited and waited. His throat was so dry he didn't even feel like talking,

The long wait at the entrance to the offices had its good points. They knew nothing about us yet; we were still mere surnames. There was till time; one could withdraw and everything could change at the last minute. Among those waiting in front of the district recruiting headquarters there was no shortage of optimists who in their heart of hearts still believed in miracles, who were in denial of all common sense, hoping that the war would be over before the sergeant called their names. Piotr Niewiadomski was not one of them. He could not care less.

On the opposite side of the street there was a school. A rectangular one-storey building with a red roof. Above the entrance to the school, Piotr noticed a bell similar to those he had seen in cemetery chapels, and on the roofs of certain farm buildings, where they chimed midday—whereas at the cemeteries...

Piotr was not afraid of death, but he preferred not to see its accessories. Then his attention was drawn to the classroom benches that had been carried out into the yard. They were mostly covered in ink-stains. They were a visible reminder of his illiteracy. On one side stood a large blackboard, which could have been the devil's own coat of arms. Many heads wearing hats and caps were leaning out of the open windows. They were not children's heads. Some were even grey-haired.

Around midday, Niewiadomski's name flew out from under the sergeant's black moustache. It was the fourth one on the list. Niewiadomski shouted out *"Hier!"* and the word, the printed word that had wandered among books and registers, became a flesh-and-blood body. Of the forty names called out, three received no response. They had disappeared somewhere in the wide world. Everyone present turned their heads to look for the lost names. But they did not find them.

Up the stone steps smelling of carbolic acid, the sergeant led the group into a hall on the ground floor. He gave orders to undress quickly, telling them smoking was forbidden. There was no smell of carbolic acid here. There was a very muggy atmosphere; an unpleasant odour given off by the naked and half-naked bodies milling around in that hall gave the impression of a fresco representing hell. Clothes deposited higgledy-piggledy on all the benches round the walls and lying about on the dusty floor made the foul air even worse. Muddy trousers, sweaty, old, threadbare shirts and coats, filthy underpants, jerkins, and shabby coats hanging from nails and pegs on the walls presented an eerie sight, rather like rotting remains of the hanged. Under the benches all kinds of footwear nestled ashamedly, from stylish, fashionable

American shoes to coarse Hutsul sandals. Numerous men's jackets, waistcoats, artificial silk shirts with upturned collars, colourful silk ties and straw Panama hats were swamped by the overwhelming mass of rustic attire. The eau de Cologne from Johann Maria Farina's in Jülichplatz, that destroyer of bad odours from time immemorial, chickened out and absconded. This is what the waiting-room for the day of judgement will probably look like, when one day all human differences are erased. Here all the men were naked, and the foul odour, that characteristic earthy smell, was the dominant element. Each body brought with it the odours of its home, the stench of its daily labours—hence the stink of smoky, unventilated mud huts. Those who worked on the land smelt of the soil and of grain, the shepherds smelt of sheep's urine and the Jews smelt of the hostelry, the mill and the Sabbath. Although nobody had brought any food with them, one could tell by their bodily odours what each of them ate. The carbolic acid did not help, disinfecting did not help; from the very first day of the inspection, the hall stank of stables and cowsheds. In this battle with smells waged by civilization and hygiene, nature was victorious. At least in this hall, which served as a cloakroom. From time to time a menacingly silent soldier entered the room, carrying a canister full of water. He refused to answer any questions put by the civilians. He smoked as he sprinkled the floor in order to quell the dust, Mother Earth ground down to powder. The dust resisted, however. Having performed his task, the self-important soldier returned whence he had come, indifferent to the outcome of his endeavours.

Nobody looked after the discarded clothing. Anybody who wanted to could steal it. However, nobody was lured by the property of others. (The owners took their so-called valuables—money and wrist-watches—with them to the inspection.) Some magic spell or charm appeared to watch over the clothes abandoned by their owners, rendering them untouchable, taboo. It was as if the souls of the owners remained in those shirts, trousers and shoes, while their bodies were being judged by the recruiting committee.

But before the bodies underwent the scrutiny of the committee, they were obliged to submit to the ordeal of the chairs. In the doorway leading to what was assumed to be the recruiting panel, the same sergeant appeared who had called out the names down below at the gateway. He was reading them out for a second time now, but just two at a time. Suddenly, Piotr Niewiadomski was flung by the voice of the sergeant into a rectangular room where rows of chairs lined the four walls. On each chair sat a body stripped bare of all its earthly shrouds, embellishments and pretences. A Jew with a long black beard went in together with Piotr. Facing the doorway through which they had entered, Piotr noticed a heavy, deep red curtain. On the sergeant's orders, each of the two fresh arrivals had to occupy the nearest available seats to the right of the door. At more or less regular intervals, some invisible hand drew back the curtain and one or two bodies emerged, making their way back to the changing room. As they did so, an imperious voice called out "Next!" And once more the curtain swallowed two bodies sitting on the nearest chairs. In this manner, all the bodies proceeded mechanically from the cloakroom door to the door behind the curtain. As though in some eerie circus, the silent, naked bodies moved on from one chair to another and from that chair to the next. In peacetime, the residents of the town of Śniatyn spent pleasant hours in those chairs, dreamily drinking beer, smoking their pipes and playing cards. But now those same chairs had become Stations of the Cross for the damned. As if there was only one possible sentence on the day of judgement: hell.

Piotr Niewiadomski shifted from chair to chair in the direction of the enigmatic curtain. It was the first time in his life that he had seen so many naked bodies at close quarters. He saw shrivelled, flabby arms alongside powerful, muscular ones; sunken, consumptive chests alongside heroic busts. Hollow, concave stomachs like deflated balloons sat alongside bulging, fattened-up, blubbery bellies; bent spines and protruding shoulder-blades alongside perfect, classical forms. Hairy torsos and shapeless masses of flesh wobbled next to smooth, shapely, svelte, supple and sometimes downright girlish figures. One man had a striking buffalo-like neck, powerful shoulders and an enormous belly, supported by very slender legs. Piotr was surprised that these spindly legs could carry such a burden. Before his eyes teemed sweaty, crooked, straight, swarthy, red, pale, hirsute, gentlemanly and boorish legs, legs, legs… Nearly all the toes were vulnerable, innocent and bashful, like little girls, even those of people whose hands looked as though they were tools for crime.

Undoubtedly all those bodies had souls of their own, speech of their own; some were garrulous while others were taciturn and reserved, even though in their nakedness they could no longer conceal anything. From chair to chair. Wily bodies and sincere bodies, cowardly bodies and brave bodies. Some were intimate with the sun, the earth and the wind, making their nakedness seem entirely natural; in fact, they would have appeared unnatural when fully dressed. Others were pale and their nakedness was alien to them, because they had never come into direct contact with the earth and the atmosphere, communicating with it only through animal skins, wool, cotton and linen. The bodies of the Jews were especially pale and unaccustomed to the earth. Their black beards contrasted uncannily with their pale complexions. Piotr Niewiadomski had never seen naked Jews before. Previously he had always seen them in their full-length black kaftans, and he imagined that these people had no white skin on their bodies, apart from the hairless parts of their faces and hands. He had always wondered what a Jew looked like without his kaftan. Now he had a naked Jew before him and he kept taking over his chair. This Jew's very prominent, hairy Adam's apple was strangely unsettled. He was still wearing his little circular velvet skull-cap.

On seeing so many bodies, so many physical defects, disabilities and signs of obvious strength, Piotr felt as though he was sitting among those savages who go around naked and live in caves. He had heard that somewhere, beyond America, there existed such people. They were indistinguishable from the animals, jumping from tree to tree, not believing in God and living on human flesh (though perhaps this was untrue). Piotr Niewiadomski fell to pondering about nudity and clothing. He recalled the first human being in the Holy Scriptures, who was a gardener in the Garden of Eden. He moved unconcernedly among the wild animals, among lions and tigers, who were as naked as he was. Wild beasts did him no harm; they did not gnaw him, they did not attack him, nor did he torment them or kill them. They mutually respected one another and all was well with them. They always kept warm, they had food to eat, the human did not have to work or plough or sow, there was no need for money—and this was known as happiness. Suddenly Piotr thought of Eve and memories of nights spent with Magda came flowing back to him. This was the sin inherited from the proto-parents. It was for this that the angel had driven them out of Paradise with a flaming sword; ever since, people have had to work for their crust in the sweat of their brows.

Piotr Niewiadomski began to feel ashamed of his nakedness, as Adam did when he had eaten of the tree of knowledge, able to distinguish good and evil. He was ashamed for himself and all those now bouncing from chair to chair. Only the marriage sacrament grants absolution from original sin, consecrating carnal pleasure, and people must go about in the world fully dressed so as not to cause a scandal. This was the only moment in Piotr Niewiadomski's life when he was truly contrite for living with Magda without the sacrament. He hid his shame under the documents he held in his hand—his certificate of baptism and his call-up papers (confirmation that his soul belonged to God and of the Emperor's claim on his body).

His embarrassment grew as he drew closer to the enigmatic curtain. He involuntarily looked towards his comrades, to see whether they too were ashamed of their nakedness. Indeed, some of them were discreetly concealing their lower parts under documents, briefcases or bags, but generally speaking there was no sense of mutual embarrassment; they were men among men. They were very concerned about looking after the valuables they were holding, removed for safety's sake from the clothes they had abandoned to fate in the changing room. A broad-shouldered, moustachioed fellow was over-cautiously clasping a bulging leather wallet with both hands. Many hands held watches—mostly the thick, onion-shaped Rosskopf pocket watch with a double lid, and a cover of yellowish mica rather than glass. On the heavy, tarnished chains hung enamelled miniatures—portraits of children, or serious women with austere coiffures. Around the necks of many hung consecrated metal tags, little crosses, medals, mementos of indulgences and pilgrimages, or cloth scapulars. One slim, close-shaven man, who might have been about forty years old, had strange tattoos on his chest—a heart pierced by an arrow, a small flag, a mouse (or it might have been a rat), the initials "F.H." and the number "1903". He had probably been in prison, or he might have served in the navy.

Nobody paid any attention to anybody else. They were all totally absorbed in themselves, everyone was trying to guess what sort of fate was in store for them behind that curtain.

During those days impetuous, mindless Mars, who in peacetime did not conceal his contempt for Asclepius, had suddenly begun to take him seriously. Ingratiatingly fawning on him, he openly sought his favours. For without the consent of Asclepius the body of no man could be placed at his disposal, inasmuch as the course of the war was determined first and foremost by the doctors. This profound change of course among the gods was accompanied by equally profound changes in the minds of ordinary mortals—mortals in the most dreadfully literal sense of the word. What this change actually revealed was how very relative the concepts of good and evil are, fixed in people's minds since the time when

Adam's eyes were opened in Paradise. Until then, health had been generally regarded as a treasure to be enjoyed and cared for. Health was a natural human instinct, whereas illness was always considered an evil. Today, the alliance between Mars and Asclepius was to be blamed for a complete reversal of values. What had been an evil before the 28th of July—for example catarrh of the lungs, heart disease, chronic gastroenteritis or a hernia—was after the 28th of July not only a source of joy but something akin to a cast-iron defence against death. It turned out that there were two ways of departing this life, namely civilian death, as a result of domestic suffering and affliction, as we call it, and military death, which is violent, attacking a perfectly healthy body. Such a death arouses panic in the human imagination because of its immediacy, and also because everything is being done, both on "our" side and on that of the "enemy", to make it easily attainable.

No wonder, then, that among the people leaping from one chair to the next in the waiting-room of the Imperial and Royal Recruiting Commission many were regretting their flourishing good health and were suddenly seeking in their mortal frame at least a hint of some defect, some blemish which would have the effect of commuting the presumptive sentence of death. Some of them sought to arouse pity in Asclepius by agonized facial expressions and gaunt figures. They had conscientiously prepared to make a bad impression by not eating or sleeping for days. Instead, they had drunk excessive quantities of black coffee in order to weaken their hearts. People who before the 28th of July had scowled at the very sight of a cigarette in the smoking compartments on trains, indignantly stepping out into the corridor, now inhaled the strongest brands of this poison, blessing the memory of Mr Jean Nicot (1530–1600), the French diplomat born in Nîmes who introduced tobacco to France. To intensify the harmful effect of the nicotine, they rolled their cigarettes using newspapers instead of delicate cigarette paper. In order to simulate symptoms of asthma, innumerable rapid ascents of staircases from the ground floor up to the fifth and sixth were undertaken. Steep hills, cathedral spires and the peaks of synagogues and minarets were climbed. These activities were known collectively as "scourging", and all such efforts for the purpose of dodging military service were known as malingering. Already here, in the waiting room, men were posing as incurable sufferers, as though they feared that their act would be unsuccessful if left until the last moment.

Piotr Niewiadomski was not among them. It's true, he did have bandy legs, the traditional Hutsul syphilis (actually dormant), as well as mild emphysema caused by many years of lifting heavy loads; sometimes he felt sharp pains around the heart, but he considered himself fit and he had no intention of deceiving the Emperor. Not only was he no malingerer, but it never even occurred to him that such people existed. Now he was only a few chairs away from the curtain. The closer he came to the last chair the faster his heartbeat became, but not because he was afraid; it was just the awareness of being about to appear naked before the Imperial Recruiting Commission. The Adam's apple of the Jew sitting next to him was moving up and down ever more rapidly. He was probably swallowing a lot of saliva. Piotr was unconcerned about what he was in for. He felt that he was committed to the Emperor now, and burdened with new, entirely unknown responsibilities. To grapple with the concept of finding ways to dodge the call-up was beyond him. It was all right for the intrepid, who never lost hope that some last-minute notion would come to mind, out of the blue, about how they could influence the Commission's decision; or they trusted that luck would be on their side, leading the doctors to discover some invaluable physical defect. From chair to chair.

There, behind the curtain, numerous bodies were ashamed of their shortcomings, but the majority were proudly paraded as tokens of certain victory. The Jews, in particular, displayed their varicose veins, crooked spines, haemorrhoids, hernias and fallen arches. They had a great respect for medicine. They were familiar with the terminology of diseases and everything concerning human pathology, so they knew the names of their allies, real or imaginary, whereas the peasants were not even capable of naming something they actually suffered from. They pointed to parts of their bodies where they felt pain. Some Jews cast trusting glances at the doctor, hopeful that they would find in him someone who shared their faith and that the underlying voice of their shared blood would—following instincts which had aided this race to make its way, over so many centuries, through all history's barbed wire fences—lead him to give them total or partial exemption. All the greater was their dismay when the doctor—who did indeed turn out to be Jewish—declared them fit for front-line service.

In Śniatyn, the fate of the bodies advancing from chair to chair in the direction of the deep red curtain rested in the hands of the regimental doctor Oskar Emanuel Jellinek, a reservist. Those delicate hands, somewhat hairy, adorned with a massive wedding ring, were allegedly not averse to taking bribes. The Jews knew this. At that time, the first letters of the Latin alphabet were a hundred times more significant to them in terms of destiny, fear and clemency, than all the Hebrew letters in the Torah and the Talmud. So they wracked their brains for nights on end, wondering how to get Dr Jellinek to replace the dreadful, deadly letter "A" by at least a "B", if not a "C". In those days not even sufferers from chronic gastroenteritis, unilateral pneumonia, cardiac neurosis or rheumatism could dream of a "D". The most merciful of all, the blessed letter "D", was granted exclusively to confirmed consumptives, epileptics, cases of incurable renal failure, the insane, the blind, deaf and lame. The fit and the frail dreamt of it as a giant chocolate biscuit. The cherubim bore it on their wings and it melted in the mouth, leaving a taste of heavenly sweetness. Those who did not merit this letter had to pay Dr Jellinek dearly for it, but it meant total exemption from military service, while a "C" (non-combatant service in the orderly room or the stores) cost half as much, and a letter "B" (guard duty, but not at the front line) could be had for a mere hundred crowns. The Jew sitting next to Piotr did not possess even that measly hundred crowns, which is why he began to shiver so much when the curtain was drawn back, swallowing up the two of them.

At a long green baize-covered table, among clouds of bluish smoke, sat a dozen men of varying ages, some in uniform and some in civilian dress. Some of them were busily writing, others were reading newspapers, and some NCO at the end of the table was consuming bread and sausage in a most laid-back manner. Nearly all of them were smoking. To the left of the curtain stood a weighing machine, identical to the one at Topory-Czernielica. Next to the scales Piotr noticed a sort of strange wooden post with an adjustable horizontal bar. This post looked like a gallows. Could it be that deserters were already being executed here? Amusing pictures were hung round the walls—red, green and yellow circles, large ones and small ones, coloured squares and dots. There were also numbers and letters of varying sizes. But the main wall opposite the curtain bore a portrait of the Emperor. Everyone in this hall was tightly buttoned up, and crosses and medals glinted on the close-fitting tunics.

As soon as he caught sight of the Jew, a stout man wearing a long white gown which fell almost to the soles of his feet, called out: "First, off with the cap!" He was standing by the weighing machine. At the heels of his brown boots his spurs clinked with a light, silvery sound. The gold facings of a staff officer's uniform were protruding from the collar of the white gown. The black ear-piece of a stethoscope was visible in his left pocket. This was Surgeon-Major Dr Jellinek.

The Jew did not want to remove his skull-cap. It isn't done. Even a goy ought to know that an orthodox Jew stands with his head bared on one single occasion only—after death, facing the Eternal. But in his lifetime and in the presence of others, even if they are the representatives of the Emperor, or indeed the Emperor himself, he may not bare his head. This is why the skull-cap is worn underneath the hat. In courtrooms and administrative offices, at court and in the presence of a mayor, only the hat is removed, while the skull-cap is kept in place.

When he continued to stand in silent defiance, refusing to remove his skull-cap, Corporal Kuryluk approached and viciously swept it off. The Jew remained silent, but his eyes emitted dark flames, scorching Dr Jellinek's white gown.

"Another candidate for the office of rabbi!" exclaimed the surgeon-major with a sneering smile directed towards the Commission, which was presided over by a grey-haired, dried-up old colonel brought out of retirement as a wartime measure. Only the two clerks gave it cognizance, while the tribunal ignored it. Notwithstanding the alliance between Mars and Asclepius, the Commission held Dr Jellinek in contempt. But nobody present despised Jellinek as much as he despised himself. He found his own remark most distasteful. From the depths of this distaste emerged the impact of all the bitter pain that had afflicted him throughout his life. It was hurtful to him that he was obliged for no good reason to pretend to the Commission, and to the whole world, on which he wanted to make an impression, that he was not Jewish. Everyone knew he was. As for the sneer, by which he intended to ingratiate himself with the colonel, the exclamation "Another candidate for the office of rabbi!" was justified in so far as so many Jews pretended to be candidates, because candidates for the priesthood of all creeds were automatically exempt from military service. Embarrassed by his failure to impress, Jellinek decided that he had to rehabilitate himself, not only in the eyes of the Commission but also in the eyes of his victim, and above all in his own eyes. Jellinek had never held a good opinion of himself, either in a military or a medical capacity. The army looked down on him because he was merely a doctor, and a Jew at that, while the medical world looked down on him because he served in the army. Even his closest relatives availed themselves of his expertise only to a very limited extent, in trivial cases such as a sore throat or stomach upsets. In more serious cases they called on "proper" doctors. And so life spared him no humiliation, and he took his revenge on life by humiliating those who were weaker than himself. Before the war, he had often had to dine in the mess with junior officers, although as a staff officer he was entitled to dine alongside the captains. And it sometimes happened that captains, especially cavalry captains, would salute him in the street in a casual, non-committal manner. There were situations in which Dr Jellinek would gladly have given up his medical degree if he could have commanded more personal respect from his fellow officers.

He wore his spurs all the time. He had the right to a mount, but he had not ridden a horse for years. His spurs were for his own encouragement, not for spurring on a horse. Those spurs were not for goading the flanks of his steed, but to spur himself on. The sound of his own spurs revived his flagging, so frequently trampled dignity. He was deluded into thinking that his spurs made an impression on those around him, not just on himself. He would not part from them all day. He wore them from morning till night, unwilling to take them off even when he was alone. He would have liked most of all to attach them to his slippers and fall asleep to the sound of their jingling. Or to his bare feet, so as not to wake in the morning to the customary unpleasant sensation. He wished to take the first step of the new day both morally and phys-ically fully armed. The jingle of his spurs sometimes called up visions of famous horsemen, proud knights that he had learnt about in world history classes—heroes, not doctors of medicine. He identified with the image of those cavalrymen.

On his imaginary charger, brandishing his sabre, he overcame every obstacle life presented him with because he was Jewish. He galloped over the dead bodies of those numerous enemies he in reality met with a friendly greeting. He massacred them with his sabre, trampled them beneath his horse's hooves. Including that German language teacher at the Gymnasium in Olomouc, who teased him for his guttural pronunciation of the letter "R". For how many Jews in Central and Eastern Europe has this letter been the bane of their lives! Including the colleagues at Prague University, who had denied him the satisfaction of the "honourable solution", and all those ladies who declined to dance with him at garrison balls. He hacked and cut his way through, and trampled, all the affronts and calamities of his life, smashed down all the doors where he had been denied entry, pulverized all the pedestals he was unable to clamber on. Such was the potency of those spurs. At this moment, however, in the presence of the colonel, who remained silent, they lost their magical power. The colonel had spurs too. There was only one thing for it: act simple. By treating the Jew "humanely", Jellinek hoped to retrieve his reputation at the Recruiting Commission, at the same time as recovering his own self-esteem. He glanced benignly at the pale, fearful body, the sunken cheeks nestling among a dark, irregular beard which must never be clipped. Beneath the heavy eyelids with no lashes, his deep-set eyes were blood-shot. Beneath the bloated belly, which was out of proportion to the narrow chest, the symbol of his manhood hung piti-fully among densely matted hair. The proud symbol of the covenant between Ephroim Chaskiel Blumenkrantz and his Creator was revealed before the eyes of Doctor Jellinek, the eyes of the entire Commission, the eyes of the whole world, and even the eyes of the Emperor in the portrait. "And God said unto Abraham, Thou shalt keep my covenant therefore, thou, and thy seed after thee in their generations. This is my covenant, which ye shall keep, between me and you and thy seed after thee; Every man child among you shall be circumcised." (Genesis 17:9–10).

This symbol therefore united Ephroim Chaskiel Blumenkrantz with staff surgeon Jellinek. But they were united only in the eyes of the Lord. An appeal to the brotherhood of Israel would be in vain, now that the war with Tsar Nicholas had turned everyone in Śniatyn and throughout the Empire into brothers of Emperor Franz Joseph. Dr Jellinek did not wish to throw the defenceless body of Blumenkrantz to the Sodomites or to the Amalekites, or even to the Egyptians, but to the Russians or the Serbs, of whom there is no mention in the Holy Scriptures of Moses. How poor now were the loins in which God had placed a promise of the eternal seed!

However, it was the arms that were most deserving of mercy. They still showed the marks of the thongs from morning prayers. They hung limply like withered boughs of trees in the Jewish cemetery. This is what the biblical Joseph must have looked like when his brethren stripped his clothes from him and cast him into a pit, later to sell him to the Ishmaelites. Jellinek was filled with pity at the sight of this man. Calmly, with no trace of irony, he asked:

"What is your civilian occupation?"

"A *Kestkind*!" replied Blumenkrantz in an expressionless voice, showing neither fear nor contempt. Jellinek was now completely taken aback. So the Jew was in no doubt that staff surgeon Jellinek would understand Yiddish? Dr Jellinek? Dr Jellinek did understand Yiddish. He knew that a "Kestkind" was a son-in-law enabled by his wife's parents to freely study the Holy Scriptures, being accepted into their home and supported at their cost. He recalled his own father and his own youth. His father had been storeman at a brewery in Olomouc. He had lain at rest in the Jewish cemetery in Prague for thirty years now. Twice a year, on the Day of Atonement and on the anniversary of his death (according to the Jewish calendar), Dr Jellinek offered prayers at Yiskor and Kaddish services for the peace of his father Hersch's soul in the reformed synagogue, where he went in civilian dress, wearing a top hat. Frequently, however, he was represented at these services by specially hired Jews. Just such a one was the Jew who now stood before him, naked and at his mercy. He gave them money for candles, entrusting to them the care of his father's soul, just as he had once, on the day of his death, entrusted them to wash his body and place him in the coffin. By then he was a medical student. He earned money as a tutor to support his mother, but he was unable to continue his expensive studies without financial support. This support was provided by the army. He became a Kestkind of the Emperor. In return for this, he undertook to stay on as an army doctor after the completion of his studies. He began his service as an assistant surgeon in the garrison hospital at Olomouc. A few years later he was promoted, whereupon they transferred him to Galicia. He was forced out of Jarosław by colleagues, army doctors, because he did not accept bribes as they did. At his own request, he was transferred to Wadowice as a regimental doctor attached to one of the regional defence regiments stationed there. There he married a poor girl who also came from the Czech lands. In Wadowice his elder daughter Klara was born. He arranged a good education for her in Prague, including piano lessons at the conservatory. Klara was unattractive. Nevertheless, a certain lawyer from Moravská Ostrava was inclined to marry her. But lawyers in those parts do not marry without a dowry. Dr Jellinek was a good son and a good husband, so why would he not be a good father? Although nothing could be proved, his growing income aroused suspicion, especially in a small town like Wadowice. So he was transferred from Galicia (where the boundary between virtue and transgression is very flexible, as is well known) to Innsbruck, this time at his own request. Tyrol is famous for its honesty, its piety and its aversion to Jews. The Alpine climate, full of ozone and Aryanism, was not congenial to Dr Jellinek. He was not at ease among edelweiss, yodellers and the traditions of Andreas Hofer. When Klara finally got married, he resigned and transferred to the reserve as a staff surgeon. The war found him in Karlsbad, where he struggled to acquire rich patients from Russia and Romania. He wore uniform once more, attached his spurs, kissed his wife and kissed his younger daughter Hermina, whose dowry he now had to muster (*"Mein Kind, mein innig geliebtes Kind,"** he later wrote to her in letters from the field)—and set off to war. He began at Lwów in Reserve Hospital No. 1, at the polyclinic. Several days later he was assigned to the Recruitment Commission at Śniatyn.

It followed that the matter of Miss Hermina Jellinek's dowry—apparently one of her father's Karlsbad failures,

---

* "My child, my dearly beloved child".

forgotten till now—had now unexpectedly re-emerged. The impeccability of Doctor Jellinek's source of income was in fact ensured by the grey-haired, desiccated colonel who (supposedly) chaired the Commission mainly for this purpose. In practice, however, he chaired it in name only. In reality Doctor Jellinek was all-powerful around here and could pass judgement in the light of his own conscience and his own needs. Jellinek was always correct in the eyes of the colonel. Injustices committed in favour of those who were capable of distinguishing between "A" and "B" and between "C" and "D", and of assigning a value to these distinctions in jingling cash, were balanced by indiscriminately declaring fit for military service the bodies of all illiterates as well as those unable to pay. However, he was not always governed by good sense and dispassionate calculation. Sometimes his heart also ruled, and whether he merely took pity on the naked Jew Blumenkrantz or whether it also had something to do with the memory of his father, he decided to give him complete exemption. For now, he wanted to forget him. He postponed the examination. Summoning what was left of his tattered pride, he pulled himself together and clicked his heels. His spurs rang out. Doctor Jellinek turned away from the Jew.

He went over to the weighing scales, on which at that moment there stood a body—Niewiadomski. Corporal Kuryluk was already moistening his chest with a wet sponge. Then he took an indelible pencil and wrote the number 67 on his chest. Sixty-seven kilograms live weight. Piotr did not understand why they were weighing him. He felt like a slaughtered beast at the abattoir. Indeed, these numbers written on human chests were reminiscent of veterinary officials' purple stamps. It was official confirmation that our flesh contained nothing toxic and was fit for consumption. Next, Corporal Kuryluk ordered Piotr to stand by the post which looked like a gallows. He lowered the crossbar onto his head. It was a device for accurately measuring height. The crossbar was reminiscent of the skimming-stick used in pubs to remove superfluous foam from mugs of beer. Here, however, it was used to remove from people's heads any delusions of taller stature their hair might have given them. Hair did not count. Having carried out this task, Kuryluk drew a slanting line below the number 67 and added the height measurement—169. Piotr was now approached by another NCO with a tailor's tape-measure.

"Raise your arms!" he shouted, seeing that Piotr was covering his private parts with the documents. He took the papers from him and put them on the table at which the Commission was seated. Then he took Piotr's chest measurement. Piotr started trembling—not because of the cold and not because he was frightened, but out of embarrassment. Only now, in this hall where all the men, both military personnel and civilians, were sitting fully dressed and buttoned up to the chin did his embarrassment reach its peak. In the changing room out there, where all the bodies were naked, Piotr's shame had been rather a religious sense of nakedness, a mournful reminder of original sin, a revelation of the secret of love and death. Here, not only did it scorch his body and torment his soul, but it turned into anger. No, there had never been anything like it! Nobody had ever seen his shame in broad daylight. He always went to women in the dark and wearing a nightshirt. He extinguished the light when he lay down with Magda. No man intentionally looked on his own shame, even in the bath.

So here was an embarrassed man standing with his body before the people. The very nakedness of this body, the last possession of a pauper, was no longer his own property. He felt like an animal, a dog, like Bass. He would not have been surprised if they had now ordered him to go on all fours. Let them kick him, let them beat him, as long as they did not look him over like this. Of course, he had come naked from the womb of his mother Wasylina, and he would one day emerge naked from the womb of Mother Earth to stand before the final Commission in the Valley of Jehoshaphat. But here no archangels' trumpets are heard. From time to time cars honked out on the road.

A storm was brewing in Piotr's body. It rose from his feet, which seemed to be rooted to the spot, so difficult was it to lift them. It rose from the tough, hardened skin of his feet, emerging through the cracks in his toenails, flowing upwards, powerful and wild. At any moment it would explode in his mouth as some inarticulate yell, the roar of a primitive human or a primitive beast, when it suddenly stopped in its tracks, settling in his knees. Piotr's knees gave way. They began to tremble. His protest was alarmed at its own vehemence and returned whence it had come—back to the earth. Piotr's body was once more submissive and patient. A fly, coming in at the window and making for the buttered bread-roll one of the clerks was eating just then, settled on Piotr's shoulder, sought some morsel of nourishment, and immediately flew off.

The gentlemen at the table, like connoisseurs of antique statuary, admired his muscular physique. These weakly citizens were torturing the physically fit, sentencing them to arduous, deadly tasks from which they themselves were exempted.

What were they staring at him like that for? Why were they scrutinizing his body so closely? What had they discovered about him? They saw only a broad skull covered with fair hair, they saw prominent cheek-bones, a drooping moustache, squinting eyes that were small, bright but sad, and a short, flat nose. The attention of the commission appeared to be riveted on the powerful, broad chest, on which the purple numbers were already fading. Unbeknown to Piotr Niewiadomski, they were only looking at his eyes to be sure that they would be able to see a target they were aiming at; they were only inspecting his ears to check whether they would hear commands and recognize explosions. The arms were valuable only insofar as they had lifting power. The legs were the most important. They were intended for marching. Anyone with weak legs was unfit for the infantry and was drafted to the cavalry. The teeth were also examined, in view of the tough regimental bread and rusks. But perhaps this was a ritual surviving from the times when the tips of cartridges had to be bitten off.

Some young officer questioned Piotr in Ukrainian and noted down his responses. They were all chatting in some incomprehensible language. Only the colonel, a grey-haired, desiccated little old man, was sitting beneath a portrait of His Imperial Majesty as silent as His Majesty himself.

Doctor Jellinek came over and stood so close to him that Piotr could feel his heavy breathing, like the softly wafting wind. First the doctor tapped him, telling him to take a deep breath. He placed his left hand over his collar-bone, tapping three times with the middle finger of his right hand on the middle finger of his left, on which he wore a gold wedding ring. He repeated the procedure on the other collar-bone. Then he pressed his stethoscope to the collar-bones. He listened at the broad, flat end, then he moved the stethoscope downwards, to the left, to the right, then back up again. Through the narrow black duct of its trumpet the reverberations of Piotr's lungs made their way into his ear, his head, his mind and his conscience. Piotr's ribs rose and fell like the gills of a fish. Suddenly, Jellinek removed the stethoscope.

"Hold your breath!"

Piotr obeyed. Then Jellinek turned him round and placed his head on his left breast. He snuggled up to it as though it was a woman's breast, a mother's breast, on which he desired to repose. The doctor's head was cool, round and bald. Yet it was a little rough and gave off an aroma of shaving-powder. For a moment, it lay motionless on Piotr Niewiadomski's breast. Doctor Jellinek was in direct contact with his heart. There was something mystical in this embrace; like the communion of a pair of lovers. At that moment of suspended breathing, Piotr saw his mother Wasylina and himself—a child on her lap. He experienced a sweet sensation and came close to tears. In his blood was heard the rustling of forests, thickets and poor fields of wheat; he heard his own blood pounding against the walls of his heart.

Jellinek listened for a long time to the subcutaneous sounds of Piotr's life. He laid his ear against the naked body, as if wishing to convince himself that under the covering of skin there really was a heart beating, and blood flowing. That was, of course, what mattered most in those days. Live reservoirs of blood had to be checked before they were tapped. So the doctors listened to the murmuring, inspecting the manometers of life, and laid their ears against the sons of the earth as though against the earth itself. The juice from these fruits of the earth was not valued highly, but it had to be fresh. The doctors examined the bodies, running their fingers over them as if they wanted to select in advance the place where a bullet would strike. This is how joiners make pencil marks on timber boards, where the nails are to go. The eyes of the Commission were as cold as lead bullets piercing through the bodies.

Something must have been amiss with Piotr's heart, since Doctor Jellinek spent such a long time examining it. He even frowned, pondering something or other, but no one noticed. Jellinek listened exclusively for his own purpose. What value could the life of a stranger have, for someone who considered his own life to have been wasted? Jellinek was sending people to their death without any pangs of conscience. He took his revenge on life (Life with a capital "L"), delivering its most handsome specimens to death. The more a body exuded life, the more readily he sacrificed it to death. What role did he actually fulfil? What part did he play in this tragicomedy? He was a supplier of bodies, a legal intermediary between the Emperor and death. The Emperor did not obtain the necessary raw material personally. For this, he had trusty Jew-boys, sworn expert factors. What was wrong with Jellinek's cheating both death and the Emperor—granting exemption to fit bodies for a financial consideration, while making up for it by delivering others that were not so fresh? This money was his commission.

When examining highly educated people, he considerately lowered his voice, and when they complained of lassitude, anaemia or nerves he would say:

"Life in the field will do you good. You will see how you put on weight in a month. Your own mother won't recognize you. If I had a son," (how fortunate that he did not!) "I would not hesitate to send him to the front line." He recommended "life" in the field as though it was life, and not death, that flourished there. But Piotr Niewiadomski was not highly educated. Doctor Jellinek did not need to lower his voice. He didn't want to talk to him at all.

He drew himself up, abruptly raising his head from Piotr's chest, then with a smile gave him a friendly tap on the shoulder. Fully cognizant of the fact that he had released two perfectly fit people that day in return for payment, and that he would release the Jew out of pity, he called out to the Commission:

"'A'! Fit for the infantry!"

Turning to Blumenkrantz, he said: "Next!"

Piotr did not know whether he should thank him, or kiss the hand with which he had so benevolently tapped him on the shoulder. The corporals told him he was "taken" and told him to go out and get dressed in his civilian clothes. He left.

Once again, the clerks noted down his name, entering it in the books and registers. In black ink, which dries immediately, they committed it for centuries to come to the white paper, from where no amount of force could ever remove it. Book would pass it to book, and so it would wander from office to office, in time perhaps wandering back to the Emperor. But that word was already converted into a soldier's body provided with a regimental number, a body to be sustained and equipped at the expense of the State Treasury. A body whose absence would be punished.

Piotr Niewiadomski found himself back in the waiting-room. The bodies bouncing from chair to chair no longer made such an impression on him. In Piotr's eyes, those still waiting to be assessed had a lesser value than his own body, which now belonged to the Emperor. There, before the Commission, he had thought they would immediately put him in uniform. Why else would they have taken his measurements? Now they had told him to crawl back into his old skin. Slightly disappointed, he dressed in his civilian trousers and his old tunic. He no longer felt at home in this garb. Only the railwayman's cap gave him a feeling of superiority over other rustic men. In the changing room he found out that after the swearing-in he could go back home. His cohort would be not be called up for another six weeks. He found this news disappointing too. The Emperor did not need him immediately, then? He was not mobilizing him on the spot? Piotr had not expected to return to his signal box, thinking that they would give him at most a day or two to sort out his personal affairs. What was all the fuss about, if the war was going to be over in six weeks? He felt good at the thought of the war being over. Perhaps he would not be called up at all? Piotr was now like a piece of furniture, commandeered by the bailiff and left for a certain period of time in the home of a citizen who has failed to pay his taxes.

The corpulent sergeant led the whole contingent of men passed fit for service out of the recruiting offices to the school building opposite. When they passed the piled-up benches and entered the school, Niewiadomski was alarmed. Who knows, perhaps they would now force him to sit down at one of these benches, press a slate pencil into his hand and order him to draw on the black slate tablet—white signs of the devil. But he soon calmed down. In the extensive hall they entered with the sergeant, there was not a single bench. On the other hand, there was a row of yellow ladders attached vertically to the wall. At the end of the room stood four polished climbing poles, reaching from floor to ceiling. Nearby, like horses' bodies with their heads, necks and tails cut off, stood two straddle-legged vaulting horses. Beyond them could be seen a springboard and some dusty mattresses. Underneath the vaulting horses lay masses of iron weights, prominent among them a heavy black bar with spheres the size of human heads attached to each end.

There was no lack of human heads here. New bodies continually flocked in. Over in the Recruitment Commission building all the diseases, weaknesses and infirmities remained. Here, where children's physical prowess was developed on the yellow ladders, poles and trapezes, only those bodies that had been passed fit by the commission were given access. But these people had not been brought to the gymnasium in order to have their strength and agility tested. Here it was all about their souls. For Emperor Franz Joseph acknowledged not only the human body. He was not an adherent of materialist doctrine or an advocate of Haeckel's theory. He was an adherent of dualism and he would not deny that even the most wretched of his subjects, the most backward Hutsul, possessed a soul. Nonetheless, he must have order. He took bodies and souls separately. They are two different things and they may not be mixed up. In the building of the district recruiting office, bodies were acquired for the Emperor; here, in the gymnasium of the seven-year provincial lower school, it was souls. Bodies one at a time, souls collectively.

Although it was strictly forbidden, they smoked and spat on the floor. Spitting could not be unhygienic, because they were all healthy. Health was somehow being made the most of. The moment the sergeant left, the hall was full of voices. The nervous tension that had built up in the room over there in anticipation of the decision was now relaxed here. The younger men leapt onto the trampoline, climbed the poles and slid down to the floor laughing. Even Piotr was tempted by the weights. Especially the large bar-bells. He raised them effortlessly with one hand.

All of a sudden, the hall fell silent. The younger men hurriedly jumped down from the gymnastic apparatus. Unfinished cigarettes were thrown on the floor and extinguished underfoot. In the open doorway there appeared a young officer wearing a cap similar to Piotr's railwayman's cap. He wore a sabre at his hip and military decorations on his chest. They stood back to let him through. He was followed at an appropriate distance by the portly sergeant carrying a sheaf of papers in each hand. He wore neither sabre nor cap.

The young officer was delegated to receive the souls, but he remained silent throughout the ceremony. Just once he whispered something to the sergeant, whereupon the sergeant burst out laughing. First of all, the sergeant divided those present into three groups, according to the languages they spoke. He separated a small German group, consisting almost without exception of Jews, from the Polish and Ukrainian ones. Everyone could take the oath in the language of their choice, because the liturgy of the military did not impose its Latin, as it were—that is to say, the German language—on those who did not understand it. In the Imperial and Royal Army only commands were to be issued to everyone in German. Then the sergeant explained to the souls, divided into three groups, the technicalities and the significance of the ritual. Everyone had to remove their caps. Including the Jews.

Piotr noticed that the Jew who had stood next to him in the queue at the recruiting office was not present in the room.

Everyone had to raise two fingers of their right hand, the middle and index fingers, keeping them at eye level the whole time, until they reached the word "Amen".

"Everyone is to repeat all the words after me, loud and clear. After swearing the oath," the sergeant explained, "all of you, though still civilians, are effectively soldiers. You are liable to military punishment. You are forbidden to do this and you are forbidden to do that. Many things are forbidden."

The young officer, an emissary of the Emperor, stood motionless and silent, like an allegorical statue. But he did not remove his cap. Priests too sometimes lead prayers in a biretta, whereas the faithful are obliged to be bare-headed.

First the German group took the oath, then the Ukrainian, and finally the Polish. Piotr Niewiadomski joined the Polish group. The sergeant read out the oath, and Piotr repeated it word for word in chorus:

"Before Almighty God we solemnly swear faith and allegiance to his Apostolic Majesty, our Supreme Ruler Franz Joseph the First, by the grace of God Austrian Emperor, King of Bohemia and so forth…"

"And so forth," came the thunderous response.

"…to the Apostolic King of Hungary that we will honour and defend His Majesty, his generals and all our other superiors, following their commands and directions at all times, against all enemies whoever they may be and wherever his Imperial Majesty's will shall demand of us."

"...shall demand of us," they chanted in unison. In Piotr's soul, invisible kettle-drums were beating and unseen fanfares were blaring.

"...On water and in the air, by day and by night, in battles, assaults, skirmishes and operations of every kind—in other words, wherever we may be, we will fight gallantly and courageously..."

Piotr Niewiadomski already pictured himself fighting on water, on land and in the air. He was dripping water and blood. Blood and water were getting in his mouth, his ears and his nostrils; he was drowning, but summoning what remained of his failing strength he thrust the enemy to the riverbed with his bare hands. The enemy was now a long-bearded Muscovite, rather like that Jew whose Adam's apple had been jumping, now a superhumanly powerful moustachioed Serb. The latter struck Piotr on the forehead with his rifle butt but Piotr dispatched him with his bayonet. Evidently, some old engraving of the Balkan war had come to mind.

"...that under no circumstances will we desert our fellow soldiers, our flag, our standards or our weapons, nor will we enter into any form of understanding with the enemy whatsoever."

No, no, no! Piotr Niewiadomski will not desert the standards and will not enter into any form of understanding with the enemy whatsoever. He would not even be able to converse with them. But why is that officer maintaining such an ominous silence? If only he would make some slight movement. Everyone would undoubtedly feel more relaxed if he did. The young officer, the Emperor's emissary, moved. The long mirror of his sabre swayed. The gilt tassels on his sword-tail swayed.

He raised a hand and covered his mouth in order to conceal a yawn. He had already had enough of all this. From morning till night—nothing but the endless "Before God Almighty". Enough to drive you mad. Better to set off for the front line. But no, actually, it's not better to set off for the front line. It's better to listen from morning till night to:

"…As obliged by military regulations and as befits honest soldiers, we wish always to behave in such a way as to live and die honourably."

The sergeant followed this with a solemn, pregnant pause, then he intoned the final:

"So help us God. Amen."

The god of the military, before whom this oath was taken, actually had no particular identity. He was inter-confessional—unlike in civilian life, where he listened to some people only when they bared their heads and knelt down, recognizing others only when standing and wearing their hats. The Imperial and Royal military god was not Jehovah, nor the Holy Trinity, nor Allah; rather, he could have been the deity of agnostics, deists and Robespierre. He abandoned any attributes of particular faiths, renounced forms given him by dogma and legend, and was insensitive to incense and wax candles. He represented that highest being to which even freethinkers and freemasons bow down. The army recognized no doubts unforeseen in the military regulations, therefore it obliged also the souls of atheists, socialists and anarchists to serve the Emperor in the name of God, regardless of what those people actually thought of him. Every non-believer, once he was judged fit for military service, thereby became a believer in God. As for God, whose existence it was forbidden to doubt, he indeed had to be an abstraction, as bland as an algebraic symbol. In the Imperial and Royal military's algebra, God was that infinite number of zeros added to the highest possible figure, which was the Emperor. That God was summoned to bear witness when the souls promised that their bodies would be faithful to the Emperor. At this spoken, obligatory agreement between the peoples of Austria and the Supreme Monarch, God acted as regent.

As the final words of the oath were being spoken, fear struck Piotr's soul. However, with his own lips he assured God that he was willing to die for the Emperor. Had the Emperor heard him make this promise? Where is the Emperor? There was not even a portrait of the Emperor in that room, and there was no cross either. The Emperor is somewhere in space, like God, whom nobody sees with their own eyes either. So they took the oath in the air. The oath rose to heaven through the ceiling of the gymnasium, puncturing the ceiling, flying up to the first floor, to class IIb, where at that moment a contingent of recruits was waiting to be transported to the front line. It soared up over the heads of the recruits from the first floor into the attic, through the layer of hot dust, between the roof tiles out into the open air. It rushed up the chimneys and vents. It also rushed out into the street through three wide-open windows. There was a clear blue sky, so the oath met no obstructions on its way to God.

But for some people God was present in that room, hovering above the souls, above the bodies, above the gymnastic apparatus.

Piotr Niewiadomski turned his gaze to the floor, as in church during mass. For he had no doubt that somewhere high up under the ceiling, on the highest rung of the yellow ladder, the Holy Spirit was sitting with folded wings. Not in the form of a white dove, but as a black two-headed eagle. In its talons, it was convulsively gripping an iron rod with black spheres at each end.

Thus Piotr Niewiadomski took the oath to the Emperor. Afterwards, he received his documents and went with his fellow countrymen to S.C. Schames's pub, where he got drunk on ninety per cent pure spirit.

Chapter Four

Blind organ-grinders at fairgrounds and carnivals had been predicting the end of the world since time immemorial. But that the predicted day of God's wrath should fall precisely on 21st August 1914—no, not even the wisest people in Topory or in Czernielica had anticipated that. Not even Hryć Łotocki had anticipated it, though no one doubted that he was the wisest man in Topory, illiterate as he was. The parish priest himself, Father Makarucha, frequently sought his advice on many important matters, for example regarding his beehives, which he looked after as enthusiastically as the Lord's vineyard. Father Makarucha had not had any inkling of such an imminent end of the world, and a man of the cloth, of all people, probably ought to have an idea about at least some of God's intentions. After all, the church does not just care for people's souls, it does not just smooth the way to eternity. The Creator also put the church in charge of all time, everything temporal, in particular the measuring and reckoning of passing time, that is to say the calendar. It was by the will of the church that a Thursday was a Thursday, that a Sunday was a Sunday, and it was by the will of the church that the current year was 1914.

All Father Makarucha knew was that the end of the world favoured round numbers. He remembered from his time at the seminary that God had already once before felt inclined to destroy the world. That was in the year 1000. However, at the last minute the Creator changed his mind, or was moved to pity; at any rate, he extended the world's sinful life indefinitely. However, the stay of execution did not amount to an amnesty. So if God felt like carrying out his sentence, he would certainly delay it at least until the year 2000. That was a round figure that had a dramatic effect. But so suddenly, out of the blue, in the year 1914? And not even on the 1st of January or the 31st of December, but the 21st of August? Father Makarucha did not attribute such idiosyncrasies or lack of awareness of their impact to celestial accounting, which, as always, was concerned with numbers on a grand scale, hundreds and thousands.

Piotr Niewiadomski had also heard something to the effect that the world was supposed to come to an end in the year 2000, so he was calm on his own behalf, and on behalf of his grandchildren and great-grandchildren too. He had no children. And as he had no children, by what miracle could he have grandchildren and great-grandchildren? May God's will be done—the Niewiadomski line would die out with him, and before the year 2000.

The Hutsul countryside was calm in those days, in spite of the approaching war. The wheat had already been gathered in, though the fields of stubble had not yet been ploughed. The old Hutsuls were in no hurry to get on with that, having a more pressing task in mind—the haymaking. They would set off in leisurely fashion to the fields at dawn, and at midday the women would bring them milk and potatoes, or even dumplings, in double earthenware pots. They ate their meal in silence, then mowed until nightfall. From time to time they would take a break, stop puffing at their pipes and contemplate the Grim Reaper, sharpening his scythe for their sons in far-away Serbia.

Fear never deserted the old mothers. It burgeoned in their wilting laps like a monstrous, fiendish bastard. They dragged themselves out of their warm straw beds covered in cold sweat brought on by the horrible haunting dreams they had been suffering. They shook off these nightmares like filthy worms, making triple signs of the cross, for themselves, for their sons who had gone to war and for their children who remained at home. Then, feeling calmer, they went to see to the cows and were soothed by the steady chiming of the brass bells hanging from the necks of their cattle. Occasionally, though, the mere sight of milk was a heartbreaking reminder for these mothers of the times long gone, when it had surged from their own breasts. After all those years, they felt a painful throbbing in their nipples, as though they were being bitten by toothless lips which might even now be biting the dust. The Hutsul mothers envied their bovine counterparts their blissful ignorance of the fate of their offspring, butchered in abattoirs. And they took it out on the cows. Wildly and furiously they wrenched at their udders, as though they wanted to draw their blood rather than their milk. And the innocent, white, warm milk flowed, sounding like a stream of peas drumming into the metal pails.

But none of these embittered mothers gave a thought to the end of the world.

Alarm first began to spread in Pokuttya in the middle of August, when the word "evacuation" was mentioned for the first time since the outbreak of war. It drifted in from the towns, where it had been unearthed, exhumed from the musty cellars of oblivion along with expressions like "victory", "calamity", "captivity", "prisoners", "attack", "heroic death". These obsolete expressions, consigned to obscurity like sleeping bats, acquired rosy cheeks and became colourful on contact with fresh air, gaining a new lease of life on everybody's lips.

Although the word "victory" was predominant and although the Emperor was continually gaining victories in Serbia, Galicia and in the Kingdom of Poland, in the district of Śniatyn the canker of doubt had embedded itself in the residents' hearts. Rumours from Lwów had it that the Muscovites were coming. At first they circulated secretly, whispered fearfully in inns and at drinking fountains, until on one warm starlit night the filthy little windowpanes of the Hutsul huts began reverberating. By then, everyone in Topory was openly saying that the Muscovites were coming. The bearded, shaggy muzhik with his long spear and *nagaika*—the Cossack lead-weighted whip. Holding between his teeth—strong as a horse's—a sharp knife. He rides his swift little steed, trampling under its hooves all that lies in his path. The stench of tar and vodka is smelt a mile off. He smashes windows with his rifle butt, robs the Jewish shops and inns, and when he is especially enraged he even burns down entire villages. He slashes the Jews' eiderdowns, cuts off Jews' beards and gives Jewish women big bellies. So it is a good idea to hang an image of the Virgin Mary over your doorway, or chalk up a cross. Although—they say—when the Muscovites are at their most vicious, Christians are not spared either. It is only the "Muscovite sympathizer elements" that are spared, those who assist them by placing logs on the track to derail trains taking Austro-Hungarian troops to the front line, or in some other way. At the invitation of the Muscovites these "elements" surface like greasy spots enticed out of the cloth by an iron and a sheet of blotting paper. They emerge suddenly from under the earth, and it turns out that they have been living among us for years, but no one in the village knew about them, not even the village headman, the parish clerk, the gendarme, or even the priest. If the priest is not one of them, that is. As recently as last Sunday, they hanged two Ruthenian priests and a deacon in Sokal for signalling to the Muscovites from the bell-tower. And in Tarnopol district they hanged five peasants for no reason at all. According to reports doing the rounds of the Hutsul inns it went like this: no sooner had the Hungarians fled from the village, leaving behind everything except their horses, than the Cossacks appeared. They came across a group of daring peasants who had not hidden in their huts like the others, but had gone to see what they could retrieve from the abandoned wagons—bread, preserves, rum, tobacco. At first, the Cossacks ordered that it should all be handed over and loaded onto their wagons. Then they took them among their horses and questioned them about this and that. So the men took fright and told all they knew. That there were this many Hungarians, not more than two squadrons, and that they had all fled—about half an hour ago. (They lied and lied and lied, for patriotic reasons, because there had been about five Hungarian squadrons.)

"Will you show us which way the Hungarians fled?" asked the Cossack *esaul*. How could you not show him when he had a pistol and a sabre and a *nagaika* and all his men were armed to the teeth? Well, the men showed him, didn't they? Meanwhile, other people had emerged from their huts, keeping their distance and watching how certain men were guiding the Cossacks. That same day two Russian infantry regiments entered the village. The officers went straight to the manor house, of course, and made merry with the squire until the early hours. They played the piano extremely well. The other ranks remained in the village. They ate and drank, danced the *trepak* and slept with the wenches. At dawn they marched on, but didn't get very far because the Hungarians ambushed them in the woods, causing some casualties and taking prisoners, and the rest took to their heels—goodness knows which way they went. The Hungarians returned to the village. They immediately found out which of the peasants had assisted the Muscovites, and summarily hanged five of them from the chestnut trees, right by the Orthodox church. Three others were tied up with ropes and taken to Lwów prison. There, in accordance with martial law, they would face criminal charges under paragraph 327 of the military code.

On 18th August, the birthday of His Majesty the Emperor, His Excellency the Governor of Galicia Korytowski arrived in Vienna. During a special audience, he placed at the foot of the throne evidence of the love, loyalty and attachment felt by the whole population of the crown lands. So much evidence had accumulated that it formed a great mountain at the foot of the throne and His Majesty experienced considerable difficulty in making his way to his study.

Piotr Niewiadomski was still carrying out his duties as a signalman at box 86. Appalling reports of traitors, spies and hanged Polish priests got through even to him. He contemplated what one ought to do if the enemy demanded assistance. If you didn't give it to them they would shoot you like a dog. (Here he glanced fearfully and tenderly at Bass. The dog was lying on the floor, licking his paw.) If you lied they would also shoot you, when they found out that you had tricked them. And if out of fear you did as they asked, your days were numbered; your own soldiers would hang you as soon as they returned. Someone would always give you away. There are so many enemies.

Piotr began counting his enemies. He did not have many, but there were always enough of them for an informer to materialize. Such a person was Fedko Semeniuk, for example. He had hated Piotr for years because of a bout of fisticuffs that had broken out over a game of cards. He would be sure to inform. But what was an innocent man to do when forced to show the Muscovites which way to go? Could a Hutsul really predict tactical manoeuvres and strategic retreats? No, Hutsuls were not brainy enough for that! A Hutsul expects that if our army has deserted the village and its place has been taken by the Russians, that's how it will stay until the end of the world, or at any rate until the war is over. Till Christmas, that is. It is best to be deaf and dumb, like that Wasyl Horoch from Czernielica. Only deaf-mutes are safe in wartime. The enemy does not ask them any questions. If it does, all it gets is "ermmmm".

So Piotr Niewiadomski contemplated quite seriously whether he should not pretend to be a deaf-mute if the Muscovites occupied Topory.

He burst out laughing so loudly that Bass was startled. What silly thoughts come into one's head! Pretend to be a deaf-mute!

Above all, the Muscovites are still far from Topory. (Although he was certain about that, he still glanced in the direction of the window to make sure it wasn't rattling. It wasn't.) And then, who around here is going to help out the Muscovites, anyway? An Imperial and Royal soldier? As if he was not bound to His Illustrious Majesty by the oath sworn by Almighty God in Śniatyn? Piotr was provided with an oath as a document bears a seal, as the deceased are administered the extreme unction. In four weeks' time at the latest he would personally be going to strike at the Muscovites on behalf of the Emperor. In four weeks' time… But they are saying that the Muscovites have already taken Czerniowce. Our illustrious regiments, the Imperial Fusiliers with their plumed helmets, the Vienna Deutschmeister and the proud Windischgrätz Dragoons are said to have been routed. The muzhiks are driving them into captivity like cattle. What about the oath? What about the loyalty? What will become of the entire 1873 intake, if the Muscovites reach Topory before Piotr is even in training?

So Piotr Niewiadomski became distressed.

The thoughts of the lone signalman in box 86 on the Lwów–Czerniowce–Ickany line were interrupted by the ringing of the bell. Topory-Czernielica station was signalling the approach of a train. Piotr donned his official cap, that tangible evidence of his loyalty to the Emperor. He went out to stand in front of the signal box with his little red flag. Deeply convinced that in doing so he was serving the Emperor, he began to turn the winch. He carried out his government function slowly, almost solemnly. He just regretted that no one witnessed it. The wires twanged and the barrier came down. And half of the burden fell from Piotr's heart. That was a good thing. As long as he felt he was useful, unpleasant thoughts were unable to penetrate to his soul. The level-crossing barrier barred the way to evil thoughts.

A long goods train full of troops passed before Piotr in the direction of Kołomyja. Soldiers had not travelled in that direction for ages.

Piotr returned to the signal box and removed his cap, carefully placing it on the shelf above his bed. Around it played the aura of Imperial majesty.

Anxiety grew in Topory day by day, and especially in Piotr Niewiadomski's heart. It almost turned to panic when troop trains began to appear on their line with increasing frequency. The soldiers, who had been so cheerful, proud and full of song two weeks earlier, were now silent, sombre and angry. The army returning from the front line looked like an army of extinguished lanterns. And even the wagons that brought them from abandoned positions back into the heartland bore the marks of defeat. They were bespattered with mud, battered, and stank of death. They sped at a crazy pace, as though falling into an abyss. They bore no trace of the drawings or slogans that had so recently reflected the soldiers' high spirits. Now they sped, crude and bare, like the naked truth of a war for which the army had already lost heart. Day and night, Piotr saw trains, trains, trains. The endless ringing of signal bells kept him awake, as in the first days of mobilization. He heard a buzzing in his head like that in Father Makarucha's beehive. The passenger coaches carried the officers. They were unkempt, unwashed, unshaven for days, without their tunics and with no insignia of rank, like ordinary people. All the finery had faded, the show was over. In one of the compartments Piotr noticed some officers playing cards. They were playing rummy, trying to forget their defeat. There followed numerous cattle wagons packed with soldiers. Some were barefoot, lying on rotting straw. Their faces wore deadly serious expressions and they appeared withdrawn into themselves, oblivious to the world around them. Some had heads bandaged with filthy, bloodstained rags or an arm in a sling. At the larger stations people stared at them, eager to catch a glimpse of those returning from the jaws of death. For all these soldiers had witnessed death; they had cheated it, and now life reeked of rotten corpses. All life's affairs had become insignificant in their eyes, tobacco excepted. Nearly all of them were smoking, eagerly inhaling the smoke of the rationed cigarettes, the soldier's last remaining solace.

At other times Piotr saw wagons marked with a huge red cross. They passed by very slowly, giving off a sharp stench of disinfectants. Piotr knew that these wagons were carrying slaughtered human flesh. He listened out for any sound of groaning, but the Red Cross wagons were as quiet as the grave. They passed by slowly, softly, silently, as though on rubber wheels. In the corridors and at the windows stood young women all in white, like angels. Occasionally, one of the angels would be smoking a cigarette.

"Crosses, more crosses," thought Piotr, and he wondered whether he ought not to raise his cap and cross himself at the sight of those red crosses.

The wagons carrying cattle to be slaughtered were less disturbing, since it was prescribed that human flesh, cannon-fodder, had to be fed on the flesh of animals. Horses too were escaping from the front line. Entire stables of horses, gently nuzzling each other's sad heads, passed by the signal box. Now and then, the approach of a train was heralded by an ominous rumbling sound. That was the flatbed wagons carrying artillery. The sprays of birch adorning the gun-carriages on the day they had set off had long since withered. The heavy and light artillery was now returning stripped of its splendour, the green paint peeling off like scabby skin. The artillery was covered by tarpaulins, hiding its shame, you might say. On every wagon a motionless rifleman stood guard over the guns. Mud-spattered cars with smashed windscreens and ripped tyres, the remnants of military equipment, the incarnation of taxes extracted from citizens—search-lights, coils of barbed wire, sheets of corrugated iron, field telephones, field kitchens—continually flashed by on flatbed wagons in a westerly direction. Imperial property must be salvaged! Like itinerant circuses, on went these pitiful supply trains, hurriedly withdrawn from endangered front-line positions. In the end the ground rumbled day and night and Piotr could no longer tell whether it was caused by the trains or by approaching artillery fire.

On 20th August, around seven o'clock in the morning, he spotted a strange train packed with civilians. It could not be an ordinary passenger train; they were no longer running. These were goods wagons with benches installed. Israel was on the move. It had with it live geese, cushions, cradles, pots and pans, sacks, boxes and a crowd of screaming children. Jewish women in shiny black wigs were bustling about just as at home, even cooking on Primus stoves. Some of the men were tightly wrapped from head to toe in long white tablecloths, bordered at the bottom with strips of black and embroidered at the top in gold and silver. The shimmering gold and silver covered their foreheads, to which they had attached little square black boxes. Beards—grey, ginger and dark, black beards—trembled among the gold and silver embroidery of the tablecloths, giving these Jews the appearance of ridiculous, pathetic kings. They rocked rhythmically to and fro to the rhythm of the clanking wagon-wheels, as though they wanted to impart to this clanking some new, more exalted meaning.

It was not the first time that Piotr had seen Jews at prayer. As a child, he sometimes used to go and peer in at the windows of an old inn, now demolished, where the Jews assembled every Saturday for prayers. In Topory there was no synagogue. Large candles burned in brass candlesticks, and praying, bearded Jews in similar shawls were swaying over massive books, virtually dancing, crying and wailing out loud. The Jews' singing scared Piotr, but at the same time amused him. One Saturday, as he stood staring and listening underneath the windows, something happened that he was unable to comprehend until long afterwards. The door was suddenly opened, and there stood a tall red-bearded Jew in a velvet smock tied at the waist with a black cord. Instead of shoes he wore soft slippers, with white stockings like a young lady's reaching up to his knees. On his head he had a weird square fox-brush cap. You could have sworn that the cap and the beard were one and the same thing. Piotr took fright. He thought this Jew had seen him through the window and had come to beat him. But the Jew took him by the hand, asking in a very kindly voice:

"You'll put out the candles, won't you, lad? You'll get five cents on Sunday." Piotr didn't understand what he meant and suspected some dangerous trap. However, he did not run away. He stood on the spot, his mouth gaping wide as though enchanted by the lure of this mysterious, alien world. Then he followed the red-bearded man into the room where the Jews were praying. In the doorway he took off his cap, not so much out of respect as out of fear. In a flash, Red-Beard replaced it on his head so forcibly that it hurt. Piotr was trembling all over. But no one present condescended to so much as look at him. They were all removing their tablecloths, folding them carefully. They then kissed them tenderly and packed them away into their little velvet bags. Piotr Niewiadomski extinguished the candles for the Jews. On the Sunday he really did receive five cents. That was years ago. But the memory of the mysterious task he had carried out once upon a time, not even knowing what his role had been, came back to him at the sight of those wagons, and his dormant fear of Jews raised its head again.

"They are always praying," he thought, "and yet they will end up in hell anyway." Piotr believed in hell.

The prayer wagon disappeared from sight. No candles had been burning in it. But in the next wagon, Piotr noticed an unlit table lamp with a light green shade. A pretty young girl with large, dark eyes, looking more like a gypsy than Jewish, was clutching it to her breast as if it was not a lamp but a very dear child. She would not let go of this lamp—as though it was the only one in the world—the only source of light, intended to light up the darkness of exile for these nomadic peoples. Where were they bound? Had they resumed their wanderings, interrupted centuries earlier? This railway line was bearing Israel across the desert, beyond which their promised land awaits. This land, by the grace of Emperor Franz Joseph, is in Moravia. Wooden huts will be the refuge for fugitives of the faith of Moses from Galicia.

These were the scenes as the evacuation of Pokuttya proceeded. State officials with their families, and some landowners and merchants, were also fleeing from the Muscovites. The Hutsuls were not running away. Hutsuls never run away from anyone; after all, you can't take your land, your cows and your sheep with you.

Piotr's duties were exceptionally onerous in those days, but he managed. He had acquired a fondness for the railway—that is, for the section entrusted to him. Every day, he walked the four kilometres to signal box 87, beyond which his responsibilities ended. He left his post only when Magda visited. She stood in for him competently, just like a legitimate signalman's wife. The sight of the young girl standing at her post with the little red flag had already on several occasions brought smiles to the weary faces of those who were returning from death. As if life itself had placed her on watch.

On Piotr's stretch of track, order always reigned. No "elements" dared to place blocks on the line. His four kilometres were loyal to the Emperor and the Imperial troops could travel here as safely as in Vienna itself. How he wished he could stay on this stretch for the rest of his life! Then life would have some value, some sense. As a signalman, Piotr would feel like a lord of the manor. For ages he had wanted to be independent. As a signalman, he would answer first to himself, and only then to the stationmaster sitting three kilometres away to his right.

To the right or to the left? This question was the sore point in Piotr Niewiadomski's heart. Although he was over forty years old, he still did not know his right from his left. Trying to work it out with his hands confused him even more. At his post, it's true, it made no difference. You didn't have to distinguish the relative concepts of left-handedness and right-handedness; you just used your eyes. Where Topory-Czernielica station stood—that was on the right, and on the left was the neighbouring signal box no. 87. But that is only the case when you are standing at the door of the signal box, or at the barrier. In the field, on the other hand, where the devil often twists the land around, what was on the left a few minutes ago is now suddenly on the right. Piotr had often been confused by this, but fortunately, so far... Better not to tempt the devil. Of course, Jesus himself had given people certain instructions about right and left, something to do with giving alms. Piotr took fright whenever Father Makarucha read out the relevant passage from the gospel. He felt he was being given over to the devil, but he wasn't brave enough to confess his affliction to anyone, not even to the priest. He felt that sooner or later this defect would be revealed, and the devil would do his worst. His undoing would actually come about from over there, but which is it, left or right? Who can tell?

Oh yes, Piotr was fond of his little signal box. It was small, but it was important, and the little man who was in residence here felt he was important. Right next to it was a Dutch barn belonging to signalman Banasik. There was not much hay left in it, as Banasik's wife had sold it to the army in good time. The crooked thatched roof, looking like a cap on the head of a massive drunkard, had collapsed. Just the four tall posts stood majestically erect, like flag-staffs with no flags. This Dutch barn was Bass's favourite haunt. He would bury himself in what was left of the hay for an afternoon nap, and he probably caught mice too. When full of hay, the barn had the appearance of a formidable tower guarding a sovereign principality, with a black crest on a white metal shield in the form of the number 86. Now the tower lay in ruins and Piotr Niewiadomski dreamt of replenishing it with fresh hay.

That same day, at about six o'clock in the evening, all his dreams were dashed. In living memory, Topory had never been anything other than an ordinary village. It numbered two hundred and eighty-one souls (according to the latest census) and seventy-eight chimneys. The term "chimney" is not accurate, since in Pokuttya few huts boasted chimneys. So let us say seventy-eight roofs. The war, at the outset, disgorged all the best men from the huts, and about forty peasants went off, all reservists and new recruits, not counting those already serving as regulars. As though someone had threshed out the best grain with a flail, the households were left like empty sheaves lying along the crooked trail, stripped bare of their young. Along with the old people and the children, there remained only the chaff of the male population, the reserve militia. Under oath and equipped with their papers, they waited patiently for the day when they would be mobilized. However, when faced with urgent economic matters, for example haymaking, that day seemed to be continually receding instead of getting nearer. In the end, many of the recruits began to feel that the day would never come at all. And until the windowpanes began to rattle, everyone tried to live as though there was no war at all.

Until suddenly, on 20th August, the tiny village of Topory gained the elevated status of a rear-echelon headquarters in the Great War. It was not even aware of this glory bestowed on it by the grace of the army high command. Once again, gendarme Corporal Durek began going round the village with his bag and his gold tooth. Once again he issued papers to the illiterates on which their lives depended. When he turned up at the signal box, Bass no longer barked at him. He had become used to the war. Piotr was no longer afraid of the gendarmerie either. Since he had been recruited into the army he felt a kind of distant cousin to all members of the armed forces. He could now hold his head high at the sight of a rifle or bayonet.

Corporal Durek, responsible for dashing dreams in Topory-Czernielica, did not come alone. He was accompanied by some soldier of indeterminate age, encumbered from head to toe. His rifle was slung nonchalantly round his neck. He was puffing on a long-stemmed pipe. One thing about him was particularly suspicious: on the green facings of his collar, next to the bone star, shone a metal winged wheel. Very clearly, this soldier had some connection with the railway.

Today, Corporal Durek was not dressed as he had been on that evening when he brought the call-up papers. Instead of the helmet he wore an ordinary soldier's cap, and grey-blue battledress instead of the black-and-green cloth uniform. The only indications that here was a corporal of the gendarmerie, and not an infantryman for example, were his bag and his sword. All the shiny objects, buckles and buttons, even the jubilee medal, had been removed—a sign that Topory was a rear-echelon headquarters. In place of the medal, a discrete, narrow red-and-white ribbon adorned the corporal's chest. The Emperor's cross was gone. "Strict incognito" is the watchword at a military staging post. The gendarme's gold tooth glinted as before, but that was all.

"This lance corporal will be taking over your duties," Durek announced. "As of today, the entire railway is in the hands of the army. Evacuation!"

The word "evacuation", like all expressions of foreign origin, served to bolster the belief of the gendarmerie corporal in his personal superiority.

"Evacuation!" he repeated. He inhaled the sound like the smoke of an enjoyable cigarette. The lance corporal meanwhile removed his backpack. He made himself at home in the signal box, paying no attention to Piotr.

"Show the lance corporal what is required," continued Durek. Mention of the soldier's rank as an NCO was intended to emphasize Piotr's comparative inferiority.

Piotr was aghast. Evacuation was all very well, but was he some Jew who had to flee? Where to, anyway? And what about his enlistment?

Corporal Durek had not come merely to relieve him of his post.

"Show me your papers!" he demanded, enigmatically.

Piotr fished out from his jacket pocket all the papers he possessed.

"That is not required!" declared the gendarme, contemptuously returning the certificate of baptism. But he studied the military papers closely. Piotr observed the lance corporal with apprehension.

"You're off tomorrow!" commanded Durek, folding up the document. "You are to report to the stationmaster for your travel instructions."

"To Stanisławów?" asked Piotr, as that was his posting.

"What do you mean, to Stanisławów? To Hungary!"

Things were becoming clearer to Piotr. The Emperor had foreseen everything, even the evacuation. The Emperor would not leave him to the Muscovites. The Emperor was now hurriedly gathering his people, like a wise farmer gathering wheat into the barn as a storm approaches. Piotr was greatly consoled. At last his heart had been relieved of the other half of the burden. The dire possibilities he had feared now ceased to exist. Now the Muscovites could enter Topory, no problem. They wouldn't find Piotr Niewiadomski there.

Emboldened by his sense of relief, he enquired:

"Are the Muscovites far away?"

This question angered the gendarme. It was not permitted to put such questions within the confines of his jurisdiction. Assuming a stern demeanour, he did his best to look like an active soldier, only his gold tooth endowed his words with a glowing warmth:

"Don't you dare sow hysteria! You'll be court-martialled! There's no cause for panic. We're winning the war on all fronts."

"*Jo, jo!*" confirmed the lance corporal ironically—he was Czech.

Durek gave him a withering glance. How tactless, to cast doubt on victory in the presence of an illiterate. Durek read military communiqués in *The New Age*.

"On all fronts the Russians are retreating!" he quoted from memory. "At Rozvadov we destroyed two enemy divisions. Cavalry General von Brudermann…"

He choked on the general's name. Not only did he know the names of the generals, but he could also pronounce them correctly. The German ones, anyway. It was only the Hungarian names that gave him some difficulty. Whenever possible, he tried to avoid them. For now, there wasn't any point in mentioning names. It wasn't worth enlightening the dark masses. Names and family titles dripping with glamour and rustling like plumes of feathers ought to be conserved for higher purposes. To astonish one's superiors, to create a favourable impression of oneself in quarters where it might enhance one's service record.

Piotr had lost the plot again. What should not be sown? Hysteria? What is hysteria? Perhaps some poisonous seed or something like tobacco? Severe punishment was inflicted on those who secretly dealt in tobacco. Piotr did not sow anything or cultivate anything other than beans, cabbages and sunflowers. The sunflowers were actually for Magda. What did he mean about the Muscovites retreating, when our forces are hurriedly retreating from the front line and we are ordered to abandon Topory as quickly as possible? The devil knows where the truth lies. Perhaps it's as the gendarme says, only Piotr can't understand it. If he doesn't know his left from his right, he might not know his front from his rear. The devil, the father of all relativity, is crafty! Once, when Piotr was a child, the evil one led him at dead of night across field after field for something like two hours. Piotr was lost and couldn't find his way home, while his house was right under his nose, just a hundred paces away. The devil had hidden his cottage underground, in order to lead an innocent soul astray. Who knows, perhaps at this very moment the devil is leading the entire Imperial and Royal Army, which thinks it is advancing whereas in reality it keeps retreating?

The signal bell rang again. Piotr ran out with his little flag and for the last time in his life lowered the level-crossing barrier on the Lwów–Czerniowce–Ickany line. His railway career was over.

Chapter Five

"So nothing is to be held up? Hello! I said—is nothing to be held up?" The stationmaster at Topory-Czernielica was on the telephone to the stationmaster at Śniatyn.

"You say it starts at 12.29 and continues until 14.50? But of course. What with this evacuation, I haven't picked up a newspaper for several days. Hello! Well, what then? Not to light up in any circumstances? No, I'm not. Such... Hello!... such things have happened before. In ancient times, during the Punic Wars, Scipio Africanus..."

Ancient history buzzed in the earpiece of the Śniatyn stationmaster's telephone. Between Śniatyn and Topory-Czernielica stations, along the metal cables the exhausted sparrows used to rest on, Hannibal was dashing back and forth at the historic moment of the evacuation of the Topory district. Meanwhile, modern history was announcing itself by the echo of distant artillery fire, the rumbling of the earth and the rattling of windowpanes.

"Yes sir, yes sir, I'll send a report, sir."

He hung up and cranked the handle. A ring of the telephone bell indicated that the call was over. Hannibal had disappeared.

The Topory-Czernielica stationmaster was proud of his classical education. He remembered the Punic Wars particularly well, since it was because of these and certain other gory facts that he had been required to retake his secondary school exams. On the first occasion, to the disgust of the entire examination board, he had said that there were five Punic Wars, waged by Philip of Macedonia against Rome. When he retook the examination six months later, he knew exactly what had really happened. Only this time the examiner was not interested in his views on the Punic Wars. On receiving more or less correct answers on the topic of Julius Caesar's campaigns, and hearing a tolerable translation of a passage from *Ab urbe condita*, he confirmed that the candidate had passed. The stationmaster remembered the Punic Wars till the end of his life. He admired the ancient Romans, not so much for their virtue and wisdom as for the fact that, thanks to a perfunctory acquaintance with their history and their writings, he was able to serve just one year in the Imperial and Royal Army, and to gain a commission as a reserve officer. He regarded those with no secondary school certificate as creatures of the lowest order. He never shook hands with them. He made exceptions only for women or members of his own family, in particular his father, who was a coach-builder in Rohatyn district. But he was indifferent towards his father, and there were few situations in which he was keen to appear in his company.

Just four more years separated him from his full pension. His only son, Tadzio, would have passed his secondary school exam by then. They should examine him on the Punic Wars or Caesar's campaigns! That Tadzio caused him a lot of worries.

He hated the ancient Romans, and the ancient Greeks even more, on account of that infernal grammar of theirs. He wanted to become a fitter on the railway. That life's ambition had to a great extent to do with Topory-Czernielica station. Tadzio was now spending his holidays with his parents. At the moment, he was rummaging among the refuse in the kitchen, searching for glass. He was determined to get a bit of glass. When he found none in the bin, he went over to where a small lamp was hanging on the kitchen wall. He lit it, turning the wick so high that the glass turned black with soot and cracked. Then he extinguished the lamp. He slipped a piece of blackened glass in his pocket. Looking around to see whether anyone was watching, he stole out of the kitchen.

In his father's office the telephone was ringing.

"Hello, yes, speaking. They arrived this morning. Yes, a provisional cadet. I don't know anything about that. The railway, right, the railway. Hello. I can't hear you. Yes. The gendarmerie. I don't know yet. I'll probably send my family to Vienna. What's that you say? Nothing like that. I handed over the cash-box yesterday. Well, what did he say? *De gustibus non est...* There's no accounting for taste. Of course. Back in ancient times, you know, they... I beg your pardon, I do beg your pardon; I thought it would be of interest to you."

He was cut off. The senior official at Kołomyja station did not appreciate the Topory-Czernielica stationmaster's erudition. Especially at such a time, when the world was collapsing and the Russians were approaching, and the military was taking over the railway.

The stationmaster swallowed this bitter pill in silence.

Without knocking, Provisional Cadet Hopfenzieher entered the office. The stationmaster could not abide anyone entering without knocking. Earlier, in normal times, he used to remark to such people that "you only enter a pigsty without knocking". (Such people at Topory-Czernielica station mostly had no secondary school certificate.) But these were not normal times, and Provisional Cadet Hopfenzieher not only had no secondary school certificate, but as from today he was actually in charge. The sign on the door that read "Unauthorized entry strictly forbidden" had become an anachronism. Who is an intruder now, and who is one of us?

"Would you care to check the inventory with me?" enquired the intruder.

"Certainly!"

They sat down together at the desk and began to check the inventory sheets.

Their work was interrupted by a timid knock. The stationmaster leapt up in annoyance and opened the door. On the threshold stood Piotr Niewiadomski, cap in hand.

"What do you want? Don't you know you aren't allowed to enter without knocking?"

"I did knock, sir."

Of course he had. But what an ass he was! Couldn't he see that this was nothing to do with him at all; it was about those interlopers who had intruded on the station that morning. They were the "unauthorized" ones who ought to have been forbidden to enter for all time.

All of a sudden, the stationmaster was overcome by compassion for Piotr. After all, this unenlightened Hutsul was one of his own, not "one of them". In any case, they had spent the last eleven years together. For the first time in those eleven years a faint sense of solidarity with the lowest official in his branch of service stirred within the stationmaster. For the first time the winged wheel on his cap, embroidered in gold thread, felt like the elder brother of the tin wheel on Piotr's cap. The lustre of the metal wheels dazzled the stationmaster, and the wings fluttered, rustling pathetically. They were no mere emblem now, not just a symbol, but the genius of the railway itself. A glance at the provisional cadet's collar was sufficient to ascertain what gods he served as a civilian. He was a militarized railwayman.

The lustre of the wheels dimmed and the rustling wings were those of an angel of mourning, mourning a ruined career. There could be no doubt that the war would delay promotion, especially in the case of officials who were obliged to escape with the evacuation. Had it not been for the war, they would have retired with a higher rank, perhaps even achieving gold-collar status. The stationmaster saw Piotr in the same light as his own son Tadzio. The stationmaster was human, even if he did, of course, box your ears.

"Come back later," he said, benevolently. "You can see I'm busy. I have a little more money for you. Come back in an hour."

There was regret in those words. The stationmaster was leaving his station. Goodness knows how long for, perhaps for ever. He was attached to it, even if he occasionally cursed it. Wasn't Piotr Niewiadomski a part of the inventory, just as much as the cupboard where the tickets were kept (the station's altar), the Morse code apparatus, the signals, the levers, the Wertheimer safe, the scales and the three clocks from the

Siemens-Halske works? He was, but the stationmaster would not hand him over to the provisional cadet. He was handing over only inanimate inventory items. Piotr was a living being. And living beings were at the disposal of the Emperor alone.

"Can I go, then?" asked Piotr.

Yes, he could go. There was no work for him to do here now. The stationmaster wanted to do him a favour by giving him one last duty.

"Perhaps you'll take down the station sign. Take care of the hooks, mind. The hooks may come in handy. Bring them to me."

Then he shut the door in his face. For the first time in eleven years the stationmaster had given him an order saying "perhaps". That conveyed a touch of solidarity.

Take down the station sign? What did that mean? Although Piotr was illiterate, he knew all about the significance of the sign. To the station, the sign was as important as anyone's own name. He knew what the black Roman and Cyrillic lettering said off by heart. He would be able to copy it. Topory was like Piotr and Czernielica was like Niewiadomski. Depriving the station of its sign was the same as taking away someone's name. The stationmaster's command shook Piotr's faith in the order of the world. The whole world was full of beautiful names, flourishing as in a wild-flower meadow. God himself had probably sown them centuries ago. There were fragrant, sweet, pleasant names and there were sharp, menacing, sullen names. Where did the name of Topory* come from, for example? At one time, there must have been just forests here,

* "Axes".

before the woodcutters came with their axes and chopped them down. And was the station now to have its pride and joy, that which distinguished it from other stations, removed?

Something began to dawn on Piotr. The station sign probably had to be taken down to stop the Muscovites finding their way around so easily. Let them find their own way or ask their sympathizers. We won't show the Muscovites where Topory-Czernielica is.

This was how Piotr understood the point of his last task on the railway.

He found the state of the platform even more upsetting. Rifles were propped against the wall outside the waiting-room. Piotr counted them: eight. Nobody was looking after them. Litter was strewn about everywhere, paper, debris, cigarette ends and trampled straw. The waiting-room floor was covered in straw as well. There were backpacks, haversacks and mess tins on the benches. Three soldiers were lying in the straw. They were smoking pipes and speaking some foreign language. Piotr reluctantly passed through the waiting-room turned into a soldiers' billet. He spat ostentatiously into the spittoon clogged with rubbish. He went to the storeroom to fetch a ladder. On his way back, he noticed that the oil lamp was missing from the lantern guarding the shed containing the ladies and gents. They had already nicked it, the bastards!

Piotr set about removing the sign. He placed the ladder against the wall. The elongated, shapely sign hung between the waiting-room and the stationmaster's apartment on the first floor. The apartment consisted of three rooms and a kitchen, but only two windows looked out over the platform. Piotr climbed the ladder and stood on the next-to-last rung.

Under the stationmaster's windows, petunias, geraniums and nasturtiums in green wooden window-boxes were on their last legs. The stationmaster's wife had planted them—she was passionate about flowers. Piotr turned his head to contemplate the flowers for a while. They gave off no scent. Then he took a pair of pliers from his pocket and loosened the hooks. The head of a boy, attracted by the noise, poked out of one of the windows. It was the stationmaster's son, Tadzio. He recognized Piotr.

"What are you doing there, Piotr?"

"I'm taking the sign down."

"What for?"

"Your dad's orders."

Tadzio chortled sarcastically and immediately disappeared.

Piotr pulled out the hooks. The white sign with its black devil's symbols tilted to one side. Piotr held on to it with his left hand, but the sign was too heavy. If he took it in both hands, Piotr could lose his balance. For a moment he stood on the ladder and hesitated. Finally, he decided to drop it. He looked like Moses destroying the tablets of stone. The sign fell with a loud metallic crash, but it came to no harm. Not a single letter came adrift.

Piotr climbed down the ladder like a hangman who had just carried out an execution. He lifted the sign as though it was a dead body and carried it off to the store-room. The soldiers on the platform looked on with indifference as the station was humiliated. From that moment on, Topory-Czernielica station actually ceased to exist. All that remained was a lonely little building beside the railway line, nameless, headless and soulless.

Late that evening, Piotr took his leave of the stationmaster. The "old man" handed him his overdue wages, adding two crowns from his own pocket. He also administered the last rites, as it were.

"Do your duty well in the army—don't get yourself killed, because if the devil takes you not even a dog will bark for you!"

This favourite saying of the stationmaster's came from the days of his own military service. Some lieutenant at the one-year service school, wanting to express utter contempt for one of his trainees and to convince him of the total worthlessness of his existence, would exclaim: "I'll shoot you, and not even a dog will bark for you!" Of course, the dog served merely as a flexible metaphor, and as such it entered the stationmaster's verbal repertoire.

The parting was an emotional occasion, but it passed without tears being shed. Piotr was not one to weep easily. His tough life had not only given him a thick skin; certain glands had ceased to function as well. Piotr kissed the stationmaster's hand. Parting with inanimate objects saddened him more than parting from living people. He felt a greater affinity with that world than with people. He was himself something of a station-supporting beam. Did not the track, the ballast and the points bear traces of his hands, were they not soaked in his sweat? Invisible as they were, those traces existed and would continue to exist until new people came to lay new tracks, to spread fresh gravel on the Lwów–Czerniowce–Ickany line. The inert, silent permanence of things to which human hands gave meaning—this is the greatest reward for heavy, rough, transient exertion. If Piotr had possessed the stationmaster's classical education, he could have said at that moment: "*Non omnis moriar*—not all of me will die."

As he walked down the track, he could recognize each object that had ever had anything to do with his work, even in the darkness. Here was the pump at which the locomotives stopped to take on water. Its blackness loomed in the dark like some weird, stiff, gigantic bird with a brass beak. So many times Piotr had packed it with straw in the winter! And over there, a little farther on, some very familiar old friends, retired rails, lay rusting in the grass.

Piotr returned home. The village lay three kilometres beyond the station. Beside the railway line stretched lush meadows, full of buttercups in spring. At this time of the year, the meadows were being mown and tall stooks of hay stood motionless like spellbound troops. Suddenly, Piotr had the impression that the stooks were moving forwards. But the illusion soon vanished. As far as the eye could see there was not a living soul about. Unless the grasshoppers, whose loud, relentless trilling penetrated the night air, have souls. The earth, ravaged somewhere in the distance by shelling, groaned at measured intervals. The night was cool. The moon had not yet crept out of its lair, which was behind the hill, beyond Czernielica, though it was already sprinkling Topory with its silvery powder. The stars twinkled encouragingly at him, but they were minute and pale, flickering like the flames of tiny oil lamps. The moon bided its time; it was up to something that night.

The village was wafting its strongest odours in Piotr's direction—the smell of over-ripe onions and parsley. As he approached the nearest cottages, he sensed the eternal reek

of peasants' dwellings nestling amid the calm of rural existence—a fusion of smoke from log fires, cheese, whey, poultry
droppings and poverty. Unglazed black pots, earthenware
pots planted with poppies and little jugs were ranged on top
of the fences like helmets on the heads of crusaders. The
lights were on in many of the cottages, as many of their
occupants would be setting off to Hungary on the following
day—the reserve militia. Their bundles and their little boxes
were being packed and food was being prepared for the
journey. Hryć Łotocki's was the only cottage in darkness.
He was sleeping soundly, being over sixty and not called up
for military service by the Emperor. Łotocki's dog leapt out
of his kennel on hearing Piotr's footsteps. Rattling his chain,
he kept barking at the passer-by for some time, as though
he was a burglar. Aroused by the barking, other dogs started
pulling on their leads, but they didn't show their solidarity
with Łotocki's sheepdog for long. One by one, they returned
to their dens.

Bass, however, recognized Piotr's footsteps from a distance
and joyfully rushed to greet him. He had been waiting in front
of the house with Magda, who had learnt of Piotr's imminent
hurried departure. She had resolved to spend the night with
him. They went indoors.

Piotr lit the lamp. It was stuffy. Magda opened the window.
At once, nocturnal butterflies, moths and fireflies flew in.
Many of them perished soundlessly in the seductive flame,
like the soldiers who were falling that night in gunfire on the
Drina, the Sambre and the Moselle, for at that moment began
the return of the Austro-Hungarian army from Kragujevac in
Serbia, and Russia's Fourth and Fifth Armies were just then on

the move from the north, and from the north-east the Third and Eighth were converging on the Przemyśl–Lwów line. The rattling of the grubby windowpanes in Piotr Niewiadomski's cottage announced the intensification of action by the armies fighting in Galicia.

Piotr sat down on his bed without removing his cap. He was exhausted and very hungry. Magda cleared out the ash that had been piled up on the hearth since before the war had started, chopped some wood and lit the fire. She had thoughtfully brought with her milk, bread and potatoes. They remained silent for some time. The heat from the fire in the kitchen slowly began to reach the couple.

Magda was the first to speak.

"You're off, then?"

Although for four years Magda had been to Piotr what polite people called his "beloved", she had not ventured to address him accordingly except at moments of greatest intimacy. Once these moments were over, she was again separated from Piotr by a barrier created by respect and by the seventeen-year age difference between them. He always addressed her as he would a spouse, but she did so only when she was serving him in the role of Venus. Otherwise, she existed only as a humble orphan, who was not permitted to forget her own low status.

"Yes," he replied.

And they fell silent again. Piotr did not speak to her again until they were having supper, the last time they would do so together.

"Look after Bass—make sure the Muscovites don't take him. Everyone is after a dog."

He stroked Bass, and then took hold of his muzzle with both hands so tightly that the dog yelped.

Magda was hurt; he had always taken better care of the dog than of her. But she said nothing, because even orphans have their pride. After supper, Piotr went outside and lit his pipe.

He sat down on the threshold and looked up at the stars. One of the stars broke away from its flock, crossed the entire breadth of the horizon and disappeared into the river Prut. Piotr paused for thought. He had heard that falling stars were seen when someone was going to die. He laughed out loud— if a star fell for every peasant who snuffed it in the war, they would have to fall incessantly like a hailstorm. Soon there would be not a single one left in the sky.

He did not know that there were more flaring and extinct worlds than there were soldiers in the service of His Imperial and Royal Majesty.

When he had finished smoking his pipe, he stood up heavily and went into the orchard. All the trees looked amazingly dark in the milky glow of the hidden moon. Neither of the apple trees had borne fruit that year, and the plums were still small and green. Still, he picked one and slipped it into his pocket. Then he walked all the way round the house, probably for the hundredth time feeling sorry about the state it was in. This house could do with being repaired.

Beneath the thatched roof hung cobs of maize. They were drying out for seeding. In the dull light, they looked like sleeping bats hanging from nails.

Piotr went back to Magda, and their night of love-making began.

The girl had washed the dishes and scoured the pans.

She had fed Bass on the leftovers from their supper. The well-fed dog ran out into the yard, but straight away he returned, looking despondent; evidently, he could not find a suitable place to lie down, so he began to settle underneath the bed. A cricket was chirruping, hidden in a crack in the floor by the hearth. Magda kneeled before the image of the Immaculate Mother, closed her eyes and prayed for a long time in impassioned whispers. Then she took off her shawl and her apron, removed her skirt, untied her two thin plaits and made one thick one. Then she extinguished the lamp and lay down beside Piotr.

At that point Bass stirred uneasily, reminding them of his presence. Piotr was embarrassed about it; this live witness made him uneasy. He had to be sent out. Piotr leapt out of bed, opened the door and tried to get Bass to go out into the hallway, at least. But the dog stubbornly refused to obey; he was unwilling to abandon his master on this last night. Piotr, humiliated, used force and with a stick, of all things, drove his only love out into the yard. The banished love howled piteously.

Piotr had never loved Magda; he just "lived" with her. Was he capable of love, anyway? Who knows, perhaps love is a luxury only privileged souls can afford. How did his love for Bass manifest itself, for example? It may have been the total trust of a downtrodden man in a downtrodden animal, a comradeship in their shared dog's life on this earth, where they went around together with a hang-dog appearance, or something else besides. Perhaps this love was concealed beneath a dull mutual submissiveness. For Piotr would often give in to Bass against his own better judgement, and senseless submission to a weaker creature sometimes passes for love. It was probably only in really serious cases, for example when the dog was in danger, that Piotr imposed his will. Apart from that, he rarely displayed his superiority. What did a Hutsul know about dogs? Piotr attributed great intelligence to Bass. He felt that the old hound could see everything, sense and understand every human gesture. For that reason, he found Bass's presence embarrassing when Magda stayed overnight, which often meant that no intimacy occurred between Piotr and Magda. The dog could not bear anyone to touch his master; it seemed to make him jealous. He would throw himself at the foreign body in an attempt to drag it away from Piotr. But even when Bass remained calm, Piotr felt his movements were restricted. This time, however, passion prevailed, enhanced by the day's events and by a vague sense that this would be his last night with Magda. He was unwilling to abandon it, but he could not see it through when Bass was there. He chased him out.

The altercation with the dog cooled his ardour and held back his advances. It was somehow silly to restart the foreplay interrupted by the dog's stubbornness. Besides, even when he closed his eyes the war was there, like an annoying insect oppressing him with persistent thoughts about the following day. He had to stir up his passion once more, shutting out logic and overcoming his fears. Eventually, victory was on the side of Venus.

No, Piotr did not love Magda. He possessed her body as one drinks vodka or takes a bath for vital health reasons. But it was not an addiction. Piotr had no addictions. Magda's slim, firm tiny body was always cool. Even at moments of most intense rapture it did not perspire. It gave Piotr the pleasure of its gentle, obedient submissiveness, which is what appealed to him. In the orphan's embrace he simultaneously experienced the sense of relief, the dulling of consciousness and the awareness of his own powers dear to every man. And finally, Magda's body was the only terrain where he felt victorious. This is something male self-love cannot easily do without. Piotr vanquished Magda without resistance, but also effortlessly, and the sterility of the insemination was the only thing that mitigated his brief pleasure. It robbed the joining of their bodies of its deeper meaning, depriving it of its dignity. But it also guarded against excess. In any case, Magda's sensuality was kept in check by other restraints—her religious faith and Piotr's age. A younger man might have succeeded in taking Magda's body to the most consummate passion and overcoming her sense of sin. "Living" with Piotr, she never forgot that she was sinning, so she attempted at least to sin in moderation. That was probably why she prayed so fervently before entering his bed. As though she wanted to beg forgiveness in advance.

Nor did Piotr become intoxicated with Magda; he always remained in control of his instincts. It was as though he was subconsciously fulfilling an obligation inherited from his unknown Polish father, Niewiadomski—Incognito.

The nights with Magda afforded him a momentary enjoyment of life, which he never experienced otherwise. For him, the orphan's body represented cafés, opera and long voyages, everything that music, sport and intellectual pleasures mean to other people. But it held no surprises—it was as commonplace as his daily bread. Piotr found in it relaxation and tenderness and for a few seconds he was transported beyond the confines of his own existence. Women, vodka and religion are the three delights that rescue the souls of the benighted Hutsul from despair and hell on earth.

But Piotr never took Magda with him into his dreams. The orphan remained on the threshold of his sleep and his wakefulness, just as she did not venture to address him as she would a husband in the daytime. Piotr was alone when he was asleep, even though he lay in her embrace. Often his mother visited him in his dreams, sometimes even his wretched sister Paraszka, but never Magda. She often dreamt of him, though. Tonight, she was completely conjoined with him. She first dreamt of him as an infant suckling at her breast, then the child suddenly grew up...

The windowpanes rattled and the ground shook rhythmically, as though in spasms of amorous passion. The dull, faint, distant explosions were not so frightening in the stillness of the night, indeed they were even stimulating. Throughout the night the cricket, that Mozart of peasants' hearths, made music for them. Only the whining of the banished Bass filled the night with anxiety and touched on old wounds.

The moon was determinedly hatching something that night. It did not appear, although it ought long since to have been looking down on Topory. Only around midnight did it majestically appear beyond Czernielica, flooding the night sky and the sleeping lovers with its cold, silvery light. Silvery Piotr and silvery Magda emerged from the gloom like two silver phantoms. Piotr was snoring. The windowpanes rattled like silver.

At that moment, death, quitting the battlefields, penetrated the confines of the Vatican. In vain the Swiss Guard kept watch with their halberds, preventing anyone from entering. Death eluded their watchfulness, forcing its way to the bedchamber where old Joseph Melchior Sarto lay. Cardinals and prelates were already administering the last rites. One of His Holiness's domestic prelates offered the dying man the cross for him to kiss. Pope Pius X's death took place at twenty minutes past one. Cardinal Chamberlain della Volpe confirmed it personally. Then the cardinals began reading the requiem mass. Death, having carried out its task, returned to the battlefields. The Battle of Lorraine was just beginning. Piotr Niewiadomski was snoring.

The stars were fading and the night was nearly spent when Magda woke with a loud cry. She was having a nightmare. She had dreamt about Piotr. He was lying in the courtyard at Iwan Bury's. He lay there stark naked, with a huge, ugly wound in his abdomen. Old Maryna Prokipczuk's sow was burying its snout in the wound, lapping blood so loudly, so loudly...

Magda's sobbing woke Piotr. Everywhere else was in complete silence. Just before dawn, the shelling had stopped, as though to catch its breath. The windowpanes were not rattling. Only the cricket continued to chirrup in the crack in the kitchen floor. Piotr was alarmed by the sudden calm of the earth and by Magda's crying.

"What's the matter," he asked, tenderly embracing the weeping woman and adding—as though he had only just noticed for the first time the orphan's misery, his own misery, all the misery of his own people—"my child?"

Magda, shuddering all over because of the cold, because of her fear, or because she was overflowing with love, stammered out through her tears:

"If... if... you wanted me to, I would love you until death."

She told him about her dream. Piotr laughed, but they now shared the word "death". She was still crying, and sighing. Eventually, Piotr calmed her down. And for the last time in his life he fell asleep in the slender arms of the orphan Magdalena Mudryk.

Chapter Six

The 21st of August dawned just like any other day that summer—bright, sunny and warm. It promised to be very fine. Not a cloud in sight. The birds' dawn chorus began early and the crowing of the cockerels lasted so long and was so fanatical it gave the impression that once again somebody was going to forsake his Master.

He who until today had been the successor to St Peter, the fisher for souls, did not forsake his Master. A few hours previously, taking his leave of the world, he had renewed his vows in the presence of the cardinals, and so he could fearlessly face the King whose earthly interests he had defended persistently, though not always with success. To the last, he had remained faithful to his motto: Restore all things in Christ.

A few days after the death the Rome *Tribune* wrote: "The Pope is a victim of the war. In his last days the Holy Father personally dictated many messages in an attempt to avert this European catastrophe." He did not avert it. By his death, which came at a critical moment, he renounced all moral association with the perpetrators of this butchery.

It was for the death of the Pope that the cockerels were crowing today in Czernielica and throughout the Catholic world.

The garrisons of the Roman God were numerous throughout the world. Even such a tiny gathering of souls as Czernielica possessed (in common, that is, with the Topory and Bogatyn parishes, the neighbouring hamlets of Nowopole and Wierbiąż, and the Biłousy settlement) its own plot of consecrated ground and a ruined relic of some saint of the Greek religion, the core of a church. And where there is a church there is also a bell-tower and a priest and a deacon or a sacristan.

News of the Pope's death reached the presbytery of Czernielica at eleven o'clock in the morning, communicated by gendarme Corporal Jan Durek. Durek had been at the station that morning and heard the news from the station-master, who had been informed by telephone. At the time the priest, Father Makarucha, had his head stuffed inside one of his thirty beehives, covered by a protective wire-mesh mask. At first he was incredulous at the sad news, for he was one of those designated by the Master as of little faith. He had not read a newspaper for a long time and knew nothing about the Pope's brief illness. The first duty of a priest on the death of any church dignitary was to toll the bell. So if the Pope himself dies, what does that call for! However, Father Makarucha did not perform his obligation straight away. The death of The Holy Father is too great an event to be believed immediately and to be acted on straight away. Besides, in those days the most incredible rumours were about and it was not becoming to the dignity of a priest to take everything seriously.

To toll or not to toll?

The decision was indeed a difficult one. For if the Pope had really died, yet the bells in Father Makarucha's parish remained silent, the negligent priest would be a sinner. But if the rumour was false, or indeed premature, then by tolling the bells he would risk being called to account for his excessive zeal. However, the soul of a living pope would come to no harm. On the other hand, a great wrong would be inflicted on the soul of a deceased pope by a failure to toll for him. That was the last thing Father Makarucha wanted. Father Makarucha wished for only one thing—official confirmation. It could not arrive quickly, because of the war, the evacuation and the general upheaval. What was to be done? Should he mourn the passing of the Head of the Church or wait a bit longer?

On that day Father Makarucha already had plenty to worry about. There were the five-kilogram pots of his purest honey, ten of which were lined up at the station, waiting to be loaded onto the Lwów train. Now that passenger and goods trains had been held up, the fate of this (purest) honey was uncertain. In fact, as of today it was quite certain; the consignment would not be despatched to Lwów. What should he do? Toll or not toll? Narodna Torhowla of Lwów had sent a deposit before the war started. This deposit amounted to only one fifth of the amount Father Makarucha was supposed to receive on delivery of the goods. Perhaps he should seek his wife's advice on the matter of tolling? But, well, what advice could a woman give in such cases? Better to decide for oneself. He would be ridiculed either way, but by whom, actually? If the rumour proved to be false, he would tell people that the bell had been tolled for a quite different reason.

It really was an outrage about that honey! Had it been worthwhile to slave away all year, and run the risk of getting stung by the bees?

It's true that Father Makarucha never went near the bee-hives without a net over his face or without wearing gloves and an apron. In this get-up he looked like the high priest of some heretical sect. But in certain circumstances he liked to emphasize the danger he faced in his bee-keeping work. All the more so since he faced no great danger in the course of his pastoral duties. Father Sydir Makarucha made no secret of the fact that he favoured the bees over those meek, mangy sheep, his parishioners. True, these sheep did not sting, but neither did they produce any honey. Nor did they make any payment for christenings, weddings or burials. Christenings, especially, were a limited source of joy for Father Makarucha; every second married couple was childless. But it was common knowledge that the Hutsuls were doing penance for the French sins of their forefathers. And while the virtues of his parishioners brought the priest of Czernielica little income, for their greatest virtue was poverty—who knows, perhaps it was indeed their only virtue—so, likewise, he gained little from their sins. People did not want to get married; they lived in sin and, what is more, they did not give birth to any children.

Sins, sins. How could one make a living from the sins of others in such an indigent, infertile parish? It was hardly surprising, then, that Father Makarucha stuck to his honey, being—if one may be permitted to say so—attached body and soul to his beehives. The more so because, although he was not a Hutsul, God had not deigned to give him children either. The sweet honeycombs, those masterpieces of insect architecture, were of greater interest to him than the sweet balm with which he was obliged to heal wounds in the Hutsuls' souls. From this wax, his wife made excellent candles for use at home and in the church. She also supplied the candles she made to neighbouring parishes, making a tidy profit.

Not infrequently, the honey flowed over from the beekeeping to the priest's actual profession. Whenever he mentioned the land of milk and honey in his sermons, those of the faithful who were endowed with a more lively imagination knew that Father Makarucha had in mind his own honey. It was indeed excellent honey. The priest never adulterated it by adding sugar.

He hated vodka drinkers. Interpreting the meaning of the Promised Land, he would say: "So you can see, dear brothers and dear sisters, that God did not promise the Jews a land flowing with milk and vodka, only with milk and honey." Once, during Easter meditation, he even committed a bad slip of the tongue, declaring that "We receive the body and blood of Christ in the form of bread and honey." He corrected this to "wine" only when it was too late and the church was filled with suppressed laughter like the buzzing of a beehive.

To toll the bells or not to toll? That was the question that continued to trouble the priest long after the gendarme had left. A further inhibition was secretly troubling the priest; if the rumour turned out to be false, the tolling of the bells would entail a grave danger. Father Makarucha recalled with horror his colleagues who had been hanged in the northern districts. He was loyal, no Muscovite sympathizer. But could all the officers of the Imperial and Royal Army be aware of that? All those Germans, Hungarians, Croats and Czechs? Only the locals know of it. The chairman of the council in Śniatyn knew as well. But he had probably already moved the council offices to some safer location. To toll or not to toll?

The deacon had been enlisted in the army and there never had been a sacristan, so if it came to anything there would be no one else to blame. Since the deacon had been enlisted, Father Makarucha himself had usually been the bell-ringer. Now that it was a matter of the peace of the soul, not of any old parishioner, but of the Pope of Rome himself, was he really supposed to have someone else stand in for him? Quite inappropriate. Father Sydir Makarucha was no coward, so he didn't want to look as if he was, even in his own eyes. So he decided to toll. But when he grasped the rope that was supposed to toll the two heavy bells, he could not rid himself of a persistent delusion that this rope was strangling him.

His self-confidence was bolstered by his imagination, which revived in Father Makarucha's soul the infamous long-standing feud between the Empire and the papacy. The priest of Czernielica now engaged in a kind of battle over the Investiture, which was not, however, resolved in Canossa. He revolted against the state's supremacy over the church and, although he valued his own life, he was prepared to sacrifice it for the faith.

All right, let them suspect him, but God in heaven knows that Sydir Makarucha is innocent; he is fulfilling his sacred duty.

He sensed the great power of his soul. His thoughts went out to all the martyrs he knew of, his thoughts went out to all the innocent Ruthenian priests who had been hanged, and with the palm of his own martyrdom before his eyes he tugged at the rope. He set both bells in motion, informing the parish of the unconfirmed death of the Holy Father Pius X.

Not long after that the bells tolled in the neighbouring parishes. So it was true; the Pope had indeed passed away.

Father Makarucha felt deeply relieved, but at the same time he was loath to see himself relinquishing the role of martyr. His palm had withered before it had time to germinate.

Soon the bells—purchased with parishioners' contributions or with generous donations from devout ladies of landed families, and the well-to-do who had recovered from their illnesses—were resounding throughout the district of Śniatyn. They resounded from church to church, from village to village, and their tones traced invisible circles in the clear, bright sky.

The Pope of Rome has died! Oh, our Pope, our Pope of Rome, of Rome, has died!

All the cardinals were mourning him, all the bishops and suffragans, the prelates and canons, the monks in their monasteries and the little sisters, all the saints in heaven and the devout on earth who had heard the news. The Metropolitan of Lwów himself, Count Szeptycki, a great man, a Polish nobleman who had resigned from the Imperial cavalry to serve God, who had renounced the Latin rites of the gentry in order to lead the Ruthenian people on the road to salvation wearing the Greek golden tiara, was mourning the Pope of Rome. And all the clerics and all the seminarists were mourning him, and the priests, deacons and sacristans were singing for him, and Father Sydir Makarucha, parish priest of Czernielica, tolled away.

Meanwhile in Rome eight Swiss Guards were at this moment bearing the body of the Pope into the Chapel of the Blessed Sacrament. The coffin was followed by a funeral procession consisting of a body of armed guards, all the courtiers and twenty-two cardinals led by Chamberlain della Volpe.

Piotr Niewiadomski was greatly surprised to hear the tolling of the bells. In those days the church bells rang only on Sundays, after the service. So was it a funeral?

No, when there is a funeral they only ring in the parish of the deceased, but now the bells were heard not only in Czernielica; the clearest echoes came from the distant bells of Horbacz and Nyrków on the Czeremosz. So if it was not a funeral, then what was it? Perhaps it was marking the departure of the last cohorts of the reserve militia? Were they bidding them farewell with the tolling of bells as if we were no longer among the living?

News of the Pope's death was first brought by Magda. She also brought provisions for the journey—a kilo of pork fat, two loaves of whole-grain bread and some cheese. With her own money she had bought a packet of cheap shag. She had been unable to get hold of goose fat anywhere (Piotr was very partial to goose fat). She was dropping by in a great hurry. She had to return to the haymaking. That was where she earned her money. She would come to the station in the evening to see him off.

Piotr found the death of the Pope very upsetting. Like the Rome *Tribune*, he believed the war was to blame. Simple people in Hutsul country found it hard to accept that great people die just like lesser people, through illness or old age. The death of the powerful on this earth is usually associated with events of world significance.

I suppose—Piotr surmised—it's because the clergy permit killing. Not only do they permit it; they expressly demand it. It now seems that the killing of a Muscovite is not a sin at all, or it is just a half-sin, like the killing of a Jew. Although it isn't the same. Jews are non-believers, whereas Orthodox Christians believe in Jesus Christ. Piotr knew some Orthodox Christians; they lived not far away, in Bukovina. They were Romanians, it's true, but they were subjects of Emperor Franz Joseph, just like the Hutsuls. They even dressed like them. On the railway, they talked of the wonders of the residence of the "Orthodox" archbishop of Czerniowce. Of course Count Szeptycki, the Golden Metropolitan himself, had visited—it must be four years ago now. On that occasion, the Hutsuls erected a magnificent triumphal arch in Śniatyn and welcomed their metropolitan with bread and salt, music and horsemen in traditional costumes. He passed this way, through Topory-Czernielica station, in a private saloon compartment. If the Orthodox congregations had been non-believers, he would not have come to visit them. This is all very confusing. You can no longer tell who is with us and who is the enemy, who is righteous and who is a sinner. They say the Muscovites are retreating, yet they tell us to run away. They say the Muscovites must be thrashed, because they are Orthodox and recognize their beloved Tsar instead of the Holy Father in Rome, and the Romanians are Orthodox as well, yet they are loyal to our Emperor and care nothing for the Tsar. But today the Lord has taken away his earthly deputy and nobody knows if that is a punishment, or…

The death of God's deputy evoked certain gloomy associations. It brought to mind the murder in Lwów of the Tsar's governor in Poland, Count Andrzej Potocki, seven years earlier. The murderer was a Ruthenian, a Ukrainian. The entire Ruthenian people were tainted with the blood of the victim of this political assassination. Piotr Niewiadomski was a Ruthenian too, though his father was Polish. One's religion was the deciding factor. National consciousness had never been Piotr's strong point. If the expression may be permitted, Piotr was poised on the very threshold of national consciousness. He spoke Polish and Ukrainian, he believed in God according to the Greek-Catholic rites while serving the Austro-Hungarian Emperor. Ukrainian insurgents had reached Topory, it's true, but they had not succeeded in undermining Father Makarucha's authority, which was dependent on good relations with the landed gentry—and not only in respect of his dealings in honey. During the elections for the Galician Diet, the priest spoke out from the pulpit, encouraging his congregation to vote for the Old Ruthenian party, but he was not too upset when a certain Polish count was elected thanks to the support of Hutsul voters. The parliamentary elections proceeded in a similar fashion, although in certain more enlightened constituencies Hutsuls voted for Hutsuls. Piotr Niewiadomski consumed the sausage donated by the Ukrainian candidate, but he voted for the count—he was a safer bet. It was common knowledge that counts, princes and the baronial classes have always ruled the world, and always will. And they are close to the Emperor. The Emperor talks to them, and he listens to them. What can some peasant deputy do? He has no chance of intruding in the gentry's circles and getting involved in government affairs.

But since the world had been at war everything had become confused. Evidently, the devil had resolved to deprive the human race of the little good sense it still possessed. Perhaps this was why the Pope had died, then. What would happen now? Christendom without a Pope is like a human being without a head, like a station without a sign bearing its name. Now would the devil begin to run riot. Piotr was overcome with a fear of the devil. Infernal visions were conjured up before his eyes. And he shuddered at the thought that the devil had robbed the Lord of the entire fifth commandment and sold it to the Emperors.

He crossed himself three times to drive away the devil. Then he went outdoors to get a breath of fresh air. It was midday. The sun was high in the sky, directly over Topory. It beat down on his uncovered head. The tolling of the bells had ceased. From the meadows came the soothing sound of the scythe and the lowing of the cattle. The rams were bleating, the geese were honking, the grasshoppers were chirping. The charming chatter of little birds twittering among the branches of the trees was heard all around and the swallows chased one another through the air—lone, dark, flitting shapes against the motionless blue sky. The sky was as blue as the Adriatic Sea. Cockerels were crowing incessantly, and once more the artillery barrage began; people were slowly getting accustomed to it. Piotr returned to the cottage and lifted the lid off a pot to see whether the potatoes were ready. Today he wanted to add to them some of the pork fat Magda had brought for his journey. He put the salt on the table and washed a spoon and a knife. He cut a slice of bread and tasted the pork fat. It was excellent. Steam was soon rising in clouds from the pot. Piotr poured off the boiling water and he was about to begin his meal.

All of a sudden it began to get dark, though there was not a cloud in the sky. With every passing second the sun lost more of its radiance and a cool breeze swept in from the orchard, even though not a single leaf stirred on the trees.

Suddenly, the sparrows had stopped twittering, taking shelter in their nooks in the trees, as they do at dusk. The swallows swooped to their nests, chirruping anxiously. The larks, alarmed at the descending darkness, swooped down to the ground, abandoning their singing high in the sky. Even the insects were seized by panic. Wasps, mosquitoes, butterflies, gadflies, common or garden flies—everything that flies in the air—tried to reach terra firma, cling on to a twig, snuggle among the foliage, crawl into a crevice in the bark of a tree, or hide among straw and moss. Everywhere a bitter chill pervaded, like that experienced inside old churches.

Piotr Niewiadomski looked up from his pot and glanced out of the window.

"What's going on? The sun is disappearing! It's in the middle of the sky in the south and it's disappearing."

Suspended in a dreary void, the sun was fading in dark red agony like an enormous round lamp, as when a fault suddenly occurs at the power station. Cold fear flowed in Piotr's veins, rushing into his heart. The ladle full of hot potatoes fell from his trembling hand. The potatoes were strewn across the floor. Bass thought they were intended for him, but they burnt his tongue. Piotr, struggling to overcome his terror, went outdoors. At the sight of the bats emerging one after another from beneath the roof, squealing horrendously and circling in their frenzy from tree to tree, he began to pray for aid to the Immaculate Mother of God.

The sun was extinguished almost completely, and the world went dark, as if people's eyes were veiled in mourning crepe.

Fear fell on the whole of Pokuttya, although many Hutsuls knew that it was a solar eclipse. Knowing the astronomical fact that the moon is intruding between the earth and the sun does not ward off that fear of sudden, unexpected darkness rooted deep in the soul, any more than the biological interpretation of the phenomenon of death diminishes our dread. It is pointless to explain to the dying that the disintegration of proteins in their bodies is caused by enzymes, that the putrefaction of the corpse is merely the passive decaying of proteins, and that the poisons forming in the corpse are the product of this decay. Not even a naturalist, when dying, is consoled by well-known certainties, and in the last moments of consciousness he does not reassure his family with the principle he has asserted throughout his life, that "nothing in nature is lost".

"It's the end of the world!" cried the Hutsuls in Topory and Czernielica. From both the Old and the New Testaments, familiar to them from the sermons of Father Makarucha, swarmed the frightful images of annihilation that beset the Hutsuls' imagination, cultivated over so many years by this one book alone, which they could not even read. In their terror-stricken souls, the little village of Topory had become the biblical city of Sodom and Czernielica was Gomorrah, and for many the valley of the Prut, with its fragrant mint on summer evenings, was now the Valley of Jehoshaphat. Everyone recalled the darknesses in Egypt mentioned in the Scriptures, remembering that when the Saviour was crucified on Golgotha the sun faded and night fell in broad daylight, just as today. And in Śniatyn district there was wailing and gnashing of teeth.

People whose consciences were not entirely clear fell on their knees, prostrated themselves before the holy icons, beating their breasts with their fists as though, this way, they could expel their lingering, unconfessed sins or those deliberately withheld at confession. Some wanted to immediately hand over everything they had once stolen, even adding some of their own possessions.

There were villains in Topory; yes, there were—thieves and adulterers. There was even a murderer. Sentenced to fifteen years, he spent only seven in Brygidki prison in Lwów; the merciful Emperor pardoned him for the remaining term when the war broke out.

For many people it now became clear why five innocent children and two pious old women had died in the village this summer. God had rewarded these righteous individuals with death so that they would not witness the end of the world. This darkness also explained the death of the Holy Father. All the prophecies about the end of the world mentioned the death of the Pope. This is how God's punishment begins. Everything is as predicted—a dreadful war raging all over the world, Christian blood being shed everywhere, the Muscovites already approaching the district of Śniatyn itself... and now the day of judgement has arrived. The Pope of Rome has passed away and the Lord has drawn a veil of darkness over the earth. Now the devil, the prince of darkness, has a free hand and he can do with the world as he pleases. At any moment now, plagues will rain down from the sky and the Antichrist will appear in his chariot of fire.

The rumble of the artillery barrage was heard even more distinctly in the darkness, swamping faint-hearted souls with black, arid waves. Mountains seemed to crack and crumble, and the pulse of the earth beat a hundred times faster. At any moment it would open up and consume that entire sinful tribe—as it had once swallowed up Korah.

The more timid could already detect sulphur in the air, and the smell of burning, and in the long-drawn-out bellowing of their own cattle they heard the apocalyptic beasts. However, a brave few wanted to run to Father Makarucha to ask if this really meant the end of the world. Others advised them to wait; perhaps the darkness would pass. But the darkness persisted and became ever more dense. The infernal ordeal of waiting for the worst began. The Hutsuls' overworked imagination ceased to function; their souls were filled with the despair of the condemned. In the general panic, no one looked at the clock. Time was moving on in the darkness just as steadily as when it was light.

At an open window on the upper floor at Topory-Czernielica station, below which the petunias, geraniums and nasturtiums were wilting, stood Tadzio, the stationmaster's son. Through the smoke-blackened glass he was observing the total eclipse of the sun. His father had told him that something similar had occurred in ancient times, in 202 BC, during the Battle of Zama. On that occasion Hannibal had uttered those famous words: "Then we will fight in the darkness."

Now too there was fighting in the darkness. They were fighting at Turynka, some twenty-one kilometres west of Kamionka Strumiłowa, and the First German Army was just entering Brussels. And in Rome, in the brightly lit Chapel of the Blessed Sacrament, the remains of Pius X, sprinkled by the Vice-Regent Patriarch Ceppetelli, were at that moment being placed on the catafalque for the lying-in-state.

Piotr Niewiadomski was the sort of person for whom the most diverse phenomena stem from a single cause and are self-evidently linked to him personally. In his mind, all events were coordinated, merging into a single entity, or rather into a single chaotic mass which this mind was accustomed to organize according to its own logic. Therefore Piotr, like other Hutsuls, saw the solar eclipse as closely associated not only with the war and the death of the Pope, but also with his own sins. Original sin was the most prominent, over-shadowing all the other, lesser, sins. And for the second time since his recruitment in Śniatyn Piotr bitterly regretted not having married Magda. He had emerged from the darkness; the darkness was his homeland, but at the moment he was mortally afraid of it, and he begged forgiveness on his knees.

The Creator graciously listened to the prayers of this poor Hutsul and for the last time, truly the last time, he forgave the sins of the world. And just as suddenly as it had fallen, the darkness began to retreat and gradually the world became visible again. Once more the sparrows twittered, the larks sang, the insects buzzed, and the beautiful, cheerful day returned. But the earth continued to rumble, shaking the windowpanes. Through his prayers, Piotr had gained only partial forgiveness for the world. Seeing that the darkened sun shone brightly once again and that everything was returning to its former state, he was almost sure that the artillery barrage would cease, and that shortly Corporal Jan Durek of the gendarmerie would appear with the joyful news that the war was over. So he was in no hurry to pack his trunk.

The solar eclipse had lasted almost two and a half hours, from 12.29 to 14.50. In those long hours of darkness the earth was enriched by tens of thousands of corpses. And there were people on the ground who wished that night would last forever, and bury their concerns, anguish and fear of war. They were not inhabitants of Topory. The inhabitants of Topory and Czernielica and other parishes of Śniatyn district enjoyed the return of the sun and the divine forgiveness and laughed at their own foolishness. But fear still gripped them, lurking in the depths of their souls; today, along with the last of the reserve militia cohorts, they were to travel to Hungary.

When Piotr Niewiadomski had recovered from his fright, and when no angel of peace had turned up in the form of the corporal of the gendarmerie, he set about packing. He could not eat now. The moment he opened the black wooden trunk, like a child's coffin, he heard ever so high above him an unusual whirring and humming. He went outdoors and saw a small bird, way up in the sky. It seemed that the bird had flown out from the very core of the newborn sun—as it were, a dove released from the hands of God. The bird was gliding gently, sometimes descending, then soaring upwards once more. It grew and grew and grew in size, and the rushing noise it made grew louder and louder, sounding like a waterfall. In the end, it flew so close that you could make out its widely spread wings, adorned underneath by colourful circles. Yet the wings were quite motionless. Huge and dark, it glided over the meadows, becoming smaller; and the sound grew quieter, as though it came from a bumblebee. Finally, the strange bird, dwindling to the size of a fly, disappeared into the blue. It was the first military aircraft flying over Topory on its way to the front line.

Piotr went back indoors and packed his little trunk. He included two shirts, a few pairs of long underpants, a towel, several colourful handkerchiefs, his prayer-books (he took them to church, even though he could not read), a mirror, a brush, a razor, a spoon; oh, and his provisions. At the very bottom he placed a handkerchief containing his money, tied in a triple knot. The knots were intended to ensure the safety of 60 crowns in banknotes and in silver. This amount represented his total savings. When he had duly packed the little trunk, he locked it with a padlock.

Yes, it was his trunk, undeniably his own property. Everything he had borne on his shoulders up to now had belonged to someone else. The Jews' potatoes, the gentry's oats, rye and barley, the suitcases of the passengers from the city. Piotr was in awe of all forms of property, but subconsciously hated it because it was someone else's. For so many years, he had to carry other people's trunks, not even having the right to know what they contained. In their mysterious depths, sealed away with a padlock, he suspected the existence of some untold treasures: gold watches, extraordinary razors. What intrigued him most, however, were the shoes. Perhaps it was because for most of the year he went barefoot. By listening to the faint rattling and rustling of invisible objects falling about in the trunk on his back, he tried to guess its contents. Piotr-the-porter's back had eyes and ears. He hated the anonymous kilograms on his back more than the people to whom they belonged. He had a particular dislike of suitcases. He preferred ordinary bags, though they were much heavier.

He preferred coal, wood and grain. He even liked them. They were honest burdens, sincere rather than sneaky. Suitcases offended him because they were locked, just as we are offended when letters we have to deliver to somebody are sealed.

The suitcases and trunks were of various kinds. Some were made from animal skins, protected by canvas covers, others were made of boards covered with oilcloth, others of woven and plaited wicker with a transverse rod passing through the handles. A padlock was attached to one end of the rod—a sacred symbol of ownership, protected by law. Corporal Durek also shackled the hands of thieves. Piotr often observed the trunks' owners checking the locks and padlocks. He would on occasion personally insist that they checked them in his presence, as he was responsible only for locked luggage. However, he did find it humiliating that they were locked at Topory-Czernielica station mainly when he was present.

This small black trunk here was his property. Piotr knew the precise contents of his trunk. Like other people, he secured it with a padlock against unknown thieves. There *were* thieves, yes there were, and not only in Topory. They would not change their spots after that two-and-a-half-hour trial of the end of the world. But Piotr's sense of ownership was such that his trunk was lighter than any of those he had carried on the railway. It was not for some passenger; it was for the Emperor. It was as light as freedom itself. Insofar as freedom is indeed light.

Going to the station with this trunk did not mean he was on his way to freedom, however. He was taking with him to war the remnants of freedom, the very essence of his civilian personality, the secret part of his outer form, which would be covered by his uniform.

Before he left his home, he had to settle three important issues: what to do with Bass, what to do with the railway cap and what to do with the key to the cottage. He had learnt from other soldiers of the reserve militia who had dogs that you are not allowed to take them with you to war. He didn't want to sell Bass. So he decided to entrust him to the dubious care of Magda. Dubious, because he thought the girl might neglect the dog. Once again he would give her strict instructions to protect Bass with her own life. As for the cap, after much hesitation he decided to take it with him. True, it would be misappropriation, but he would create a better impression if he joined wearing a cap like this. And as for the key, he abandoned his original intention of giving it to Magda. He did not trust her. She was a well-meaning girl, but unreliable. Who knew whether the war really would be over by Christmas? And if it did not end and the Muscovites occupied Topory and Magda had a key, then goodness knows what might go on in his house. It was definitely better to take the key with him. So that is what he did. What confidence people have in their keys! These cold pieces of iron lying in people's pockets like hostages, to ensure the safety of houses, cabinets, cash boxes and drawers. We can be a hundred miles from our homes, but the keys to gates and doors accompanying us on our travels give us the illusion that we are still masters of our property. Keys in pockets are like the souls of those abandoned places, which when locked up lose their meaning and lose their lives. Piotr locked up his house with the key, and although the windows almost reached the ground he believed that no thief would break in. He trusted even the Muscovites; surely they would respect locked doors, not daring to break them down with rifle butts.

He locked the house containing all his possessions: the bed, trunks, pots—and all his hopes. The hopes could have escaped through the door if it was left unlocked; now they would be secure. When he came back from the war Piotr would find them intact, just as he had left them. And who knows if in the meantime they would not multiply? Piotr Niewiadomski had locked up his life's ideal, his career, and that wonderful, imaginary wife with a dowry. Let her wait for him here until the war was over. Let her thrive, reflecting on him and their marital happiness to come. So Piotr had locked up two houses with his rusty key: the actual, ramshackle one, half of which belonged to his sister Paraszka Niewiadomska, a girl of easy virtue, and the other—the house of his dreams—renovated, with flower-pots in the windows and a mousetrap.

There was a loud rattle as he turned the key, checking that the door was properly locked. Then, without looking back, he set off with Bass, carrying his little trunk on his back.

It was four o'clock. Although the train was not due until six, many villagers were already making their way towards the station with their trunks and bundles. The women and children were going along to see them off. There were even several carts standing outside the station building; the wickerwork seats were more comfortable to sit on while waiting. Topory-Czernielica station served many settlements scattered across the hills and in the valleys of the two rivers, so a motley crowd had gathered outside the station, in the waiting-room and on the platform. Some Hutsuls still wore their hair long, shiny and greasy, although everyone knew that the army razors would crop it close. The Jews were also unwilling to part with their beards and side-locks prescribed by the Holy Scriptures. The army would cut them off, the army would shave them—well, the Emperor would be called to account for that, not they. They would not willingly perform sacrilegious acts.

The station was teeming. Everyone had arrived much too early, as they felt that hurrying off to war was unseemly, just as unseemly as hurriedly burying the deceased. Going to war is a solemn affair, so a long time should be spent saying good-bye, and waiting. Everyone was in a state of great agitation, especially after those stressful hours of darkness. Those who had been the most terrified by the eclipse were now coming out with the boldest jokes about the end of the world. The stationmaster in his red cap bustled about like a master of ceremonies at a ball, appearing every now and then on the platform and immediately disappearing again. Provisional Cadet Hopfenzieher, the actual stationmaster, carried a sabre, and the Czech soldiers bore rifles. Three gendarmes—the entire gendarmerie of Czernielica—were keeping order today: two corporals, one of whom was Durek, and their commander.

That day, the platform was crowded with people who had never travelled by train before. All the old women had emerged from their cottages, the Wasynas, the Horpynas, the Warwaras, the oldest women and the oldest men had shuffled their way here. Children and dogs chased all over the platform, so that the Czech gendarmes had difficulty keeping order. Even deaf old Wasyl Horoch turned up, moving from group to group, arousing general hilarity with his slurred gibberish. Those now departing were grateful to him for coming to provide a distraction from their dark and gloomy thoughts. They teased him, but only good-naturedly. The men were trying to keep calm at all costs. And to put a good face on things. Some were dead drunk, staggering about and tripping over their bundles, embracing strange women, singing obscene songs, punctuated by hiccups. Some tousled peasant vomited on the platform, to the anger of the Czech corporal. *"Ty prase!"*— he yelled in Czech—bloody pig!

The station was filled with the stench of vodka, sweat, woollen scarves and aprons. Emotions grew in intensity as six o'clock approached, but with the increasing agitation the noise gradually subsided. All eyes kept turning in the direction from which the train was expected to approach. Everyone was waiting for Father Makarucha; he had promised to come and bless those who were going to war. The deaf-mute Wasyl Horoch wandered about the platform like anxiety incarnate until one of the soldiers seized him by the scruff of the neck and frog-marched him off. Horoch struggled with the soldier, pitifully protesting: "Mu-mu-mu…"

Around six o'clock, the whole of Topory and the whole of Czernielica had gathered on the platform. One had the impression that all the cows in the village would be turning up as well, and all the horses, all the sheep and the pigs, that the stream flowing through the middle of the village would come by, and that the sacred Hutsul rivers Prut and Czeremosz would break their banks to bless the men who had come to them to bathe and to water their horses and cattle.

The station was seething. Final words of advice, final exhortations and final curses flew back and forth in a heavy atmosphere of anxiety, fear and pain—muffling the pounding of the artillery. Nobody was thinking about the approaching Muscovites now; everyone's thoughts were directed far beyond the sapphire evening horizon above which the reborn sun reclined, reconciled with earth and people. Everyone's thoughts were drifting towards the unknown little Hungarian towns, where the sons of the Hutsul land were already being expected in the barrack yards by the dreaded sergeants with their threatening bushy moustaches. The heads of anonymous corporals, sergeants and captains kept emerging from nowhere, from out of the ground, sprouting from the gravel and from the railway tracks, popping out from behind telegraph poles. Not even obtaining a platform ticket, death wandered at will all around Topory-Czernielica station, breathing cold air down the collars of one man after another.

Six o'clock came and went, but there was no sign of the train. Those waiting to depart became really impatient. They would have preferred to be on their way, rather than endlessly prolonging the moment of parting. After the strange events of that day, the sun was setting like a splendid, perfectly round dish, and shortly mist and haze began to form above the rivers.

It was not until a few minutes to seven that a heavy rumbling sound was heard, accompanied by wheezing, and finally the clanking of iron moving at speed. Everyone held their breath. Silence fell on the platform and the silence was so profound that you could hear the telegraph tapping in the stationmaster's office. A brief, hysterical whistle brutally pierced the silence. Preceded by clouds of white steam and black smoke, a long train made up entirely of goods wagons pulled into the station. It was hauled by an iron camel, the product of Floridsdorf locomotive works. The camel with a massive hump, the boiler, was sweating. Its iron skin was covered with long, winding veins of copper pipes. It passed the station building, coming to a halt far beyond the pump.

All the ironwork was clanking. The locomotive's buffers had struck the buffers of a coal wagon, and they passed the impact on until it reached the last wagon. All the chains clanged and the train reversed a step, like someone bumping into a wall in the dark. The pistons, the locomotive's sinews, relaxed their tension. The camel relieved itself by letting off steam.

Although he was a railwayman, Piotr Niewiadomski felt as though he was seeing a train for the first time in his life. The wagons were already full of reserve militia who had boarded at previous stations.

The boarding of the train began. The great commotion resumed. Mothers and wives, sisters and fathers kissed and hugged the departing men. Everyone jostled each other, as if all of a sudden they were in a great hurry. The gendarmes and the soldiers had to chase away the old women crowding towards the wagon, using their rifle butts. Magda sobbed softly, not venturing to embrace her man in the presence of all these legitimate wives and mothers. She could not bring herself to express her illegitimate anguish. She wept in some impersonal way; her inward sobbing might just as well have been for all those departing men as for a particular man. Piotr shook her hand as if it was that of a man, once again giving instructions to take care of Bass. At the moment when he had fought his way through the crowds to reach the wagon, the incident with Bass occurred. Doing his damnedest to get into the wagon, the dog dug his teeth into Piotr's tunic. Gendarme Corporal Jan Durek noticed this and separated the dog from the man, delivering a heavy kick with his hobnailed boot. Bass gave a pitiful whelp and sprang back, tearing off a piece of cloth. He clenched this relic saturated with Piotr's scent

firmly in his teeth. Piotr turned to the gendarme and, all red
in the face, shook his fist in anger. But the gendarme did not
notice. Before the dog was able to launch a renewed assault
on the train, he had already been separated from his master
by the boots, trousers, backs, bundles and boxes of strangers.

"Get in! Get in!", shouted the soldiers and gendarmes.
Everyone boarded. And when they were all aboard, the stationmaster gave the signal with his whistle, but, not sure
that the driver had heard it among the great commotion,
also raised his hand. Yet the train did not move. It refused to
obey civil authority. It was standing on the track as though
spellbound or as though waiting for someone else. Then the
stationmaster shouted in a thundering voice: "Ready!" The
call was echoed by the soldiers on duty at the station. This
had the required effect. A military cap leant out from the
footplate of the locomotive and immediately a hiss of steam
was heard. A prolonged whistle sounded and the wagons
juddered. The station fell silent. Even the dogs went quiet.
The steam concentrated in the boiler was forced through the
internal pipes into the cylinders and the pistons came to life.
Puffs of heavy black smoke burst from the stack and slowly,
slowly, like caravans leaving a house of mourning, the wagons
began to move, pushing away, repelling, tearing away, literally
tearing away the bodies of those who were going to war from
those who remained in Topory.

At that moment, two old Jewish women gave a loud scream.
In their withered wombs the juices stirred once more, reviving
the pain that had seared them in childbirth like the scorching
heat of the desert. Deadened by the passing years, it now
flared up like embers below the ashes. This was the signal for

universal weeping. The whole station caught fire from the Jewish flames, shaking and sobbing. The women yelled like tragic choir leaders, the Hutsul women yelped like bitches being whipped, toddlers whimpered, dogs, led by Bass, who had released from his teeth the scrap of cloth torn from his master, barked. The gendarmes beat them with rifle butts and chased the women away. Only the old men and women sobbed without shedding a tear. Not a sound came from their throats, not a single drop of moisture drove out the grief from their glazed, sunken eyes. They shivered and trembled like withered shrubs in the wind. Father Makarucha had not come.

The train made its way through human pain and despair as through snowdrifts in winter. The stationmaster stood to attention, visually checking each wagon in turn, as though counting them. He gave a military salute to the guard on the train and for the last time Piotr Niewiadomski saw the golden winged wheel on his red cap, glinting in the rays of the dying sun.

For a long time after the departure of the train, silent, motionless women remained standing on the platform. Their helpless eyes were glued to the track. This track had once led to the world, to life, to Kołomyja, Stanisławów, to Lwów. Now it led only to war, directly to death. A cloud of white smoke, the last visible trace of the train, floated for a while above the track and slowly descended to the embankment, torn by the branches of the spruce and fir trees like fine gauze. Until it dispersed into nothingness.

From the group of silent women some old woman emerges. She hobbles to the middle of the track. Her colourless hair, dead as crumpled hemp, protrudes from under her white headscarf. She mumbles something toothlessly. From her eyes devoid of eyelashes some liquid drips, like resin from rotten bark. The old woman is saying something to the rails, explaining something to the rails, which no one hears. Then in a hieratic gesture she raises her trembling bony hands and makes a gigantic sign of the cross on the rails, the triple Greek sign.

Chapter Seven

The Austro-Hungarian Monarchy was, as the name indicates, made up of the countries represented in the Viennese parliament, namely Austria and Hungary—that is to say, the lands of the Crown of St Stephen.

The Crown of St Stephen (in Hungarian "A Magyar Szent Korona") is very old and very heavy. Nevertheless, every Hungarian king must place it on his head once in his life. Clad in a magnificent cloak and wearing the crown, he rides on a white steed to the top of the highest hill in Buda, where he symbolically brandishes a giant sword. This is the culminating moment of the coronation ceremony. After that, the crown sleeps for years in a vault in the castle of Buda, awaiting a new king. It rests peacefully, unless someone steals it. This has occurred more than once in Hungary's history. For this reason, in 1846 it was buried by patriots near the village of Orşova on the Danube. It lay in the ground for ten years. But the gold and precious stones did not put out any shoots. Only the cross on the top of the crown worked loose and today it leans to one side—as when Christ fell beneath it. Everyone in the kingdom, even a beggar into whose outstretched hand they drop 20 hellers, knows what the Crown of St Stephen looks like. Because actually the mint was common to both countries, as indeed was the entire treasury; it issued the coinage in both countries—both the Austrian and the Hungarian. So even Piotr Niewiadomski carried around many Crowns of St Stephen in his pocket, and he often wondered why its cross was crooked.

During peacetime in Śniatyn district, people showed little interest in Hungary, close neighbour though it was. And yet every Hutsul child knew that the Hungarians' emperor was no emperor, only a king. Truth to tell, no one in Śniatyn district gave any thought to why that was the case. It only became an issue when certain of the Emperor's subjects, and the best of them at that, had to go to Hungary.

The wagons in which Emperor-and-King Franz Joseph was transporting his soldiers (40 men), or his livestock (8 horses), were secured in two ways, depending on who the passengers were. If they were horses, cattle or pigs, a single wooden door without windows was drawn. People enjoyed greater freedom; anyone who wanted to could even jump off the train, because instead of a door the way to death, disability or freedom was blocked merely by a simple iron bar.

Leaning against this bar were Piotr Niewiadomski and his compatriots. It was a privileged place, the only one in the dark, stuffy wagon where there was access to oxygen and nitrogen and where the world could be seen slipping away. The small opening in the roof was good only for animals' lungs. As for humans, it wasn't even any good for their morale. It was covered by a grating, as in a jail. Piotr owed this benefit to his fellow passengers' ethical principles. An unspoken pact applied in the wagon—those passing through their home territory had the right to stand at the front. Then, when the train entered unfamiliar districts, you were supposed to give way to others (let them too get their breath, let them have a look), and lie down on the straw in the reeking, gloomy inner depths.

All were supposed to take turns in this way throughout the journey, because they still believed there was justice in this world. Piotr also believed there was justice in the world, but only as far as Delyatyn station. He stood by the bar and everything he could see was still familiar, close, sometimes even intimately known to him. First of all the train passed the plot of land the railway had given him in fief. Magda's sunflowers were already drooping, and Piotr thought this meant they were turning their heads towards him, black and yellow like Imperial and Royal banners. The spreading, steel-blue cabbage leaves were eaten away by caterpillars; what a shame. For some considerable time, the wooden church on a hill in Czernielica was reluctant to disappear from the horizon. It circled around the train, showing now one side, now the other (was it on the right or on the left?), playing hide-and-seek with the train. It would suddenly disappear, and then its three cupolas would unexpectedly re-emerge from the ground like the heads of three divers in a swimming pool. Piotr had been christened in this church; here he was given his name—once a year he went to Father Makarucha for confession, and before that to the old parish priest, who had died sixteen or seventeen years ago. He would undoubtedly have got married there if he had eventually found a wife. And certainly it would be nowhere else but in this consecrated ground where Czernielica church stood that he would be buried. His mother lay there. Suddenly, the memory of his mother, still so close to the train, pierced his heart like a sharp bayonet, filling it with condensed regret for everything he had lost that day. But the church had already disappeared from view, this time irrevocably.

The train redoubled its speed, as though spurred on by a whiplash. It plunged down the wooded slopes. The telegraph poles passed by at regular intervals like the refrain of an old, never-ending song. The cables stretched between them undulated rhythmically, turgid with news of the war. On the mown meadows horses leapt at their tethers—the train had startled them. Keeping close to the mares, unfettered foals were frolicking. Motionless regiments of geese stirred at the sight of the roaring train and without breaking formation, without spoiling the symmetry, menacingly distended their necks. The most exposed ranks of geese spread their wings wide, and beating their wings as if in response to a command rose effortlessly above the ground. These goose storm troops, prepared to attack the train, looked like a detachment of white, heraldic eagles. All along the track, particularly on marshy riverbanks, the mobilization of storks was under way as the 25th of August approached, the traditional holy day of departure to warmer countries.

The train reached the first station, took on new people with bundles and trunks, and again women were crying. And so it went on until Kołomyja. Piotr noticed that all the station signs were in place, although the army was in charge everywhere. So the relegation of Topory-Czernielica station had been the stationmaster's whim.

The ancient rule of travel imposes on passengers a heightened reserve towards new passengers. In this wagon too, those who had been travelling to war for over an hour looked down on the newcomers for a while. However, after half an hour they were all equals. At each station, an invisible hand stoked the iron furnaces of war with fresh fuel—human bodies. But nowhere did so many reserve militia soldiers board the train as at Topory-Czernielica. Apparently, the rest had gone by other trains. Piotr wondered how many trains carrying this cargo for the Emperor were running at the moment on all the monarchy's railways? A hundred, maybe even more?

None of these hordes of travellers, who for the first time in their lives were allowed to travel free, knew where they were going. Everyone knew only one thing: they were going to Hungary, where people gobble paprika and where His Imperial Majesty is merely a king.

But Hungary, the land of the Crown of St Stephen, is a big country.

The wagon was overcrowded, and the train had long since left Piotr's homeland. Despite this, Piotr still occupied his privileged place. This was thanks to his railwayman's cap and his railwayman's manner of speech. One of the new passengers insisted on knowing when the train would reach Kołomyja. It was as though his concern involved some urgent business in Kołomyja, not that he was on his way to Hungary in the interests of the Emperor.

"Should be there at twenty-one sixteen!" Piotr declared in the tones of a timetable compiler. To say "nine sixteen" would be beneath the dignity of a railwayman, for whom there are neither mornings nor evenings, and day and night are one body like a husband and wife, the twenty-four-hour body. A true railwayman knows only one nine o'clock—the one in the morning.

So Piotr was regarded with a certain deference right from the beginning of the journey. Some men in the wagon, including of course those who knew him, were almost certain that he was travelling with them in his official capacity, not joining the army like everyone else. He was himself also imbued with the magic of his cap. Seeing how people looked up to him, he began to regret his stupidity, his fear and his shame—goodness knows why he didn't mention his civilian occupation when he was called up. He might have been posted to some railway division. But when he was at the recruiting station he had no idea that such divisions even existed.

The army is the army, he thought, and the railway is the railway. Who would have thought that there might be such a thing as a railway army? Too late now. Now he was going to war as an ordinary member of the reserve militia. He was taking with him to Hungary an oath which he could not revoke in the slightest. It bound him hand and foot. Carrying burdens on his back was better than this. He had only himself to blame. He could have said he was a railwayman. He would have sworn an oath to serve the railway.

Piotr had often sworn oaths in his life. Twice even in court. But these oaths applied only to the duration of the case. When he left the courtroom, he was free. And how many times had he sworn at the station, to the stationmaster, of his own volition, for his own benefit, and not under duress? That he had not stolen, had not seen, had not heard, that he would never do it again, that it was someone else... In his younger days he had also sworn in church that not a drop of vodka would pass his lips all year. That was a hard year, but it shortened with each passing day and he could count the days that remained before he would again be allowed to visit the tavern.

An oath sworn to His Majesty the Emperor was something else. That meant pledging your own life away. On credit. But you only have one life. How good it would be to have two lives, one for the Emperor, for your homeland, and the other for yourself. After giving your life for the Emperor on land, on water or in the air, you could still always go home with your second life. As it is, though, you can please neither yourself nor the Emperor. If you want to live you become a deserter, cheating the Emperor, and the Emperor rewards you with a bullet in the head. That would be his right, because you swore the oath. And you rot in the ground. Or you press on to the front line and expose yourself to the heaviest firing and you end up lying in the ground anyway. Either way, it's dreadful.

Piotr Niewiadomski dearly loved the Emperor. However, he was not completely indifferent to his own fate. We even have a good deal of evidence that he liked life. This is why he was greatly troubled by his oath, especially since God alone knew how long it would be in force. And how it would end. In promotion to lance corporal or in death for the sake of the Emperor? Neither one nor the other, perhaps. Piotr could not become a lance corporal. An NCO has to be able to read and write. He could become a corpse, though. You didn't have to attend school for that, but he hoped that the war would end in six weeks. The training would just about account for the six weeks. The war might drag on till Christmas. Between mid-October and Christmas you could die for the Emperor a hundred times over... But does every soldier have to die? If that was the case, the Emperor would not win the war. And, as is well known, he must win. After all, an entire train-load of Hutsuls is rushing to his aid.

The whole train was bound by the oath just as those horses in the meadows were tethered by ropes. The soldiers escorting the convoy were casually playing rummy in the only "human", i.e. passenger, carriage, immediately behind the tender. They were unconcerned about the troop transport. The oath took care of them. If necessary, it would invoke the dreaded Articles of War and a court-martial. It already gave the corporals the right to punch recruits in the face. The escort could play cards at their leisure; there would be no deserters.

Constrained by an oath more powerful than chains, the men proceeded towards their appointment with fate. At that moment, all other emotions were subordinate to their curiosity about their new life and new conditions in Hungary. This curiosity overshadowed any fear of foreign surroundings or any suggestion of homesickness. Any day now, however, perhaps in a week or a month, the homesickness would kick in and in the railway wagons, the barracks and the camps they would be retrieving those faded photographs from shabby bags, greasy notebooks and envelopes. They would be showing off the crumpled charms of their wives, children and lovers, seeking in the indifferent eyes of their comrades a flash of recognition, admiration, or even jealousy. Today, it's too soon for that. The deadly germ of longing has not begun to have an effect. Besides, everyone in the wagon believed in an early return to those beings whose lifeless portraits—thanks to the incredible wizardry of the Frenchmen Niépce and Daguerre— they could take with them to war. Piotr Niewiadomski had only one photograph—of his mother. It was at the bottom of his trunk, in a prayer-book, among the unread litanies.

It was still light when they stopped at Kołomyja. Piotr was mistaken; it would not be twenty-one hours for another thirteen minutes. The sun had long since set, but, desiring to compensate the earth for the two and a half hours of darkness, it had hesitated for a long time before depriving it of its setting rays. In Kołomyja the last of the reserve militia came aboard. A second locomotive was put on at the rear. After that the train stopped only occasionally, and then only to pick up coal and water for its own needs—but no soldiers.

At the first bridges beyond Delyatyn, Piotr's dignity as a railwayman was dealt a painful blow. He ceased to believe there was any justice in the world. Although the night was drawing in, a sight met his eyes that the others merely found amusing. Down below, just beyond the bridge, stood some bizarre armed figures. As the wagon approached the bridge and these figures became clearly recognizable, Piotr saw two bearded Jews wearing long kaftans girded with a military cartridge belt in place of the ritual cord which during prayers separates the clean upper half of the body from the unclean lower half. On their heads they wore standard army forage caps. Shouldering rifles, with bayonets fixed, they were guarding the bridge. Guarding a bridge over the Prut! Well, is there any justice in this world?! Is the Emperor not ashamed to have such dopes guarding his bridges? As if he did not have proper railwaymen. What sort of an army is this anyway? Why aren't the Jews in uniform? The railway suddenly became alien to Piotr; it was shamelessly mocking a man who had faithfully served it for so many years and who knew many of its secrets. Again there was a bridge and again a Jew in a kaftan. Accompanied by a Hutsul, it's true. In other words, they had not yet had time to get all the reserve militia men into uniform. Piotr was up in arms now. He would gladly have got rid of that railwayman's cap, if he had another. He could now think of only the bad aspects of his career.

The telegraph poles passed by, one after another, the train was breathing hard, the terrain became steeper and steeper and the Prut became narrower and narrower, its roar louder and louder. A beautiful night settled over the track after that day of torment and terror. Piotr was growing indifferent to it all. Nothing was of interest any longer, neither the night nor the Prut, not the waterfalls, the bridges or Hungary—all that and the whole railway could go to hell. What had become of the railway? It was a slave to the war, having only one task—the delivery of its human cargo. And it seemed to Piotr that the railway had never had a civil purpose and it would never do so ever again. The bridges were guarded by men in kaftans and he was travelling as an ordinary reserve militia man. This is what he had to thank the Emperor for! At that moment, Piotr was minded to break his oath to the Emperor. But how could it be done? By jumping from the train? He would only succeed in breaking his arms and legs.

So he took offence at the railway, vented his anger on the landscape, giving up his privileged place at the bar. With a feeling of relief he found his trunk, as if he had found himself. If it had been possible, he would have hidden in that box where his money was kept. No one needed to know that he kept it in the trunk. No one can be trusted in this world, not even your own brother. He carefully opened the trunk, took out the bread and pork fat and vented all his rage on the meal. Then he lay down in the back of the wagon like a kicked dog. He was angry, unapproachable and a stranger even to himself. With every passing kilometre, this journey was tearing him away from the part of the world where his life had been more or less acceptable. Piotr could not cope anywhere other than Topory-Czernielica. This seems to be the fate of all people who spend their lives in one place. When a higher power abruptly snatches them from their homeland, they become strangers to themselves. And so Piotr clung to his trunk, curled up against its hard but protective side and fell asleep as one falls asleep in the shade of one's family cottage. He slept for a long time. He dreamt of swarms of black Jews with rifles and bayonets.

Meanwhile, the train reached the border station of Köresmözö. Here the camel from the Floridsdorf locomotive works lost the comrade that had been attached at Kołomyja to provide a push from the rear. The terrain had begun to decline. The shunting took quite a long time. But Piotr did not hear it. In a deep and unpleasant sleep he entered the lands of the Crown of St Stephen.

He woke up several times during the night, had a smoke and something to eat, relieved himself at the iron bar and spoke with his fellow Hutsuls, mostly about the military service that awaited them. Someone was arguing that in a few days they would elect a new Pope in Rome, and then the war would be over for sure. Another complained that they were transporting them like cattle, without even telling them where they were going. Everyone agreed it was scandalous and they all wondered how much longer it would take. Hardly any of these people had ever experienced such a long journey. Some of them were bored, but there were also some who wanted it to last as long as possible. They had presentiments about what awaited them, and feared the worst. There was no lack of optimists either. They were going to war as if they were going on holiday. But most of them were already afraid, not so much of being in the army as of being in a strange place.

There was no lamp in the wagon, there was no candle, just occasional ragged shafts of light cast by the moon through the open door. The train pressed into foreign lands, penetrating dense pine forests, poisoning the nocturnal balsam of the sleepy trees with its carbon fumes, trundling through serpentine bends, cutting though passes, disappearing into long dark tunnels, filling the wagons with acrid smoke, the railway's ubiquitous companion. It was taking human fear, human anxiety and a good deal of self-love over the mountain by night.

By dawn, everyone was terribly thirsty. There was no water on the train. If only it would make a stop somewhere. But the engine-driver deliberately avoided both smaller and larger Hungarian stations where electric lights were still on despite the rising sun. It was not until about seven o'clock that he deigned to bring the wagons to a halt at Huszt station. There water—and the devil—awaited the sons of the Hutsul land.

They all thought they had reached the barracks, and they wanted to leave the wagons. The escort stopped them in time. It was the first time since they had set off that they had taken any interest in the recruits. The armed men lined up on the platform, ensuring that no one got out. Their compatriots became unruly. They immediately started grumbling, and then their protests became vociferous. Some even adopted a threatening attitude. The great god of all armies and all wars, Discipline, had not yet had taken these people under its wing. As long as they were still wearing their civilian trousers and were unfamiliar with the regulations, they could still yell, regardless of the oath. And they yelled. What right had the escort to deny them drinking-water after a night spent in that stifling wagon? Let us get to the water! But the senior members of the reserve militia making up the escort were unrelenting. No one was allowed to get out. The comrades must obey the escort's orders; they were bound by their oath.

New wagons were attached. In the blink of an eye they were filled with Slovak peasants in colourful jackets. They too were joining the army. They were yelling in a language the Hutsuls did not understand, although many words sounded familiar. There were women weeping at the Hungarian station too. Evidently, tears were popular in the lands of the Crown of St Stephen too. The locals, especially those who were not going to war, stared with curiosity, and considerable mistrust, at the new arrivals. They considered themselves superior. It took some time before the escort condescended to allow the men off the wagons. The comrades swarmed onto the platform like a pack of hungry wolves. The more mistrustful of them took their trunks with them in case they got stolen. The escort was very concerned about that. If they were taking their baggage with them they might desert. And in the first instance it was the escort who would be held responsible for deserters; it was only afterwards that the deserter himself would be charged—if he could be caught, of course. So in each wagon someone was detailed to look after the baggage. He would get a drink later, when the others returned.

Piotr pushed his way with the rest of them towards the water. His cap got him through. All around he was bombarded by Slovak and Hungarian speech. He stood in bewilderment amid surging alien life that was completely strange to him. If it were not for the wailing of the women, that international language of pain comprehensible in every latitude, Piotr would never have believed that he was surrounded by mountain-dwellers from the Carpathians like himself.

Within a few minutes at Huszt station, an indifferent animosity was born in the souls of the Ruthenian peasants and of the Slovak and Hungarian peasants, stirred up by a shared helplessness regarding their fate. Unable to take their revenge on fate for having brutally torn them away from their fields, pastures and forests, they shoved each other about, exchanging hateful glances. Assailed by foreign words, resounding in their ears like insults, the Hutsuls struggled towards the well. That was where the devil stood. A giant devil. In the guise of a Hungarian gendarme. On his head, instead of a helmet, he wore a black hat decorated with a cock's tail-feathers. Similar hats are worn on ceremonial occasions by the "hares"—the Landwehr and the Chasseurs. On his breast glinted the same medal as Corporal Durek's. The only thing missing was the gold tooth. The Hungarian devil's teeth were all sound. His perfect black moustache and side-whiskers and his dark gypsy complexion sharply contrasted with their predatory whiteness. No sooner had the Hutsuls fought their way through to the well than lava began spurting from behind those teeth. The devil greeted them at the well with a seething torrent of dreadful bellowing. For fire, that devilish element, has been at war with water through the ages.

In Śniatyn district, especially since war broke out, any number of foreign languages had resounded in people's ears. Hutsul eardrums were gradually beginning to get used to the incredibly harsh-sounding German speech and the so-called Army Slav, that mishmash of all Slav languages. They had started to come to terms with the Czechs' snub-nosed manner of speech, apparently devoid of all vowels. They had long been familiar with the melodic Romanian of their neighbours in Bukovina, and even that established resident of the region, Yiddish, with its garlic and onion flavour, sounded familiar to Hutsul ears. In Śniatyn district people sometimes worked certain Jewish words into their speech, indeed even entire phrases, in most cases using them incorrectly. So they could not be suspected of total ignorance or hatred of foreign languages. It was something else, though, to hear incomprehensible babble at home, where both Ukrainian and Polish are, always were and always would be, master and landlord, whereas foreign speech would always take a back seat, like a tenant or a guest. And it was a different matter altogether when you suddenly found yourself surrounded by foreigners, where no one understood anything you said—apparently out of spite. At home you could laugh, you could mock those who spoke differently, but abroad not only did they make fun of you, but you were quite lost. You were as helpless as a little child, as a blind man groping in the dark. Piotr suddenly realized what a great crime, what a great sin it must have been to build the Tower of Babel, since it was on account of it that the Lord had confused people's languages. Piotr had never given any thought to the magnitude of this disaster before. He had never wondered why people cannot understand one another. It was not until he reached Huszt station in Hungary that he felt terrified by the utter profundity of the fact that this gendarme had eyes, ears and a mouth just like anyone else, and yet this mouth did not emit human sounds. No, Hungarian speech was not human. It was fire, brimstone and paprika. The gendarme had ears, so why could he not hear what Semen Baran, a very wise man, was explaining to him in German? (Baran had spent three years in Saxony and he had travelled widely.) He could hear, he could hear all right, but between him and Semen Baran there was a massive, impenetrable wall. A fragment of the Tower of Babel. If only he had been an enemy, a Muscovite or a Serb, but he was supposed to be one of the Emperor's men... No, he was not one of the Emperor's men. An Emperor's man always understands an Emperor's man somehow, in German at any rate. This gendarme is the King's man. Because to the Hungarians the Emperor is only a king. Evidently, the Hungarians did not even deserve an Emperor. Not with mugs like that, and not with a language like that!

And what does this devil want, exactly? Is he banning them from drinking the water? Perhaps he is afraid the Emperor's men would poison their stinking Hungarian water? Why doesn't he speak like a human being if he wants people to pay attention to him?

The Emperor's men ignored the gendarme. They offered him passive resistance, as they were in an overwhelming majority and felt they had a God-given right to the water. Even cattle have the right to quench their thirst, and they were not cattle. The Royal gendarme, in order to defend not so much the water as his own authority, resorted to force. He took his rifle from his shoulder, expecting to repel the Emperor's men from the well by lashing out blindly with the butt. He trusted in his uniform and cock's feathers, otherwise he would have held back. He was facing an entire mob on his own. But his stars of office and his cock's feathers let him down. The Emperor's men considered themselves obliged to obey only the Emperor's authority, not the King's. Their passive resistance turned to action. They pushed the gendarme aside, wresting the rifle from his grasp. They began swearing in their own language, assailing the devil with the ugliest curses and insulting his mother. Of course, many of them were well aware what active resistance to the gendarmerie entailed; Piotr in particular was afraid of unpleasant consequences. But the Hutsuls' keen sixth sense, their awareness of reality, told them they were in command of the situation by dint of their sheer numerical superiority. They knew perfectly well that the attack on the Hungarian gendarme would go unpunished, since they were going to war.

Pandemonium ensued. Other gendarmes who had up to that point been busy getting the Slovaks onto the train now rushed to the assistance of the devil under threat. They hit out with their rifle butts, and soon restored the dignity of their colleague, along with the seized rifle. At the same time some soldiers, all Hungarians of course, dashed over and drove the Hutsuls back. Alarmed by the hellish uproar, the escort, who had overall responsibility, rushed out of the buffet. They did not understand Hungarian, but they did understand that people had a right to drinking-water. They reacted rather hesitatingly and ineffectively. And if it had not been for the Jews, who were around even before the Tower of Babel, and who knew all languages, a great war between the peoples of the Emperor and the peoples of the King might very well have broken out at Huszt station. A railway official called on the Jews in broken German to explain to those savages that the gendarme was keeping them away from the well in their own interest. In their own interest. It was suspected that the water in the well was infected with typhus, dysentery and other diseases, which accompany all wars, as is well known. Drinking-water, sterilized water, was to be found at the other end of the platform in a wooden barrel. Too late. Some of the Hutsuls had already slaked their thirst and their rage with typhus and dysentery.

It could just be that on that particular day at Huszt station the notorious seeds of hatred towards the local population had germinated among Galician soldiers quartered with Hungarian regiments, above all towards the Honvéds and the Hussars. This animosity was restrained at first, but later fierce brawls frequently broke out.

And many litres of superb Imperial and Royal blood were spilt in Hungarian taverns and inns instead of on the fields of glory for the monarch's benefit. At the time, they managed to stop the fire spreading, and not only by dousing it with water. Wine also had a good deal to do with it. One Izrael Glanz, a spice merchant from Kołomyja, casually remarked that there was no point in fighting over water when you could get cheap wine at the station buffet.

Wine?—Piotr Niewiadomski suspected this was some Jewish swindle. He had never drunk wine in his life. Vines grew only in the Holy Land, in warm countries, in Rome, which is why priests drank it during mass. It was hard to imagine Hungary as the Holy Land—quite the opposite. A few minutes later he was quite happy to declare that wine was also a layman's drink, available in Hungary even to ordinary mortals. The gendarmes, now operating hand in hand with the military escort, had difficulty separating the Emperor's men from the Hungarian wine. But they managed it. Without protest or resistance, they returned to their places in the wagons. The wine was already coursing in their veins, awakening the muses. Polyhymnia and Terpsichore. Especially the younger recruits sang melancholy heroic ballads about past military expeditions or imitated the bleating of rams, bagpipes and shepherds' long pipes. The kołomyjka dance broke out, with a lively drumming of heels. Three wagon-loads of Slovaks listened in to the Hutsul bacchanalia. Stirred to indulge in friendly competition, the Slovaks summoned up their finest songs from the depths of their souls. They too imitated the bagpipes and shepherds' horns. They were on the point of fraternizing with the Emperor's men, but this was prevented by the devils in cocks' feathers. The Slovaks were strictly forbidden to leave the wagons.

The train moved on, resounding with song. Only Piotr Niewiadomski kept a straight face. It turned out that he was a *vin triste* type. Once again he stood by the iron bar, in the company of the wagon's older men who had not been affected by the wine. But the pagan god Dionysius had his way; Piotr was reconciled with the railway.

Suddenly, Telesfor Zwarycz, a man from Widynów, remarked that such loud singing and dancing was inappropriate when they were supposed to be in mourning for the Holy Father:

"The Pope of Rome is still warm, they haven't laid him in his coffin yet."

Indeed, the Pope was not yet lying in his coffin. Not in the first one, made of cypress wood, nor in the second one, a lead casket, nor in the third and last one, made of elm. The people of Rome were still viewing his catafalque in the Chapel of the Blessed Sacrament.

Of all Zwarycz's arguments, what most appealed to the Hutsuls' conscience was this:

"What will these Calvinists think of Greek Catholics carousing when the Pope has just died?"

"Calvinists? What Calvinists?"

Apart from the Jews, no one in the wagon had heard that some Hungarians subscribe to the doctrine of Calvin. Telesfor Zwarycz was of the opinion that there were no Catholics at all in Hungary. They were all heretics, worse than Lutherans. Piotr was not inclined to believe this, somehow. Heretics, yet St Stephen is their patron saint? Can a saint be a heretic?

Matters of religion were debated at length. In the end, Piotr allowed himself to be convinced that Hungarians are not Catholics at all. Secretly, he was even pleased about it when he finally realized why in this accursed country Emperor Franz Joseph is only a king. At the same time, the mystery of the leaning cross on the crown of St Stephen was solved for him. Wherever the Christian faith falters, the cross leans over. All his fellow Hutsuls felt very proud to have not one but two reasons to feel superior to the Hungarians. Firstly, as soldiers of the Emperor, and secondly as true Catholics. Naturally, everyone fell silent and everyone was saddened when the Pope

JÓZEF WITTLIN

died. And once again the Church of Rome had vanquished
the pagan deities—wine, song and dance.

For some time now, ever since they had left Máramaros-
Sziget, a companion had latched on to the train, not leaving
it for several hours. This was the river Tisza. It ran alongside
the train, as though to win a bet on who would be first. Hour
by hour it became wider and its roar grew louder. But the
landscape had not changed much since the previous day. The
Hungarian Carpathians were very similar to the Galician. Only
the style of the buildings on the hillsides and in the valleys had
changed. The wooden cottages and huts had long since disappeared, long gone were the little wooden churches with their
triple layered roofs reminiscent of Chinese pagodas or sailing
ships with three masts. This was what temples inhabited by
the true God looked like. Temples of the false God were stone-
built, white-washed, and had plain or red galvanized roofs.
Most of them had slender clock-towers. There were many
walls in this country, lending the villages a very urban appearance. Telesfor Zwarycz exaggerated grossly, however. Not all
Hungarians were Calvinists, and in any case there were none
here in the land of the Slovaks. The train had not yet reached
the Calvinist districts. But the Hutsuls, educated by Zwarycz,
had already formed their own opinion about the Hungarian
churches. They considered them all to be nests of heresy.

In spite of that, they did like the Hungarian countryside. As
a child, Piotr had always taken an interest in any new scenery.
Why should he hide the fact? This was not just the longest but
also the most beautiful journey he had ever undertaken. And
if he had not been aware that he was going to war, he would
have enjoyed it very much. In peacetime he would never have

travelled so far. What interest could he have in Hungary? What surprised him most about the journey was that, while being ever closer to the war, he was continually moving away from it. What could be the explanation for that? The Hungarian land was extremely quiet; the war zones lay somewhere beyond it, hundreds of kilometres away. Here, deep peace reigned. Everything had an air of prosperity and security; this carefree land was not shaken by artillery barrages, nor did it anticipate the coming of the Muscovites. Ordinary passenger trains were running, nobody was guarding the bridges, and the railway crossing guards stood by their booths, wearing the same caps that Piotr used to wear. But, of course, he was going to war.

The mountains came to an end. The train sped alongside the broad river Tisza, and when the latter was suddenly lost in the steppe the train came to a stop at Beregszász station, as if it had lost its power along with the river.

No, there is no justice in the world. When they resumed their journey, they found the vast steppe quite charming. These Calvinists have such a beautiful land, while the Catholics were close to snuffing it on their hillsides, which could yield for them at best a little rye and miserable oats. Oh, and maize in the valleys. And the cattle the wretched Hungarians had? Those pigs! Even the Hungarians' worst enemies, contemplating the countless masses of cattle on the steppe, had to admit, objectively, that they had never seen cattle like this. The horns of the oxen were perhaps a metre in length. But why do the shepherds in these parts go around in skirts like women?

Already on the last slopes of the Carpathians vast plantations of some unknown species of beans had been seen. Then, where the steppe began, the beans disappeared. They spent half a day traversing the steppe with the hot sun beating down (Piotr wondered whether the end of the world had not occurred here too the day before), and suddenly the beans reappeared. More and more of them kept coming, climbing up higher and higher poles.

"How is it that these Hungarians wolf down so many beans?"

"It's vines, not beans," explained one of the Jews. He kept scribbling and sketching in his notebook, calculating—it seemed—the annual income from these vineyards.

They travelled on and on among vineyards along the river Bodrog. On and on. All of those who had shaved before setting off to war had heavy stubble by now. They had grown weary of this unending journey. The passing milestones were bringing them closer to the war and the elapsed miles felt like years. On a long journey, time is sometimes measured in spatial terms. Some people were deluded into thinking that the war would end once the journey was over. They would arrive at their post, and the sergeant would say, "Go home. You are not needed now. The Emperor thanks you. We are at peace."

The men, dazed by a great rush of impressions, were experiencing their second night on Hungarian soil... Time and space had knocked the stuffing out of them. They were subdued, resigned to their fate. So they fell asleep, but this lasted for two hours at most. Suddenly, in the middle of the night, they were exposed to broad daylight. The opposite of a solar eclipse. Bright daylight amidst the dark night. They were awakened by a powerful jolting as the entire train staggered and regained its balance, swaying as it swung over the points, again and again. They passed an entire encampment of wagons waiting in countless sidings. A deafening medley of sound: clanking iron, bells and whistles. Slowly, very slowly, they pulled into a colossal shed of glass and iron resembling the nave of a massive church. The vault of the glass domed roof was supported by arched iron girders. A great hubbub filled this remarkable church of the railways, where a dozen locomotives prayed fervently, emitting columns of smoke and incense in steam. Suspended at various heights, huge opal glass apples shone as brightly as daylight. They were the source of that brilliance. Large illuminated clocks showed the sacred railway time.

It was only 23.13.

"Everybody out! Get your luggage!" called the escort. Everyone rushed to collect their belongings and jumped down from the wagons. "Follow me! Follow me!" called the authority-conscious members of the escort. "Mind you don't get lost! Keep together!"

So finally they had reached the garrison. Piotr's country-men staggered like drunks, making their way among the crowd of strangers—soldiers, officers, civilians and women. Such a commotion, such a row had erupted here, regardless of the night-time hour! This was not night-time; the war had abolished night-time—it was broad daylight. From all sides the Hutsuls were inundated with torrid Hungarian speech.

It was not the barracks, but the railway station in Budapest. Like a flock of frightened sheep, they shuffled along after their guides, awkward, bemused, at their mercy. They dashed down the steps, through dimly lit underground labyrinths and again up the steps to reach the brightly lit, noisy platforms, from platform to platform—when would they finally escape the railway's vicious circle?

Again they were told to get in the wagons, but this time they were passenger carriages. Thank goodness, there are benches; they would travel as human beings. As they had not had a hot meal for ages, they were overcome with delight when benevolent ladies came along the carriages, distributing coffee, tea and even sausages and cigarettes. They were very polite, very refined, and they smiled, but they prattled away in Hungarian. They kept saying *"Teszek, teszek"*—"Here you are… Here you are."

The eagerness of the patriotic women was so great that it extended beyond the uniformed heroes. Their kindness was lavished even on those who were only just on their way to join the army. They anticipated their heroism, committing to it with coffee, tea, sausages and cigarettes.

Fed, watered and delighted by the kindness of the Hungarian women, they travelled on in high spirits. They contemplated their earlier impressions, reviewing their premature judgements. Gradually, they began to show conciliatory tendencies.

"You know," explained Semen Baran, "they are Royal and we are Imperial, but only in civilian life. In the army it's all the same. The military is Imperial and Royal. Only the Honvéds, the Hungarian Landwehr, is Royal, not Imperial. I tell you, lads, don't ever have anything to do with the Honvéds!"

Piotr was already dozing off. He was aware only of snatches of what Semen Baran was on about: "Imperial and Royal…"

He was sitting on a bench by the window, nodding and sleeping. He began to have visions of honking geese, then the geese were followed by heavy Hungarian oxen with metre-long horns and wonderful, wonderful pigs. Suddenly, the geese started gabbling in Hungarian, German and Slovak. Even the oxen were talking in Hungarian. Even the pigs spoke Hungarian. Then all the languages mingled in their beaks, snouts and muzzles, merging into a single dense mass of sounds, that proto-language spoken by the human race once upon a time, before the construction of the Tower of Babel. Piotr Niewiadomski understood every word, every single word of that proto-language.

Suddenly he was dazzled by a massive glare of electric light. Piotr entered the focus of that glare, and what was revealed to him? The interior of the church in Czernielica. Hungarian ladies were singing the wedding song 'Long Life to You' in Ukrainian. The parish priest, Father Makarucha, wearing a floral robe embroidered in gold, leads him to the altar. He is wearing a cap with cock's feathers. At that moment, a gorgeous young bride blooms forth at his side. Father Makarucha anoints Piotr's forehead with some oily, viscous liquid. (He recalls the moment when Father Makarucha brought holy oil to his dying mother, Wasylina.) Unexpectedly, the priest takes a gleaming golden crown from the altar and places it on Piotr's head. Piotr groans. This crown is too heavy to carry; it weighs perhaps fifty kilos. No one can wear fifty kilos on his head. Piotr collapses under the weight of the crown. The Crown of St Stephen.

It was dawn when they reached the military post.

Chapter Eight

They arrived at the garrison and sat on their trunks, waiting for the war to end. But the war was not about to end. It had not even been unleashed in earnest, although many fortresses, particularly in Belgium, lay in ruins and numerous Gothic cathedrals had lost their spires, many Ruthenian villages had been consumed by fire, and lead had rent hundreds of thousands of souls from human flesh.

Newspapers throughout the monarchy were publishing enthusiastic reports from the "theatres of war", which differ from other theatres in that the actors are also the audience and the audience are the actors. Every day, images of the directors and prima donnas of the war looked out at you from the newsprint, profiles of old men in uniform, avidly seeking applause, flaunting their own immortality gained at the expense of the deaths of others. As to the spectacle itself, the newspapers illustrated their enthusiasm not so much in photographs, which often speak with the grim and distorted mouth of truth, as in fanciful drawings of crowd scenes in which the artist's ingenuity, adapted to the requirements of propaganda, triumphed no less gloriously than military victories. In such drawings it was only enemies who perished, their mutilated corpses trampled by the splendid regiments of our cavalry, galloping in perfect calm and in perfect formation. If sometimes, to set a good example, it was appropriate to depict wounded Austrians or Germans, there would be at most one soldier, slightly wounded in the leg. And if for the sake of decency it was necessary to include in the composition several dead on our side as well, these trivial losses never caused a breach in the ranks of the victorious and they never spoilt the harmony; on the contrary, they added a certain piquancy to it.

However, the lists of casualties published in the same newspapers told a different story, growing longer and longer every day. Few families could congratulate themselves that their names were not among those endless litanies of people killed, people wounded, missing and captured. Fortunately, not all families in the monarchy were able to enjoy the benefits of the written word and the art of printing. Hutsul families, for example. So our people did not know why the flags were out all over the town of Andrásfalva, through which they walked from the station to the garrison. Huge red, white and green as well as black-and-yellow bunting hung triumphantly from turrets, balconies and windows, fluttering above the passers-by, responding obediently to gusts of warm breeze, which playfully blew them onto the roofs or wrapped them round the flagpoles. How could Piotr's comrades know that this fairy-tale display of bunting in the Hungarian town was to mark the battle of Kraśnik and the victories of the Imperial and Royal Army under Cavalry General Viktor Dankl? They did not even know the fate of the regiment whose losses they would be adding to with their own bodies. This regiment belonged to another army, as famous as the Imperial, but not for its victories. For that reason it should remain nameless. The lists of casualties were saturated with names of the fallen in that army, which would probably have ceased to exist in a few days if their decimated ranks had not been continually replenished with fresh recruits.

No town in the monarchy raised black flags to mourn General B—'s routed army. They sat in the courtyard at the garrison in the scorching heat of the midday sun, waiting for the end of the war.

The garrison was located in an old disused brewery belonging to Farkas, Gjörmeky & Co., with wooden sheds added. The planks these sheds were made of still gave off an aroma of the pine forest. Their inner life had not yet died out. Here and there drops of sticky resin oozed from the planed walls. The recent hot weather had prevented them from setting and they dripped onto the soldiers' straw mattresses like fragrant tears.

The huge complex of buildings comprising the garrison was four kilometres away from the town of Andrásfalva, reached by a fine, smooth asphalt road. On both sides there were extensive ploughed fields. The rich black furrows gleamed in the sunlight. Dense vegetable gardens, already wilting, bore witness to the fertility of the soil. Tall, sweetly scented linden trees, their foliage covered in grey dust, lined the road to the nearest village, obscuring the view. The towers and chimneys of the town could be seen only from the second floor of the main building, where the officers and the one-year volunteers were quartered.

One set of regulations, one timetable, was in force here, and a different one in the town. Over there, the factory sirens announced noon at twelve o'clock, whereas at the garrison it was an hour earlier. The town's nightfall was in accordance with the seasons and the duration of sunlight; the military nightfall disregarded the revolutions of the heavenly bodies; in winter and in summer lights-out was sounded at the guard-house at nine o'clock. Then the lights were extinguished throughout the garrison (with the exception of the officers' and NCOs' quarters, the canteens and the sick-bay) and the bodies of the privates, uniforms removed and stretched out on straw mattresses, obediently awaited the blessing of pre-scribed sleep. Sometimes sleep lingered, came late, unwilling to interrupt the stories whispered in the darkness from pallet to pallet, but in general it complied with the regulations. It arrived from its distant nurseries a few minutes after nine, removed weary souls from the weary bodies and released them for a few hours of freedom.

The garrison remained aloof from the town. It lived a life of its own, creating a small town apart, a world apart—men only. They were divided from the world of women and Hungarians by high fences, barbed wire and—speech... However, town life found its way in. It crept onto the parade ground, into the huts and into the brewery as distant voices and muffled rumbling; it made its way inside by way of howling factory sirens and the ringing of bells. It was disturbing and provocative, and tempting, even though it seemed to be such an alien, hostile intrusion—indeed, perhaps for that very reason. It should not be forgotten that most of the inmates of the garrison were country people.

At first they were allowed to walk into town during off-duty hours. After all, the battalion was made up of men who had served in peacetime and were used to discipline. However, after the regimental doctor Dr Badian began to be approached by increasing numbers of victims of the Hungarian Venus needing to be referred to specialist hospitals instead of being sent to the front line, this liberal regime came to an end. From then on, you could go into town only with a pass, and a pass was not easy to obtain when you were serving at a garrison of His Imperial and Royal Highness. Under these conditions, the soldiers took risks and went out without a pass. Sometimes they got away with it, but military police patrols, always Hungarians, often rounded up these risk-takers in the town, in the taverns and brothels, depriving them of their dignity, that is to say their bayonets, and escorted them to their own guardroom. Men seduced by the siren song of the town had to appear the next day before their company commander, and persistent offenders came before the regimental commander himself. Punishment ranged from ten days' confinement to barracks to twenty days' solitary confinement. On two occasions, the regiment marched into town in full complement: once to church and once for rifle practice. The rifle range lay far beyond Andrásfalva, on the other side of the railway in the north. These official marches went down the middle of the road, preventing soldiers from making individual contact with the civilian population. A man in the ranks is only one of the strokes or spots on the move making up the geometric figure called a "column on the march". But even the smallest speck among the ranks has eyes and a mouth, which can send a smile to a woman in a window or on the pavement.

Sometimes the town itself came close to the garrison. It virtually rubbed up against it, passing by just below the fences and barbed wire. But it brought with it no life, only death.

Before dawn, before the souls of the soldiers returned from their nightly holiday called to awareness by bugles sounding the reveille, herds of cattle, calves, rams and pigs passed by. Soon afterwards, when the entire garrison was already on its feet, the frightful squeals of the animals being slaughtered were heard in close proximity. And in the afternoons, at least once a week, funeral processions passed slowly by along the road—hearses preceded by Catholic or Calvinist clergy, sometimes even with music and banners, but usually ordinary black boxes on trolleys, without ornamentation or wreaths and without the presence of priests. Only a cross carried by a boy with his head bared testified to the fact that a poor dweller of the town of Andrásfalva also had a soul worthy of heavenly grace.

So the closest neighbours of the garrison were two public institutions, the municipal abattoir and a cemetery. It might seem that people going to their death were deliberately accommodated near shrines of death so that they got accustomed to it in good time. But people having to go to their death had no time to think about it. The proximity of the abattoir—well, it was even enjoyable. At any rate it was a reminder of food, and therefore... of life.

Our people were hungry now. For hours they had been sitting on the vast square between the brewery and the huts, surrounded by barbed wire, beset by uncertainty and growing fear. They had already finished off the last of the bread grown on their stony home ground, and when they had swallowed the last morsel they were overcome by misery. Everyone had the feeling that only now they were truly parting company with their homeland.

From now on the Emperor was supposed to feed them. The Emperor was supposed to provide seven hundred grams of bread and three hundred grams of meat per head, per day. They had not yet rendered him any service, but already His Majesty deigned to cook a whole ox for them in in the regimental kitchen. Not personally, of course, but through Lance Corporal Mayer and his assistants, the so-called "spud-bashers".

At home, the Hutsuls rarely ate meat. Once or at most twice a year, usually at Easter. Unless a calf happened to die on them. But now, under the Emperor, every day would be Easter. Every day (except Fridays, because on Fridays even the army had to fast) they were to get fresh beef, sometimes pork, not something that had just happened to die. Those were the days!

At eleven o'clock barracks the world over are filled with the smell of broth. This pleasant aroma reached the nostrils of Piotr and his companions long before the duty corporals announced dinner. The general rejoicing was marred only by technical difficulties; what were they to serve the meat on, what was the soup to be eaten out of? It was a Sunday, and the demigods of war, that is to say the NCOs, were unwilling to issue the mess kits. Mess kits are issued together with the entire kit only after a roll-call, when it is confirmed who is to be "incorporated" and "drafted to a unit", and who is to be sent on—to hospital, to a different unit, or to hell. It was a Sunday. No self-respecting garrison holds a roll-call on a Sunday. God himself, after creating the world, rested on the Sabbath. So even demigods, who are more susceptible to exhaustion than the Creator, ought to rest. God created the world in six days and then he rested, whereas NCOs have to spend weeks on end turning people into soldiers, that is to say into real men. For man as created by God is—you have to admit it—merely material for making a man, the raw material.

"I will make men of you!"

That is how the garrison's iron-fisted Regimental Sergeant-Major Bachmatiuk had greeted each new cohort of recruits for the past sixteen years. It was no idle boast. In a few weeks, he produced truly excellent specimens of humanity. But today Bachmatiuk was absent. He was enjoying a privilege that no one else in the regiment shared, not even platoon commanders, and of which no superior dared to deprive him. Contrary to regulation, on Sundays he was allowed to vanish unannounced for the whole day. No one knew where Bachmatiuk went. According to some, he wore mufti. But it is easier to imagine the devil getting baptized than Bachmatiuk wearing mufti. At any rate, no one had yet seen him dressed like that.

He returned from his secret expeditions well after midnight, dead drunk—he whose sobriety was supposed to set an example to all ranks. On his return, he was incredibly aloof, not recognizing anyone, not responding to the smart salutes of the night sentries, and not saluting anyone in return either, not even the garrison commander. The officers he met on the steps when leaving the mess pretended not see him, averting their gaze. The entire camp could go up in flames and the whole Imperial and Royal Army could desert without disturbing the RSM's Sunday indifference, which ceased at dawn with the first notes of the reveille. After several hours of deep sleep Bachmatiuk sobered up. It was unknown for him to be as much as one minute late on a Monday. And during the sixteen years Bachmatiuk had never been off sick on a Monday. In general, he was rarely taken ill. And if his body had to part with his uniform for a few days as he was confined to bed, the RSM's mind would never sympathize with his body, remaining on duty, fully conscious, alert and all-seeing. If garrisons have souls, Regimental Sergeant-Major Bachmatiuk was the soul of this one. And the garrison had to come to terms with the fact that its soul deserted it every Sunday.

When Bachmatiuk disappeared, the pulse of life at the barracks weakened and all ranks, even including the officers, fell into a stupor. Duties were carried out aimlessly and carelessly, and blunders occurred.

Today everyone had a grievance against Bachmatiuk, for not making preparations for the arrival of the new draft, such a numerous one at that. He had not even arranged for the warehouse to issue mess kits. What is more, he had taken with him the keys to the "supplementary" stores. In vain the garrison commander Lieutenant-Colonel Leithuber and his aide Lieutenant Baron Hammerling tried to conceal their impotent fury. They did not have the courage to grumble out loud about Bachmatiuk. Both of them felt dependent on him. And, in the absence of the regimental sergeant-major, the NCOs could not be bothered. They did not even read out the list of names, merely accepting the escort's general report and passing it on to the duty officer—transport arrived, consisting of 567 men. None of these men yet existed as far as the military were concerned, either as a person or as a surname. Today the only statistic was 567 stomachs.

It was the responsibility of the duty officer to ensure that the kitchen issued 567 servings. This obligation was carried out. By what means those servings were to reach the stomachs of the new arrivals was another matter, and its solution was not the responsibility of the duty officer. Let the men sort that out themselves.

At about twelve o'clock the battalion returned from church. They were a good three quarters of an hour late for dinner, because on this Sunday Lieutenant Smekal was in command.

Reserve Lieutenant Smekal, a removals contractor in civilian life, enjoyed inspecting the parade on the town square after the service. During the week, he was just a company commander, but on a Sunday he sometimes led the whole battalion to church. Andrásfalva market square is very broad and is ideal for this kind of display. Especially on Sundays, when many of the civilian population of the female species gather on the footpaths shaded by double rows of chestnut trees. Lieutenant Smekal's dream would actually be a parade on the market square of quite another town, namely the one where he was born, where he went to school and where his furniture removal vans often passed by. Well, unfortunately war cannot make all dreams come true. Having duly gathered his laurels on the Hungarian market square (for this purpose he adopted a picturesque pose beneath the small statue of the great Hungarian statesman Ferenc Deák), and after momentarily slaking his thirst for power, Smekal felt the pangs of mundane physical hunger. It was purely thanks to this circumstance that the exhausted battalion was finally allowed to return for dinner. To the thunderous tramping of rhythmically moving feet, the battalion entered the garrison quadrangle in a cloud of dust. Fortunately, they were marching on that occasion without full kit and without rifles. Now, had it not been for Piotr Niewiadomski and his 566 comrades, the lieutenant would undoubtedly have dismissed them.

At the sight of such a large crowd of civilians, the removals contractor could not resist temptation and although there was not a single woman among the new arrivals he decided to hold a minor parade. Once again he set in motion the living, two-hundred-metre-long strip of grey-blue cloth, bordered by two bright rows of sunburnt faces and hands. Once again the steady tread of hobnailed boots was heard, trampling, trampling the foreign soil, as if wanting to trample to death every last blade of grass. For several minutes, this entire resounding wall of uniforms passed before the dumbfounded Hutsuls. Everyone began to realize that behind this rhythmic display of hobnailed boots lay a deep hidden meaning, something inhuman, even though it was produced by human feet. The beauty of the march was out of this world. Some invisible forces were at work here, probably the same ones that generate electric light and the power that drives distilling machines. People were marching, but they were not people. And it seemed that even the magician himself, Lieutenant Smekal with his short legs, was nothing but a tool of these invisible forces, obediently carrying out their will.

Suddenly the lieutenant cast a new magic spell on the wall of electrified cloth and the entire wall made an about-turn on the march, without changing its rhythm or pace. Then at one point, suddenly prompted to make a decision, Smekal took about ten rapid steps backwards. In a changed voice that rose two octaves, he let out a fearful bark. In response to this bark, four nimble figures wrested themselves from the depths of cloth, springing to one side with sabres drawn. All four barked in unison, whereupon in an instant the monolithic wall split open, forming four walls marching in sequence, separated by a few paces. Each company now formed two ranks, marching one behind the other, facing the commander. The trained kilograms of human bodies struck the ground heavily. The sleeves swung rhythmically, left, right, left, right, as if mowing either some invisible meadows or simply the air, accompanied by the metallic clanking of bayonets held to the left hip. A prolonged, harsh cry came from the lieutenant's throat. The squad took one more step and froze. Silence fell on the square, as though not a single living soul was present. The only interruption was a hoarse singing coming from a gramophone record in the officers' mess:

Puppchen, du bist mein Augenstern
Puppchen, hab dich zum Fressen gern![*]

The bewitchment lasted only a few seconds. Casting a new spell into the sweltering midday silence, the lieutenant broke up the entire rectangular structure. But he did not destroy it. He barked in monosyllables and the walls swayed and shook slightly as all left legs were extended. Then the tension was relaxed. All the heads and arms swayed individually, out of rhythm. But the cloth walls stayed rooted to the spot. At that moment, the respective components of the structure revealed themselves so that you could distinguish the faces imprisoned in the grey-blue cloth, the sweaty faces, human faces. And

---

[*] "Little doll, you are the apple of my eye,
   Little doll, I could gobble you up!"

it turned out that the battalion's grand title referred mainly to residents of Śniatyn, Kołomyja, Nadwórna and several Bukovina districts who had joined up at the beginning of the war as reservists. Our people found it strange to see that their fellow men looked so different, and that they were capable of performing such difficult routines. They took fright at the invisible powers which would probably succeed in making moving walls of them too.

"What will happen," they wondered, "when we are ordered to march like that?" Fortunately, however, not everyone had enough imagination to anticipate the torture of parade drill.

Lieutenant Smekal was about to go to the mess with the officers and cadets when the duty officer came running from the building. He stood to attention, saluting sharply, and for a few minutes they discussed something or other. Suddenly the lieutenant yelled across the square:

"Doroftein!"

Sergeant Doroftein detached himself from the right flank of the leading company. He ran up at the double and stood to attention. Smekal gave him the order to stand at ease. For some time they spoke naturally, as though they were equals. Meanwhile, the men in the ranks, enjoying the command to stand at ease, lifted their caps, which were soaked in sweat, from their close-cropped heads and mopped their sodden brows with handkerchiefs. The men in the front rank turned to look at the civilians.

And when the officers had gone off to the mess, to which they were enticed by toreador Escamillo's aria, Sergeant Doroftein took command of the battalion. Facing the squad at an appropriate distance, he shouted in a gruff voice:

"Battalion! On my command—Atten—tion!" And he turned the people back into a wall. But immediately he ordered them to stand at ease and then addressed them in Ukrainian.

"Lads," he said, "the battalion will be issued with its meal as usual, by company. The first two companies are to eat up promptly and wash their plates. They will then pass them on to these recruits. The corporals of both companies are to be present at the issue of the meal, but each man is to ensure nobody steals or refills his plate. Understood?"

The "lads", many of whom were over forty, understood. And even if they had not understood, no one was allowed to speak up. The sergeant's question was rhetorical. Many such questions are put in the army, and woe betide the soldier in the ranks who dares to respond. But some soldier in the second row of the first company carelessly gave himself away. A feeble grunt came from the pit of his stomach rather than from his mouth, but it was his mouth that betrayed him. He grimaced in doubt or protest, God knows what that grimace meant.

Sergeant Doroftein suffered from persecution mania. This ailment often affects weak people who find themselves in positions of power. He thought every soldier was laughing at him. If they laughed at him when off duty, well, he couldn't do anything about it. But on duty, well, there were plenty of ways of dealing with that! Sergeant Doroftein had a beady eye, though nothing like Bachmatiuk's, which could see through walls. Picking out the soldier who had apparently mocked him, Doroftein first insulted him in particular, and then carried over his anger to the entire company. That was how he operated. Casting aspersions on the mothers of more than two hundred men was quite something! It gave him a sense of self-importance and he took pleasure in it. In being just one man, capable of reviling a whole company with impunity.

Streams of invective in Romanian, Ukrainian, German and Polish now poured from his mouth, defiling the squads standing there in silence. But the company preferred to hear their mothers besmirched by the sergeant to doing punishment drill, which he was accustomed to inflicting first on the culprit and, later, on the whole detachment. However, Doroftein's rage usually died down as quickly as it flared up. In a voice still shaking with rage, he now yelled:

"Attention! Double file! Right wheel!" And having achieved what he intended by that voice, he relaxed into a familiar tone, issuing the command "First Company! Follow me—quick march!" and he led the First Company into the barracks. The other companies followed under the command of their own sergeants. Only civilians remained on the square.

Earlier, when Sergeant Doroftein was talking with the officers, Piotr Niewiadomski had convinced himself that magic was practised in the army. Discovering familiar faces in the squad, he and a few civilians took the liberty of approaching them. He wanted to greet his fellow countrymen, to speak to the familiar faces. It was in vain. The men in the ranks turned out to be as dumb as that Vasyl Horoch of Czernielica. What had happened? Why didn't they answer, why did they stay silent? Only their eyes seemed to say: "Keep away from us! Run away from here!" And with their hands, which could move quite freely, they desperately warded off their countrymen. But it was only the privates who had lost their tongues. The NCOs had the gift of speech, and most unpleasant it was too. They also used it to ward off the civilians, for between the army division and the rest of the world lay an invisible but very dangerous zone which nobody was allowed to cross in either direction. It was like a zone of death, if not physical death.

And suddenly these civilians realized that terror reigned in this garrison. It controlled all this demesne given over to the war; this is where the oath solemnly sworn to the Emperor leads you. Terror, terror turns living people into rigid rectangular formations, rhythmically marching columns. All these fine marches and parades arise from human terror. Terror would one day lead these penal formations beyond the confines of the Farkas and Gjörmeky brewery, it would lead them beyond the Hungarian land, driving them far away, to their encounter with death. Terror—in the face of something more menacing and more powerful than the officers and sergeants, maybe even than the Emperor himself, and death. They did not yet know the name of this deity, but they could already sense that they were in its sharp clutches. They did not know about Discipline, but they were already frozen by its icy breath.

The former brewery's spacious machine room housed the soldiers' kitchens. Here too terror reigned, here too there was Discipline. It could be sensed even in the aromas from the cooking and the smell of bulls' blood. Thanks to it the serving of meals was carried out fairly calmly and in a fairly orderly manner, even though Bachmatiuk, the great high priest of Discipline, was absent today. Our people had already unwittingly submitted to it. Voluntarily imitating the behaviour of men in uniform, they had fallen into line of their own accord. But what ranks they were! God of war, have mercy!

The recruits took their meals in company messes III and IV. I and II would take their turn last today. Every day a different company went into the kitchen first. Justice prevailed under the Emperor.

At lunchtime it became clear that no one in the battalion had lost his tongue in the army. Everyone continued to talk as freely as at home. Not on parade, however, when the command to stand at ease did not permit conversation. Not with companions, and even less with someone who was on the other side of the danger-zone.

The recruits were clumsy with the mess kits. Many of them spilt the entire liquid contents of the metal dishes over their own and others' trousers. The especially thick, hot mashed beans, ladled onto shallow dishes by the spud-bashers. In less than an hour a whole ox, the pride of the Hungarian steppe, disappeared into the Hutsul bellies. Such fine, long horns it had only the day before!

Food banished terror from the Hutsuls' souls. The army was not so bad, since it even fed you with meat, and soup, and beans. At least you knew you were not serving for nothing.

After issuing the rations, head chef Lance Corporal Mayer noticed that he still had thirty-six portions on the wooden counter, not counting those put aside for the detainees. What did that mean? Had the administration made a mistake? That was impossible, the administration never made mistakes. What then? Perhaps not all the new arrivals had reported to the mess?

That was actually the case. Not everyone had reported. Thirty-six men could not stomach that dinner. They found the mere sight of the meat repulsive. And even though they knew it was not pork or hare or venison, or meat of the weasel, eagle, griffin, ostrich or owl, or of any other animal that does not chew the cud or have a cloven hoof and is therefore unclean—it was from the ox, which chews the cud and has a cloven hoof—yet they did not want to touch it. For how could they be sure that the muscles and all the veins of the ox had been removed before it was cooked? How could they be sure? No, there was no such certainty. The meat had probably been cooked in its own blood along with the veins. But did not the Lord say unto Moses, "Ye shall eat the blood of no manner of flesh: for the life of all flesh is the blood thereof: whosoever eateth it shall be cut off"?

Thirty-six reserve militia recruits declined to eat the soul of an ox, so as not to die and lose their own souls. And when was death more likely than in these times of war? And who was going to suffer it if not the soldiers of His Imperial and Royal Highness, who on enlistment had been assigned to category "A"? And although the Sons of Israel (including those who failed to observe the rituals of cooking) would not be the only ones to perish in the war, they might be more likely to die. Of course, this whole war was not kosher and it reeked of sins a hundred times worse than eating unclean food. Flesh, veins and all, was wallowing in rivers of its own blood and the slaughter of human cattle was by no means according to ritual, no! But as long as the Jewish bodies wore kaftans rather than uniforms, as long as Discipline did not force them to eat, they could and must abstain from everything unclean. As the ancestors of these thirty-six righteous men did, so would they. Tomorrow their beards would be shaved, tomorrow their side-locks would be cut off, and the Emperor would dress their submissive bodies in uniform, like shrouds. Tomorrow, but not today. Tomorrow they would be delivered to higher powers and they would therefore be free of the obligation to be kosher. And they would go to the regimental kitchen with their mess kits, like goyim, for their unclean meal.

And they would eat. One day the Emperor himself would answer to the Almighty for their tainted souls.

Although food is something we are accustomed to consider subordinate to so-called higher needs, a serving of beef may also provide comfort for the soul. Every meal prolongs our existence on this earth, offering our bodies the promise of their continuation. Otherwise the idea of last requests for the condemned would make no sense. How often they abandon the consolation of religion, the last rites rendering their souls immortal, to request immediately before the execution just one thing—pork roast, veal stew or fish. Perhaps they are subconsciously clinging to the false hope that it will enable them to live a little longer, that death would not so easily claim a healthy body containing freshly introduced life-giving substances. Perhaps, for those who do not believe in the immortality of the soul, food is the only drug capable of anaesthetizing the terrified soul?

Piotr Niewiadomski was not a condemned man in the true sense of the word. And he did believe in the immortality of the soul. But the hot beef consumed before the soup gave him courage to fight the terror that permeated the atmosphere of the whole garrison. It was not the fear of death. The chemical composition of the terror in the garrison could not be precisely defined. It was some invisible, odourless gas. It exuded from the flaking walls of the Farkas and Gjörmeky brewery, it wafted powerfully from the ten barracks buildings which stood in rows, one next to another, new, wooden, oblong, like giant coffins. In the shadow of these coffins, emitting an odour of resin, now sat uniformed men next to men in civilian attire, resting, eating and smoking. For the duration of mealtimes and while the food was being digested, an armistice with fear prevailed.

The men in uniform were very pleased by the arrival of their compatriots. The latter, for their part, were glad to find in Hungary so many of their own kind. A good number of them came from the Śniatyn district, from Iliniec, Biełełuja and Chlebiczyn. Hutsuls made friends with Hutsuls, Poles with Poles, Jews with Jews, German settlers from Mariahilf in Kołomyja and Baginsberg with Germans. People of the same nation recognize one another by their sense of smell. Hutsuls can sense Hutsuls, Jews can sense Jews at ten paces, even if they are wearing Turkish rather than Imperial uniform. It was heartening for all concerned when they mingled. For a moment both parties even accepted the illusion that the distance separating Hungary from Pokuttya had lessened and that the homes left in the care of their women were on the move and were to be found somewhere just around the corner...

The civilians brought a great deal of interesting news from their home, about their cattle, their wives, children and lovers, about the harvest and also about the war. It turned out that the battalion soldiers were actually less well informed about the war than the civilians. They were far away from the fighting, but any day now they would have to go to join it. The war had not started for them yet. It was just being born in the safety of the barracks courtyard, the surrounding stubble fields, the calm, sweet meadows and the shooting range. They had come here to refresh the strict ABC of war, which they had forgotten during the years that had passed since they had been on active service. Since that time a few new letters had been added to the ABC, but it had also been simplified. They already knew how to march, they were able to drop to the ground on command and get up again, to kneel and crawl on their stomachs; they were familiar with the Mannlicher and Werndl rifles, they could use small spades to dig trenches to protect themselves from gunfire. But above all they knew how to listen and keep quiet. On the other hand, the civilians had heard with their own ears the roar of real guns, and seen with their own eyes trains full of real wounded. For they had come from the war zone, from a land burning underfoot. This was the advantage they had over the battalion soldiers and they were proud of it.

The men in uniform talked about the great victory at Kraśnik that the commanding officer had solemnly announced in an order of the day. They were not very enthusiastic about it, somehow. The great victory at Kraśnik was all very well, but a matter of much greater importance was the weapons inspection scheduled for the next day. Only someone unacquainted with Regimental Sergeant-Major Bachmatiuk could consider the victory at Kraśnik of greater importance than a weapons inspection. Only someone who had never seen Bachmatiuk squinting his left eye, applying his right eye to the muzzle to check the rifling, and checking for pollen, soot or rust, could take this ceremony lightly! The civilians did not yet know Regimental Sergeant-Major Bachmatiuk, but they were also indifferent to the victory at Kraśnik. For them, everything taking place at the front line at the time was merely a prelude. The real war, unless it ended in the near future, would begin in earnest only when they took part in it. It could hardly be said that they had a burning desire to get involved. They could easily get over the fact that the greatest victories were occurring without them. Victory or defeat—they were as bad as each other. Not even Piotr Niewiadomski was so naive as to suppose that lives were not lost in times of victory too. He remembered from the Russo-Japanese War that victors die as well as the vanquished, sometimes even more of them. As they said in 1905, the Japanese fell "like flies" at Mukden. Piotr had never seen any Japanese, but he had seen flies expiring on long yellow strips of honey-covered flypaper. He had himself hung up such flypapers in the stationmaster's office at Topory-Czernielica. He had thrown them in the rubbish himself too. The Japanese died like this, and yet it was they who won the war, not the Russians. So what did the Japanese corpses gain from such a great victory? Probably about as much as the dead flies.

"When a war is over," Piotr told himself, "the emperors sit down in their palaces, take paper and pencil and count corpses. It would seem to be just like a game of cards; whoever lost more is the loser. But what actually happens? Quite the opposite. At Kraśnik too we probably lost more men than the Muscovites did."

He ate the soup. Next to him sat a soldier, Dmytro Tryhubiak from Czernielica. An old acquaintance. He had lent Piotr his bowl. He talked about relations at the garrison, explained the mysteries of parade-ground drill and the sequence of military training, and complained about the NCOs. They hit you in the gob, although physical assault was banned in the army. Victims of physical violence could complain on parade, but woe betide anyone who did so. Tryhubiak talked at length about punishments. He described the different forms of detention. It apparently gave him satisfaction. Personally, he even preferred detention to marching in the heat in full equipment. You could always get some rest.

The things the soldier was talking about seemed trivial compared with the real war in which people killed one another. Piotr was surprised to hear the soldiers exaggerate the importance of garrison life, as if "the field" existed for the benefit of the barracks and its detention regime, rather than the other way round. Suddenly he stopped listening to Tryhubiak, because he saw a woman's face emerging from the tin mess bowl. The eyes and mouth immediately seemed familiar. Whose face could it be, unless, unless... Piotr had a shock. He recognized her. It was his mother's face. Not the worn-out, hieratic woman she became in the last years of her life (Wasylina Niewiadomska's face looked like that in the photograph he kept in the trunk). It was still a young, wrinkle-free face, as he barely remembered it from his childhood. He had never seen it with such clarity before. And that is what scared him. In other circumstances, he would undoubtedly have been very pleased. But why, after all these years, had this forgotten face appeared to him? What paths had it taken to make it all the way here, to Hungary, to find the troops? She became clearer and clearer to him. He recognized the red scarf on her head. He recognized the strings of corals around her neck, corals hanging over him.

It was the aroma of the Imperial soup that had lured his young mother from the netherworld. Memories sped at a staggering pace on invisible waves of fragrance. They floated around in disorderly heaps like thawing ice floes on the Prut. Suddenly they came to a standstill, gathering around clearly recalled events. Into Piotr's mind came a now distant winter, as severe as the disease which, as he was only a small boy, debilitated him for weeks. In Śniatyn district illnesses have no names. They visit people namelessly and namelessly they pass. Piotr lay for weeks on end behind the stove, wrapped up in any scarves and any rags that were to be found in the house. It was as though his mother concentrated all the heat in the cottage on her dying child. For Piotr was dying. Hutsul children's illnesses mostly end in death, since there are no doctors to treat them. A mother's last resort in that part of the world is a bath. In the case of chest pains and fever, a bath of incense, sage and thyme. Wasylina Niewiadomska repeatedly bathed her son according to this ancient superstition, but in vain. So she took to fumigation. She fumigated the boy with smoke from burning horses' hooves and from wild poppies, but it was no use. The Jewish divine commandments propagating fumigation of a sick child, and the Jewish matzah blessed in the church with the *paskha* at Easter, were not accessible to her. Well, she gave up her superstitions. She had stopped believing in them. But she took advice from a certain wise old woman who in her younger days had been in domestic service in the town. This old woman believed passionately in God and in hot soup. From then on, Wasylina prayed every day before the holy images and daily brewed greasy, hot broth with beef bones. She bought the bones from a Jew in Bogatyn. She added liberal amounts of groats to the soup— millet, barley or ordinary buckwheat, Piotr didn't remember which it was now.

Meanwhile Dmytro Tryhubiak kept on complaining. During night exercises in the fields he had lost three blank cartridge shells. "I thought—silly me—'Your pay will be docked slightly and that's the last you'll hear of it.' But you don't know the army, my lad! The army doesn't tolerate the slightest loss. For something like that you have to join the left flank, to answer on parade. Each lost cartridge means one day confined to barracks, so for three cartridges you get three days. That's the going rate."

Piotr listened with one ear. He could not distinguish blanks from live rounds. And he had no idea where the left flank and the right flank were. And anyway, what had flanks to do with making a report on parade? Flanks were what beasts had. The aroma of Imperial soup acted like chloroform. It was destroying the present, desensitizing him to the real and imaginary threats of all military penalties. Piotr saw only his young mother and a glimpse of his childhood. But he could not for the life of him remember what kind of groats they were—millet, barley or ordinary buckwheat. The long journey and the intense heat had made him drowsy. The apparitions summoned up by the aroma of the soup were becoming blurred. Blank cartridge casings were floating in his soup. He would have fallen asleep if he had not been suddenly reminded of his mother's words:

"Eat up. Piotr, eat up, it will keep you alive!"

These words drifted soundlessly from the abyss of forgetfulness like birds from warm countries, playing in his ears and scaring away sleep. Piotr sat bolt upright and an expression of strained attention came over his face as he listened intently, absorbing all the resurrected music of the past. Perhaps he would hear something more, perhaps some more words would come from his mother's lips. He heard no more. "Eat up. Piotr, eat up, it will keep you alive!" That's all.

"Keep me alive? Of course it will!" The soup had saved him at the time. But what meaning did that have now? Could the Imperial soup also save you from death? Who knows? Was that why the Emperor feeds it to his soldiers, his children, every day?

His mother's young face vanished into thin air. In vain Piotr tried to recall her with all the forces of imagination he could muster. He closed his eyes. It was in vain. God alone knows what powers govern apparitions of the dead! An opportunity like that occurs once in a blue moon. If you squander it, that's your own fault. Piotr lost the opportunity. There was no need to think about barley! Instead of his young mother he was only able to summon up an image of old Wasylina as he had seen her for the last time. There was nothing special about that memory, which often haunted him. His mother lay dead in her coffin, in all her glory, on a bed of wood shavings. Her eyes were closed. Piotr had closed his mother's eyes himself, though he was under the impression that it was done by the hand of death. What horrified him most was the large wart on the dead woman's upper lip, and her thick black moustache. While his mother was alive he had not paid any attention to it, but he was surprised that the wart and the moustache did not disappear after she died. (He considered the blemish on his mother's skin and the mannish hair on her lip to be the effects of pipe-smoking.) There was something shameful about the wart which his mother took with her to the grave. It was indecent to look at it.

Piotr also had a glimpse of the funeral. This was the moment when he was carrying the nailed-down coffin from the cottage with the help of his neighbour Biłyk. It was so heavy it might well have contained not only her body but all the worries that had plagued her throughout her life as well. (Piotr would often recall that coffin while working on the railway, as he shifted heavy loads.) The women sang devotional songs as he and Biłyk lifted the coffin over the threshold three times, setting it down three times. That was the correct ritual, honouring a farmer's wife. At that point the vision vanished.

Now Piotr started thinking about himself—was he young or old? Such were the thoughts that haunted him whenever he thought about dying. Actually, he was not old. He could live on for twice as many years as he already had behind him. Well, he wasn't young either, but he still felt strong and healthy, and as for women…

As always at such moments, Piotr felt a sudden wish to have a child, as if he was not a man but an ageing, infertile woman. Why couldn't he have children? Why should he have to die without an heir? What had he done to deserve that punishment which God imposed on the entire Hutsul tribe? Paraszka, that dissolute sister of his, she could have a baby! Evidently, as if to spite his own sacraments, God sometimes blesses the iniquitous. A fine blessing that was! What can you say? After all, Paraszka's child died! He did not even survive for ten years. No soup had come to his aid.

Piotr was very fond of that child of sin, so looked down upon in the village. Who despised him? All those who were childless, out of envy. After giving birth to the bastard Paraszka wore the shawl of a married woman, but it didn't help her much. The shawl incited the women to greater resentment. Paraszka was right to leave the child in her mother's care and go to town. Except that she could have found better employment than in a brothel.

Piotr was often visited by the dead little one in his dreams. He always asked for something, always wanted something. After such dreams, Piotr regretted having been so severe with the boy. He did beat him, yes, he did, even though he was very fond of him. Considerable pain is caused by memories of harm inflicted on those who are no longer alive. Especially children… If Piotr had known that Paraszka's child would not survive, he would never have raised his hand against him. But then how could anyone know?

He was immediately reminded of the bastard's funeral. A Christian burial, but without a priest. A priest is very expensive, and the child's soul was still without sin, so he could go to heaven free of charge. It is true that in the first weeks after the funeral, Piotr feared that bastard would walk about at night haunting the village. He was not sure whether the souls of illegitimate children, like the souls of unbaptized children, turn into wood-nymphs after death. Especially as there had been no priest. But little Wasylko was baptized in the church. Why couldn't he remain an angel, like other Greek Catholic innocents? Piotr was also troubled by the uncertainty as to whether a bastard can be saved at all. After a long deliberation he always came to the conclusion that of course he can be saved. For death in childhood is the redemption of the mother's sin, and the all-knowing God is not so vindictive as to deny the little innocent his rights.

"Oh dear! Why is my head so full of nothing but illnesses and burials today?"

Piotr crossed himself three times, so that the dead might return to their after-life, and leave the living in peace. He was a little embarrassed about doing this in the presence of Tryhubiak, though the latter thought this was Piotr's way of parting after the meal, following his pious custom. Piotr took out his cigarettes, those from the charitable ladies in Budapest. He offered one to his companion and lit one himself. He hoped this would unite him closely with the living.

Yet it was not the dead who were the threat here; it was the living. They were truly vampires from hell, sent to drink human blood in broad daylight. Tryhubiak spoke about his superiors. They either had hearts of gold or they were sons of bitches. Somehow, there were more dogs at that garrison than hearts of gold. Entire packs of dogs. Tryhubiak was full of names. From the sound of these names Piotr tried to work out for himself what their bearers were like. He tried to imagine what they looked like and to guess at their character. He didn't trust Tryhubiak. He knew people and he realized that those who have had bad experiences like to scare novices. Longer-serving prisoners and veteran soldiers take pleasure in this. Some names had unpleasant associations. The name Garbacz, for example, belonging to a certain young cadet for whom Tryhubiak was full of praise, was particularly off-putting, suggesting "hump-back" in Polish. Lieutenant Zelenka, on the other hand, although Tryhubiak counted him among the worst of the dogs, Piotr found congenial. Something green, sylvan and meadow-like was associated in Polish with Lieutenant Zelenka's name.

And after all, there are good dogs, aren't there—Bass, for example?

When Tryhubiak started talking about lost cartridges for the third time, Piotr got up and went to the well, where his comrades were washing up the borrowed dishes. He waited his turn, returned the mess kit, and headed in the direction of the happy crowd. In the shade of the first barracks shed sat Semen Baran. He was entertaining a sizeable group of military and civilians. He knew the world and he was not afraid of the army. He was doing card tricks. Suddenly the fun was over. Lance Corporal Zubiak of the First Company wanted to bet a packet of Herzegovina tobacco that the next day, or at the latest the day after, the Tyrolean or Italian or even Bosnian reserve militia men would turn up, and the devil alone knew who else. The Emperor had enough nations under him. He wanted to bet that half of our men at most would be staying on at the garrison. Zubiak, as an NCO, had occasion to visit the orderly room and he had heard the sergeants discussing it. Now they were supposed to mix together men from all lands of the crown, to prevent treason.

At the ominous sound of that word, they all drew closer, tightening the circle, as if they wanted to keep treason at bay with their bodies.

On the Russian front, said Zubiak, treason was being committed. Our men were deserting to the Muscovites with their rifles, machine guns, their banners and their bands... even entire companies and entire battalions... And now they are packing each company with Germans, Italians and Czechs— there will be no more desertions. The nations will all be watching each other.

The sons of the Hutsul land took this news badly. They had expected to go to war as a family, with their own people, but now the Emperor wanted to take revenge on them for the guilt of others; he wanted to disperse them among foreign regiments and mix the languages, as God once did when he built the Tower of Babel.

"None of us has ever committed treason or ever will!" exclaimed Piotr Niewiadomski.

But now all the men were wondering where they would be sent on to, since only part of the draft was to remain in Andrásfalva.

Treason! Treason! The entire garrison reeked of it. Had Piotr defeated the phantom of treason back at home only to have it follow him all the way here with the army, to Hungary? He even wanted to pretend he was deaf and dumb… He never expected that treason could wear an army uniform.

This uniform, he thought—implying the oath sworn before God—was adequate protection from treason. Well, but if entire battalions are going over to the Muscovites with their banners and bands there is no place left to hide. Except in death. It's all the work of the devil, who stole the fifth commandment from the Lord. The devil tells them to play the wrong marching music, changing the musicians' scores so that the brass trumpets play only Russian tunes instead of Austrian ones.

An oppressive heatwave hung over the garrison. It mollified people's brains and madness seeped through invisible fissures in their skulls. But although they were exposed to a fierce blaze from the skies they stood firm. They crowded around the wells, huddled in the limited shade offered by the huts, from which the sun devil was licking the last of the sylvan moisture. The resin constantly dripped in honey-like tears. It was weeping for the regiment's dead. Those who were to replace them sat patiently on their trunks, sticking to the melting paint or covering their heads with wet handkerchiefs, lying on their stomachs, waiting for the end of the war. Dead, organic tribal odours arose from their sweaty clothing. Their baking-hot shoes split open. Anguish and boredom were written all over people's faces. The blinding glare showed up every skin defect, flourishing like mildew on their cheeks. Only a few faces managed to preserve their masks. The heat seared through most of them, exposing the brutal truth. The old, hirsute contingents from the Upper Czeremosz and Prut regions were panting like tormented, dull-eyed lions. They were battling with the terror of the garrison. The armistice was over.

The mysteries of military discipline, like the Eleusinian mysteries, already here on earth gave mortals an intimate relationship with death; they were accessible only to the initiated. Here and there were two stages of initiation: the lesser mysteries applied to recruits and the greater mysteries (*epopteia*) applied to the soldier already serving at the front line. But whereas the voluntary cult of Demeter gave initiates complete freedom to assess the taste of death, the taste of death for the Emperor, King and Country was laid down in regulations. For centuries, it had invariably been sweet.

The men of the battalion were initiates of the first stage. For now, they were in contact only with symbols of death, whose true sweetness was to be revealed to them only after their so-called baptism of fire. Here, in the garrison, they became worthy of this baptism by idolatrous worship of Discipline. The religion of Discipline was not exclusive. On the contrary, it was dependent on the masses, forcibly converted. Anyone unwilling to be converted and initiated into the mysteries of Discipline suffered death on its orders, but a bitter, shameful death, not a sweet one. The cult of Discipline required many ritual practices and gestures. And do not be surprised, my grandson and my great-grandson, to whom I am telling this long story, that in those distant days millions of men had to freeze as they stood still, saluting strangers because they bore gleaming stars of rank. We had to salute all the Messrs lance corporals, and the Messrs corporals, and the Messrs sergeants, and the Messrs colour sergeants, and especially the Messrs officers, from second lieutenants up to Their Excellencies the field marshals. And we had to salute even higher authorities—it is frightening to think how high. All these star-bearing powers, however, required the same salute, although it would make sense to take into account such great differences, and salute a corporal in a quite different way from a general. If a corporal was saluted with one hand, a general should be saluted with two hands. That would make sense. One soldier whom the patient reader will get to know later in this story, actually did so. That soldier was later dismissed from the Imperial and Royal Army as a lunatic.

Up till now, the men of the battalion had been freely chatting with civilians, taking advantage of the armistice between them and fear. Suddenly they began leaping to their feet, standing to attention, adjusting their caps, fastening buttons and throwing lighted cigarettes on the ground. Their faces turned into dead larvae, their bodies stiffened and their eyes glazed over. Like puppets, they swung their heads to the left, to the right, to the left, to the right. The stars hypnotized them from afar, and the soldiers' hands shot towards their caps, striking the peaks, striking the peaks, striking the peaks. After the prescribed number of seconds had elapsed, they dropped back down. Limbs relaxed, releasing the deadly cramp. The hypnotic effect of the stars wore off. The men turned into wood recovered, as if from a long journey to the after-life. Every pore of their skin exuded fear. Fear spread to the civilians. But they did not move from the spot. The stars had not worked their deadly fascination on them. Civilian dress acted as protective armour.

Piotr Niewiadomski was well versed in military constellations. He knew that one bone star was for a lance corporal, two for a corporal, three for a sergeant, three stars and a yellow stripe for a colour sergeant. He could distinguish NCOs' stars from those of commissioned officers, on cloth lapels and even gold ones. As he wore an Imperial railway cap, he joined the soldiers in saluting the officers returning after dinner from their mess. Contrary to all appearances, they were men. Older men, paunchy, moustachioed, bearded men. There were also quite a number of younger men who were clean-shaven, following the foreign fashion. They looked like priests in uniform. Almost all of them wore the same field caps as privates, and if it were not for their long swords it would be difficult to distinguish at a distance their silk stars, embellished with silver or gold circles, from bone stars.

During those honeymoon months of the war, the officers responded with evident satisfaction to the deference accorded to them. The reserve officers were especially proud that they had suddenly become objects of respect. From all sides, ordinary teachers, salesmen, clerks and students were greeted with military salutes, in the prescribed rhythm and tempo, and they caught them like balls in the air and returned them. The cult of Discipline was observed conscientiously. However, minor aberrations did occur.

Two young men of the rank of cadet had just emerged from the officers' mess. Against the background of the square occupied mostly by peasants, their smart, tight-fitting tunics, breeches and long boots gave them the appearance of a pair of young landowners on their estate. One of them was toying with a riding-crop that had a shiny handle. In the military hierarchy, cadets were akin to centaurs. They were officers only above the waist, the rest of their bodies belonging to the rank of private. In peacetime, they had to march carrying both a rifle and an officer's sabre. Those battalion soldiers whose proximity required them to salute the cadets did so impeccably. Only one of them, a stout older man, evidently exhausted by the constant saluting, the oppressive heat, or by life in general, did not manage to coordinate his movements in time and he saluted while still getting to his feet. The cadets noticed. The one with the whip and ruddy, childish cheeks approached the sinner. Like a careworn mother, he enquired:

"What kind of a salute is that, old man?"

This familiar address coming from the youngster sounded strangely inappropriate. The old man remained silent, standing rigidly to attention. He stuck out his belly in an exaggerated manner. For a moment, the cadet looked at him pityingly. Suddenly he drew himself up and in a changed, inhuman voice called out in German:

"Setzen!"

The old man sat down, as he was ordered.

"Salutiert!"

The old man rose, as required by regulations, paused for a second, and saluted. Once again:

"Setzen!"

The old man sat down.

"Salutiert—eins! Zwei! Drei!"

The old torso rose with a struggle and the hands carried out the salute in the three stages.

"Setzen!"

The old eyes, like a couple of beggars, sought mercy in the eyes of Discipline. But they did not find it. Discipline could not see human eyes. It watched only hands, feet and caps. Intoxicated by the rhythm of its own command, it chanted:

"Salutiert—eins! Zwei! Drei!"

The old body hesitated for a moment, as if slightly swaying, but in good time rose from the ground. This was repeated five more times. In the end, eyes met eyes. After the eighth *"setzen!"* no further *"salutiert!"* followed; relief came from the commands to stand at ease and carry on:

"Ruht! Weitermachen!"

After that, the old man could do with his body as he wished. Having eaten its fill of salutes from a sitting position, Discipline smiled kindly from the young man's mouth, showing two rows of strong, healthy teeth.

"Garbacz!" whispered one of the soldiers in Piotr's ear.

So that was Cadet Garbacz! Piotr compared him with the conception of the man he had formed on the basis of his surname. Wrong! Tryhubiak had been right. Garbacz did not look like a "dog", although he had tortured a tired old man. Everyone who knew Garbacz was aware that, personally, he could not care less whether people saluted him. He was indifferent to polite greetings. But bad saluting he could not tolerate. Only those officers who considered bad saluting a mark of personal disrespect could overlook it, as it was they who were looking, not Discipline. Cadet Garbacz had no right to give away something that was not his own property. On the other hand he could, for example, offer people his own cigarettes. He actually wondered whether he should give one to the old soldier. He did not give him one. The uninitiated might think he regretted what he had done. But he did not regret it. He had a clear conscience. If people saluted so badly in the very first month of the war, what would happen later on? The war might last until Christmas. Was it permissible to condone sloppy saluting in the presence of the new recruits, who were still civilians? It was actually because of the civilians that he had to react so strictly. He would not give him a cigarette. On the other hand, it would be good to speak to the civilians. Don't let them think that they are dealing with some blunt, bigoted blockhead of an official.

"Well, you fellows, was the meal all right?"

He knew it was all right, although he himself did not eat in the soldiers' canteen. He was on his way back from the officers' mess, where he had been dining on something akin to ambrosia and nectar. His question was intended to indicate that he was partly human, even if the rest of him was not.

He did not wait to hear the response, which was a positive one of course, chanted in unison. He saluted first, and, arm in arm with his companion, who had observed the spectacle with indifference, set off in the direction of the town.

Piotr Niewiadomski now knew for sure that this was no "son of a bitch". But how could you recognize those with a heart of gold round here?

If Cadet Garbacz had been a son of a bitch, by now he would have been running around with his tongue lolling out, in this heat. The stuffy Hungarian air was contaminated with rabies germs. Piotr thought of his Bass—would he be able to stand this inferno? Of course he would. The men were dreaming of the cool mountain rivers, of the Prut or the Czeremosz. The feebler souls among them were ready to sell themselves to the devil and betray the Emperor in return for the chance to soak their bodies in running water. They enquired of the soldiers whether there was a river, a pond or a brook anywhere nearby. There was a pond, on the other side of town on the way to the firing range, but it was dried-up and abandoned. So they eyed the luxuriant row of linden trees lining the main road, the garden surrounding the brewery officials' cottage, but help was not forthcoming from any direction. One by one, the soldiers abandoned their compatriots and retired to the straw mattresses in their quarters, where it was cooler. Although it was a Sunday, there was still work for them to do—cleaning weapons for the inspection on the following day.

Presently, two figures appeared from somewhere inside the red walls of the brewery. First came an unshaven giant of a man in crumpled uniform. He shuffled along in ungainly fashion in boots from which the laces had been removed. His trousers were slipping down and he kept pulling them up with his elbows. Both hands were full—he was carrying buckets. He was closely followed by another soldier. His trousers were not slipping down, his boots were no problem, on his shoulder was a rifle with fixed bayonet. At his waist, on both sides of the brass eagle on his belt, hung two bulging pouches like a pair of black udders filled with the leaden milk of death. The space between these two men was charged with some deadly current. Again a death zone. This time a physical one. It was amazing that the insects carelessly flitting between the two soldiers did not drop dead.

"A deserter," thought Piotr to himself at the sight of the prisoner. "Perhaps he is a traitor, one of those who, carrying the colours…"

But this was no deserter, nor was he a traitor.

"Hello, Huk! Hello, Ilko! Come over here and roll one! Oh, you've grown a beard!" called out the giant's comrades from the third company. Some of them temptingly offered him their tobacco pouches. But no one was seriously thinking of giving any to him. Ilko Huk had had enough tobacco in detention. Throughout the monarchy detainees secretly obtained tobacco. The soldier carrying the buckets threw his comrades a friendly glance, winking at them knowingly, and gestured with his bearded chin. The soldier with the rifle kept his eyes on the other's back. He was obviously afraid.

"He's going to the kitchens to fetch rations for the men under arrest," explained one of the soldiers.

"Who is he?"

"Some Polish comrade. Very fond of girls. After he went out last Saturday, without a pass of course, he didn't come back until Monday, after the physical exercises. But the man's in luck! The captain likes him. He only got twelve days. The captain would give anyone else twenty-one, and irons as well, because it was the second time he'd bunked off."

"What are irons?" asked Piotr Niewiadomski. Tryhubiak had not said anything about those.

The initiates of the first category burst into ironic laughter and Lance Corporal Zubiak shook his head:

"Don't you know what irons are, conductor, sir? Have you got a mother?"

"No, I haven't."

"That's a shame, because when they cuff your left hand to your right leg or your right hand to your left leg and you have to sit like that for two hours, three, four—whatever you've earned—your liver will swell and you'll curse your mother that you were ever born."

The initiates roared with laughter once more. A few civilians joined in. Piotr frowned. Snippets of the vision of his mother feeding him soup flickered before his eyes and her words still echoed in his ears. And a stranger tells me to curse such a mother? Perhaps the devil deliberately evoked this image in the infernal heat of the midday sun? Curse her! What for? For the left hand, for the right hand, for the right leg... Piotr looked at his hands. For God's sake, which is the right and which is the left? Was he never going to learn that unless he was placed in irons?

The soldier carrying the buckets and the soldier with the rifle had already passed the most menacing place in the garrison, the command headquarters, from where they could be observed by the officers. The tension between them had subsided a good deal. The soldier carrying the rifle was now more relaxed, walking like a human being instead of marching. As they were about to turn towards the machine room, the prisoner turned, lifting the buckets without caring what happened to his trousers. He struck them triumphantly and they resounded like cymbals.

Piotr was still upset, despite the amusement the prisoner had aroused among his comrades. The soldiers lost no time in explaining to the civilians that the guard with the loaded rifle was infantryman Ołes Hnidej from the same third company as infantryman Ilko Huk. That day, the third company was on guard duty. Lieutenant Smekal was to blame for a two-hour delay in the changing of the guard. Ilko Huk had been guarded by his comrades for twenty-six hours instead of twenty-four. In half an hour, new men from the first company would take over. Ołes Hnidej would lay down his weapon and be released from guard duty. He would hand over to the guard commander in person the live cartridges, which he was obliged to fire at a comrade should he attempt to escape. The gendarme, the detention guard, the enemy, would become a friend once more. The prisoner was also one of the initiated. He was familiar with the metamorphic nature of discipline. He knew that in a few days, when he was released from detention, everything could be reversed. Today's gendarme could become a prisoner, and the prisoner become a gendarme.

Piotr Niewiadomski could think of nothing else all day until evening came with the sweet black coffee. Arrests, solitary confinement, dark cells, fasting and the irons. Enough of this in the service of the Emperor, enough! And the worst of it is that comrades face each other with loaded weapons, like Corporal Durek and the bandit Matviy, known as The Bull.

Except that a gendarme was a gendarme all his life, a thief was a thief, but under the Emperor you are a gendarme today and tomorrow you're a thief...

He could not come to terms with this new order of things. He had been around in this world for forty-one years and still he was rediscovering it, and always from different perspectives that kept getting worse and worse.

"All right," he told himself, "it's war. We know that. But why has the Emperor visited so much fear, so much anger, so much punishment on his own people? Would it not be better to save all his anger for the Muscovites? After all, it's them he is at war with, not us. Why spill good, Catholic Austrian blood?"

Piotr Niewiadomski was a friend of Emperor Franz Joseph's. He considered the whole Imperial and Royal Army to be friends of the Emperor's. With the exception of traitors, of course. "My beloved peoples, my beloved army," wrote His Majesty in his proclamations. Perhaps he did not write this? But writing, the devil's signs, is one thing, and the truth is something else. "My beloved peoples..." A fine sort of love that is.

After the coffee he relaxed. Military caffeine had exactly the opposite effect from the civilian variety; it soothed troubled hearts. Nevertheless, many hearts were now beating rapidly on the square, by the huts, and the cause of this was not the heat, it was fear. Nightfall was approaching, and no one knew whether they would have to sleep under the stars. Among the civilians there were those who had never slept on the bare ground. Somehow it seemed unlikely that they would be given accommodation for the night. People who were now afraid of the night, the starry sky and the bare earth were descended from an old tribe of shepherds. Centuries ago, their fathers spent many a night in the dew and many a night sleeping in the desert, with burnt grass, hot sand or hair of live camels as their only bedding. When storms raged in the sky, they sheltered in canvas tents. In the darkness of the night they feared only God and jackals. Oh, how long ago it was that the tents of Israel had crumbled to dust! The descendants of ancient shepherds, pursued by sneering, evil fate, now wander the deserts of brick cities and towns, afraid of the land, afraid of the sky, and afraid of the rain.

Since the beginning of the war, almost four weeks ago now, there had been no rain. It was as if the sky had renounced the privilege of watering the soil, waiving it in favour of human blood. But human blood, however profusely it flowed, brought no benefit to the land.

Around seven o'clock clouds began to gather on the horizon to the west. The clear blue sky darkened in many places. The sun had not yet reached its final position beyond the town of Andrásfalva; it had only just left the garrison boundaries. It floated down towards the clouds. And the clouds swelled, growing dark. People who in other circumstances would welcome the relief of a storm now anxiously watched this mobilization up above. Where could you shelter from the downpour, which could last all night? No one was allowed to enter the huts without express permission. Only a command could release them from their oppression, but no one gave such an order.

By eight o'clock, it was clear that it was not going to rain. When the sun collided with the cloud bank, the clouds parted. Then, as if blushing with embarrassment, the clouds separated into numerous flocks of fleeing dirty sheep, chased by the fiery dog into an abyss. The sun's victory was something wonderful, like the victory at Kraśnik. Jews and town-dwellers breathed a sigh of relief.

The night beneath the Hungarian sky held no terrors. Stars flashed on the clear firmament, one after another, glorious, mature, brilliant. It was nights like these that gave birth to astronomy. The close atmosphere which had been so oppressive during the daytime seemed to have relented in the face of people's anxiety before the storm. The sky set in motion its hushed, invisible fans. A pleasant coolness wafted from the north. A northerly breeze gently caressed the faces of the new arrivals. The moon had not yet appeared.

In distant huts they were singing, in chorus, each verse beginning with "Oi!" It was a sigh developed into a melody, sheer Ukrainian nostalgia condensed into sound. Homesickness, longing for the steppe, the mountains, for love, for a lost paradise. Our men lay on their trunks and their bundles. They were waiting for their dreams to come true, they were waiting for the war to end.

The summer night slowly slid down on them. It rendered their features gentler, erasing their dullness and roughness. The night covered the commonest of faces with a patina of holiness. It closed mouths, but opened hearts. But no one here had anything to confess. They had not yet experienced the kind of shared misery that robs souls of their pride and their shame. Everyone kept their secrets to themselves. There would come a day when no one could keep them in any longer. In the absence of a priest they would confess to one another.

Nobody could sleep. The first night in the army held some secrets. Everyone was waiting for something.

As a cloud drifted in front of the moon, from the depths of the brewery came a long-drawn-out bugle call. The Emperor's lullaby for well-behaved children. The communal singing in the barracks died down. Nine o'clock. Soldiers throughout the monarchy go to bed at nine. With the exception of those on the front line. A few moments later, from the mysterious depths of the brewery, from where the prisoner had been led that afternoon, and from where the notes of the lights-out bugle call were now drifting, a small detachment of armed men emerged. Bayonets glinted on the rifle barrels. They marched in double file. They came to a halt in front of the command headquarters. An officer or a sergeant gave a lengthy explanation to the soldiers. The light from the windows of the headquarters building was reflected in his sabre. He spoke in a hushed voice. Then they set off towards the square. They paused here and there to leave one soldier behind. The stars on the NCOs' collars glinted. The garrison was posting the night sentries. The duty sergeant was positioning them at the boundary fences, at each barracks hut, by the barbed wire and at the main gate, embellished with fir branches and banners in honour of the victory at Kraśnik—an armed soldier now paced to and fro.

They did not trust us. We were surrounded on all sides as in a prison camp.

Piotr Niewiadomski could not swear to it, but he imagined that one of the sentries was Dmytro Tryhubiak from Czernielica.

The prisoners fell silent, although no one had forbidden them to speak. They spoke to each other in whispers. In the army, night-time of itself ordered silence. Nervously, they lent each other matches and seemed to be smoking furtively, even though no one had banned it. Eyes wandered round at night, clinging to the walls of the brewery, red in the daytime and now white as chalk, clinging to the huts, and plunging into the dark mass of linden trees lining the road. Neither the walls nor the linden trees could restore their lost freedom.

"Thus far," said the borders of the earthly horizon, "and no farther!"

So they raised their eyes towards the heavens, where constellations with names known to astronomers but not to dwellers of Śniatyn district shone with ever greater radiance. Piotr Niewiadomski did know a few stars. He knew which was the Great Bear, the Plough. He knew that the path of stars strewn across the sky was the Milky Way. It was there that the Plough broke an axle. The prisoners' eyes anxiously ran backwards and forwards across the Milky Way like starving dogs. Maybe the sky would throw them a bone as consolation?

At this time of year only stars fell from the sky.

Seeing how often they fell, a merchant from Kołomyja, Izrael Glanz, thought God was dismantling the heavens. Perhaps the stars were going over to the Muscovites as well.

The camp was going to sleep. Disappointed by sky and earth, the men curled up and retired into themselves. They drifted away into the dark depths of their beings. Piotr Niewiadomski looked at his comrades and saw them all placed in irons. The left hand to the right foot, right hand to the left foot. Everyone silently cursing their mothers. There was a great silence, interrupted by snoring, coughing and groaning, and there were stars in the sky, and stars on the collars of the NCOs.

Chapter Nine

The alarm clock on the table rang shrilly. It shook as it made its sharp but impotent attack, merely obeying its own spring. No need. The man who had wound it up the evening before was no longer asleep. He was lying here on the bed, half-covered with a white woollen blanket, smoking a cigarette. (This smoking on an empty stomach was probably the reason for his hoarse voice.) The alarm clock ejected the extent of fury prescribed by the mechanism, then it fell silent. Now it was just an ordinary ticking clock.

This had been going on since time immemorial. Since time immemorial Regimental Sergeant-Major Bachmatiuk had awoken a few minutes—sometimes even more than ten minutes—before the alarm clock launched its attack. All the same, he would set it every evening. In summer for five o'clock, in winter for six o'clock. Was it just an old bachelor's unthinking, eccentric habit? Regimental Sergeant-Major Bachmatiuk was an old bachelor, but he was not eccentric. Everything he did had a purpose. This alarm clock fulfilled an important function for him. Every day it noisily acknowledged the superiority of the RSM over the forces of the night. Additionally, on Mondays it sounded his victory over alcohol. Punctuality and discipline were not imposed on Bachmatiuk by powers alien to his nature. Over the dozen or so years of his service, these virtues had entered his bloodstream and penetrated his tissues like lime. Bachmatiuk demanded nothing more from his alarm, just a loud affirmation of this fact, which he wanted to hear repeated every morning. It was his soaking therapy. And when the alarm rang Bachmatiuk had the impression that he was in control not only of himself, his will and conscious-ness, but also of the time he allotted to himself. The alarm clock faithfully carried out its duty; it did not wake him. So far, it had never failed. It was obedient, eating out of the hand that wound it up, as it were. Bachmatiuk never disappointed either. He always woke up of his own accord; he was always the first past the post. But whose hand wound up the springs that worked Bachmatiuk?

The RSM battled Chronos not only on the minor scale of the clock. He also fought against time's heavy calibre, that is to say his own ageing. He had already passed fifty, and it was not only his temples that were turning grey; he had a grey moustache too. He could shave it off, thereby maintaining a semblance of youth. He did not do so, because he served in the infantry, and infantry regulations expressly encouraged the cultivation of a moustache. In the Imperial and Royal Army only one reg-iment had the right, indeed the privilege, of shaving the beard and moustache, in honour of their famous ancestors who fell in the prime of life. That was the Windischgrätz Dragoons. Bachmatiuk was not a Dragoon but an infantryman by vocation and he respected the regulations of this arm of the service to a fanatical degree. As for outward signs of ageing, he had means of suppressing them which were just as effective as the razor.

After finishing his cigarette, he closed his eyes and immersed himself in deep meditation. After a while he sat up in bed and barked a loud command to himself: "Get up!" Accustomed to obey any command, even from his own lips, he leapt up in a flash, put on his morning slippers and marched towards the wash-basin that rested on a chair. He plunged his head into the cold water to wash away the remnants of sleep from his large, dark, badly bloodshot eyes. He shaved in front of a little mirror which maliciously distorted his handsome, weather-beaten face. Then he cleaned his teeth. After that he engaged in a struggle with time. From a table drawer he produced all his armoury: a little box of blacking, some muslin netting and a child's toothbrush. He spent a long time dyeing his broad, dense moustache, which overnight had lost its artificial lustre and its black, artificial symmetry. Finally, he applied a pink strip of muslin, attaching it round his ears. It looked like a bandage, drawing back his upper lip to reveal the pale gums and the long, yellow, equine teeth.

He sat back down on the bed and meditated. He was wondering which trousers to wear. The short grey-blue breeches to go with his tall boots, or the long black evening ones? He chose the latter, although he would not be visiting any drawing-room. Huts, storerooms and dust were what awaited him. Black trousers were impractical on duty, of course, but they did have a certain advantage, not to be underestimated. If you were asked about Regimental Sergeant-Major Bachmatiuk's stature, you would have to say it was Napoleonic. Short stature is no disadvantage to anyone, of course. But the majesty of the Emperor of the French, who usually appeared before his troops on a historic white charger, clad in the historic grey greatcoat—well, that is one thing; quite another matter is the authority of a chief instructor in an Imperial and Royal Galician infantry regiment. Sometimes, long black trousers were to Bachmatiuk what the charger and greatcoat were to Napoleon. They elevated his status, enhancing his authority over subordinates. In those days Bachmatiuk set great store by authority. The trousers for evening wear were old and shabby and the seat was shiny. But all down the outer seams on both sides ran two narrow purple strands. Modest miniatures of general's stripes. The choice of trousers determined the choice of footwear. In the nature of things, the tall boots standing to attention against the wall had to give way to the ordinary shoes that the orderly would bring along with the coffee.

The orderly appeared just as Bachmatiuk was combing his thick black hair; it was naturally black, not dyed. A white, perfectly straight parting ran down the middle, as if traced with a ruler. It ran from his forehead all the way to the nape of his neck. The parting in his hair and the stripes on his trousers all seemed to make the same statement.

In the doorway stood a soldier, a paunchy fellow with the complexion of a hermaphrodite. The skin of his pale, bloated face resembled parchment and it glistened like butter. Nature had endowed him with a perpetual lack of facial hair, making him an ideal Dragoon for the Windischgrätz regiment. However, he had been drafted into the infantry. Since the beginning of the war he had been unofficially polishing the RSM's shoes, tidying up his quarters and bringing his meals. Now he was holding the polished shoes in one hand and a mess tray in the other, as the RSM was accustomed to drink black coffee from a pot like an ordinary soldier. He did not avail himself of the facilities of the NCOs' kitchen, which issued white coffee in glasses and mugs.

He did not even look round. With an experienced eye, he glanced in the mirror, quickly scanning the shiny surface of his shoes to establish that they had the correct appearance. He did not acknowledge the creator of this shine with a single word. In general, he rarely conversed with him. He had only had him since the outbreak of war and he did not want them to be on too familiar terms. He issued all commands in an official tone. Fatso generally carried them out conscientiously. His name was Hawryło (Gabriel) Kistoczok and he came from Bukovina, Bachmatiuk's homeland. It was probably to this circumstance that he owed the privilege of his position. Bachmatiuk seemed to like him. Once, in a fit of good humour, he made a joking allusion to the fact that the shoe-shiner had an archangel's name. In the presence of several soldiers, he called out:

"Hey, Hawryło, Michajło, Rafajło, go to the orderly room and fetch the orders!"

After that, wherever infantryman Gabriel Kistoczok appeared, he was met with calls of "Hawryło, Michajło, Rafajło!"

The battalion's soldiers taunted him, but instinctively they showed him respect. In any case he roamed at will in the lion's den, sweeping it out every day, and he dwelt at the very source of fear; he was steeped in the intimate aroma of power. Someone like this must know a thing or two. So they bombarded him with questions—such as when would there be a weapons inspection, when was the general's inspection to take place, when would they be entering the battlefield, when would the war be over. They sucked up to Hawryło and even tried bribing him with vodka, sausages and tobacco. Hawryło acted as though he really did know something. He intimated that he was a confidant of the RSM, and his smile was as moronic as it was enigmatic. But his answers were mostly vague and ambiguous. In the end, the soldiers decided that Hawryło, Michajło, Rafajło knew about as much as they did. Nevertheless, they still looked up to him, so that every day his self-esteem grew and grew. Alongside Bachmatiuk, however, he felt increasingly insignificant.

Now he blurted out, with some difficulty:

"Regimental Sergeant-Major! Reporting, the straw has arrived, sir!"

"Dis—miss!"

Hawryło clicked his heels, silently put down the coffee and the shoes, silently took away the basin of dirty water and silently departed. He would return to the tidying up once the RSM was no longer in the room.

The RSM had a small room to himself on the second floor of the regimental headquarters. The other "professional" NCOs were quartered two or three to a room. Mostly they were married, with children. In the Stanisławów garrison they had apartments, with sideboards, gramophones with huge loudspeakers, chamber-pots, rubber-plants, rhododendrons, little dogs and canaries. The war and the evacuation had suddenly driven them out of their cosy nests. Deprived of their creature comforts, they found it difficult to adapt to the new conditions at their Hungarian barracks. Bachmatiuk was in his element here. For almost thirty years he had lived with the regiment and it was all the same to him where the regiment was stationed. He never had his own furniture, he did not even possess his own bed-linen, and as for the family—the military was his family. It was hard to imagine him ever having had parents. Regulations seemed to be his father and Discipline his mother. While Bachmatiuk was on military service, he sometimes spent his holidays at "home". He used to visit his father, the mayor of a prosperous municipality near the river Sereth, and his younger siblings. But after transferring to the regular army, he broke off relations with the whole family and he was seen in the affluent municipality by the Sereth only once—at his father's funeral. "He that loveth father or mother more than me is not worthy of me," said the Lord to the apostles. Like a nun, married to the Lord in her innocence, Bachmatiuk lived for years away from his family, loving the deity more than himself.

The earthy parents he chanced to have, as if foreseeing that their first-born son would one day become a source of support for the military might of the Habsburgs, christened him with the archducal name of Rudolf. Throughout his life, Bachmatiuk sought to prove himself worthy of that name. He was Ukrainian by birth, but in the course of many years in the army his nationality dissolved without a trace in the black-and-yellow substance. Today he was simply an Austrian. It would also be naive to mention his religious affiliation as indicated in the register of baptisms and like-wise in the regimental records, according to which he was a Greek Catholic, since the only faith that he ardently professed and nurtured was the army. He attained the rank of RSM by honest means; he was as strict with himself as with his subordinates, selfless and pure as a vestal virgin. His vows of purity were addressed to his own conscience, but it was the late legendary Captain Knauss who ordained him a priest of Discipline.

Bachmatiuk knew he had no chance of further promotion. The rank of RSM was the apogee of his career. He did not care about promotion, as he was not a careerist. He served his deity disinterestedly, maintaining his celibacy. He treated his task of turning men into men as that of a missionary. He not only created foot soldiers fit for parade and for combat, but above all he turned out Austrians. The duty of a priest, especially his missionary work, makes exclusive demands on a man. That was why Bachmatiuk was not married. Those unable to understand the meaning of true faith had their own explanations for Bachmatiuk's avoidance of women. Some considered him to be impotent from birth. The fools! In any case, we have scant knowledge of the RSM's private life. He did not keep the company of anyone in the barracks when off duty. Apparently, he had acquaintances in the town at Stanisławów. As the sole RSM, he occupied a totally isolated position in the regiment. He treated the sergeants as beneath him, but on the other hand he was modest and considerate enough not to approach the cadets and the junior officers, the subalterns.

His little room at the Farkas and Gjörmeky brewery resembled a monk's cell, indeed that of a monk belonging to some strict order. A camp-bed, a shelf above the bed, and on the shelf—bread, salt, butter, tobacco and an old parade helmet. Everywhere in the room—on the window, on the table, on the walls and on the floor—everything you saw had some connection with the army. Dummy ammunition, magazines with blank rounds in colourful boxes and odd spent shells. Everywhere there were piles of paperwork, old typewritten orders of the day already carried out, service notes, report books, forms, maps and service reports. On the floor, leaning against the walls, were faulty range-finders which he was repairing, rifle-practice targets, a large wooden box with live ammunition and two heavy, padlocked trunks. It could be that in one of these trunks he kept the civilian clothes about which the wildest rumours circulated. On one wall hung a brass trumpet. The following sacrosanct books lay on the table:

Service Regulations, Part I, i.e. D.1
Service Regulations, Part II (Field Service), D.2
Service Regulations, Part III, D.3
Exercise Regulations for Infantry, I.
Rifle Training

and a small manual for NCOs—the *Handbuch für Unteroffiziere* by H. Schmidt, with a portrait of the Emperor in colour on the cover. There was no trace of his private life anywhere. The wall above the bed was adorned with picturesque ornaments—a sabre, a belt and a pistol in a brown leather case. Nearby was the only picture in the cell—a large photograph in a black frame, under glass. It contained the figure of a handsome middle-aged officer in field uniform with field-glasses on his chest and a bunch of flowers. This was Captain Knauss. Captain Siegfried Knauss, setting off into the field, had offered Bachmatiuk only a small amateur photograph. He perished in the first days of the war on the Russian front. Bachmatiuk idolized Captain Knauss. Everything he knew about the army, that is to say about life, he had learnt thanks to him. None other than Captain Knauss had turned Bachmatiuk into a "man". At the news of the captain's death, the regimental sergeant-major—the man of iron—reportedly wept like a baby. After that, he lost interest in the fortunes of the regiment at the front. If the entire regiment were wiped out to the last man, it would be less of a loss than that single death. With that death, the regiment had already lost the war. Bachmatiuk took the likeness of the dead man to the best photographer in Stanisławów and ordered an enlargement, to be set in a beautiful black frame. Nobody would have been surprised to see an olive lamp burning underneath this photograph one day.

After the orderly had left, he looked out through the closed window. Hundreds of people were milling around down below. On the main route leading from the brewery to the highway a convoy of wagons fully loaded with straw was drawn up. The horses were impatiently stamping their hooves. Bachmatiuk opened the window and leant out over the window sill. The hubbub from the people on the square seemed to calm down slightly. The regimental sergeant-major's torso made an impression even in his vest. Civilians were washing at the wells. The soldiers were fetching coffee. From the east, from the direction of the abattoir, came muffled bellowing.

"Reszytyło!" yelled Bachmatiuk at the NCO standing by the wagons. "What are you waiting for? Move on to the fourth barracks building! And see to it that nobody smokes! If fire breaks out you will be in for it, not me! Get a move on!"

The wagons started moving. Bachmatiuk remained standing by the window for a while. This window and two storeys separated him from the anonymous masses which he had to knock into shape. He was supposed to infuse spirit into these ostensibly living beings who were ignorant of discipline. This work had aged him. Before the war, he had trained sixteen intakes. But what had previously been achieved calmly over a period of years now had to be done while you wait, in the stifling heat, in the space of a few weeks. Besides that, up till now the raw material had been young men of similar ages and types, whereas these days nothing but old clapped-out recruits were being rushed in from all over the place.

The migration of Imperial and Royal peoples was already under way. Throughout the monarchy, reserve militia recruits were being transported from the mountains down to the plains, from the Carpathians to the Alps, from Dalmatia to Tyrol, from Galicia to Bosnia, to Bohemia and to Hungary. Some Hutsul transports had already proceeded from Andrásfalva to Styria. To replace the Hutsuls, about seventy Styrians had arrived. Mostly miners from the Knittelfeld region. The one-year volunteers, those "lawyers", as Bachmatiuk contemptuously referred to them, were despatched to their special training centres, and the sick and the malingerers were taken to hospital. Hundreds of healthy bodies, mostly peasants, were waiting down below for the privilege of being enrolled and given uniforms trimmed with the regimental colour, a beautiful orange. In peacetime, the "owner", that is to say the regimental commander, was a certain Balkan sovereign with whom the Imperial and Royal Monarchy was at war today. Despite this the regiment's name was unchanged. It could still afford the luxury of this courtesy. It continued to be the 10th Infantry Regiment of King N.

At the mention of King N, Bachmatiuk smiled. He had seen him during the great Imperial manoeuvres in 1904. King N had visited "his own" regiment at the time, along with His Majesty. Until the carriage stopped in front of the first company, who were the colour-bearers, it was difficult to identify who was the guest and who was the Emperor. Franz Joseph sat dressed in Balkan uniform with broad silver epaulettes, wearing a white fur hat with a red plume, while the Balkan ruler wore a shako and the full-dress tunic of an Imperial and Royal infantry colonel (with orange lapels and cuffs). Such masquerades used to be common before the war. They were part of the official routine of royal visits. Many foreign uniforms hung in the wardrobes at the Burgtheater and at Schönbrunn Palace. Intoxicated by the mothballs, they dreamt of bygone days of friendship between the crowned heads.

"What will they do now with all those enemy uniforms?" wondered Regimental Sergeant-Major Bachmatiuk when war broke out. "Will they return them or take them prisoner? It is uniforms, after all, that are taken prisoner, isn't it? It is of no consequence what bodies are wearing them. An Austrian in Serbian uniform is a Serb."

When war broke out, Bachmatiuk got drunk, although it was not a Sunday, but a Tuesday. At one point he thought he could see his Emperor, strolling in Balkan regalia on the streets of the Austrian garrison of Stanisławów. He was frightened, and began to shout so the whole tavern could hear: "Turn back, Your Majesty, take cover!" He very nearly got arrested by the gendarmerie.

Now he was sober. He was looking out on the world through the window of his cell. He made a rough estimate of the quality of the material from which he was obliged to produce a new battalion for the Emperor in the shortest possible time. The Emperor! Well what concern of his was the Emperor, actually? The army can exist and fight without the Emperor! Franz Joseph was the supreme leader, of course, a supreme god like Zeus on Olympus, but the RSM served a greater deity, invisible as Moira, the goddess of destiny before whom Olympus, with all its military might, trembled.

On the days of the migration of peoples it was very hot. As the War Ministry commanded, the most variegated species and the most multifarious kinds of human beings were cast into the melting-pot, elements whose fidelity had been tested along with elements of betrayal. The Ministry entrusted this difficult task to the respective units. Commanding officers were to decide for themselves which of the thousands of names stored for years in paper archives deserved to be trusted, and which should be transplanted to foreign, more reliable, lands. No commander got involved personally. This was what his adjutant was for.

However, predictably, our adjutant, Lieutenant Baron Hammerling, could not cope. He could not even pronounce the names of those whose fate he was supposed to determine. How, then, could he tell which of them sounded loyal and which sounded suspicious? In such cases, an honest adjutant does not rely on his own instincts but seeks the assistance of an experienced NCO. And that is what he did. Regimental Sergeant-Major Bachmatiuk requested alphabetical lists from the orderly room. Under each letter of the alphabet he selected at random a few names and marked them with a little red cross. Those marked with a cross answered "present" and left for Styria. What motivated Bachmatiuk's choices, and why he despatched Semen Baran and Telesfor Zwarycz, while he kept Izrael Glanz and Piotr Niewiadomski behind—that remains his personal secret.

Although they worked from morning until late evening in the orderly room (a few recruits with some education were requisitioned to fill in the regimental record books) Bachmatiuk was not satisfied. Registration dragged its feet as though there was no war on at all. It was difficult, of course, to sort matters out with this uncouth lot. Many of them arrived without their birth certificates and could not remember their parents' first names. One had to take their word for it that they really were who they said they were. But still, Bachmatiuk believed that registration and enlistment could have been completed two days earlier. Baron Hammerling cost the recruits two whole days. No surprise there, since he played the violin in the evenings instead of sitting in the orderly room working. He should have been made leader of a string orchestra, not a regimental adjutant. Out of all the new arrivals they only managed to enlist one company. As for the rest, they were spending their fifth day lazing about without taking a bath or getting de-loused, still in mufti. Living like that was bad for morale. There had even been reports of theft. If Captain Knauss had been alive, if he hadn't gone to the front, everything would have been different at the barracks. Captain Knauss's watchword was "tempo". He remained faithful to it until his death. And even the haste with which he died for the Emperor seemed to be merely a confirmation of this principle. Tempo, tempo! No sooner had he turned up at the front than he fell. Now Bachmatiuk had inherited all his principles.

He closed the window and removed the net from his smoothed black moustache. The tips were curled up to form the fine ornamental shape of a large shiny letter "W", like the German Emperor's monogram. He drank a cup of coffee, rolled a cigarette and glanced at the alarm clock. There was still time; he still had several minutes to himself before he needed to appear before anybody. Actually, he was hardly ever really alone. For many years, his deity had always accompanied him everywhere. It always crept after him, invisible, stalking him like a tiresome informer, spying on every thought, every word, every step. It even slunk into his dreams. From this deity he took refuge every Sunday in alcohol, hoping he would be out of its reach. No chance! It caught up with him in his drunken hallucinations, torturing him with remorse. It was as though his soul had been mangled by a mad dog; in this state Bachmatiuk returned to his cell. For years and years he wrestled with the deity; in the end, he surrendered meekly, dissolved himself in it and was lost. These days he was enslaved by Discipline; he was in love with it.

He spent hours enthralled by the fact that he was quite alone with the holy spirit of military service. He celebrated silent holy mass with the Regulations, and like any mystic found the greatest bliss in direct communion with the Mystery. Often, after midnight, when the entire barracks was asleep and the officers' mess was long since deserted and even Baron Hammerling's violin had fallen silent, the light was still on in the RSM's lonely cell. He lay in bed, reading. Not newspapers or comic strips like the other NCOs, but D.1 and D.2, those Old and New Testaments. Like a Talmudist, he leafed through the same old pages, for the hundredth and thousandth time, pondering over the same old statements, and sometimes he managed to get to the bottom of them. He was mainly attracted to difficult and intricate matters, inaccessible to average minds, but what gave him the most pleasure was the contemplation of elementary things. Such beauty was hidden in such seemingly simple commands as "Attention!", "Stand at ease!", "About turn!", "Company, quick march!", "Quick march!", "Slow march!", "At the double!", "Halt!" Any child can understand them, yet they are a mystery. How passionately Bachmatiuk immersed himself in the cavernous depths of "Attention!" The command to stand to attention transforms a man; it transforms a phalanx of men into a single dead vessel of obedience. "Attention!" means intense alertness, from which everything military, that is to say everything human, can be derived. When a man is standing to attention, you can fling him to the ground, you can tell him to run, kneel, throw himself into the water, to shoot, to stab, to trample! "Attention!" This is the golden key to understanding the history of nations!

For many years the Regulations were Bachmatiuk's only, and his favourite, reading matter. He was cultivating a pure army as some cultivate pure poetry. The army for its own sake. And although he knew by heart the primeval books of soldiery and understood their infallible, unfathomable content as no one else in the barracks did, he constantly read and re-read them, and each time he discovered some new truth, new revelations.

Knew them and understood them? Does that not sound like blasphemy? What mortals really know and understand D.1 and D.2? Not even generals or senior staff officers could make that claim. Nor officers in the War Ministry or the Ministry of National Defence! Not even Captain Knauss! And who knows whether the authors of the Regulations themselves, those fathers of the militant Imperial and Royal church, were capable of understanding everything written by their pens so endowed with grace? Certainly they were not, much less so a humble NCO in the regular army...

And even if he could grasp something or other with his feeble intellect, would it end there? Does understanding and fathoming the Regulations not mean living strictly according to them, carrying them out to the letter, blindly following every paragraph, every item? Day and night, in peacetime and in times of war, on land, on water and in the air? Oh perfection, you would be Rudolf Bachmatiuk's dream! You meant more to him than promotions and decorations. He dreamt of perfection as someone who was still far from achieving it. He did not know that he had gained it long since. For how else, if not by perfection, could he inspire such fear? He paralysed not only the soldiers, but the officers as well, and especially the officers of the reserve. They took great care lest they— God forbid—commit some blunder in his presence. He was dangerous, yet he was the one who before now had rescued many a second lieutenant from an embarrassing situation, as he knew everything and was never at fault. It was indeed a rare case in the history of discipline when a subordinate did not fear his superiors, but instead they feared him. The officers feared him—that's right, they feared him, because in their eyes he was the embodiment of all virtues, and nothing terrifies people so much as virtue.

He was proficient in everything to do with the infantry, as capable of handling the toughest combat missions as an old staff officer. His intelligence and powers of observation were alarming. He was an excellent marksman, bugler and drummer, and he could dismantle and reassemble a machine-gun in a few minutes. Crouching, squatting, side-stepping, adopting a firing position, holding the rifle butt when on parade— all this ought to be done as demonstrated by Bachmatiuk. Correctness personified, he was a living model, photographed for textbooks.

And his style, his fairness! He never wronged soldiers or favoured them; he had no prejudices and made no compromises. He never struck anyone or swore at them, never humiliated them or stooped to using foul language. On the other hand, his three hours of disciplinary exercises meant three full hours, not two hours and forty minutes! When he checked the fitting of the irons, not even the most lenient of corporals would dare, in his presence, to make them looser than the regulations prescribed. The recruits preferred to get a slap in the face and to hear the worst words of abuse rather than endure the cruel torture of his derision. When angered, he would invariably address the victim as "Your Grace", "Sir" or "Your Excellency". There was terrible power in his words. When he exclaimed: "I will make a man of you!" the poor creature thus addressed felt he had before him a veritable creator; he anticipated that dreadful things were about to happen, the ultimate events of the book of Genesis, that the Creation was about to begin. God the Father no longer came into it, because the RSM's small, swarthy, hairy finger emitted an electrical current capable of killing anything living and bringing it back to life. And when in a moment of great anger he approached the offender and—blanching—whispered in a hushed voice, virtually in his face: "My son, I will banish your soul!", that "son", the son of the earth, the son of a woman, knew for sure that he possessed a soul, for any moment he would lose it.

Such was the power Regimental Sergeant-Major Bachmatiuk seemed to possess. What was the source of this supernatural power, if it was not the Regulations? He made nothing up in his own imagination. Not even an enemy could accuse him of any arbitrary act. His every gesture, his every action, adhered strictly to one of the paragraphs D.1, D.2, or D.3. Everything had been devised, designed and calculated with such wise foresight! It was only thanks to the Regulations that the world took on some semblance of meaning, and life ceased to be a concatenation of blind fortune and fatal misunderstandings. These are not dead formulas without any practical application, but a rigorous, precise plan of existence, covering everything, absolutely everything from buttons and belts to death itself. Military death, Imperial and Royal death, as distinct from civilian death, was not considered a catastrophe even in peacetime. Thanks to paragraphs 702, 703, 717 and 718 D.1 any soldier could die calmly, neatly and safely, just as he had lived. All aspects of mortality in the army were accounted for as follows:

Diagram

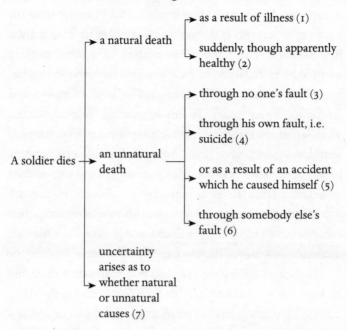

A soldier dies

a natural death
→ as a result of illness (1)
→ suddenly, though apparently healthy (2)

an unnatural death
→ through no one's fault (3)
→ through his own fault, i.e. suicide (4)
→ or as a result of an accident which he caused himself (5)
→ through somebody else's fault (6)

→ uncertainty arises as to whether natural or unnatural causes (7)

The procedure in cases 4, 5, 6, 7 was established by the War Ministry under a special regulation of 29th October 1910, Clause 14, no. 1416, appendix 39.

How could one fail to admire the Regulations, that Bible of Order, the only order in this vale of chaos leased out to civilians? Regimental Sergeant-Major Bachmatiuk could not understand why there were so many blind people in the world, so many befuddled people, whose eyes had to be opened by force. But those whose cataracts had been removed found themselves dazzled and sometimes they were admitted to the fount of light; they became candidates for promotion to the non-commissioned ranks. They learnt by heart the commandments and dogmas, and attempted to emulate their master. No one had yet managed it, however. If a saint is someone who obeys to the letter all the commandments and observes the letter of the canon, then Regimental Sergeant-Major Bachmatiuk was a saint. And like a true saint he regarded himself as a great sinner. He remembered his own sins, which people had long since forgiven and forgotten; he remembered them very clearly. He remembered all his lapses along the only path leading to perfection, the path of military duty. Several times during such a long service career he had been in detention, and his punishment had always been deserved. To this day, the detentions were a blot on his pristine copy-book. And how could he regard himself as perfect, when every Sunday he got roaring drunk and behaved in a manner inconsistent with the Regulations?

He glanced at the alarm clock: it was nearly six o'clock and in a moment he would have to go to meet the men. There down below, the early-morning hubbub of voices and the shrill whistling were growing louder, as the companies lined up by the barracks, ready to march out into the fields. From the dawdling stragglers now hurriedly joining the ranks came a rattle of iron. Again the day promised to be fine and hot. The bellowing from the Andrásfalva municipal abattoir was becoming continually more intrusive and more trenchant.

Bachmatiuk hurriedly finished his grooming. As every other morning, today he had managed to dye his old age. Banished from his face, it settled in his bones and his knees. But no one inspected his bones or his knees. He went to reach for his dark blue tunic, which had spent the night on a hanger. In the morning sunlight all its glory came to life. It sparkled with false and real silver, the sewn-on badges, gold medals and

stars glittering. Bachmatiuk reached for the daytime capari-
son of his corporeal ego and the row of medals and crosses
pinned to the breast of his cloth tunic chimed to announce
all Bachmatiuk's glory, all the toils of his life congealed in the
metal of his decorations.

For a moment, he stood gazing at his decorations. He
rarely studied them closely, but he never parted with those
medals. Today he was charmed by the flickering crosses on the
triangular coloured ribbons. This cross, a medal on a red-and-
white silk ribbon, featuring a bust of His Majesty, looked very
fine, but it was unimportant. Every soldier who was serving in
1908 received this memento from the monarch on the occasion of the latter's jubilee. Similarly, there was the medal for
the pointless mobilization against Serbia in 1912—it was of
no importance. Nor was the cross with a yellow ribbon with
black edging and Roman numerals on its face, announcing
to the world that Regimental Sergeant-Major Bachmatiuk
had served the Emperor faithfully for XXIV years, actually a
medal in the proper sense of the word. It was just a "military
service badge", first class. As to how Bachmatiuk had actually
served the Emperor for twenty-four years—well or badly—on
that score the cross was silent. Only the fourth decoration,
pinned in the place of honour, right over his heart, celebrated
Bachmatiuk's personal merit. This was the silver Cross of
Merit, with a crown. This was the prize for Bachmatiuk's
turning sixteen annual cohorts of recruits into men. That was
what his life's work looked like in effigy. A small cross made
of silver, coated with red enamel. In the middle was a silver
shield with some Latin inscription and Franz Joseph's initials,
the whole surmounted by the silver Austrian Habsburg crown.

Oh, arduous was the path Bachmatiuk had to follow before he won that cross. A true *Via Crucis*. Frequently he had fallen along the way; often he had been weighed down by the burden of the actions that were counted among his merits. But what of it? Crosses like these were also awarded to civilians in peacetime. Every postmaster, every tax-collector, every clerk, every veterinarian was eligible to receive the Silver Cross of Merit with a crown. And not only the silver one, but even the gold one.

Regimental Sergeant-Major Bachmatiuk was, without a doubt, on his way to the gold cross. No, he did not set great store by decorations. But when he stood face to face with his awards something tugged at his heart. The regimental tailor had left plenty of room on the breast of the RSM's tunic, and if it were to be occupied in the future by both of the crosses that it was possible to acquire—the small gold one and the large gold one (with a crown)—then how pale and false their glitter would be by comparison with the most modest of medals awarded for gallantry! Any of Bachmatiuk's louts, any of his illiterate recruits, the lowest of the low, could acquire the small silver medal, the large silver medal or the gold medal for gallantry! For a wound, for bravery in the face of the enemy, for bringing in a prisoner. But Bachmatiuk himself never could! A man who dedicated his life to the craft of war would never be able to see the face of the enemy! Why was it that he had to forego this honour? Was he physically handicapped? Mentally? Perhaps he was cowardly, and through some proposition made to his superiors he had gained entry to a category releasing him from front-line service? For sixteen years the regimental sergeant-major had held the office of regimental religious instructor. He conscientiously prepared young and old, Christians and Jews, for their baptism of fire. But religious instructors of other faiths must themselves be baptized. Otherwise they would not gain the trust of the catechumens and their fervour could arouse suspicion. Bachmatiuk had not been baptized. He knew about war only from hearsay and from the Regulations. He had smelt gunpowder only at the shooting range; he had never seen with his own eyes that death in the name of the Emperor for which he so skilfully trained thousands of his fellow men. He never would, even though he was as fit as an ox and assessed as "A1". He never would face it as long as Lieutenant-Colonel Alois Leithuber was commanding officer. He never would face it.

Bachmatiuk was not afraid of death. He was afraid of nothing that was provided for in the Regulations. To suggest that he was shirking from front-line duty would be despicable slander. He did not go to the front, but his conscience was clear. And not only in his own eyes—everyone at the barracks, from the lieutenant-colonel to the last recruit, considered it to be in order. Well, were pedigree bulls slaughtered in the Andrásfalva municipal abattoir? Did they slaughter stud stallions in the abattoirs? The regimental sergeant-major was also kept for purposes of insemination, for the breeding of new battalions. This was his historic mission. What would the Emperor have to gain from the death of the best instructor of recruits to King N's Imperial and Royal Infantry Regiment? It would be madness to lose such a powerful asset! It would be madness to give Bachmatiuk his marching orders, placing him in command of a platoon! Lieutenant-Colonel Leithuber was not crazy. Bachmatiuk was not only the most senior NCO and the best in the regiment. He was the only trusted man—indeed the only man at the barracks—Leithuber had known for a considerable length of time. The officers, the adjutant included, were all new people, reservists or regulars, transfers from other regiments or cadets fresh out of military college. Leithuber could not rely on anyone as he could on Bachmatiuk. That was why Bachmatiuk was not sent to the front line.

All at the barracks understood this. But the regimental sergeant-major was sometimes troubled by doubt, though he realized that he was indispensable to the barracks. He was often haunted by the call to battle which is the lot of a soldier in wartime. A soldier who has not experienced battle is like a woman withering in virginity. Why should he be the only one to wither in the barracks, in the Farkas and Gjörmeky brewery, while thousands of less worthy men were undergoing the baptism of fire for which he himself had prepared them? Bachmatiuk was tempted by martyrdom, although he was a martyr in the barracks too, a martyr to duty, to discipline and to perfection. Perfection! Can anyone achieve it who has not tasted all the events described in D.2 (Service in the Field)? Is it possible to achieve perfection in the way of duty without even once having been exposed to "unnatural death by the fault of another" (case no. 6)?

Today, like a gentle reminder of the deity, like a call from the netherworld, the peace medals chimed on Bachmatiuk's breast. It seemed to him that by comparison with the sound of gallantry medals they all had the ring of counterfeit coins.

At that moment he felt very old. He felt the weight of his whole life on his shoulders, bearing him down. It lasted only a second, but that second encapsulated dozens of years spent on the barracks square. Immediately Bachmatiuk called himself to order with the basic command to himself: "Attention!" He stood bolt upright, fastened the buttons on his tunic, one by one, pulled it straight and adjusted it. He sighed like an old man no longer battling against time and not dyeing his moustache. Simultaneously, he gestured with his hand as though waving temptation aside.

He donned his cap, stiffened his posture, glanced in the mirror, tweaked his moustache a little and went out, banging the door after him. In the long, dark corridor he never met anyone except the two shoe-shiners. The officers were still asleep, but the sergeants were already down below. Bachmatiuk descended the steps with the heavy, uneven tread of an old civilian. To start with, he even leant on the hand-rail.

There were already large numbers of people gathered on the first floor. A large group of civilians was waiting outside the sick-bay waiting to be examined. In the charge of the duty corporal, a dozen or so soldiers without cartridge belts or bayonets were standing around. These were men from the battalion who had reported sick. At the sight of the regimental sergeant-major the men reporting sick quickly stepped aside to make way for him. Bachmatiuk had rejuvenated his gait, putting a spring into his step. His eyes, which had been somewhat dull up on the second floor, now took on a cold glint. Signs of weariness in his face disappeared as the tension in his facial muscles smoothed out the wrinkles.

The appearance of the regimental sergeant-major had a healing effect on the men reporting sick. A blush came over the faces of the sufferers. But the malingerers turned pale. The mere sight of Bachmatiuk banished their hypochondria. He looked at no one and spoke to no one, scarcely acknowledging the salutes. Lieutenant Baron Hammerling, adjutant to the garrison commander, suddenly hastened by. As they saluted one another simultaneously, the Baron smiled. Bachmatiuk respectfully let him pass, but did not return the smile. He now proceeded down the steps in such a dignified and commanding manner as if he were marching at the head of an entire company. But there was not a single soldier following him; he was alone on the steps. At the moment he emerged through the gateway and stood in the full light of the sun he might almost have been a young man. Perhaps this is an exaggeration, but Regimental Sergeant-Major Bachmatiuk down there on duty was certainly a different man from the Bachmatiuk at home upstairs.

Chapter Ten

For a long time now, Piotr Niewiadomski had been unable to fathom how it could be that his regiment, the Imperial and Royal regiment, the Austro-Hungarian regiment, which swore allegiance to His Majesty Franz Joseph, belonged to a Balkan king. After all, was that king not at war with His Imperial Majesty? If that is so, why is the regiment not fighting on the side of its owner?

Piotr Niewiadomski was also an owner. He had half of a house, half of an orchard and a dog. A fine thing it would be if Bass bit him, Piotr, instead of attacking strangers and enemies! Unless he had rabies! This whole matter smacked powerfully of the devil. Another of the many mysterious tricks that he played on people in this war. Who knows, he might tell them to shoot themselves instead of shooting Serbs and Muscovites. Clever people like Hryć Łotocki or Semen Baran would probably have managed to unravel this mystery. But Hryć Łotocki had stayed behind in Topory, and Semen Baran had gone to Styria. And so, left to his own devices, Piotr Niewiadomski once again became caught up in a snare left by the devil. Everywhere the devil sowed fear and it was futile to take flight; the efforts of a poor soul expelled to Hungary were in vain. Fortunately, this war cared more for bodies than for souls. It prepared them for its own needs, changing their appearance to suit its requirements.

Since early morning, scissors had been chattering. Those with beards had to lay them on the altar of the homeland. Thanks to the resourcefulness of hospital orderly Lance Corporal Glück, that altar had been erected in one of the brewery sheds. Only the most pious Jews were permitted by the Emperor to retain a small Spanish goatee. Side-locks were mercilessly removed! The Chasidim were seeing themselves in a mirror for the first time in their lives. Lance Corporal Glück (a barber in civilian life) had bought it with his own money. Now he was cutting hair and shaving officially, so he was unpaid. Some orthodox Jews, horrified, closed their eyes so as not to see their reflection. To see your own face was a great sin, because God created it in his image and likeness.

Under the scissors, gloomy, enigmatic Asia disappeared; tragic antiquity perished, and the first outlines of Europe emerged on the pallid faces, revealed for the first time in many years, as if dredged up from the sea bed. But it was not only the Jews who had their hair cut; it was Christians as well. It fell from their heads, from their chins and from their faces onto their shoulders, their backs, onto the floor, into the dust, dark and fair, straight and curly, Catholic and Jewish all mixed together, though it is written, clearly written, that except by the will of God not one hair of your head shall fall.

Piotr Niewiadomski sat on a stool, stiff and solemn as a bishop. The clippers no. 0 travelled up and down, backwards and forwards across his head like a harvesting machine over a field of wheat. That was the first harvest of the war, from his own scalp. He was not sitting in front of the mirror and he did not see the devastation done to his head. But he was highly amused by the heads of his colleagues. Half of the head looked like a kneecap, while the other half was like a haystack. It was reminiscent of the sheep-shearing back home. But what did the Emperor want with all this human hair? Was it for stuffing mattresses, perhaps?

After they had had their haircuts, they were ordered to go to the barracks to stuff mattresses. No, not with their own hair but with fresh Hungarian straw. Piotr had been allocated a place to sleep on a bunk-bed in barracks hut no. 4. The day before, they had been issued with straw-filled pillows. Piotr deposited his trunk, all his possessions, on the bed. This was where he would be sleeping now, from lights-out till reveille. Until they got their marching orders to proceed to the front, this is where he would be spending the nights, between two companions. They were separated by a narrow gap of just a few inches. In fact, it was a matter of kilometres or miles, because on the left he had been given some Pole as a neighbour, a count's butler, and on the right a Styrian, a Kraut.

The sweat standing out on his brow, Piotr stuffed his mattress with dry, rustling straw, the leftovers from the Hungarian harvest. He looked kindly on this Hungarian straw. It would soothe all the injustices done to him during the day, absorbing the sweat of his brow and the anxiety in his soul. Perhaps they would be living in the barracks for just a short time. Perhaps the war would really be over in a few days' time, and not last till Christmas? Why would it not end, since Austria had already defeated Russia at Kraśnik? Piotr was weighing up the odds like a card-player. Once you win a game, collect your money and get off home! No need to tempt fate! The second time round you can lose everything! What a surprise that will be for Magda! Bass will jump for joy! Piotr reached into his pocket and felt the cold iron. It was still there; he hadn't lost it. He had not lost the key to his house, the key to their hopes.

He stuffed away, not grudging his pallet any straw. He wanted the mattress to be nice and firm. In any case, it would settle down later.

Suddenly Bachmatiuk appeared. Piotr had already got used to his appearance. The terror of the barracks had so far not made any great impression on him. A burly character, clearly, and morose, but then not so strict. He ignored the civilians. Actually, Bachmatiuk found them somehow repellent. He was ill at ease in their presence. He did not look at them. Could it be that civilian dress intimidated him so much? He would chat only to people in uniform.

"What am I known for?"

Corporal Reszytyło, in charge of a group of recruits, kept silent.

"I said, what am I known for?"

"It is known that you are not to be taken lightly, Regimental Sergeant-Major, sir."

"Why did you permit smoking near the straw, Reszytyło, against my orders?"

"I did not see it, Regimental Sergeant-Major, sir."

"What are your eyes for, Corporal?"

Without waiting for an answer, he disappeared. Corporal Reszytyło flew into a rage, insulting the mothers of the recruits and stubbornly repeating his question—who was smoking? He got no response. The silence among the crowd of strangers infuriated him still more. The crowd had the advantage over him. Again he insulted their mothers. It was no use. Breathing heavily, silent as the grave, they packed the straw into the mattresses in the ever more intense heat.

"You'll pay for this! You'll pay for every day I'm detained in the stinking cells because of you sodding recruits. You can be sure of that!"

The "sodding recruits", covered in sweat and caked with dirt and straw, were afraid. As though it was a form of defence against the repayment Corporal Reszytyło had promised them, they hid behind the huge pallets. They lifted them onto their freshly shaved heads and onto their backs and scurried, cowering, into the huts. Piotr Niewiadomski was beginning to understand the threat posed by Bachmatiuk. He did not personally shout or swear himself, or do anyone any harm. But he aroused anger in his subordinates.

So the Hutsuls assigned to barracks hut no. 4, along with a few Styrians, recognized in Acting Corporal Ivan Reszytyło their first enemy in this war.

Before he can wear a uniform, a man has to take a bath to purify his body, as must a bride before she receives the bridegroom. Led by Corporal Reszytyło, they proceeded to the baths, which were set up in a special hut attached to the kitchen block. Space was restricted, so they entered in groups, while the rest waited outside. Suffocating clouds of steam billowed from the open doors as from the boiler of an invisible locomotive. Wild laughter, shrieks and hoots were heard. Strange things were going on in the bath-house. From time to time all other sounds were lost among the mighty roar of the waterfall. When Piotr Niewiadomski went in, at first he could see nothing. A heavy damp mist filled the room, which was already quite dark. Only after the noise ceased, the mist dispersed and Piotr Niewiadomski saw a crowd of wet, naked bodies. They were panting and snorting and leaping about on the wet boards, slapping their backsides to shake off the water.

Piotr had never been in a bath-house before. He could only imagine bathing in a river. He had also heard that gentlemen in big houses in towns would wash in their own baths. Here there was no bath, just boards underfoot, or perhaps they were ladders. Rusty iron pipes above your head. That was all. But where was the water? Some older man in a white coat such as a doctor would wear, with a trimmed grey beard, was in charge here. Perhaps he was a doctor? Corporal Reszytyło issued the order to undress and step onto the boards. Piotr undressed, untroubled by any sense of embarrassment. His embarrassment gradually got lost in the army. Piotr was very curious about these Imperial baths. But he did not know what to do—should he lie down on the boards or sit on them?

"Come on! Get under the water! Don't be afraid!" squawked the white-coated man in a wheezy voice. "Into the *mikveh*! Into the *mikveh*!" he laughingly taunted the Jews.

He was no doctor or even an NCO, just an unarmed category "C" private. He was distinguished from other reserve militia privates by a thin yellow stripe on his sleeves, the so-called "intelligence stripe" or "toilet badge", guaranteeing exemption from certain tasks such as cleaning the toilets. This Imperial and Royal badge was given to older reserve militia men without a secondary school certificate, but who followed a civilian profession requiring "intelligence". This distinction was accorded especially to owners of larger enterprises, industrialists, merchants and landowners. The man in the white coat was called Izydor Parawan. He fulfilled light duties in the barracks and he enjoyed considerable privileges. He was the owner of one of the most popular venues in Stanisławów. Many officers of the regiment were among its regular customers. His "light" duties, in addition to those of bath attendant, involved assisting in the sick-bay during the weekly sanitary inspections known as "dick parades".

"Move along! Move along! Don't be shy of the water!" he shouted to the peasants and Jews, finding their hesitation amusing.

"Now, young ladies! Susannas in the bath! No one is peeping at you, you don't have to hide your charms! Fine flesh, fine flesh, healthy cannon-fodder! All steaks for the Russian artillery! I'll prepare you a Diana's bath in no time."

And he vanished behind a wooden partition like an executioner preparing the electric chair. Piotr found him extremely disconcerting. He felt sure he was the devil in a white coat. That grey beard, his incomprehensible yelling, his horrible laugh... hopefully he wouldn't drown them!

Suddenly, warm rain gushed from the wooden ceiling. Streaming from imperceptible holes in the pipes, thin but sharp jets of water sprayed heads and bodies like so many whips. The men cringed in terror beneath the sluices. Some even lay on the boards, convinced that the water from the pipes would fill the whole room and that they would be swimming in it. Their fear soon gave way to laughter. The bath was not at all bad; it was very pleasant. But suddenly the water changed. From warm it turned to cold. Brr... Only the devil could cast a spell on the water like that in the blink of an eye. And the devil in the white coat emerged from his hiding place, laughing, laughing away through his jagged teeth, rubbing his hands and shrieking loudly, trying to make himself heard above the noise:

"Well? Nice bath? Not a single louse left on you! Word of honour! Fine flesh! Dry yourselves and get dressed! Next lot!"

You couldn't tell whether he was joking or whether he was angry. He was the devil, wasn't he?

This way, the men's bodies were cleansed, and not only of bodily uncleanliness. Beneath the artificial rain, all the impurity of their former civilian life was removed from these people. The bath restored lost innocence to bodies and souls. But their feet kneaded the thick mud. The black pastry of the devil.

Although he had been given a haircut and a bath, Piotr Niewiadomski still hoped he would not be going to war, because they seemed to be in no hurry with the uniforms. That same morning they had received their first pay. For ten days. In addition, each man received six crowns for the purchase of necessary supplies—thread, soap, brushes, boot polish, flax and grease for their weapons. Regimental Sergeant-Major Bachmatiuk was present at the pay-out by barracks hut no. 1. He sat at the table with the NCO paymaster and another NCO. He was checking the payroll. One of the NCOs called out the names. Another's deft fingers felt in the little canvas bags and arranged the coins in piles, occasionally reaching into a green wire basket for the paper money. It was hard to work out why he gave one soldier the amount he was due straight away, while he gave another one a large banknote to be shared among two or three of them. The Hutsuls stepped aside and counted their money out loud, as they would do at market, passing it from hand to hand, making mistakes and arguing. These calculations were not easy.

Here was the Emperor giving himself away, in greater and lesser denominations, to those who were to give their lives for him.

"This is bad!" thought Piotr Niewiadomski, taking the money.

"They're paying us, so they won't be letting us go." The clinking of silver and nickel coins drowned out the last hopes of a speedy return home. Piotr was surprised that the Emperor, whom he considered a good player, was still trying his luck instead of calling it a day after the great victory of Kraśnik.

"What are you waiting for?" snapped the sergeant at the table, when Piotr, instead of moving away, stood there lost in thought.

The sergeant did not know that Piotr Niewiadomski was waiting for the war to end.

Bachmatiuk suddenly leapt to his feet, knocking over a chair, and briskly walked in the direction of the regimental headquarters. He had heard a familiar clatter on the main road. In a cloud of dust, a carriage drawn by two graceful bays was arriving at the main building. Adjutant Baron Hammerling dashed out through the gateway, but Bachmatiuk beat him to it. Saluting almost simultaneously, they stood before the carriage, from which an impressive-looking, well-built officer was just stepping out in a tall peaked cap. Despite the heat, he wore a long black cape, picturesquely folded. It covered his arms. He quickly freed one arm from under the cloak—the left, and returned the salute. The adjutant wanted to help him down.

JÓZEF WITTLIN

"No thank you, I am not that old."

He really did not look old, despite his grey hair. He had the fresh, shapely, clean-shaven features of an actor, with grey sideburns, one of those Austrian faces that so effectively combine features of the Latin, Germanic and Slav races. Thick black eyebrows. Something of the Roman and a hint of "old Vienna" in Colonel Leithuber's general appearance created the type much sought after in later years by film studios.

The regimental commanding officer resided in Andrásfalva, at the Hotel Hungaria on the market square. He came to visit the regiment in a carriage belonging to the battalion, sometimes earlier in the day, sometimes later, depending on how soon he managed to read all the Viennese daily newspapers in the Café Budapest.

On stepping out of the carriage, he exchanged a few words with the adjutant, then with Bachmatiuk, who spoke perfect German, after which he made straight for his office, his spurs jingling. Bachmatiuk did not return to the paymaster's table. He looked in on the sick-bay to check how many of those reporting sick had been confirmed by the doctor as indeed being ill, and he went upstairs to his office. Without removing his cap, he sat down on the bed and looked through the papers, preparing material for his daily conference with the lieutenant-colonel.

The lieutenant-colonel's conversations with Bachmatiuk would have been on a perfectly sincere basis if Alois Leithuber had had it in him to be honest with himself. The discussions with the RSM were held mostly face-to-face, which of itself indicated a need for sincerity. Actually, they were

290

not conversations but monologues for two voices. Leithuber expressed out loud all the doubts that troubled him, and he resolved them with Bachmatiuk's help. When he had something to reproach himself with or when he was dissatisfied with himself, he shouted at Bachmatiuk. The latter put up with it all, obediently and calmly, but he often had objections. He knew that he was the only man at the barracks who had not only the right but indeed the duty to disagree with the commanding officer. The officers, who were all uninitiated newcomers, always shared the views of their commandant. But Leithuber did not consider himself the infallible oracle by any means. To be able to give orders with a clear conscience, he needed someone who would raise doubts. Whenever Bachmatiuk suggested something that was contrary to his—Leithuber's—wishes, the lieutenant-colonel looked away, but actually he pricked up his ears at the same time.

There he sat, behind his desk, gazing at a photograph of a lady with an elegant coiffure. The desk-top concealed his massive torso, and his arms were hidden.

"That's impossible," Bachmatiuk was insisting in his calm, hoarse voice, which sounded as though it was scorched. "The battalion will not be able to set off at the beginning of September. The machine-gun crews are not yet ready... Lieutenant Lewicki..."

Leithuber suddenly slammed his left hand down on the table so hard that the lady with the elegant coiffure fell on her back. He picked her up and carefully put her back where she belonged, appearing to give her an apologetic look. But he could not control his rage. What angered him was that he trusted Bachmatiuk's judgement better than his own. Whenever he felt that he had to concede, he flew into a rage and pounded the table with his left hand.

He had no control over the right arm. It had long since been withered. On account of this he never removed his black leather gloves in front of anyone. The colonel found this disability no less humiliating than his dependence on the RSM. He never appeared before his men without the cape. He also avoided situations where he would be obliged to turn up with his sabre unsheathed. The disabled right arm was wonderfully compensated for by his left. Not only did it take over all the functions of his right arm, but it did so with a kind of super-efficiency. Leithuber used his left arm for saluting, eating and writing. His handwriting was very elegant and legible. The orders issued daily by the barracks command in ten cyclostyled copies, bore his clearly written signature:

Leithuber, Col.

With his left hand he could fire a pistol and he could probably manage to handle his sabre, but somehow it did not seem appropriate to wear it on his right side. What made the greatest impression, however, was his left-handed slaps. To get a right-handed slap in the face was something to be expected. But when Leithuber struck you with his left hand, while his right hand was dead as the dodo, dangling under his cloak, this was something incredible, something contrary to nature. Actually, the lieutenant-colonel was a kindly man, benign in the way some tumours are. But he often got carried away and lost his self-control.

His right hand was, literally, Bachmatiuk. Although they were roughly of equal age, the RSM behaved like an old clerk towards his young boss.

"Colonel," he explained, "we work from six to eleven, and from two to five. The men get exhausted. In this heat you can't do more… Night exercises twice a week—"

"You can! You can!" interjected the lieutenant-colonel. "You have to! High command informs us that the general will be inspecting at the end of the month!"

"With respect, sir, may I request that you give the order to work from five to twelve and from two till seven?…"

They were both aware that such an order was impossible, being contrary to the regulations regarding working hours in summer. Leithuber glanced at the photograph, then he changed his tone and changed the subject. Now he wanted to explore Bachmatiuk's views about his decision to send Captain Slavíček to the front. He wanted to get rid of this captain, because he could not stand Czechs. His dislike of Czechs went back to his childhood. The family house was in a working-class district of Vienna and it was attached to a wine bar owned by the lieutenant-colonel's father Johann, popularly known as Leithuber-Johnny. Leithuber-Johnny was a member of the Christian-Social Party and he venerated Mayor Lueger… In the noisy arguments with customers around little green tables covered with red-and-white chequered tablecloths, he predicted the imminent fall of the monarchy at the hands of the Czechs and the socialists. Leithuber's son (Leithuber-Al) became convinced of the accuracy of his father's predictions many years later, on the outbreak of the infamous *zde* affair. Czech reservists were unwilling to announce their presence

in German: *"Hier!"*, calling out in their own language: *"Zde!"*
This scandal echoed loudly round the walls of the neoclassical
Parliament. He could not forgive the Czechs for 1912. During
that partial mobilization, reservists in the Czech infantry
regiments—the Imperial and Royal 18th, the Imperial and
Royal 36th, and the 8th Regiment of Dragoons—had openly
mutinied.

"Captain Slavíček," respectfully remarked Bachmatiuk,
"is a professional officer. He has served in the regiment for
eighteen years, without a break. Captain Castelli came to us
out of retirement. I don't know what he did previously. With
my own ears I heard him utter an obsolete command that is
no longer in the regulations. It was used back in the days of—"

"I said Captain Slavíček will leave with the battalion while
Captain Castelli will be in charge of the recruits. That's that
and there is no more to be said!"

"Yes sir!"

Bachmatiuk clicked his heels, took out his notebooks and
began giving a detailed report of everything that had taken
place at the barracks during the last twenty-four hours. In this
way, as he did every morning, he confidentially conveyed the
most important information to his commanding officer. As
he listened to Bachmatiuk, the lieutenant-colonel occasionally
jotted down names and numbers on a separate pad. Bachmatiuk
reported every incident. Yesterday, around eleven at night,
he had passed by the guardhouse and looked in through the
window. It turned out that the commander of the guard had
been asleep. This morning in the baths a certain Jew had felt sick.

"It's amazing what sort of human material they're sending
us now!" he complained, like an estate steward to the heir.

The recruits' state of health was of no interest to the lieu-tenant-colonel. It was a matter for the doctors.

"Pachmatiuk!"—Leithuber pronounced his "B"s, in his Viennese accent, as "P"s. "See to it that you get me all the recruits into uniform by tomorrow. Done and dusted! I will attend the swearing-in."

"Yes sir!"

Someone knocked at the door. It was the adjutant—with two bulky folders. He also had sideburns, but they were black, shiny as satin. And a moustache to match.

"Pachmatiuk, dis—miss!"

Bachmatiuk saluted both superiors in turn, then he left.

Leithuber disliked the adjutant. For a start, he was offended by the title of "Baron", though he derived considerable satis-faction from the fact that the son of a bar-keeper had "under him" someone high-born, even born in one of those romantic feudal castles perched like birds' nests on top of wild rocks, to the delight of passengers on the Vienna–Venice railway line. He was offended by the baron's appearance. A fop. Shirker in the barracks, son-in-law of some influential field marshal in the War Ministry, wearing field uniform as though he was leaving with the battalion this very day. Instead of medals he wore thin ribbons, covering the stars on the collar with a silk handkerchief, so they would not accidentally be revealed to the enemy he was never going to meet. Leithuber could not bear comedy and pretence. He ostentatiously wore peacetime uniform. He did not conceal his gold collar. He also disliked the adjutant for his affected manner of speech. No, he could not swallow it! Why had they sent this dandy to the Galician regiment, not understanding a word of Polish or Ukrainian?

But speaking fluent French! There was not a single Frenchman in the regiment. There were no Frenchmen in the entire Imperial and Royal Army. Even in conversations with him—with Leithuber—he used French expressions. *En attendant!*... On one occasion, Leithuber could not stand it any longer and he yelled in his face:

"*Am attandan*, Lieutenant, I don't think it is right for an Austrian officer to speak to his superior in the language of a nation with whom we are at war!" Lieutenant-Colonel Leithuber could not speak French.

Today the baron turned up once more in battledress. In a voice quivering with submissiveness, he reported on all the day's occurrences, presenting paper after paper for signature, and finally reading out the draft orders of the day. Reluctantly, Leithuber listened to him. At Item 6, he lost patience, interrupting the adjutant and ordering him to find a pencil and take down, in shorthand:

"It has come to my attention that some guard commanders, guard commanders—are asleep while on duty in the guardroom. I order, no—I draw attention to the fact that it is a serious offence, punished severely—severely punished, not as a disciplinary matter but according to the code of war. If anything similar occurs again, the offender will be immediately brought before the divisional court. Divisional. Full stop. Let no one think that I can be deceived. I can—are you taking this down?—I can see everything and I forgive nothing. Full stop.

Item 7. PENALTIES. As of today, I impose the following penalties on the following NCOs and privates—you will fill in the names yourself, but please write clearly, so the typists make no mistakes. Names have been misspelt in the orders several times before. When I pointed this out to Sergeant Kandl, he reported that they transcribed the adjutant's shorthand accurately in the orderly room. Where did you learn your shorthand, Lieutenant? In the conservatoire?"

A delicate allusion to the baron's violin-playing, which Leithuber hated. At each gathering in the mess, it was always the same pieces: Schumann's 'Träumerei', Chopin's Nocturne no. 2, and *Si j'étais roi*. Like a lovelorn cadet at the military academy.

"Please take this down: Item 8. ASSIGNMENTS. As of today, Captain Erwin Castelli is assigned to the 1st Battalion and will enter the field as commander of the second company. Command of the battalion recruits will be assumed by Captain Jaroslav Slavíček... have you got that, Lieutenant?— Jaroslav."

Can you imagine a war conducted in frock-coats, jerkins, kaftans, ties, bowler hats and Jewish skull-caps? No, not even Piotr Niewiadomski could imagine such a war. He clearly understood that you were only allowed to kill a man when wearing uniform, and death in the name of the Emperor only counts if bodies are packaged in the official state wrapping and intact. You see, besides his monopoly in tobacco and salt, the Emperor also had a monopoly in the killing of people. But God created man in his own image and likeness, so the Emperor too gave men a uniform in order to create at least some likeness. Of course, there was a great difference between the uniform of the Emperor himself and that which Piotr Niewiadomski was to wear today. Yes, but there was also a good deal of difference between those two mortals.

Ah, what fine caps and costumes people have worn as they die for their kings and emperors! They have died in all colours, in iron armour, and in shining coats of mail. They have snuffed it in helmets, in busbies, in enormous headgear the size of wine jugs with glittering brass plates, in capes and helmets sporting birds' feathers or horsehair. And so that a private could not be distinguished from his comrades in the regiment, so that he totally lost the appearance he had in the world as a son, a father and a husband, emperors ordered military tailors to make the same caps, the same tunics and the same trousers for everyone in the regiment. The only regret they had was that they could not convert all the faces to conform to a single model.

But long gone were the days when a foot soldier went to his death immaculate, colourful and resplendent as a peacock. Now, emperors were more concerned with hiding infantry-men from the eyes of the enemy than dazzling those eyes with a fine uniform. So everywhere armies adopted uniforms that were grey, matching the earth or the sand. They had the illusion that this way they would manage to fool the enemy and their long-range field glasses. In their concern for the life of the soldier they tried to make him look like the Mother Earth he was supposed to defend with his body. But Mother Earth has more colours than the cloth dyers have dreamt of. If only they could come up with a material that changed like opal, according to all the colours of the terrain and all the seasons! Now white as the snow, now yellow like the stubble, now grey-blue like the forest or colourless like water. Who knows, perhaps not a single Hutsul would die in the war. But what kind of war would that be, in which no Hutsuls perished?

However, the most garish colour of all—red—was not immediately banished from the Imperial and Royal Army. In the first months of the war they kept it on the trousers of the Uhlans and the Hussars—to let them enjoy it for a while longer. But when this speeded up the wiping out of the cavalry, red was completely banned in the army and from then on red was represented only by blood. It would be untrue to say that all soldiers were immediately dressed in field uniforms. In Andrásfalva, for example, the reserve militia received old castoffs from their predecessors to wear during training. The issuing of uniforms was a ritual carried out under the super-vision of Regimental Sergeant-Major Bachmatiuk.

Before Piotr Niewiadomski's eyes there opened up stores containing everything due to him from the Emperor. A soldier consisted of a tunic, trousers, an overcoat, boots, a rifle, belt, two cartridge pouches, a bayonet, knapsack, haversack, spade (or pickaxe), bowl, flasks, two blankets, one canvas tent sheet, a large quantity of straps, and himself. Oh, and a cap. Without a cap, he was almost a cripple, he was like a lamp without a shade, a stem without a blossoming crown.

The barracks clothing store was stacked to the ceiling with shelving full of grey-blue and dark blue uniform garments. All this cloth smelt of malt barley, because the store was set up in the former brewery malt house. With a long pole ending in a fork, the storekeeper reached for the uniforms and cast them on the ground. In a fragrant cloud of dust, cloth legs and cloth sleeves descended, birds of cloth one just like another, thread for thread, button for button. The old tunics had orange squares on the collars; the new ones had only a narrow braid showing the colour of the regiment. The recruits casually tried on the Imperial uniform, but some pulled faces; this was too wide, this was too tight. They were behaving as though they had paid for these uniforms to be made to measure. Pious Jews recoiled from putting on old sweaty trousers and smelly caps. Who knows what the previous owners had put in their pockets as they crawled about? Perhaps they were getting all this from men who had fallen in the war?

Bachmatiuk stood to one side, staring at the empty uniforms. He cast a loving eye over the most beautiful creation to come from the tailors' shears. An empty infantry uniform was dearer to him than the man who was to wear it. He begrudged each item taken away by some dolt. He begrudged Piotr Niewiadomski the uniform he was trying on. He stood gazing at the piles of tunics, coats and trousers and the pyramid of caps, as if giving them his blessing.

They collected more or less everything from this store that was due to them from the Emperor, throwing the whole load over their shoulders, then they set off, following Bachmatiuk.

A thousand rifles with fixed bayonets in dull sheaths awaited them in the murky arsenal. They lay in rows on the shelves—quiet, innocent, sleeping. But the tawny barrels and rusty butts glinted disturbingly. How powerless were rifles without human hands! Now the hands were reaching out that would extract the roar of death from this mute iron. Slowly, slowly! Regimental Sergeant-Major Bachmatiuk watched intently as the platoon gunsmith handed the weapons to the recruits, recording a number against each name. If a uniform was dearer to Bachmatiuk than the man, what then of a rifle, the chief organ of the infantryman, more important than his heart and his brain! For Bachmatiuk people did not exist;

there were only annual intakes, material that was cheaper than the Mannlichers produced in Steyer at over 100 crowns apiece. And what was a man in comparison with a Mannlicher, and even an old Werndl that lives longer than a man? That is why Bachmatiuk became so indignant when people said of a regiment that it consisted of three thousand soldiers. An infantry regiment is made up of three thousand rifles, a cavalry regiment of two thousand sabres.

Piotr Niewiadomski received a Mannlicher and bayonet no. 46 821. He knew his numbers, but such a long number, engraved on the flintlock and on the hilt of the bayonet, was not easy to make out. As for memorizing it, that was out of the question. Piotr had not yet had to deal with such large numbers. His salary on the railway was 15 crowns, the signal box where he worked as substitute signalman bore the number 86. And now all of a sudden forty-six thousand eight hundred and twenty-one. Such a powerful number associated with his person filled him with pride and he felt more important than before, but at the same time he realized that from that moment he was no more than an additional property of the number 46 821. This weapon was not new. Many others must have made use of the number 46 821 before Piotr. God knows if they are still alive. And if God permits you to come back from the war with a healthy weapon, you have to give it back to the armoury; let it rest, let it have a good sleep—until the next war. Yes, Piotr himself felt that the weapon was more important than he was. Wagons were also more important; they too had big numbers written on them.

"How many dead bodies can all these weapons cause?" he asked himself, looking at the hundreds of rifles in the hands of the recruits. Five thousand? Ten? He was reminded of the Hutsul legend of self-firing rifles and of weapons inside which the ghosts of those who had been shot would hide. And suddenly ghosts began to circle round beneath the vaulted ceiling of the murky brewery cellar. Silently they swooped down, catching hold of arms and snatching at legs. Phantoms emerged from the darkness, arms pulled elongated grains of lead out from torn breasts, bellies and foreheads, pleadingly offering them to Piotr. Piotr was terrified, thinking that the Hungarian brewers Farkas and Gjörmeky were not brewers but devils, and that it was not beer that they stored here, bitter beer made from hops and barley, but blood.

Piotr expected that when they issued the rifles they would give them ammunition as well. Obviously, he had never served in the army. Who would give recruits live cartridges? And not only recruits! In this armoury there was no ammunition anyway. There are no barracks where firearms are held alongside their little leaden souls. This cruel separation would not end until they were at the front.

Laden like a mule, Piotr returned to his hut. "Piotr, Piotr, what will you look like now? Your own mother will not recognize you! Wasylina Niewiadomska!"

Under the supervision of the NCOs, they began changing into their uniforms. When they took off their civilian clothes, there was a moment similar to that separating night and daybreak. Day is not yet day but night is no longer night. So it was with the men; they were no longer civilians, but not yet soldiers either. The human being passed from one form to another, like a caterpillar turning into a butterfly. Some regretted parting with civilian life, but many cast it off gladly.

They all had to pack up their belongings and attach tickets with names and addresses and take them to a warehouse for safekeeping. Those who believed in God felt the bitter truth that he alone knew how many of them would reclaim their bundles. Piotr Niewiadomski believed in God but he could not write. He asked a comrade to do it, but first he retrieved the key to the cottage from his trouser pocket, and together with his money and a dried plum transferred it to his army pouch. He did not miss his civilian clothes. He was sorry about his railway cap, but as for the soldier's cap, that was the Emperor's as well. Maybe even more so.

They were also issued with state underwear, but those who wanted to could wear their own underneath the state issue. Waistcoats were not confiscated. The military did not stick its nose into what is beneath the uniform. As long as everything looked uniform on the surface.

The draft of peasants, shepherds, miners and traders was soon converted into soldiers. The glaring differences that had divided the men until now were gone. Hutsuls were no longer Hutsuls, Jews were not Jews. Old men looked a little younger in the Imperial disguise, moving like teddy bears in billowing pantaloons or like village lads in their fathers' short kaftans. A major change also came about in their souls. They were no longer the same people. Suddenly they became childish and they began to pay attention to trivialities like buttons and straps. The NCOs now began explaining to them the purpose of each strap and each flap. For everything on the soldier, every part of his accoutrement, has a serious purpose; no button is superfluous, every centimetre is part of a careful design. One thing connects to another—the knapsack covered with furry calf hide to the cartridge pouches, the cartridge pouches to the bandolier.

Only now did Regimental Sergeant-Major Bachmatiuk take cognizance of them. Only now that they were all wearing the same uniform was he struck by their memorable individual features. He made careful mental notes of their faces and bodies, which from now on he would be permitted to mock openly. The defects or unwitting physical absurdities of his fellow men would no longer be tolerated. He saw Piotr too, whom he had not noticed before even when he was wearing his railwayman's cap. He looked him up and down with undisguised contempt. He despised the new cohort, even though they were now in uniform. And suddenly they were all gripped by fear. Until then, fear had been something external; now it settled within them. It penetrated into their bodies from the coarse fibres of the uniforms. They all felt that this fragrant apparel smelling of malt consigned them to death. A miracle had occurred; this undrilled crowd had been overtaken by Discipline. It crept into their bones, mingling with the marrow and stiffening their movements. It even altered their voices.

Until late at night in the barracks the NCOs taught them how to walk properly, how to fold their coats and make their beds. They were taught new manners. To the question: "Who are you?" recruits were to reply: "Reserve militia infantryman so and so, of such and such a company, of the 10th Regiment of King N…" Such was their initiation.

Was the man who fell asleep that night on a bunk between the count's butler Bryczyński and the Styrian miner Guglhupf still Piotr Niewiadomski? No, he was no longer our old friend from Topory-Czernielica station; he was no longer Piotr

Niewiadomski, son of Wasylina, brother of Paraszka the girl of easy virtue; he was simply reserve militia infantryman Piotr Niewiadomski. This was something very different.

*   *   *

Next day they were all summoned by a bugle call to the square outside the barracks command post and drawn up in line forming three companies, each consisting of four platoons. Piotr Niewiadomski found himself in the first platoon of the second company. Fourth on the right. He made a good impression in his uniform. They waited for the arrival of the lieutenant-colonel, who had announced his intention to be present at the swearing-in ceremony, because the Emperor wanted to make sure once again that they would be faithful until death on land, on water and in the air. They had to wait a long time for the lieutenant-colonel. This day, as every day, it was sunny, and it looked as though it would be very hot. It seemed that the war had concluded some secret pact with this heat-wave and that it would be over once it started to rain. Despite the heat, the men in the ranks held up well. They were allowed to talk. Two soldiers in white linen tunics were painting some gigantic red letters on the outer walls of the huts.

Something important must have detained the lieutenant-colonel in town, as it was past nine o'clock and he had still not arrived. The officers took refuge from the heat in their mess. Captain Slavíček stood in the gateway, chain-smoking. Bachmatiuk alone stayed with the ranks. He kept his eyes on the rows of boots. He was worried that the long, straight lines might become distorted. It had been such a hard job to get them into this condition that morning! It was also important to him that the boots of the recruits should be faultlessly polished. When they entered the square at eight o'clock, all the boots shone like glass. Now, after the long wait on dry sand, they were all dusty. There would be no point in giving an order to repolish them. The laboriously assembled ranks would fall into complete disarray. Bachmatiuk was upset about the boots, all the more so because the men were not to blame for their appearance. It was after ten o'clock and the lieutenant-colonel had not turned up. The ranks were beginning to break up.

Bachmatiuk went all round them and with the help of the corporals he kept re-dressing the ranks. In vain. In his view, many of these foot soldiers were better suited to the cavalry, with their short, crooked legs. Bachmatiuk could not stand the cavalry. He could not stand the cavalry, he could not stand the artillery, he could not stand sappers, pioneers, the service corps, the medics, men or women, even if they were in uniform. He hated officers and one-year servicemen, because they were recruited from the upper classes, he could not bear privates because they were people of his own sort. But it would be wrong to think that he was capable only of hate. He could also love. And how! Like a passionate lover in the prime of life, and like an older man lusting after an under-aged girl. He hated each soldier individually for his mouth, for his soul, it is true, but he loved the symmetrical lines created by his body, uniform and shoes. He worshipped ranks, double files, columns of four—either stationary or on the move. He loved quadrangles and phalanxes. Any irregularity, any breach in the formation caused him physical pain. He considered standing to attention to be mankind's fundamental state, the attitudinal norm. Everything else was aberrant. For him, the value of humanity was measured by the extent to which it was formed into regiments. Was he capable of real love? He loved the dust kicked up by the impact of rhythmically tramping feet; this was the music of the spheres, and he regretted the fact that men do not have more feet with which to tramp in time with the beat. He loved the clash of weapons, and sacred military silence: that most exalted of all silences played for him an echo of eternity. His nostrils greedily drank the scent of a soldier's sweat. He watched himself reflected in the shining boots of the infantry as in the mirror of truth. The only, absolute truth.

The boots of the recruits were covered in ever-deepening layers of dust. The sun began to undermine the already fragile square formation; scorched by its rays, the ranks began to droop like melting candles. Before long they would begin to melt. The corporals continued to redress the ranks, fastening buttons, raising the heads of the recruits, lifting drooping belts, pushing the protruding bellies in with their fists. They bustled around these old men like anxious mothers preparing their daughters for their first ball. If the commanding officer did not arrive now, everything would fall apart, the whole painstakingly constructed building would fall into ruin.

He arrived at last, looking morose and deeply perturbed.

When a superior officer approaches drawn-up ranks, they are required to acknowledge him in response to the command "Eyes—right!" Neither Captain Slavíček, the newly appointed battalion commander, nor Bachmatiuk, did so. Quite rightly. It would have been ridiculous to produce a collective nod when the men had no idea how to do it. A sufficient mockery had already been made of the recruits. All the lowest-ranking barracks staff, including the shoe-shiners and the malingerers, had taken to the square, eager for fun at the expense of others. Hawryło, Michajło and Rafajło kept his distance by the huts, grinning. He felt safe at some distance from the RSM.

Lieutenant-Colonel Leithuber did not even accept the report. With his left hand, he signalled to Bachmatiuk that he did not require it. Wrapped in his cape, he looked more like the leader of a gang of conspirators than the head of a military formation. He went upstairs to his office and did not re-emerge for a long time. He was reliving, this time alone, the alarming news. All the daily newspapers had screamed in bold headlines: LEMBERG STILL IN OUR HANDS... Everyone knew what that meant. In a day or two, perhaps even now, the splendid city of Lwów, the capital of the largest of the Crown Lands, the jewel of the Habsburg crown, the headquarters of the 11th Corps, an enormous garrison, the dream of all officers stationed in smaller Galician towns, Little Vienna, would be occupied by the Russians. All the barracks, the Citadel, the High Castle, the Kortumówka rifle range would be occupied by the Russians. All the cafés, the Corso and the Colosseum! Leithuber could already see the terraces of Lwów cafés full of Russian officers. Still in our hands! What sort of hands were those of generals who could not keep hold of Lwów? Perhaps the generals' hands were also withered.

He hurried down to where his numerous retinue awaited him below, Adjutant Baron Hammerling, Captain Slavíček, three company commanders and the ensigns. Leithuber took no notice of the retinue or the squad of recruits. He was looking at the barracks and the painters.

"Pachmatiuk," he shouted angrily, "Whose idea is this? How can you paint generals' names in red? I suppose you'll order the recruits to sing socialist songs next?"

Yes, they were the names of those thanks to whom Lwów was still in our hands. But the command had come down from Military Headquarters to immortalize those names on the walls of the lodgings so that people could commit them to memory more easily, and they had no choice but to obey. (Although the Military Headquarters ought to have been aware that most of the men in this regiment were illiterate.)

Bachmatiuk did not feel guilty. The commanding officer had given no instructions regarding colour. Bachmatiuk had chosen red because it stood out. Immediately he ran over to the painters and told them to use white paint. Leithuber was impatient. "Get on with it," he yelled at Bachmatiuk as he was returning. He did not like those sheds.

When a squad of soldiers had to take an oath, the command was "Take the oath!" Our people, though they were now in uniform, were not yet a real unit of soldiers. They were ordered, as civilians, to remove their caps and raise two fingers of the right hand to eye level. Bachmatiuk pronounced the oath in three languages. Choirs began, in the name of God Almighty, taking a vow of faithfulness and obedience to His Imperial Majesty and all his generals. All of them, including, therefore, those whose hands could not keep hold of Lwów. Piotr Niewiadomski thought that at such a solemn moment music should be playing. He did not know that the orchestra was with the regiment at the front. So he had to settle for the music that was playing in his soul. And very beautiful it was too.

In a voice that got lost in the collective elation, for the second time in his life Piotr assured the Emperor that he would "never under any circumstances desert his fellow soldiers, flags or banners". Until that moment, Lieutenant-Colonel Leithuber had not been listening to these assurances. In his mind, he was going over the speech he was to deliver to the recruits in Ukrainian. He was quite fluent in that language, but he was wracked with nervousness at the prospect. The awareness of being nervous was humiliating, all the more so because he was to address people of a standing so much lower than his own. He was suddenly struck by the word "banners". It would spoil his fine oratorical moment. High above in the blazing blue sky loomed the yellow standard edged in black and red. With the double-headed eagle in the centre. In Leithuber's soul, a vision of the regimental flag fluttered noisily. "Where is it now? How many bullets have pierced it? Perhaps it has been captured, soon to be flying over the St Petersburg arsenal?" In his youth Leithuber had read of heroic standard-bearers who died on the battlefield, refusing to let go of their bullet-riddled banner... Would Ensign Stiasny, regimental standard-bearer, be able to achieve something like that? Ensign Stiasny was regarded as a great skirt-chaser. But the one does not exclude the other. On the contrary... When the regiment was being moved from Stanisławów, Leithuber personally brought with him the standard's empty oilcloth case. It rests in a cupboard in his office... "...and thus we will with honour live and die," chanted the choir.

Before the banner disappeared into thin air, the lieutenant-colonel saw Ensign Stiasny's hand clinging tightly to the staff. A moment later, it also disappeared into the sky, as if together with the regimental standard it had been granted the grace of ascension. There remained only the honour with which these people "wanted to live and die". He had to tell them something about honour. Leithuber winced. His throat was burning with nervousness. The men lowered their hands and replaced their caps. The smell of spicy soup, becoming ever stronger, told them eleven o'clock was approaching. For a split second, Piotr Niewiadomski again saw the face of his mother. Ah, those groats, barley and millet!... Lieutenant-Colonel Leithuber took a few steps forwards, looking for a spot from where he would seem taller. But the square was as flat as a pancake, so he moved back onto the steps and cleared his throat.

"Soldiers!" he began in a gentle, fatherly tone.

Piotr was reminded of Father Makarucha's sermons. He too used to begin in this soppy manner: "My brothers."

"You have been given your uniforms." Leithuber raised his voice, reaching the heights of raw pathos. "You have been given your uniforms, in which you will go to war..."

At this point his voice suddenly broke, falling to the ground like a wounded bird. Leithuber was not telling the truth. He knew perfectly well that they would not go to war in these uniforms. Before leaving for the front they would be issued with new uniforms. It was of no matter. Again he raised his voice:

"To fight for the Emperor and the homeland..."

Nervousness began to choke him like a big Czech dumpling. Nervousness, and something worse than that. It would be best to finish now. Who was he, to tell these people anything about fighting? Already an invalid in peacetime, he would never see any fighting! When war broke out, Leithuber had volunteered for active service. Not because he loved war (although he longed for it in time of peace, like any professional officer). He did not love war, but he wanted to escape the circle of eternal pretence; he had had enough of continuous fruitless preparation for something that was never going to happen. He had spent years preparing for situations that would never occur; it was unbearable. And when war finally did break out, carrying everyone before it in its vehemence, was he to continue firing blanks at non-existent enemies? Throughout his army career he had been continually firing into a void. He had volunteered for front-line service because he wanted to see real war at last.

In the presence of people who were to go to war, he felt like a healthy man at a patient's bedside. He considered himself fit despite the arm. He had volunteered for the front line. A regiment in the field can be commanded with your left arm. And anyway, who today commands with his arms? What colonel rushes into the fray with bared sabre? That's what it was like in the days of old Radetzky. Today you command with your head. He had a sound head. A much sounder one than that of Colonel Martin, who was wasting a regiment at the front... And if the medical commission ruled that he was not fit for front-line service, why did they not bury him in some office, for example in the War Ministry, where he would not have to come into direct contact with people destined for the fire? ...Why are you staring at me like that, you foul brutes? I was a volunteer, wanting to go to the front...

Lieutenant-Colonel Leithuber was now making two speeches at once, one out loud and the other unspoken.

"The honour of the uniform," he shouted across the square, "is a great thing! Take care not to sully it. ...Blood alone will not sully it... Do not get the impression that I am a shirker. I am an invalid, but in spite of that I volunteered for front-line service."

But none of those men he addressed in both speeches accused him of shirking. It did not occur to anyone. Everyone listened religiously, with the exception of the Styrians, who did not understand Ukrainian. Everyone wanted this formal ceremony to be over as soon as possible. They were hungry. Piotr Niewiadomski kept looking at his tunic; it was still unsullied, thank goodness. And when the commanding officer had finished his speech Piotr breathed a sigh of relief, as if he had received absolution for sins he was yet to commit.

The lieutenant-colonel approached the battalion. Accompanied by the officers, he began inspecting the ranks. It was an age-old ritual, followed ever since armies existed. Commanders judge the worth of a soldier by his appearance, drawing encouragement from his sprightly bearing. When a man stands firmly on his feet he offers a pledge of victory. The bearing of our men was not good. Everything was now up to Bachmatiuk.

No, the regiment Leithuber had the responsibility of bringing up to scratch was no élite force. As far back as anyone could remember, this regiment had always had a poor reputation. And no one knew why. In the Imperial and Royal Army there were good regiments and bad regiments, likeable ones and unpopular ones, regiments that were fortunate and regiments that were unfortunate. Regiments are like men. Some are forgiven everything for their charm or their smart bearing, or because they have a good band. They are spoilt and fussed over like women. Then there are others who are never permitted the slightest mistake and who, even when they perform miracles, win over no hearts and gain nobody's trust. Nothing could damage the reputation of the Deutschmeister, for example, and you didn't have to search that far. The 11th Corps also had its favoured regiments, such as the 30th Lemberg. On the other hand, the entire army assailed our regiment with the bitterest jibes, and the alleged stupidity of the Hutsuls was legendary. Officers of other units would say to their recruits who failed to understand or made mistakes that "even a dull Hutsul of the 10th Regiment of King N could understand that!"

Lieutenant-Colonel Leithuber became despondent when inspecting truly awful parades. From time to time he would stop in front of one of the recruits to enquire about the year and place of his birth. He did not stop in front of Piotr and he did not ask him anything. The officers followed the commandant; Bachmatiuk came last, walking with his head bowed, tenaciously following the line of boots. On reaching the first platoon of the third company, Leithuber became tired and turned back. He thumbed through the first pages of that empty notebook and on losing interest he abruptly closed it. All hopes were focused on Bachmatiuk. Casting him a meaningful glance, the commander and his retinue left the square. The soldiers immediately broke ranks.

"As you were! As you were! Who said you were dismissed?" yelled the NCOs. Whistling at them, they chased the scattered flock of sheep back into their ranks. Regimental Sergeant-Major Bachmatiuk waited until they had re-formed, re-dressed and settled down. And when they had re-formed, re-dressed and settled down, he shouted:

"I will make men of you!"

The uniformed men's skin crawled. They wondered what he was going to do with them now. What had they been until now, exactly? What physical or mental torture did this threat entail? Everyone had the feeling that this man in long trousers, with medals on his chest, was wiping out and revoking their entire previous life. They were grey, bald-headed moustachioed infants that the great mother Subordination would teach to suck from her breast. Their life had only just begun, on the day they first wore uniform.

In the beginning was the Word. The Word that calmed the waves, a Word whose sound was followed by a deathly silence. Bachmatiuk screwed up his eyes like a zealot at the most important moment during mass, or like a music-lover at a symphony concert. He drew himself up like a crowing cockerel and gave the long-drawn-out command:

"A—t—t—e—e—n—shun!"

For some time he kept his eyes closed for fear of seeing something that would be a total abortion. And indeed, not everyone understood the command. The corporals facing them showed the dullards how to stand erect. Regimental Sergeant-Major Bachmatiuk opened his eyes, adjusted his cap, and reached into his pocket. He pulled out a slim pamphlet—the thirty-seven articles of war, the articles of faith. He calmly deluged the recruits with the list of crimes and offences which carried the risk of death or long prison terms. The recruits hurried to plumb the depths of their souls to test their resilience. After this confrontation, very few of them felt any self-confidence. Piotr Niewiadomski feared cowardice most of all. Not to show cowardice in the face of the enemy was no insignificant matter. The Emperor demanded courage from every man, as if everyone was born brave. Perhaps the RSM could teach them courage.

When the RSM had finished reading the articles of war, the spectres of the thirty-seven deadly sins of the Imperial and Royal soldier hung over the recruits.

"At this point you should say the Lord's Prayer," thought Piotr. "Or at least cross yourself." He wanted to raise a hand, but he could not do so. It lay dead on the seam of the Imperial trousers, as if paralysed by Bachmatiuk's words.

Bachmatiuk gazed, as though in a trance, at the expressionless faces, the uniforms and the boots. The perfect silence engendered by his words filled his ears. He inhaled the sweet fragrance of obedience and fear. And he was happy. On this first day of the Creation, as he took possession of the souls of the oldest reserve militia intakes, he could already see his work completed. And he saw that it was good.

HEALTHY DEATH

(A Fragment)

A NOTE FROM THE AUTHOR

I would like to remind readers who have not read (or do not remember) *The Salt of the Earth*, first published in 1935 as the first part of a trilogy entitled *The Saga of the Patient Foot Soldier*, that it is set at the time of the outbreak of the First World War, initially at the railway station of Topory-Czernielica in the Galicia-Bukovina borderlands, and later at the garrison of an Imperial and Royal Infantry regiment transferred after the Russian invasion to the town of Andrásfalva, deep inside Hungarian territory. Both Topory-Czernielica and Andrásfalva are figments of the author's imagination, not to be found on any map. The chief protagonist of *The Salt of the Earth*, met in the first part of *Healthy Death*, is Piotr Niewiadomski, whose mother was a Hutsul, his father Polish. In the beginning he was a porter, later a signalman, at the said railway station of Topory-Czernielica. On his recruitment under the general mobilization he is transported with others for training at the Andrásfalva garrison. The next most important character of *The Salt of the Earth*, and to some extent also of *Healthy Death*, is Regimental Sergeant-Major Bachmatiuk, the fanatical expert and high priest of Military Discipline. He considers it his mission in life to turn human beings into real people—soldiers, that is. The character Łeś Nedochodiuk, whose "soul is let out" by Bachmatiuk, appears in *Healthy Death* for the first and last time. "Healthy death" is Bachmatiuk's term for the death of a soldier at the front line.

I n the entire garrison there was not a single louse, not even
for medicinal purposes, for Łeś Nedochodiuk, who lay in
the sick-bay dying for the Emperor. They had been so thor-
oughly exterminated by the great de-louser Izydor Parawan,
a man with a grey goatee and a yellow "intelligence stripe"
on his sleeve, an unarmed reserve militiaman, category "C".
All the lice had left for the front line with King N's Imperial
and Royal 10th Infantry Regiment band and standard. A pity,
that! They would have come in useful now at Andrásfalva,
oh, so useful! But opinion was divided in the garrison as to
whether reserve infantryman Łeś Nedochodiuk was really
dying for the Emperor. Some claimed that you could only die
for the Emperor on the battlefield, in the open air—where the
lice were, actually—and not on a bed in the sick-bay. Others
admitted that while you could die for His Illustrious Majesty
only from an enemy bullet, bayonet or piece of shrapnel,
it was—for goodness sake—of no consequence whether it
occurred on the spot, on the bare earth of the battlefield or
a little later in hospital. The main thing was that it was death
in battle and not from some illness that you could equally
well suffer in civilian life. But most of the countrymen were
of the opinion that it made no difference. Every soldier who

dropped dead in the Emperor's tunic, even if he had not smelt gunpowder, died for the Emperor.

"You'll see," said reserve infantryman Bryczyński, a count's valet in civilian life, a man of the world. "They will arrange his funeral with a parade and military honours, which means he croaked for the Emperor."

"Croaked! He hasn't croaked yet!" protested Piotr Niewiadomski, Bryczyński's comrade-in-arms. "The man you're talking about is still alive!" But he was fascinated by those military honours and he wanted to see them with his own eyes.

For the Emperor or not for the Emperor, Łeś Nedochodiuk gasped his last, although Regimental Doctor Badian did everything in his power to save him. But then, what did Dr Badian actually have at his disposal? Drips? Injections? Digitalis, coramine, camphor? Medicine like that was just a joke. It might do for officers, Jews, lawyers, but not for Hutsuls. Now Łeś Nedochodiuk was a true Hutsul, a farmer from Dzembronia by the river Dzembronia, not a hybrid, not someone from a village in some neighbouring territory, like that Piotr Niewiadomski, his comrade from the 3rd Company of the 2nd Battalion. Łeś Nedochodiuk had sixteen head of cattle in his shippen, sixteen head of cattle grazing on the Carpathian mountain pastures. And those sheep! A rudbeckia would have helped him, that magic herb! Just give him some hooch with toad, befuddle him with smoke from a burnt broom used to sweep a Greek Catholic church. Or with smoke from the dried testicles of a stallion! Nothing would have helped him so much now, nothing would have saved him from perishing in a foreign land, in a Hungarian brewery, as surely as the ancient tried-and-tested drug—half a dozen or a dozen lice downed in a gulp of vodka! But what can doctors know about this?

And why was it that Łeś Nedochodiuk had to die so young, without being granted his baptism of fire? What had struck down such a tough lad, leaving him lying there like a log, gasping like the bellows in Kłym Kuczirka's forge at Żabie-Słupejka? Had some Hungarian devils overpowered him? Had some Hungarian seductresses beguiled him? They said Łeś was impervious to such inducements. He prayed regularly to St Nicholas, the favourite of the gods, to look after him and protect him from all dangers, and from evil fate, on the hills and on the water. The Lord's Prayer had evidently been of no use, because Nedochodiuk did not even live until the Feast of the Veil of our Lady. What had happened to him?

The cattle were already returning from the mountain pastures in the distant Hutsul land, the beloved cattle, the Christian cattle. The lights had been extinguished in the shepherds' cottages, where apparitions, the souls of people who had been killed, were settling back in for the winter (this year there were more apparitions than cottages, although it was only the third month of the war, the beginning of October). The land in the mountains was drying up, the herbs were dying, the larch trees, or rather dwarf pines, were turning black. The mullein, leaves drooping, protruded dismally and rigidly, like extinguished candles in the church. All the grasses dried up, losing the juices that nourished the cattle on the mountain pastures from St George's Day until the feast of the Veil of Our Lady. So the cattle that did not go to the winter hay barns descended from the mountain pastures. Day and night, the valleys and ravines were echoing with lowing and bleating, the complaints of the driven beasts, drowning out the roar of the sacred Hutsul rivers, in full flood at this time of year—the White Czeremosz, the Black Czeremosz and the Prut. The whole Hutsul land vibrated with the pounding of hooves, cloven and uncloven. Thousands of bells, large and small, jingled on the fattened necks of cows, calves and rams on the march. The heavy stench of bovine excrement mingled with the smell of steaming hide and wool, the scents of trampled meadows, mown hay and milk yet to be collected. Only rarely were the shepherds' long wooden horns to be heard.

Already the cattle were returning from the mountain pastures, and our men in the garrison were not yet real men. They could go to the front line now in the event of dire necessity, but only in the event of dire necessity. The garrison commander Lieutenant-Colonel Leithuber would have sent them, but he was not the one who decided whether the men were now real men. This decision belonged exclusively to Regimental Sergeant-Major Bachmatiuk.

Rafting on the Czeremosz rivers had ceased. The sluices had been closed and the rafts had been immobilized, probably because the best helmsmen had been called up anyway and were rafting Serbs and Muscovites into the other world for the Emperor. The winter was coming, and our men at Andrásfalva were not yet real men. The Muscovites had now occupied Pokuttya, running affairs among the Greek Catholic people as they did back home, installing bearded Orthodox priests in the parishes, hanging images of Tsar Nicholas in offices, while our men in Hungary who were supposed to drive the Muscovites out of Galicia were not yet real men.

They were not real men, although Regimental Sergeant-Major Bachmatiuk had been pounding the Hungarian ground with them, hurling them into the stubble and the potato fields, soaking them in swamps and bemiring them in mud. For the rainy season had already begun, although the war was not over despite the universal expectation that it would end with the first rainstorms. Throughout the dry month of September, the comrades had inhaled Hungarian dust mingled with their own sweat; their hands were scarred by long hours of exercises by day and by night, their feet were sore from forced marches with full kit, their bodies were covered in bruises from falling and getting up again, falling and getting up again, from the digging of deep trenches, from lugging boxes of ammunition, from firing in erect, prostrate and kneeling positions, from crawling on their bellies with dozens of kilograms on their backs.

But they were not real men.

For is a creature like reserve militiaman Piotr Niewiadomski a real man if, at the most important moments in his life, such as when taking part in battalion drill or when on guard duty, he forgets which is his left hand and which is his right? Is anybody a real man who does not know what "line of fire" means? Anyone who does not know that according to the sacred firing instructions for the Imperial and Royal infantry it is an imaginary line extending from the eye of the rifleman through the rear and front sights on the barrel to the target itself? And even if he knows what "line of fire" means, is he a real man if he cannot focus on moving objects in simple, level terrain like this whole Hungarian lowland? And can you call a uniformed being a real man if he does not know what to do when his Schwarzlose machine gun barrel overheats and there is no water?

No, they were not real men, though Regimental Sergeant-Major Rudolf Bachmatiuk had let out the souls of many of them. But the souls let out by Bachmatiuk's words eventually returned to their bodies and returned to their uniforms like birds to the nest, or they were no longer the same souls as before. They had already been transformed by that great deity of the Imperial and Royal hosts—Discipline.

Anyway, you can live without a soul. You are even a better soldier. For often the soul prevents you from carrying out the orders of higher powers. You can live without a soul.

In the 2nd Battalion there was a reserve militia private called Stepan Basarab, a native of Podolia, very close to the Russian border. As a young boy, he had acted as a guide to a poor blind minstrel. He heard oh so many tales and songs that were older than the Emperor Franz Joseph. These tales knew no borders, freely crossing it in both directions, unafraid of Russian and Austrian guards alike. Stepan Basarab told his comrades in the barracks of one Orthodox man who lived without a soul. His body was in one place and his soul was somewhere else, and this Orthodox man did not even know where it was. But he really needed his soul. Because in church, over and over again, he had been promised immortality, like everyone else, whether they were Orthodox or Greek Catholic.

"Well, what does it mean to be immortal?" asked reserve militiaman Stepan Basarab, squinting. Is your nose supposed to be immortal? Are your innards supposed to be immortal? Perhaps your belly, eh? Or what's down below it? It's better if all that you have sinned with in your life rots in the ground, but your soul lives forever. And this Orthodox man, said Stepan Basarab, was looking everywhere for his soul into his old age. He kept looking for it but he couldn't find it anywhere. The devil knows what became of it. It was now close by, now far away, somewhere near Kyiv, but he knew nothing about it. It was not until he was dying that his soul returned to his body, just for a moment, *eins*, *zwei*, *drei*, just to leave it again, according to the rules. For good now. For ever and ever, amen. Thereupon this man died.

At the garrison things were not as in Basarab's story; at the garrison all the souls were returning to their bodies. It was only on one occasion that Regimental Sergeant-Major Bachmatiuk let out a soldier's soul for it never to return.

That concerned Łeś Nedochodiuk's soul. What was it like, big or small, pretty or ugly, or—well, we don't know. For the human soul is like that line of fire; it is known to exist, but who has ever seen it?

The body is different. Even Łeś's worst enemy could not deny that he was handsome. Łeś Nedochodiuk was tall and slim, but the gracefulness of his movements was in harmony with his strength. He walked lightly, even in heavy army-issue boots, and he swung his hips as if wafted by a gentle breeze. There was something tree-like about him, so it seemed strange that he did not rustle in the wind. The dark skin covering his entire body gave the impression of delicate bark. Cut it or saw through it, and surely resin would flow. And no flesh would be revealed, no bones, just the rings of a tree. And no stench would erupt from Łeś's belly, but the aroma of a sawmill.

His element was the forest. He worked in the forest and he was imbued with its spirit. He had no great devotion to his herds. The beasts smelt like liquid manure. The army abused him—they cut off his shiny chestnut locks, but they did not touch his light moustache. He trimmed it himself in the English manner. His sweaty exercise uniform did not look good on him. In uniform, Łeś looked like an animal whose charm and dignity are in its nudity, whereas in any attire, not necessarily belonging to the circus, he arouses only pity and laughter. The Imperial cap also sat uneasily on his shaved head. His big blue eyes stared out from under its peak with the innocence of an animal. His long eyelashes softened the cold, wild look in his eyes. The bloodshot left eye seemed particularly severe.

Apart from his handsome appearance, Łeś had no distinguishing features. And yet he was respected by his countrymen. They respected his strength, his breeding and his family origins. He had only one claim to fame—his success with women. It was said that he had several wives simultaneously, but that was not true. There was one woman he was married to, also good-looking and of noble birth and, well, one mistress. And if there was some coquettish woman who could not resist the handsome young man from Dzembronia, she was the one to blame, not Łeś. Łeś Nedochodiuk found it hard to resist Hutsul women, and not only Hutsuls, as a spreading oak offers shade to anyone who lies down beneath it. Even the goddess of the forest would succumb to him.

He had three legitimate children. About the illegitimate ones never a word was spoken in the land of the Dzembronia and Czeremosz rivers. The father and mother still lived in their cottage, but the whole farm had long since been in the hands of Ostap's eldest son. This Ostap had brought his beautiful wife Kajetanna from Kuty. She looked a little Jewish, but she was not a Jew—heaven forbid! She was Armenian.

Good times and bad times, peacetime and wartime passed over Łeś like a waterfall on the Czeremosz. Noisily, but without any harm to him. Łeś Nedochodiuk paid no attention to historical events. It was all the same to him who ruled the world, Austria and all the Hutsul lands. He was unconcerned about the Emperor or the enemies of the Emperor. He could read, but he did not read newspapers. Łeś was not alone in this. Many generations of Hutsuls had been buried with their eyes closed to anything that was not Hutsul. It was only extra-terrestrial matters that Łeś cared about. He believed in heaven, he believed in hell, the holy saints, angels and archangels, but also in Arch-Judas, the king of the devils, evil spirits, spirits of the night, spirits of the forest, and in the whole supernatural world of his pagan ancestors.

This man of the wood was incompatible with machinery. He was decidedly inimical to products of the metallurgical industry. Machines were not well disposed towards him either. Not just machines, but metal in general. Twice in his life he had been tricked by iron. Once, in his childhood, he was almost blinded. At Kłym Kuczirka's forge in Żabie-Słupejka, a spark from a red-hot horseshoe flew into his eye. He had to go for treatment to a quack doctor in Kosov, who gave him herbs and ointments that helped Łeś regain his sight after a few days, though his eye was painful for a long time afterwards. It was a miracle. Perhaps St Nicholas himself, the children's friend, helped the Kosov quack. Many years later, when Łeś was working on his own, the axe with which he was chopping wood to make a raft cut off half of the thumb on his left hand. In peacetime, a minor disability is sufficient for exemption from military service. But in wartime you can enlist with half a left thumb missing. As long as the other hand is all right.

This was the heyday of iron rather than of wood. It was manifested in the persecution of bodies of all kinds—human, animal, vegetable—by means of machinery. The infantry had not really ceased to be the queen of armoury, but her realm was no longer that of a world that killed with rifles and bay-onets. The Mannlicher had been superseded in the Imperial and Royal Infantry by the Schwarzlose automatic rapid-firing machine gun, model 07/12, calibre 8. At the outbreak of the war, two machine guns were allocated to each infantry battalion. But when it turned out that Tsar Nicholas had actu-ally won a victory over Emperor Franz Joseph thanks to the superiority of automatic weapons, the high command of the Imperial and Royal armed forces began rapidly creating new machine-gun units, but also training as many of the infantry as possible to operate this weapon.

Sometimes, in combat, the enemy would manage to take out all the machine-gunners, who would then have to be replaced by whoever was at hand, without waiting for qual-ified replacements to be sent from the rear. Therefore, in Regimental Sergeant-Major Bachmatiuk's opinion, no march-ing formation was ready for the front until all its members were familiar with the machine gun, at least superficially. Of course, not every cretin could be permitted to have access to such a delicate and unpredictable machine. Piotr Niewiadomski, for example, was not under consideration here. It would be criminal to allow any man (if he was indeed a real man) to come into close contact with the Schwarzlose not knowing his left hand from his right. He did not know which was which, although he already had experience of being clapped in irons. He did not know which was which although the garrison commander himself, Lieutenant-Colonel Leithuber (the one with the withered right hand) had struck him twice in the face with his left hand. If necessary, you can entrust the less important parts of the machine gun to anyone—the shield, the tripod base, the ammunition boxes. But only to carry them. Piotr Niewiadomski was a porter on the railway in civilian life. Let him do the carrying. In peacetime, mules and Hutsul ponies of Turkish origin, which fed exclusively on hay, were used in the Imperial and Royal Army to transport machine guns. In our garrison there were actually mules, but not enough to carry the increased numbers of machine guns. So the machine guns were dismantled and people had to carry them.

Bachmatiuk took a liking to Łeś Nedochodiuk at first sight. If the RSM had still been capable of loving anybody after Knauss's death, he would have loved Łeś. Much in the way that a man of the cloth might sense that someone had a vocation to serve God, Bachmatiuk spotted Łeś as a potential NCO. He wondered whether to recommend him for NCO training before the battalion set off for the front. He gave Łeś numerous special, but on the face of it insignificant, dispensations, avoiding doing so ostentatiously. Nedochodiuk seemed not to notice. He did not realize that Bachmatiuk exempted him from cleaning latrines or helping in the kitchen, or clearing-up jobs, more often assigning him to more subtle tasks. For example, he was honoured with the functions of an inspection lance corporal, and during training exercises Bachmatiuk sent him on patrol as leader of a reconnaissance detachment. Łeś did not notice any of this. It also escaped his notice that Bachmatiuk never mocked him, did not address him as "Your Excellency" or "Your Grace". He accepted these privileges as if they were conferred by the Emperor himself and were not even worth acknowledging. Throughout the training of the recruits Bachmatiuk waited for some response from Łeś—for at least some small sign of approval, if not gratitude. He saw none. Łeś Nedochodiuk carried out all orders impeccably, but nothing more. When the battalion began practising with machine guns (all of iron and steel, only the rear handles being made of wood), Łeś's behaviour changed. It was very obvious that he found it repulsive to touch the machine gun. When it came to firing, Bachmatiuk asked Łeś if he would care to transfer to the machine gun detachment permanently. Łeś drew himself up on the command to stand to attention.

"Begging your pardon, Regimental Sergeant-Major, I cannot."

"Why can't you?"

By way of answering, Łeś Nedochodiuk showed his left hand. Bachmatiuk understood this: with a missing thumb you cannot fire the Schwarzlose. So he ordered him to lie down beside the gunner and the gun-layer, hold the ammunition belt and collect the cases of used rounds. Drowsily, sluggishly, Łeś fed the cartridge belt through his fingers. He did so with an expression on his face as if he was feeding acorns to pigs rather than handling Imperial and Royal ammunition. And when Bachmatiuk, taken aback by this attitude, ordered him to remove the barrel from the tripod, Łeś took hold of it as if it was something unclean.

Other Hutsuls did not trust the machine either. They could not get on with it. How does a Hutsul know how a machine gun lives and breathes? Had his mummy taught him that?

And so they lay in the fields at Andrásfalva alongside the Emperor's machine guns, as if they were guarding some precious livestock, as though they were watching over it as it grazed there. They pretended to be caring for its well-being, although they would rather have drowned it. Łeś Nedochodiuk made no such pretence. He openly displayed his disgust for the machine gun. Bachmatiuk took it all in and it troubled him, but he was unable to fault Łeś, who worked impeccably. But when Nedochodiuk displayed aversion to this beautiful weapon for a second and third time, as it were spitting on it, this was too much for Bachmatiuk. With a voice coming from the depths of his suppressed anguish, he cried out in a tone in which he had never before spoken to Łeś:

"Careful there with the machine gun, Your Grace! A machine gun is no slut!"

No slut! There was a flash in Nedochodiuk's bloodstained eye. Open conflict had occurred only after live firing of the machine gun.

It was a beautiful autumn morning when the third company of the 2nd Battalion (2MB / III) marched through the town, singing as they went. The chestnuts at the market were displayed in the glory of yellow leaves gleaming with water droplets. The rain which had lasted all night had cleared the dust from the pavements and streets. The great Hungarian statesman Ferenc Deák stood with his foot of stone protruding as if he was tapping it in time to the Ukrainian song. Then the recruits, tired of singing, were relieved by the company trumpeter Hryć Podbereznyj.

Our men were in good spirits. They preferred live firing to the boring parade drill by the barracks, to the accompaniment of bellowing from the Farkas and Gjörmeky brewery's bloody neighbour, the municipal slaughterhouse. Down the middle of the road at the head of the detachment marched Regimental Sergeant-Major Bachmatiuk with a sheathed sword. The officers walked on the pavement so as not to stain their puttees.

When they reached the field where live ammunition drills were held, Lieutenant Lewicki, the battle training manager, ordered the burdens to be removed from the mules and the men. He allowed a short break. The mules were fed, and the men stretched out on the damp ground, which had been flattened by the garrison's constant practice manoeuvres. Soon a sharp whistle interrupted the hubbub. The men jumped to their feet. They stiffened. And one of those military silences ensued as when words with the significance of life and death were uttered. On Bachmatiuk's order to "Fall in!" the men rushed for their rifles stacked in pyramids, to their dismantled machine guns, and to their equipment, prepared according to regulations. The Indian summer had enfolded the damp rifle butts in thin silvery strands. On the command to shoulder equipment, they hurriedly took up their packs and fastened their belts. When they were ready, Bachmatiuk ordered them to shoulder arms and stand at ease. Then he posted sentries to check the boundaries of the firing zone and chase away all living creatures, Hungarians and cows, if they came near. After the sentries had left, the machine guns were assembled and set up in trenches.

The firing began. At first with hand-held weapons only. Soon the machine guns supported by their tripods started shuddering epileptically in their muddy nests. Fiery tongues flared out of their narrow muzzles and the whole space was filled with an incessant clatter, as though storks were indulging in insane orgies. It was a simulation of the company's means of defence against a frontal attack by the enemy. Live fire saturated the foreground cleared of all living beings perceptible to the naked eye or field glasses. Moles and mice were burying themselves in the shelters they had made in good time. To begin with, on the Emperor's orders, the men had to use their imagination to picture the enemy in the wasteland before them. But soon there was no need for that. Suddenly, our men spotted the enemy they were shooting at. Through his binoculars, Bachmatiuk picked out something in the wilderness and he started waving two flags, a blue one and a yellow one. He was sending secret signals to invisible forces, and there, no more than a hundred and fifty metres away, blurry grey-blue figures began jumping up. They were Muscovites. As they came under fire and were hit, they tottered and fell to the ground; then they reappeared, now here, now there, ever more clearly silhouetted against the bright sky. This was how Regimental Sergeant-Major Bachmatiuk had power here even over the Muscovites. He killed them and brought them back to life again.

The sun was now getting hot; the machine guns, churning up the mud, were rattling away, firing deliriously, when one of them began to falter; then it failed completely and fell silent.

Bachmatiuk came running, touching the barrel as a mother feels a sick child's forehead, and hissed. He waited until the barrel cooled a little, then checked the radiator. Of course, the water had run out. Three litres was not that much, given the continuous firing. The radiator needed refilling. But what with? The water was far away, where the "Muscovites" were dug in. Where the mules would be fed after the exercises. But you couldn't go to the enemy emplacements to fetch water for the machine guns that were strafing them! You had to sort it out yourself. The men had water in their mess tins, but Bachmatiuk did not want to deprive them of their drinking-water on such a hot, strenuous day. Besides, he wanted to simulate with them the "extreme eventualities" likewise provided for in the Regulations concerning firearms instruction.

"Nedochodiuk!" he shouted. "Pick up the barrel and piss on it!" Łeś Nedochodiuk did not understand. He just stood there, not making a move.

"Nedochodiuk, did you hear what I said?"

"Yes, Regimental Sergeant-Major."

"Well, why aren't you pissing on it?"

Nedochodiuk still did not understand, so some of his comrades tried to help by making appropriate gestures. To no avail.

"Nedochodiuk!" shouted Bachmatiuk. "Why are you standing there like an idiot?"

"Regimental Sergeant-Major, I, I—"

"'I, I'! What do you mean, 'I'? In the army there's no such thing as 'I'!"

"Regimental Sergeant-Major, begging your pardon, I can't."

"Who says? Your Grace Count Potocki? His Excellency Prince Schwarzenberg?"

Not only was Nedochodiuk's left eye all bloodshot, the redness began to spread to both his cheeks. Nedochodiuk reported:

"Regimental Sergeant-Major, Reserve Militiaman Leś Nedochodiuk…"

Bachmatiuk did not let him finish.

"Your Grace cannot? Why not? Has he caught the clap?"

For a short while they exchanged fierce glances. Suddenly, Bachmatiuk turned away from Leś and shouted:

"His Existence Reserve Militiaman Niewiadomski!"

"Present!"

"Unfasten His Grace's trousers!"

Piotr Niewiadomski went up to Leś, but when he was about to face him he hesitated. He could not even bring himself to face him. Bachmatiuk yelled right into his ear:

"That's an order!"

He had received an order. His Existence Piotr Niewiadomski stretched out his hands before him like a blind man or a sleep-walker. With trembling fingers, he began searching for Leś's buttons.

Something extraordinary occurred. Leś's hands, motionless along the seams of his trousers as he stood to attention, rose and pushed Piotr away. They pushed him with such force that Piotr lost his balance and would have fallen on top of the RSM if the latter had not supported him with the cooling machine gun barrel. Without losing his temper, Bachmatiuk gave Piotr the barrel to hold and slowly approached Leś like a predatory animal. He knew that Leś would not dare to raise a finger against him. And with calm deliberation he unfastened his buttons. Then he tore the barrel from Piotr's hands and in a voice trembling with supernatural force he declaimed:

"In the name of the Highest Command, I order you—piss!"

Łeś Nedochodiuk was trembling. With his right hand he reached for his trousers, but he immediately withdrew it. Bachmatiuk paled. Was this the end of the world, or wasn't it? Bachmatiuk knew he must make a decision immediately, if the world was not to end. But what was that decision? If Łeś's behaviour was an offence, or, as the Regulations stated, an infringement of discipline, he should arrest him on the spot and court-martial him. However, it could not be a question of insubordination unless there was no doubt that Reserve Militiaman Łeś Nedochodiuk could urinate on the Schwarzlose barrel, but was unwilling to do so. Difficult to prove, if there is no evidence and no doctor is to hand. Here, it was necessary to appeal to the deity and save one's own authority, taking care to avoid inviting ridicule by interfering in the laws of nature, which could be just as intransigent as discipline in the Imperial and Royal Army.

Bachmatiuk chose a solution that satisfied both the deity and himself. Since it was not clear whether this was a case of insubordination or not, it was better to accept that it was not. So Bachmatiuk did not arrest Łeś and he did not even order him to give a report on the left flank. However, he had to do something with him. So, in a silence pregnant with the dread of the day of judgement, a silence that could not be drowned out by the clatter of the two "healthy" machine guns, he came so close to Łeś that the glittering peak of his cap struck him in the neck. As if his neck was struck by the blade of a guillotine. He was, however, shorter than Łeś, so he had to look up in order to meet his gaze. He found the bloodshot pupil of the Hutsul and saw there a readiness to murder. They looked at one another with deadly intensity. Bachmatiuk looked away from the bloodshot eye as if he was withdrawing a bloodstained bayonet. He closed his eyes, but there was a sea of blood even in those closed eyes. He did not open his eyes, but his cold breath, soured by alcohol and tobacco, wafted onto Łeś's neck:

"My son, I'll let out your soul!"

Then he leapt away from Łeś like a hangman from his victim. He gave a shrill whistle. Officers and NCOs followed his example and the whole company broke off the exercise.

In the third company there was no swine who would rush to report Łeś, so as soon as Lieutenant Lewicki ordered a half-hour break, Łeś Nedochodiuk went with the others to a place in the open field where there was a lone oasis of shrubs—wild roses and blackberries, and there he relieved his full bladder. Although Bachmatiuk had portended the letting out of Łeś's soul so quietly that only those closest to him, Piotr Niewiadomski for example, had heard him, mortal fear overcame everyone. They all felt they had a soul too, for here was someone who could let it out, if only for a day, an hour, a moment. Everyone also sensed that Bachmatiuk's prediction was not just a threat that would lead to the familiar punishments. They knew something they had never experienced before would happen that day. A sixth sense told these defenceless people that their comrade Łeś Nedochodiuk's soul would shortly depart from his body, flying from his mouth and his nose, his immortal soul for whose redemption he had prayed from a book with gilt edges.

Piotr Niewiadomski sensed the presence of the devil. He could have sworn that he saw the devil evaporating from the barrel of the Schwarzlose machine gun and forcing himself into the soul of a Hutsul who was unwilling to expose himself in front of others.

None of the witnesses of the incident had the courage to approach Łeś, let alone speak to him. Łeś was already taboo. An invisible chalk circle had been drawn round his body. No living person dared to cross this borderline between life and death. But Łeś Nedochodiuk walked among his comrades, who fell silent at the sight of him, like a king who had just been excommunicated by the church. The faithful are supposed to shun even an excommunicated king. So the disciples of Imperial and Royal Discipline avoided Łeś, while at the same time admiring him for daring to challenge the deity, endangering his soul in an unequal battle. Some were rash enough to mutter about the incident, fearing to speak of it out loud. They tried to guess what Bachmatiuk would do now, and by means of what punishment he would expel Łeś's soul. Meanwhile Bachmatiuk, like Łeś, stood to one side, smoking a cigarette. He was probably wondering the same thing as the men.

He did not devise anything special. The sanctions he had at his disposal were rather mild. Bachmatiuk had no right to impose disciplinary punishments. Only the company commander could impose detention or solitary confinement, while *szpanga* (clapping in irons, cuffing the left arm to the right leg and the right hand to the left leg) and *Anbinden* (tying hands behind the back and binding to the post) were the exclusive privilege of the commanding officer.

However, even within his limited powers, Bachmatiuk had enough ways of letting out Łeś's soul.

And he did let it out.

Nobody could tell exactly how it happened.

Most of his countrymen supposed that Corporal Reszytyło, whom Bachmatiuk had instructed to carry out punishment exercises with Łeś, tortured him to unconsciousness with constant sit-ups, "frog leaps", running, falling and getting up again in full marching gear, all while holding a Mannlicher. Łeś collapsed from exhaustion, they said, although he was such a strapping fellow. Or maybe he suffered a sudden haemorrhage. Some saw him fall on the second day of his punishment exercises, dropping the weapon and failing to get up after repeated commands to do so.

"He's malingering," said Bachmatiuk when Corporal Reszytyło reported it. But Lieutenant Lewicki was disturbed. He drew his sabre and applied the blade to the lips of the man who had fainted, and when he had convinced himself that he was breathing, ordered stretcher bearers to carry the unconscious "malingerer" to the sick-bay.

However, many Hutsuls, among them Reserve Militiaman Piotr Niewiadomski, were convinced that Regimental Sergeant-Major Bachmatiuk had accomplices from another world. She-devils had come for the soul of Łeś, of whom it was known, and not only in Dzembronia by the Dzembronia River, that he had sinned and sinned as an adulterer. And now the same devils that had incited Łeś to commit this sin out there in the remote Hutsul land—and Łeś committed adultery not only with the wives of strangers, but also with his brother Ostap's wife, that beautiful Armenian from Kuty,

Kajetanna—those same devils suddenly turned into guards and avengers of the flouted sixth commandment. The cursed she-devils took advantage of the fact that there was a war on, that their patron Arch-Judas (one should spit at the very mention of his name) had stolen the whole fifth commandment from God and sold it to the Emperors. Because it was only thanks to this that Regimental Sergeant-Major Bachmatiuk was able to drive out Łeś's soul. And the she-devils had come to take it off to hell.

On the third day, Łeś Nedochodiuk was lying in the sick-bay, behind a Chinese screen, fighting for his life. The sick-bay consisted of only one room with ten beds. Not all were occupied. When it became clear that Łeś's condition was hopeless and that not even the leeches bought at a pharmacy in town by medical orderly and garrison barber Glück were any help, Regimental Doctor Badian ordered a Chinese screen to be brought from his quarters in Andrásfalva. He wanted to spare others, mostly patients with mild ailments, the sight of the dying man. True, this happened in the army and during the war, and perhaps it was time to familiarize the soldiers with death. But Dr Max Badian, the regimental doctor in reserve, preferred to shield the dying patient with a screen, since it was otherwise impossible to isolate him. However, since in such a sad situation neither Łeś's healthy comrades nor the sick ones who came to enquire about his health were amused by the comical figures of Chinese men with long drooping moustaches and locks of hair on shaved heads painted on the screen, Dr Badian had the screen covered with a sheet.

There was another, more serious, reason why Dr Badian shielded the dying Łeś with this screen.

Leś Nedochodiuk felt that he was dying. He was not afraid of death, but he was afraid of hell. He requested a candle and a priest. There was no candle at the garrison. There was neither a Greek priest nor a Roman Catholic one. The regimental chaplains of both confessions were in the field, that is, at the division headquarters. It had been correctly agreed at the Department of Pastoral Functions of Christian Faiths of the Imperial and Royal Ministry of War at the Stubenring in Vienna that care of the souls of soldiers is needed first and foremost where the soldiers are constantly in danger of death, and therefore on the front line, not in the safe garrisons. Especially when they had been evacuated from the home garrisons presently occupied by the Muscovites. So our people, at least for now (since the Stubenring promised to send a Greek-Catholic priest later), were deprived of their own pastors and pastoral sustenance. Not entirely, however. Every Sunday and on every church holiday Catholics marched to the garrison church in Andrásfalva, where the parish rector of the church and the military chaplain simultaneously celebrated mass in Latin, only the sermon being given in Hungarian. Regimental Doctor Badian, like so many physicians in those days, was an atheist. If he believed in anything at all, it was just the laws of nature. The development of natural sciences was supposed to guarantee mankind a bright future. This belief was slightly undermined by the war, which Dr Badian considered a senseless anachronism. He saw in it only the last convulsions of the dying world of irrational, and therefore false, ideas. However, as a true liberal, he respected all religions. He understood that even in the army Christian mortals should not be deprived of the sacraments in the face of death.

So he went to the garrison commander with a proposal to bring a Honvéd chaplain to the dying soldier. It was the first fatal accident at this garrison, and Lieutenant-Colonel Leithuber responded favourably to the doctor's initiative. But, personally, he did not want to call the chaplain of the unpopular Honvéds. So Dr Badian dealt with this. He drove to the city in the garrison commander's carriage and found the priest not in the barracks but at the rectory of the garrison church. Father Dr Géza Szákaly, a chaplain with the rank of captain, immediately agreed to Dr Badian's proposal. However, scarcely had he (in German) expressed his agreement to prepare Łeś for his death than he came up against a brick wall. The wall of the Tower of Babel. It was supposed to bring people closer to heaven and therefore to God, but the result of this undertaking was the opposite; it was fatal. The Tower of Babel had distanced people not only from God, but from one another. They ceased to understand one another. So Father Géza Szákaly hesitated. He spoke only Hungarian and German. How could he undertake confession for a man who does not know these languages? Łeś Nedochodiuk spoke only Hutsul dialect, and a little Polish. Dr Badian, wishing to help the priest out of such an embarrassing situation, proposed confession with the help of an interpreter. Father Szákaly, surprised rather than shocked by this unheard-of proposition, seeing the good will of a doctor unfamiliar with rituals, explained to him that confession through an interpreter was impossible. It would be a violation of the seal of the confessional. After a long struggle with his own conscience, however, he acknowledged that mercy is more valuable than knowledge of foreign languages. In any case, God, in whose name he, a modest priest, was to receive the confession of a dying Hutsul in an unfamiliar language, certainly knows all languages. Ukrainian too. After all, the Merciful Almighty punished only human pride with the confusion of tongues, not Himself. Therefore, the confession requested by the poor sinner in the 10th Infantry Regiment of King N would be valid despite the language difficulties. So Father Szákaly decided to go to him. Dr Badian wanted to take the priest back with him, but he declined. He had to prepare first, for such important functions as taking the confession of a dying man, holy communion and final anointing. He promised to follow soon. He only asked for a table at the bedside, covered with a white cloth, two candles and a few balls of cotton wool. The crucifix he would bring himself.

Father Szákaly's arrival caused a sensation in the garrison. The sight of the old priest in a white surplice, worn over a long black coat—neither frock-coat nor uniform—was extraordinary. On both sleeves there were three gold straps. The purple stole did not cover the officer's stiff collar. He wore an officer's cap when off duty, but he was now bare-headed. The priest was accompanied by a moustachioed Honvéd, also wearing a surplice, bearing a lit lantern. But without a bell.

It was late afternoon and the garrison was completing its military activities and the men, although they were hungry, were not hurrying to the mess. Curiosity prevailed over hunger. Almost everyone in the square before the command post crossed themselves and kneeled; and those who did not kneel removed their caps and stood to attention.

Although the Regulations contained a "Kneel to pray" command, Regimental Sergeant-Major Bachmatiuk considered that in the army kneeling only makes sense when an infantry division is firing in two rows. The first row kneels, and the second, behind them, fires in a standing position. So he removed his cap, but stepped back inside the gateway and went upstairs to his room.

The priest, carrying a white chequered pouch containing the viaticum was conducted to the sick-bay by the adjutant, Lieutenant Baron Hammerling. Dr Badian discreetly retreated to his office adjoining the sick-bay. He had previously instructed Glück to prepare several balls of cotton wool. Father Szákaly sat down on the patient's bed behind the Chinese screen. He made the sign of the cross over Łeś and heard his confession, of which he did not understand a word. And Łeś kept beating his breast and confessing in such a loud voice that Father Szákaly gestured to him to speak quietly, because he could be heard by other patients. Indeed, they heard him continually crying out "Forgive me! Forgive me!" and they could hear how frequently the words "brother, brother's wife" occurred in the confession... Łeś continued to beat his chest. He did so with such force that the priest wondered how the dying man could summon up such strength. Evidently, the merciful God himself gave him the strength to help cleanse the soul of its sins. They must have been dire sins, since Łeś Nedochodiuk took so long to confess. The priest thought these sins were resisting, that they were unwilling to emerge from Łeś's soul. Łeś was suffering like a woman in difficult childbirth. Father Szákaly, observing how painful it was for the dying Hutsul to "give birth" to his sins, sought to assist him. Forgetting that the repentant man did not understand Hungarian, he whispered something in his ear in that language and the dialogue proceeded for a few moments in this fashion, yet another consequence of the unfortunate attempted construction described in the Old Testament.

Exhausted by this extraordinary confession, Father Szákaly recognized that enough was enough, that the repentant man had already cleansed his soul of the sins that oppressed him. But he did not stem the flow of incomprehensible words and Łeś's voice weakened, his words turning to an incomprehensible mumbling. The confessor seemed to notice an expression of relief on Łeś's face, which was covered with perspiration, and he gave him a sign that it was enough. The evidence of his repentance was all too visible. In view of that, Father Szákaly lit the candles on the table and began preparing Łeś's soul for the Particular Judgement Court and the Last Judgment. First he forgave him all his sins in a language that neither Łeś nor his countrymen, nor Father Szákaly's Honvéds understood. It was incomprehensible even to some of the officers, especially the professional ones trained in military academies. Dr Badian alone would have understood it, if he had been present:

Misereatur tui omnipotens Deus, et dimissis peccatis tuis, perducat te ad vitam aeternam. Amen.

Then Father Szákaly administered Holy Communion to Łeś and with cotton balls dipped in holy oil he anointed his eyelids, nostrils, lips, palms, loins and the outside of the arches of his feet.

Reserve Militiaman Łeś Nedochodiuk could now die in peace.

As to whether it was for the Emperor or just for himself alone, so far history remains silent.

Author's Postscript

I began writing *The Salt of the Earth* in 1925, when many people in Europe were still prepared to believe that wars on a world-wide scale, such as the last one, were a thing of the past and would never happen again. To numerous participants of that war, many of whom were so-called intellectuals, the idea that any government made up of people in their right mind would dare to bring about another, similar catastrophe seemed so grossly absurd that they could not accept it. Thus, in 1925, the Great War was so deeply buried in the consciousness of the author of *The Salt of the Earth* that he had had to strain his memory to recall the imponderables. As I perused memoirs and diaries of veterans and old newspapers and examined prints and photographs from the years 1914–18, I had to artificially stimulate my imagination to visualize events of such relatively recent years. Today, such a procedure would be unnecessary despite the elapse of half a century since the experiences of my youth. It is paradoxical that the war of 1914–18 is now closer to us today than it was in 1925, the year of illusions about peace, reinforced by the signing of the so-called Geneva Protocol. Time, instead of distancing us from the 1914–18 war, has now inevitably brought us closer to it. The Second World War, with all its infernal terror, resulted not only in a violent shift of perspective compared with our view of the First World War, but normalized, as it were, our sensibilities regarding everything that in 1925 appeared to us absurd, immoral, and therefore inhuman. Furthermore, The Second World War and its appalling results accustomed people to suffering disgrace and humiliation, and rendered them immune to shocks that threatened the health of their souls.

From today's perspective, the war of 1914–18 can be considered primitive in the light of the technology of mass annihilation perfected in the years 1939–45, but it must also be seen as the forerunner of the second, total world war and all the present-day threats of catastrophe. In our so-called civilization, something we would call cadaverism has become established. Press, radio and television feed us every day with corpses, calling on us to rejoice in the high numbers of murdered enemies and the low numbers of our own people. For the author of *The Salt of the Earth* it is hard to accept a civilization based on cadaverism.

I completed *The Salt of the Earth* in 1935. Germany had been under the rule of Hitler for three years, and he was preparing them for conquests and victories to assure them domination for a thousand years, if not over the whole world, at least over the whole of Europe. Then, when in the summer of that year I was reading the proofs of the Polish edition of this book, Mussolini began the Abyssinian war. At the end of 1935, the first edition of *The Salt of the Earth* was published in Warsaw, and one critic wrote that "this work shows how the theme of the great war has matured into song." He was probably thinking along the same lines as Friedrich von Schiller: "What is to live in song must perish in life."

The First World War was caused mainly by people for whom war was an abstraction or the result of dispassionate calculations carried out in ministerial offices and in the offices of the general staff. Few of the participants in previous, generally limited wars in Europe and outside Europe had a decisive influence on the outbreak of the Great War. When in one of the residences of the old Emperor Franz Josef a so-called crown council was held at which Austria declared war on Serbia (as I attempt to represent it in the Prologue to *The Salt of the Earth* it is not to be considered entirely authentic), the eighty-four-year old Austro-Hungarian monarch reportedly asked the war-mongering ministers and generals trying to break his resistance:

"Have you ever participated in a war? I have been in several!"

Even if this episode is just one of the legends surrounding Franz Joseph, it testifies eloquently to the sense of responsibility and the isolation of a monarch who knew from his own cruel experience in his younger years what war meant.

So the Great War was caused by people who were unaware of its ramifications and its effects, and by cynics, careerists or reckless, though honest, patriots who were unaware of the whole raw reality until it had broken out, or as it proceeded.

Undoubtedly, from the perspective of modern times, so full of hatred and enmity, the war in Austria, on which *The Salt of the Earth* is based, may seem a mild absurdity—at least as far as the episode familiar to the author of *The Salt of the Earth* is concerned. In this war he served in the Austro-Hungarian infantry from the autumn of 1916 to the autumn of 1918. Like most of his comrades, he did not feel any hatred for the "enemies" as he was ordered to consider Russians, Italians, Serbs and Romanians. On the contrary, during this war he made friends with Russian prisoners of war, who carried out nursing duties in Austrian field hospitals, often with devotion, and often with great dedication. They showed their wounded and the sick "enemies" much compassion. With gratitude I remember the tender care afforded me in one of the field hospitals, in the infectious diseases ward, by a young Russian prisoner named Zakharko. I never knew this man's name, but I can still see his kind face, the face of a simple, sincere peasant, as if transferred to the reality of 1917 from the books of Leo Tolstoy.

For the rest of my life, I will also remember the friendship shown me by the Italian prisoners of war for whom I acted as interpreter at one time. Despite all the horrors of that war, at least in situations familiar to me, the "enemy" away from the battlefield, the enemy disarmed and taken prisoner, ceased to be an enemy, and he was just our colleague, wishing just like us that this war would end as soon as possible.

Today, it is difficult to understand in the name of what the soldiers of the army in which I served, especially the soldiers of Slav nationality, killed and were killed. That irrational mechanism was operating which I attempted to reveal in *The Salt of the Earth*. I think that thirty-five years later I can talk about it objectively. All the characters in this book, other than the historical ones, are completely imaginary, although some of them incorporate characteristics of the people I encountered during my military service. Piotr Niewiadomski is a product of syncretism. I met people more or less similar to him in the formations of the general mobilization of the Imperial and Royal Army. They belonged to the oldest generations and came mainly from eastern-Galician regions bordering on Russia or Romania.

But Piotr Niewiadomski as a fictional character appeared to me only a few years after the war, strictly speaking three years after I wrote the Prologue to *The Salt of the Earth*. I saw him in Paris in 1928 on the glistening tarmac of the Place de la Concorde, which was swarming with cars gleaming like that asphalt. My imagination was struck by the glaring contrast conjured up by the image of a peasant from a far-away world, a primitive civilization so alien to Paris. In the Place de la Concorde, Piotr Niewiadomski was not yet a railway porter. He was a shepherd from the Carpathians and with a baton in his hand he went barefoot amidst noisy, hooting cars, holding the reins of a pair of Hutsul horses hauling a cart loaded high with hay held down by a crossbar over the top.

This vision never left me throughout my Parisian years until it transformed Piotr the barefoot shepherd into a porter at the imaginary railway station of Topory-Czernielica.

The second most important person in *The Salt of the Earth* is Regimental Sergeant Major Bachmatiuk. He was created in the Thirties, a prefiguration of fanatics who were later to destroy with a clear conscience the bodies and souls of millions of people in the name of the most various ideologies.

The railway wagon in Chapter 7 of *The Salt of the Earth* can be considered as the seed from which those nightmarish sealed wagons grew and multiplied during the Second World War in which prisoners destined for extermination, innocent people, civilians, not soldiers, old men, women and children, were suffocated.

The recruitment camp at Andrásfalva, the benign captivity of the men trained by Regimental Sergeant Major Bachmatiuk as automatons for killing people, turned out years later to have been the seedlings of all those camps surrounded by barbed wire, where armed, well-fed people tortured defenceless starvelings. The mild harm inflicted by the army on pious Jews in *The Salt of the Earth*, forcing them to consume non-kosher food and forcing them to have their beards shaven, leads directly to the violence and crimes committed with impunity in concentration camps against millions of Jews, and not only Jews...

But let us return to Piotr Niewiadomski.

I share his view that only He who gave someone life has the right to take it away. My friend Piotr Niewiadomski loved his Emperor, of course. In his hierarchy the Emperor takes second place after God. He thinks of the Vienna Burgtheater and Schönbrunn Palace as the vestibule of heaven, in any case as buildings in direct communication with heaven, something like today's hot line. Still, my friend was not so naive as to think that Emperor Franz Joseph gave him the gift of life.

He knew that life was given to him by the Creator through the mediation of his mother, a Hutsul named Wasylina, and his unknown Polish father. If Piotr Niewiadomski was able to think in terms of the popular slogans and metaphors current during the war, he would have called Austria his mother too. We know, however, that Piotr does not think in the metaphors which people often meet in books and newspapers. Perhaps it was because he could not read. He created his own metaphors and myths, partly inherited from his ancestors. In this, he was a kind of poet.

New York, June 1970